The LAST WISH of BRISTOL KEATS

The
LAST WISH
of
BRISTOL
KEATS

A Novel

MARY E. PEARSON

FLATIRON
BOOKS
NEW YORK

THE LAST WISH OF BRISTOL KEATS. Copyright © 2025 by Mary E. Pearson. All rights reserved. Printed in the United States of America. For information, address Flatiron Books, 120 Broadway, New York, NY 10271. EU Representative: Macmillan Publishers Ireland Ltd., 1st Floor, The Liffey Trust Centre, 117–126 Sheriff Street Upper, Dublin 1, DO1 YC43.

www.flatironbooks.com

Map designed by Virginia Allyn
Designed by Donna Sinisgalli Noetzel

The Library of Congress Cataloging-in-Publication Data is available upon request.

ISBN 978-1-250-33200-4 (hardcover)
ISBN 978-1-250-33201-1 (ebook)

Our books may be purchased in bulk for specialty retail/wholesale, literacy, corporate/premium, educational, and subscription box use. Please contact MacmillanSpecialMarkets@macmillan.com.

First Edition: 2025

10 9 8 7 6 5 4 3 2 1

For my husband,
I walked through a door with you,
and it was magic. I never looked back.

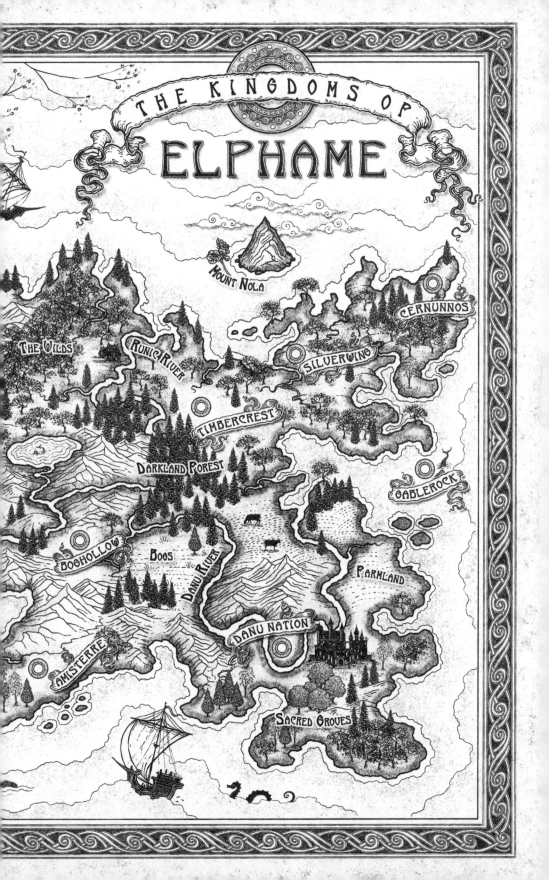

It was the stuff of legend, the torrid love affair between the Queen of Elphame and the Prince of Danu and how they became the most bitter of enemies. In a fit of rage, the prince turned the young and lovely queen into a frog, and a passing crow snatched her up in its beak. She was never seen again. The story blossomed as most do among bored and idle gentry, speculation abounding, until no one knew which version was true, but it didn't really matter because, in the end, everyone knows all legends have a secret life of their own.

—*ANASTASIA WIGGINS'S*
ENCYCLOPEDIA OF FAERIELAND

The LAST WISH of BRISTOL KEATS

CHAPTER 1

Four pink petals lined Bristol's windowsill, softer than silk, promising to brighten the darkest day.

"More," Deek whispered. He and the other sprites left in a frenzied cloud, returning to the garden until the rose was plucked bare and the wide stone sill was full.

Was it enough?

Deek had already told the other sprites why. *By day's end, this room will be filled with misery*. He had tasted the tears coming in the air, in the way only sprites could, a sweet saltiness that warmed the skin but crushed the heart.

And he didn't want the mortal's heart bruised more than it already was. He was afraid it might stop beating altogether. He tasted that in the air too.

⚷

Bristol's room was spotless, her rampage erased. A fresh vase of hyacinths rested on her breakfast table, and the floor was free of shattered dishes. Butterflies glided over the forest floor–patterned carpet once again, and her fox's green eyes peered from his woven burrow in the corner. Even the smoky singed ceiling above her bathtub was white and pristine again. The evidence of their bitter argument was gone, but inside their hurtful words still lingered. Those would take longer to clean up.

She skimmed past the thought instead of sinking into it, her sights set elsewhere. She raced through her room, stripping off yesterday's clothes as she gathered her riding gear and boots. Tyghan was doing the same in his room, rushing to get ready. Their nearly sabotaged quest had been given a second life. Today, with their team, they would rescue Cael. She remembered the cheer that rang out in Timbercrest Castle on Beltane Eve, when the smoky vision revealed that Cael was still alive. And even if he wouldn't admit to loving his brother, she saw the relief that washed over Tyghan's face. No one, not even a king, should have to choose between duty and his brother's life. Today, Cael would be coming home.

She sat on the chaise to lace her boots, but the open wardrobe doors drew her attention instead. Her stomach fluttered. Tyghan's clothes hung beside hers once again. The hobs who had discovered them thrown out in the hallway probably hadn't known where else to put them, and she was surprised at the lightness unfurling inside her, a grip loosening in her chest. His clothes were back—and she was glad.

Forgiveness is a thing of the heart . . .

Had she forgiven him?

That morning, in the predawn hours, their legs still tangled beneath bedsheets, he pulled her close and kissed her palm. *We'll work this out, Bri, I promise*, he whispered. But the full meaning of *this* remained unclear. Maybe for now it had to stay vague, so they could patch together one part of their life before they tried to fix the rest. Tyghan told her he had Eris working on the council, sending messages to them in all their far-flung homes, recalling them to the palace for a new vote concerning her father, and he had already rescinded the kill order for her mother. *But that doesn't mean your mother won't be taken prisoner. She will.*

Bristol understood that, at least for now. Being a prisoner would give her mother the pause she needed to shake the spell Kormick had cast over her. Strangely, Bristol's worry for her father had eased. Trows hadn't taken him after all, Kormick still believed he was dead, and Tyghan was working to stop the hunt for him. She guessed her father would be fine. Logan Keats, Rían Kumar, Kierus the Butcher of Celwyth, was a man of many faces and lives. He always landed on his feet, always had a plan, his own determined ways. Those determined ways had always kept his family safe. He had managed to outwit two kingdoms for over two decades, after all—with three children in tow.

But perhaps, most importantly, she couldn't keep worrying because he had refused Bristol's help or advice. That part, after all she had done, still hurt. *You need to go home*. Like she was interfering instead of helping. His goals were focused only on her mother and his own secret plans to find her. She reconciled her hurt and worry by remembering that Logan Keats wasn't only an artist but a clever warrior too. A wonder, even without her. He would evade his enemies a little longer.

His enemies. The thought dug into her, like a cat's claws in flesh, a sharp reminder of the differences that still lay between her and Tyghan. The anger she still felt for all the cruel years her family had spent on the run, but also her remorse for the horrible torture Tyghan had endured. They would eventually have to talk, to wrestle their harsh words and choices into something they could both live with, but at least he was making an effort to meet her demands, which was no small thing. Julia's words rang clear again: *Every heart is wounded and mended in its own way*. Tyghan's heart still bled from her father's betrayal. He had suffered greatly, and forgiveness was still nowhere inside him. But if Logan Keats hadn't betrayed Tyghan all those years ago . . .

The hard truth was that Bristol only existed because of her father's horrendous act. Her violent argument with Tyghan in the rotunda still rattled inside her.

You were going to kill my mother!

She wasn't your mother yet! She was a monster terrorizing Elphame!

The facts made her head pound. Tyghan had lost his best friend and had to endure unknown horrors, but because of that betrayal, she was here. It was a dark puzzle with a thousand pieces that didn't quite fit together.

Light peeked through her drapes, and she stood, grabbing her knife from the wardrobe shelf. She sheathed it in her belt, an act that was now as natural as brushing her teeth. Who had she become? Had she reinvented herself the same way her father had? She glanced sideways at her mirror, barely recognizing herself. Riding boots, leather wrist cuffs studded with protective amulets, a knife hanging casually at her hip—a knife she was fully prepared to use if necessary. She shook her head. Courage came from unlikely places, and hers had sprung from fear. It was the powerful elixir that had pushed her to come here—a deep, breath-robbing fear of always being on the run.

She had never wanted a life like her parents', and she didn't want that for her sisters either—especially not Harper. Happy endings? Maybe that was what she was still trying to give her little sister. Bristol had a shot at creating a lasting home for Harper, a place where she could watch the seasons change, watch the elm tree in their front yard grow past the roof, where the front porch would sag a little more with each season, where Harper would sleep in the same bed month after month, year after year, where continuity would become a solid history inside her, something that anchored her to the world in a way Bristol never had been. She took the long dirk from the wardrobe and shoved it in her scabbard. Courage didn't feel strong or wise. It just felt necessary. Bristol would never underestimate the power of fear again.

It was even fright that drove her to Tyghan's room yesterday. She barged her way into his room because she was more terrified than she was angry, terrified that Tyghan might give up. Afraid that this time, the demons would win, and she would forever lose him to the monsters her mother had unleashed.

"May I come in?"

Bristol whirled around. Tyghan leaned against the doorframe, the color back in his face, the icy glint back in his eyes. In that brief glance, she knew she had saved him, and her own eyes suddenly stung. Maybe it was how close she came to losing him that burned inside her, or maybe it was all the things they had said that couldn't be taken back. *Yes*, she thought. *Come in. Let me hold you and kiss you and feel your heart beating strong against mine. Come to me like the last two days never happened.*

"Yes, of course," she said.

But curiously, he remained in the doorway, four days of stubble shadowing his face, making him impossibly more handsome. "Why did you come back for me yesterday?" he asked.

He was the picture of a warrior—confident, lethal, his shoulders wide, his sword ready. From the outside. But she saw the crease between his brows, the uncomfortable set of his jaw, the uncertainty that resided beneath the confident exterior. She saw the prince he had been only months ago, carrying out orders, carrying out a plan her father helped devise. And then fate had intervened. *Love*. The unexpected but abiding love of Kierus and Maire turned all their plans on end.

"I came back to you because second chances are more compelling than first ones," Bristol said, trying to keep her voice steady. "Because I loved you more than I hated you. Because I was sorry for what you've suffered, as much as I was sorry for what I have suffered. I didn't want us destroyed by past decisions that we weren't fully part of. I didn't want to lose you and never get the chance to fix this."

This. What they had. And it was worth fixing.

"So this is a fresh start?"

She shook her head. "No. Not a fresh start. It's holding on to everything we still have, working out the knots, and moving forward from here."

He entered her room like she had unlocked an invisible door, and drew her into his arms. "I wish we didn't have to go," he whispered.

She pushed him away. "But we *do*. This mission is another second chance for us—to finish what we started. I didn't rip out Kormick's hair just for fun."

"You were smiling when you pulled it out of your pockets."

She shrugged. "Okay, maybe it was a little fun."

She took a last sweeping glance of her room to be sure she hadn't forgotten anything and spotted the pink line of petals on her sill. She grinned, wondering what had prompted Deek to place them there.

"Let's go," she said, and she and Tyghan left, hand in hand.

CHAPTER 2

Master Woodhouse had the horses saddled and ready. Their coats gleamed in the misty dawn light, and the beasts' breaths curled in the brisk air. They stamped and whickered, eager to be on their way—except for August, who moped in his stall. He was being left behind because the king wasn't well and had taken to his bed, and August was quite put out to miss the glory and excitement of the rescue mission.

"It's all right, boy," Master Woodhouse consoled. "Next time—"

"Everyone ready?"

Master Woodhouse hobbled around to face the voice.

Tyghan stood in the doorway of the barn with Bristol by his side. Three recruits followed on their heels. The old stable master stumbled over himself, apologizing for not having the king's horse ready. "Your Majesty! I think I misunderstood Kasta's orders."

Tyghan breezed past Master Woodhouse. "It's not a problem. I'll get August ready."

As speechless as the stable master was, no one was more surprised than Kasta, who had just exited the tack room. The rope she carried slipped from her shoulder. "What are you doing here? I thought—"

"I'm better." He glanced at Bristol. "A good night's rest, I guess."

"Rest?" Kasta replied, still confused. Tyghan had been furious with

Bristol just yesterday, and the last time he'd been plagued with demons, it took him weeks to recover. "All right," she answered cautiously. "But why are they here?" She flicked her hand toward the recruits still standing in the barn doorway. "This is not what we planned—"

"It's the plan now," Tyghan answered, and moved quickly to gather August's tack. He grabbed his blanket and saddle and carried it to his stall. "The recruits should all stay together," he explained. "Olivia and Esmee both confirmed their strength as a team. They feed on each other's magic. Brief the others." Meaning Julia, Sashka, and Avery, who weren't supposed to come along. And, of course, Bristol. "And we're including that stop on our way," he added. "The one we originally planned."

Tyghan was so energized, Bristol was certain he didn't notice the cold cut of Kasta's dark eyes. They skimmed over Bristol, as if assigning blame for this deviation from the plan, but Kasta shook it off quickly, snatched up the coil of rope she had dropped, and continued her preparations. As always, she was the model soldier and knight, moving forward and following the orders of her friend and sovereign. Bristol admired her scalpel-like focus, not wasting time on her feelings but absorbed only by duty. Today wasn't about Kasta or egos, but about the goal, which was common to them all. Not about past grievances, because those were plentiful and evenly sown. Today was about the future survival of Elphame—and the mortal world. Betrayals and angry demands were put on hold, disputes to be settled later. With less than three weeks until the Choosing Ceremony, time was running out.

Still, when Tyghan affectionately touched the small of Bristol's back, she saw the sharp turn of Kasta's head. Unspoken questions seared the air. Things had changed drastically since the day before.

A certain guilt filled Bristol, like she had undermined Kasta—the very officer who had secretly given her father a second chance. *Secretly.* A very big secret. Kasta had discovered Kierus and Maire in the forest all those months ago, but she walked away when Tyghan couldn't. *Why?* Bristol wondered. At least now with a new plan on the table, she showed no signs of agitation. She was too busy briefing them as the king had ordered.

This wasn't a drill. It was the real thing. Step one, remain undetected. Step two, get Cael. Step three, get home alive. There were a myriad of other steps between, rules and assignments that Kasta reviewed with them, but those three were the basics. She emphasized that complete silence was essential once on the ground, even if they were under the veil of invisibility. That veil didn't suppress sound. Whispers could be heard, twigs could snap beneath boots, tree branches would bend if brushed by a careless shoulder. Not to mention Kormick had powerful wizards, and a suspicious one could cast a sweeping ward to reveal them.

"But we will give them nothing to suspect, correct?" Kasta asked.

The recruits nodded.

"Only if I approve it will we shed our invisibility, so our full powers are available to us. Understood?"

"Understood," Julia answered for them all.

Surreptitious movement had been covered in drills too, but now its necessity wasn't theoretical. They were heading into enemy territory—a place where Bristol's mother lived with Kormick. Where she *worked with* Kormick. Bristol's mouth went dry, and she glanced at her fellow recruits. They were also paired with knights on horses for the ride. Rose and Hollis glowed, their spirits soaring, noticeably relieved that the others were going too. But Bristol saw her friends differently this time.

More knights might die.

Their vulnerability screamed at her in a way it never had before. *My mother won't harm them*, she said to herself, almost as a mantra. *My mother would never—*

But the restless dead would.

Kormick's hideous warriors would.

Kormick himself would.

How far would you go? she had asked Kormick, and he easily answered: *As far as I need to go.* He would do anything to become king of Elphame and gain control of the cauldron that would put them all under his thumb.

Bristol closed her eyes, seeing his soulless stare again when he trapped her in the alley. Unseelie. Her father's despair swept over her. *When she's with him, she is not herself.* But who was she? Had Bristol ever really known her mother at all? The answer was obvious. No. Her mother was good at hiding things, at playing roles. When she was with Kormick, maybe she was being exactly who she wanted to be, someone more powerful than any nightmare.

"Don't forget this," Cully said, and handed Kasta a small sleeping hare, calmed with magic. Kasta lowered the animal into her saddle-bag. The proxy. A powerful kind of glamour would transform it, one that could stand the test of time, the difference between a castle made of sand and one made of granite. A hare that would become Cael for weeks. This was a magic Bristol had never seen. Only the most power-ful sorcerers could conjure it, and Olivia was one of them.

Julia sidled close to Bristol. "So I assume this means you two have resolved your differences?"

Bristol nodded. "We haven't had a lot of time to talk it out yet, but we're working on it."

"Good," Julia said. "Be sure that you do, or those differences will eventually catch up with you."

"I know. Thank you, Julia. And thank you for letting me crash in your room, and letting me cry on your shoulder."

She smiled, creases lighting her beautiful cat eyes. "That's what friends and shoulders are for."

They walked with the others to the waiting horses.

Avery's newfound confidence glowed on her sun-kissed face, freck-les traveling like stars across her cheeks, and Rose and Hollis were engaged in excited chatter. Breath rippled lightly in Bristol's chest. *No knights will die on this mission*, she promised herself. *None.*

She wished Glennis wasn't still away on patrol. She always had a calming and encouraging word for the recruits. They needed that now more than ever. A single word could be more empowering than all the magic and might in the universe.

August bowed, allowing Bristol and Tyghan onto his back, and Tyghan slipped his arms around Bristol to hold the reins. "Let's move out," he called, and the Tuatha de horses leapt forward in unison, taking to the air.

CHAPTER 3

The border of Danu passed beneath the company of knights in a green haze. Tyghan lifted his hand as a signal to go dark. One by one, the knights and their horses faded from view and became part of the sky, invisible to anyone above or below. Since Bristol hadn't acquired the ability, and perhaps never would, Tyghan swept her into his circle of invisibility. Only an amulet created by Master Reuben made them partially visible to one another.

The company stayed in formation behind August, like a wedge of white swans performing a ballet in the sky, dipping, rising, turning in unison, a magnificent and ruinous wonder. Their grace belied their lethal power.

Tyghan glanced over his shoulder and gave another signal—one to Kasta to take the lead. She eyed him uncertainly, and he repeated the signal. She moved forward, and he and Bristol dropped back. He knew Kasta had been flustered when he showed up at the last minute with four extra recruits in tow. Especially with Bristol at his side. That was not Kasta's strategizing style, and he hadn't meant to catch her off-balance in front of everyone. Not to mention, she was the one who had drilled and prepped the recruits for the mission. It was best that she lead. But it was more than that. She wasn't just smart and prepared—she was loyal, a lifelong friend. He owed this trust to her.

He had another motive too. A self-serving one. He wanted every bit of his concentration on Bristol and her safety. They were going down to an area a dozen scouting parties had identified as the likely location of the Abyss portal—a deep, slender gorge half a mile long. Numerous swarms of restless dead had been spotted in the sky near the eastern end by the watchguards at Mistriven, though the exact spot remained elusive. It was an odd location for the portal, unlikely even—on the fringes of Fomoria instead of deep within its interior. If it wasn't there, odds were they would never find it before the Choosing Ceremony, which meant they wouldn't be able to stop Kormick from claiming the throne of Elphame.

And if it was there—

His chest tightened, a fusion of hope and terror clutching him. Knights didn't depend on hope, and there was no room for terror when heading into battle. Confidence and cunning were the fevers that usually raced in his veins when he faced an enemy. He shook off this new feeling with logic. This was what they had all trained for. What they had trained *Bristol* for. She would be safe.

The gorge came into view, and Tyghan's blood raced hotter. "We're going down now," he whispered into Bristol's ear. "Keep watch on the east end. This might be our last chance to find it. On the day of the ceremony, there won't be time."

"Last chance. No pressure there, right? Thanks a lot, Your Majesty." Though she tried to keep her voice light, he heard the breathless flutter in her words.

"You'll be fine. Just take your time. Remember, the only thing we're doing today is finding it."

There was an order to these things. If they closed the portal now, it would raise suspicions over who had done it. Kormick would look straight to Danu and have Maire reopen it and summon every demon out of hell. It had to be closed at the last minute, when there wouldn't be time for Maire to do anything about it. While closing a portal was a quick affair, opening one took more time, not unlike a construction project. According to the historical records, a portal could take several days to open, and the Abyss portal, perhaps even longer. Once Kormick and his entourage had arrived for the parley and were caught up in the pageantry—that was when Bristol would close the Abyss.

Tyghan was glad she would be nowhere near the battle. She'd be far away while Danu and the hidden forces of Elphame descended on the Stone of Destiny and kept the path clear for Cael to claim his throne. No doubt a battle would ensue, but it would be one the Danu and Elphame forces could overcome. Once Cael stepped up, Kormick's quest was over—the Cauldron of Plenty would be out of his grasp.

August circled and Bristol scanned the landscape.

"Anything?" Tyghan asked.

"Not yet."

They circled again. Nothing. "Maybe we need to go farther east—"

Kasta drew close. "She may need to shed her invisibility to have her full powers available."

Kasta had read Tyghan's mind, but still, he hesitated.

"We'll have you surrounded. Nothing will get past us," Kasta added.

"Let's do this," Bristol said, and Tyghan released the veil hiding them.

Bristol immediately flinched.

"What is it?" he asked.

She pressed her hand to her breastbone. "My chest is so tight."

"Should we leave?"

She shook her head. "It's here. Somewhere close." She peered south. "That way."

Tyghan looked in the direction she pointed, confused. That wasn't what the scouts had indicated. "Are you sure—" *Of course*, he thought. South. Just over the mountains. It was the closest straight shot from Fomoria to the Stone of Destiny. Only a short ride away if Kormick encountered resistance and Maire had to summon more demons to the ceremony at the last minute.

They headed for the ridge. As they neared, Bristol lifted her palm, as if reaching for something. She nudged August slightly west. They had only gone a dozen yards when she tensed back against Tyghan.

"*Hold*," he ordered, and midair, August hovered, his legs still pumping.

Bristol stared at the base of a cliff, tilting her head to the side, listening for something. Tyghan didn't move or speak, afraid he might break the magic in her.

She reached out, trying to connect with whatever it was. And then she froze. "There. At the foot of that cliff. That wall of rock. I sense . . ." She jerked her hand to her stomach, clutching it like she'd been stung. "That's it," she said. "It doesn't feel like the others. It's different."

Only seconds later, a writhing demon emerged from the solid rock, only to be yanked back by a tentacle curling around its throat. The demon squealed and clawed against its captor until it disappeared into the solid rock once more.

Bristol shivered, still holding her fisted hand to her stomach.

"Let me see," Tyghan said. When she opened her palm, it oozed with bloody blisters.

Tyghan cursed. Some wicked part of that portal had reached out and burned her. He whispered words of general healing, and for good measure, other spells to counteract poisons, as he cupped her palm between both of his. "*Miche obray*," he said, sealing the magic. "*Doman fi.*" He felt the fiery sting of her skin against his, a thousand razor-sharp cuts, and then a gradual cooling. When he pulled his hand away, the blisters were gone.

He glanced back at the portal. Even from a distance, its malevolence was caustic. It wouldn't be gone soon enough. If only his archers had their sights on Maire, he could let Bristol try to close it immediately. If only Maire was already dead so she couldn't open it again. But he had promised Bristol he would call off the kill. Now he questioned if that had been the right decision.

At least they had finally found the Abyss portal, and that was victory enough for today.

"Let's get out of here," he said, and nudged August back in the
direction of Queen's Cliff. "It's time to get Cael."

CHAPTER 4

Queen's Cliff belonged to no one. It never had. Not even to a
queen. Mostly because no one wanted it. An old haegtesse,
who wished to be left alone, claimed it for a time and chiseled
out a fortress at its pinnacle. Its name came from the queens and kings
who paid her handsome amounts of gold to watch and report threats
from the northern seas, back in a time when giant dragons—and the
more cunning smaller varieties—were a danger. *Easiest money I ever
made. Royals are fools*, the hag was reported to say after she collected her
debts. But for centuries now, the dragons mostly stayed in their northern
isles, tucked in the icy caves, preferring their own company to fae, and
once the hag's value disappeared, so did she. Some said she was eaten by
the beasts she had spied on, but others said she only moved on with the
great chest of gold she had accumulated to find more gold elsewhere.

Being adjacent to Queen's Cliff, the Fomorians mostly claimed it
now, but no one cared. It wasn't a destination spot on anyone's list, as
Sashka proclaimed, until Kasta hushed her.

The squad hovered offshore, waiting for Dalagorn to determine
the exact landing spot, based on their old maps. They gazed at the towering rock rising up in the middle of the Mirthless Sea like a hungry
siren. A headdress of ghostly clouds floated above her, and a bloom of
forest skirted her middle.

Rose's upper lip lifted in disdain. "Hard to believe anyone could live on that dreadful thing."

"Which makes it the perfect place to hide someone," Julia replied.

Avery pulled in a deep breath, like she was preparing to dive into something that was way over her head. Maybe it was.

Bristol's heart skipped. *We trained for this*, she thought. She tried to remember that they were all here because they wanted to be, but guilt still nagged at her that Rose had almost died at the hands of the demon her mother had summoned. That her whole squad might—

"This way," Dalagorn said softly, cutting off her thoughts, and he signaled for them to follow. They landed on a flat, rocky ledge just below the tree line. The northern winds whined through the forest above them, and Bristol's hair whipped across her face, the icy air biting her cheeks.

She looked north, far across the sea, and made out the distant islands of Tattersky—realm of the dragons. Ribbons of purple clouds drifted over the islands. They appeared peaceful, and yet only giant dragons and the banished avydra lived there—power-hungry shapeshifters like Pengary, who burned and ate a queen and her children. Still, for a brief moment, Bristol wished she were there instead of on this rocky mountain that seemed void of any life at all.

When viewing through the magical smoke, Cully and Quin had only seen two guards at the fortress, but like Rose, Bristol couldn't imagine even one person living here. How Cael had survived, she wasn't sure.

At Kasta's silent signal, they dismounted and the team moved forward in precise formation single file, eight feet apart, weapons drawn, each shedding their veil of invisibility once they entered the forest. Here, they would need every power available to them. The wind hissed through the twisted pines, masking their footsteps. It was hard to gauge their progress because all they could see around them were the thick trunks of trees, and the forest undergrowth of ferns and ruffled fungus, and the occasional holly bush with thorns so long they could run a person through as sure as a knife.

There wasn't even the sound of creatures or birds in the trees, just the whine of the wind, but when they took a turn a low, menacing rumble vibrated through the air. Kasta raised her hand, and they all froze. An animal? A storm? Dalagorn's ogre stomach?

There was a loud rustling, the sharp snap of a twig, and the trees to Sashka's right shook violently. Before the knights could react, the earth cleaved in two, and a churning sandpit opened up near Sashka's feet. It reached out, grabbing one foot and then the other, slamming her to the ground and pulling her under. Sashka didn't even have time to scream.

Avery reacted just as fast. "Grab my legs!" she yelled to the others, and dropped to the side of the pit, reaching in, her head, shoulders, and chest disappearing. Tyghan, Bristol, and Julia pounced onto her legs, gripping them as they lengthened, twisting into long, sturdy vines. Avery disappeared deeper into the pit, her trunk thrashing back and forth like she was waging a great battle beneath the sandy surface. Olivia saw the commotion and ran back down the trail toward them and pulled a vial from her bag. She poured it into the sand as she chanted a sleep incantation. Almost immediately, the sand stopped churning and the tug-of-war eased. Avery's legs rapidly shortened again, and she emerged from the pit, Sashka firm in her grip, both of them gasping for air. Quin, with his arms of steel, yanked them both clear. The two lay side by side on the forest floor, their chests heaving.

"Fuck," Sashka said, still gasping for breath. "I didn't know you could do that."

A nervous laugh shook Avery's chest. "I didn't either."

Olivia knelt beside them, rubbing balm on the bloody nicks on their faces and hands. Tyghan knelt beside them too. "Well done, Avery. You two need to go back? Or can you go on?"

They both pulled themselves to their feet in reply, looking like bad-ass weathered soldiers in their torn clothing. "Onward," they said.

"I never thought I'd be so thankful for those drills," Rose whispered.

Silently, Bristol agreed.

They continued without incident, though all of them were hyperalert. When they reached the last twisting climb that led to the fortress, the forest thinned. There was no more cover. From here, only Kasta, Cully, Hollis, and Olivia would proceed under a veil of invisibility, but Hollis would venture the deepest, because, as a mouse, she could slip up the last narrow path and beneath the door of the cells to determine exactly which one Cael was in and who, if anyone, was guarding him. And once in her mouse form, even an unexpected ward couldn't reveal who she actually was. Kasta carried the sleeping hare in a bag on her shoulder, ready to switch their proxy for Cael. If necessary, Quin, Julia, and Dalagorn would provide distraction to draw away the guards, and lastly, Tyghan, Avery, Sashka, and Bristol would keep the exit route clear and help whisk Cael back to the horses waiting on the plateau. Rose was their eyes in the air, already circling in her hawk form to report anything suspicious. But first, everything hinged on what Hollis found.

Kasta, Cully, Olivia, and Hollis disappeared up the steep rocky trail, while the rest of them maintained their positions, waiting for word. Minutes passed. Then more long minutes. Tyghan shook his head. Bristol searched the sky. Rose still circled, nothing apparently amiss. Tyghan finally waved Rose down and motioned to Quin to move forward, to check on Kasta and the others. The trail swallowed him as he climbed out of sight.

Rose landed near them and transformed.

"What's taking them so long?" Tyghan asked. "Did you see anything?"

"I saw Hollis go in, and, a few minutes later, Kasta, Cully, and Olivia followed."

"Guards?"

"No. Nothing."

"Maybe Olivia is having trouble with the proxy," Bristol suggested.

"Or Cael," Tyghan said. "We'll wait a little longer—"

And then Quin came stumbling down the trail, and everyone ran to meet him.

"They have them," he whispered in breathless starts. "A troop of warriors. Kasta, Cully, Olivia," he gasped. "They're all pinned to the ground, crossbows at their backs. Cully's bleeding with a bolt in his shoulder, and Olivia's out cold—or dead."

Dead? The only thing that knocked Bristol out of her shocked state was Quin's next words. "And one of the warriors is dangling Hollis by her tail, ready to feed her to their hounds." Quin wrenched Tyghan away from the group and whispered even lower. The only words Bristol heard were "She's there with them! It's time! You have to use Keats! They're about to die!"

The sound of Quin's desperate voice saying her name, curdled beneath Bristol's skin, but it was even more frightening to see Tyghan's face when he turned to look back at her, his eyes cold steel. He drew his knife and came toward her. His steps were methodical, determined. He pulled her close with his free hand, the knife still clutched in the other, and whispered just as desperately as Quin. "You know I love you. I would never hurt you. But I need you to be afraid right now. Very afraid. Fight me. Hate me. But trust me, please, or Hollis will die. They all will."

And with that, he spun her around, holding the knife to her throat, and dragged her up the trail. "You're going to be our hostage."

CHAPTER 5

Tyghan—" Bristol cried, trying to pull away.

"Quiet!" he ordered, still dragging her up the trail, her feet barely touching the stony path. Blood pounded so fiercely in her head, she couldn't make sense of anything. *Be afraid.* She was! This was nowhere in the plans—at least none that she knew of. But Quin's words pounded in her head too. *It's time. It's time.* Quin had known about this plan.

The world blurred around her, her hair whipping in front of her eyes, and the salty taste of blood swelled in her mouth. She didn't remember biting her lip, but it throbbed. They emerged at the top of a small plateau, and Tyghan jerked her roughly, his arm pinning Bristol to his chest, his knife still poised at her throat. Serious. Intent.

"Maire!" he yelled. "I have someone you want to remain alive!"

Maire. The name foreign but familiar. Maire. The Darkland monster. Leanna.

Bristol peered through wild strands of hair lashing across her face. Standing between six armed warriors was a woman. Her mother. The version of her mother she had mistakenly glimpsed in a motel bathroom twenty years ago. *Your mother is only playing dress-up.*

But she wasn't.

Her eyes were glowing pieces of jade, her skin cold alabaster, bright against her indigo gown. And there were horns. Deeply ridged horns that looked like they were dipped in gold. They wound around her head like a thorny crown, and her long copper hair flowed freely in the wind, wrapping around her body like a royal banner. And lastly, her right hand—the one that was always colder than the other—was fashioned out of silver like elegant filigree jewelry.

"Let them go, and I won't hurt your daughter!" Tyghan yelled.

"Hurt who?" her mother answered. Her voice was regal, authoritative, a voice Bristol didn't know.

When she regarded Bristol, her eyes held no recognition.

"Your daughter Bristol!" Tyghan shouted again.

Maire smiled, now eyeing Tyghan, unmoved by his threat. "Your tricks are beneath your station, Prince Trénallis. Go ahead, kill the creature. She means nothing to me."

Bristol couldn't breathe. Was this really her mother? But she noticed the familiar movement of her thumb brushing her finger, the old nervous itch to perform magic that Bristol used to think was just an odd habit.

Tyghan didn't move, and Maire laughed. "It seems we're at an impasse, then, and all the favor is mine. Pay better mind to who you are dealing with." She looked down at Kasta, Cully, and Olivia, still pinned to the ground. Cully's quiver of arrows was strewn across the rocks and trampled beneath the warriors' boots. Olivia was still, her eyes closed. Hollis dangled in her mouse form from a warrior's hand just above the frothing jaws of a snapping hound. "These trespassers have killed one of our guards. They must pay. Who should we kill first? Your elven boy? He already looks half-dead. Pity our first bolt didn't do the job."

The warrior who pressed a crossbow between Cully's shoulder blades shifted his weight, like he was about to launch another bolt.

"Shoot one more, and she's dead!" Tyghan yelled.

"Mother!" Bristol called. "Please! It's me. I swear! Your Brije. I'm begging you! Let them go, or he'll kill me!"

Maire's eyes narrowed, the smile gone, replaced with a fury Bristol had never seen before. Her nostrils flared and her eyes sparked. "Go ahead, young prince," she said, taunting him. "Kill her! What are you waiting for?"

Bristol felt Tyghan's forearm straining against her shoulder, trying to maintain the sharp blade a hair's width from her throat. She had to do something, and there was only a split second to think it through.

Bristol leaned forward imperceptibly, appearing to struggle against Tyghan's hold, forcing the sharp blade to slice into her neck. She winced at the sting of cold steel cutting her skin. It went deeper than she expected, her skin like butter beneath its razor edge. Warm lines of blood instantly trickled down her neck, calling the bluff and making Tyghan's threat real.

Maire's pupils shrank to tight pinpoints, jolted by the sight of the blood. For long, taut seconds she was frozen, but then she snapped, "Enough!" as she took a threatening step forward. "You're not worth my time! Leave and take your worthless underlings with you before I summon my legions and order them to pick your bones for the rotten carrion you are! You have five minutes before I unleash my pets." Her hand swept the air, and a blast of thick, hot mist exploded around them. When it cleared, Maire, her warriors, and the hounds were gone.

Kasta ran to Olivia's side, trying to rouse her, while Dalagorn scooped up Cully and began running for the horses. "Five minutes! You heard her!" Tyghan lifted the unconscious Olivia and threw her over his shoulder and Quin snatched Hollis from the ground. She was still a mouse, apparently too terrified to change back, and Quin secured her in his vest pocket.

Julia shifted to her lion form, saying she would help safeguard the rear, that she was best equipped to fight off the hounds if they should follow. But Bristol was certain that the *pets* her mother spoke of weren't the hounds but the legions of restless dead from the Abyss.

Kasta was in the rear with Julia, already summoning a mist that followed at their back, as thick and dark as solid wall. It crested over their heads like a protective wave.

They ran, stumbling as they rushed down the rocky trail. They all believed Maire to be true to her word. *Five minutes*. And their horses were a long way down the mountain. Tyghan held the limp Olivia secure on his shoulder with one hand while summoning magic with his other, heedless of the noise as his powerful sweeps of energy cleared the path of boulders, branches, and thorned holly. "Your neck," he yelled through the clamor. "Hold your—"

"It's only a flesh wound," Bristol yelled back. "Mind the path! I'm fine."

But she really didn't know how bad it was. She only knew she was soaked in blood and running for her life because her own mother had threatened to kill them all.

CHAPTER 6

The city was in lockdown. There were no evening gatherings in the plazas, as they prepared for a retaliation. Every watchtower was manned, and the garrison sent squads to border villages to watch for trouble there. It was rare for music not to be playing somewhere in the palace. Instead, there was the strangled thrum of waiting.

By now, Kormick had to know they had nearly breached Queen's Cliff.

Nearly.

Cully, Bristol, and Olivia were being treated, and Hollis was being observed. She still hadn't changed back. She had literally been held in the jaws of death, and Esmee said she was still too shaken to resume her human form. No bones appeared to be broken, but a piece of her ear was missing. Sashka and Rose were with her, trying to coax her back.

The rest of them had gathered in Winterwood, an interior salon rarely used in the spring and summer months. Recruits and officers milled in the corners of the room. Ivy had dinner and drink brought in for them, and a fire blazed in the hearth. The fire was unnecessary, considering the season, but there was something comforting about it in the darkly furnished room. It was something bright to focus on, the crackling embers a needed distraction.

"It was the hounds," Kasta fumed. "Two fucking shape-shifting guards." Quin and Cully had been right about there being only two listless guards, but they were also shape-shifters, and in their flea-bitten form, their keen noses had smelled the knights coming from a mile off and alerted Maire and her warriors. For a terrifying moment, one of the hounds had Hollis in his teeth. When Cully drew an arrow to shoot him, he was shot from behind with a bolt. After that, it was pandemonium, warriors closing in on all sides, a wizard striking Olivia with a magical blow before she could turn to stop him. Kasta only managed to kill one guard before she was struck down and pinned.

"An ambush," Tyghan said.

"Yes," Kasta confirmed. "Maire smiled through it all."

Dalagorn rubbed his bristled cheek. "First time I've ever seen her. Not what I expected. She doesn't look anything like her daughter."

It was Tyghan's second time seeing her. The first time she only said a few quiet words to Kierus from the cottage porch. She had seemed stoppable. Today was different.

Eris ambled over when there was a break in the conversation. "I know this may not be the right time," he said, "but I need to tell you something." He pulled Tyghan over to a private corner. "There hasn't been a single response to my summons to the council."

Tyghan was distracted, his mind only on Bristol. Eris was correct, this wasn't the right time. "Most are still on holiday after Beltane," he replied.

Eris shook his head. "It is not the holiday keeping them away. Their absence is their reply. There will not be a new vote. Their order to kill or capture on sight still stands."

As Knight Commander and king, Tyghan could make unilateral decisions regarding war, security, and almost everything else, but on matters of high crimes committed by Danu citizens, the council's decisions were final. "Send them another summons. Add some threat," he replied.

"I will," Eris answered, but he didn't look hopeful. "On a brighter note, the painting is on its way. But it's large and will take a while."

It had already taken a while, and it wasn't exactly a bright note, more of a dark curiosity, but Tyghan knew Eris was only trying to distract him, to give him a break from his thoughts. He didn't want a break. He nodded in reply and sought out another quiet corner to await news on Bristol and the others.

Quin came in after checking on the watch and sank into the leather chair beside Tyghan. A dark golden glow from the fire reflected on his bare muscled arms. "Everything's still clear," he reported. He poured himself a drink from the decanter on the table and stared at the fire. The silence between him and Tyghan was thick. "You did the right thing," he finally said.

Tyghan didn't reply.

Quin fidgeted in his seat. "Did you explain to her?"

"There wasn't time." Quin knew that. There was never enough time, never enough breathing room. Tyghan had ridden back with the unconscious Olivia in his arms, and as soon as they reached the palace, they rushed her, Cully, Bristol, and Hollis to the treatment rooms. From there, Tyghan left to speak to the garrison commander and had set the watch through the city and countryside. There was no time for any explaining.

"She knew, though," Quin said, still prodding. "She knew what you were doing. Look what she did to—"

Tyghan set his whiskey on the table. "Dammit, Quin, are you trying to make me feel better or yourself? Yes, she knew what I was doing. Does that make it all right?"

"You did what you had to do. Otherwise, they all would have died."

And that was the crux of it. As Knight Commander, he had made decisions like that a hundred times, but this one was different. This one terrified him. He had held the knife so steady, so carefully—but close. Believable. He felt Bristol trembling beneath his arm, afraid. *He'll kill me.* Convincing. He still wasn't certain if his hand had slipped or she had pushed forward.

He sat back and watched the log on the grate splinter, its fragments joining the glowing embers below. "How much more can one person take, Quin? Her father's betrayal. Her mother's. Mine."

"She seems strong enough to me."

"She is strong." Tyghan hissed. "But everyone has a breaking point. She had to beg her own mother for her life while her lover held a knife to her throat!" The murmurs on the other side of the room quieted. In a softer voice, he added, "We only reconciled last night. This is going to tear us apart again."

"I'm sorry if I pushed you—"

Tyghan's hand brushed the air to stop Quin, his frustration still mounting. "I'm not blaming you. I'm the one who—"

Footsteps sounded in the hall outside the salon. Soft footsteps. Tyghan and Quin jumped to their feet as Bristol entered. The room went silent, all eyes turning toward her. A bandage circled her neck. Another covered her hand. Though the room was large, with everyone scattered around it, Bristol's eyes instinctively turned to Tyghan.

She smiled. It was a small smile, mostly around her eyes, easy for others to miss—but it was a look that sank into Tyghan like medicine and magic, warming his insides, the tension in his shoulders easing. She was glad to see him.

Julia and Avery closed in on her, hugging her while the others held back, waiting. After a few quiet words with her friends, she turned, looking back at the rest of the room, and said, "You'll all be happy to know that Hollis is back to two legs instead of four, Olivia is sitting up and drinking tea, and Cully is awake, and Madame Chastain is cursing at him to stay in bed." At the news of Cully, Ivy burst into tears and ran from the room, presumably straight to him. Murmurs circled the air. The couple may have thought they were keeping their relationship under wraps—at least from her parents—but anyone with eyes could see they were smitten with each other.

"And your neck?" Eris asked, his tone hesitant.

"Only a minor flesh wound. I've had worse," Bristol replied. She touched the bandage circling her neck like it was a decorative choker. "This will be off by morning."

Tyghan knew if it was minor, a bandage wouldn't be necessary at all. The others knew it too, but a tentative ease returned to the room, like a clenched muscle relaxing. By appearances she seemed to have taken being used as a hostage well, but Tyghan sensed something in her was still off, and his apprehension returned. She was too cheery. She crossed the room and whispered in a lower voice to Quin, "Hollis wanted me to give you her apologies. She's pretty much mortified that she may have soiled your vest pocket during the escape. She says a mouse's constitution, especially in dire situations, can be, well, unpredictable."

"I didn't notice my vest," Quin answered. "Blazes, I may have pissed my own pants. How's her ear?"

"Definitely notched like an old alley cat, but she doesn't seem too bothered by it. Madame Chastain gave her something for the pain, though. It's left her a bit loopy."

Tyghan noted that the High Witch gave at least some of her patients pain medicine.

"Is she taking visitors?" Quin asked.

Bristol smiled. "I think she would welcome a visit from you."

For the first time in Tyghan's recollection, he saw Quin blush, his dark skin reddening at his temples. *Quin and Hollis?* When did that happen? How had he not seen it? Quin eagerly excused himself, and Bristol turned her attention back to Tyghan. He saw the fatigue in her face, the heaviness of her lids, a sadness in her eyes she was trying to hide. The day had punched something out of her. It was a wonder she wanted to be with him at all. Did everyone in the room see it too? Or was it just his own guilt, conjuring something that wasn't really there?

He reached out and took her bandaged hand in his. "What happened here? I didn't heal it?"

"It required more layers of spells and balms." She told him Madame Chastain explained that the Abyss portal was different from other portals because it held eons of the powerfully evil. And since it was a caustic cauldron of the worst the world has ever seen, it wasn't surprising that it could burn deeply into a hand that tried to reach inside. "Madame Chastain said the goddess Brigid never meant for it to be opened again, and she suspects only the strongest of bloodmarked can open or close it."

Tyghan saw the concern in her eyes. *The strongest of bloodmarked* did not describe her. She blinked, forcing a smile. "Can we go rest in our room for a little while? I know there's a watch, but—"

He nodded. "Everything's quiet, and the watch is set. We have time to rest." He told Kasta where he'd be and to alert him if there was any change, then let Bristol lead him to her room, which was apparently "their" room once again.

But as soon as they entered, she slumped into his arms, her breath coming in gulps. His arms circled her protectively. "I'm sorry, Bri. I am so sorry."

CHAPTER 7

Bristol pressed into the broad darkness of Tyghan's chest, like it could block out the world. All she wanted to do was hide.

He whispered words gently against her hair, his voice soothing. It wasn't the words that mattered, but him, something solid and true in a life that was slipping from her grasp.

"Bri." Tyghan gently lifted her chin so he could look into her eyes. "I'm sorry."

"What?" she said, uncertain what he was apologizing for. "I told you, it's only a flesh wound. And I was the one who did it. Not you. I pressed into your knife. There was no other choice."

"Not the wound," he said. "That we used you as a hostage."

Hostage.

The thought circled back, one of many shattered moments of the day that had assaulted her since she had stared into her mother's eyes and heard the words *kill her*. She shivered, seeing her mother's cold jade eyes again. *Go ahead, kill the creature*. Bristol had no value as a hostage, not even for her own mother.

Her knees wobbled. The room swayed.

Tyghan scooped her up, holding her tight like he would never let her out of his arms, his lips resting against her forehead. He carried her to the sofa and laid her down, then swept a blanket over her shoulders and turned his attention to the hearth. It was already set with logs, and with a gentle motion of his hand and a whispered word, the logs ignited. When he looked back at her, his face was pure misery.

She shook her head. "I don't blame you, Tyghan. We saved Hollis and the others. That's what matters. It was an impossible situation, and a hard choice had to be made."

"I didn't want to do it—"

"You think I didn't know? That was obvious. It was a chaotic moment—there wasn't time to think, much less explain. I would have done the same thing." Splintered images shot through her mind: Quin's troubled whispers, Tyghan drawing his knife and turning toward her—the unknown. A plan she hadn't trained for. "When you grabbed me, I was shocked . . . but that shock paled—"

She shook her head. Tyghan sat down beside her. "Tell me."

She stared at the crackling fire. "The way she looked at me . . . I was nothing to her. A stranger. I can't shake it from my mind. She pushed you to kill me. More than once. She didn't care."

"That's how she looks at us all, Bri. That's who your mother is. I'm sorry."

"It's not who she used to be."

Tyghan had no response. This Maire was the only one he had ever known.

"My father warned me that she might not know me. I'm not sure that she did. How can a mother forget her own child?"

"She must have remembered something. She let us go."

Bristol tried to make sense of it, reliving the moment when the knife sliced into her neck and her mother's eyes widened. A second later, she sent them on their way. "Maybe it was the blood that saved us. My mother always hated the sight of blood. When we were small, my father was in charge of our skinned elbows and bloody noses." Bristol reached up and traced the faint line on her forehead where a scar disappeared into her hairline. Her mother had fainted at that one. She'd been unloading her loom from the top of the van when it suddenly jerked free and hit Bristol in the head. Heads bleed magnificently, and her mother collapsed in a heap when she saw the gash.

"Forgive me," Tyghan said, "but I have a hard time believing Maire is bothered by blood. Buckets of it have been shed by her hand, and she bragged about shooting Cully. I don't think it was just the sight of blood that made her stop."

Bristol couldn't argue with that. Still, her mother had reacted when Bristol's neck started bleeding. Maybe the sight of the blood made her mother stop thinking Bristol was only a clever deception. Or maybe it jolted a sliver of memory free . . . a memory that she'd had a daughter once. *Three daughters*. Did some lost part of her remember, or was Leanna Keats gone forever?

Tyghan wished he could erase Bristol's pain, make it disappear with the right words, but there was no magic that could undo what she heard and saw that day. He was grateful for the knock at the door and jumped from the sofa to answer it.

"It's supper," he said, taking the tray from the servant so Bristol wouldn't have to endure any more sideways glances. "After all the blood you lost, you need extra nourishment." He also hoped some routine and normalcy would give her a break from the thoughts that were overwhelming her.

He set the tray on the low table, spreading out plates and silver, but at the first rattle of dishes, the fox she'd been feeding emerged from the burrow woven into her carpet—art come to life at every meal. He sniffed at the table, investigating. "Back to your burrow, freeloader," Tyghan said, trying to shoo him away, but Bristol intervened.

"No. Give him something."

Tyghan sighed and handed over a red pear from the fruit bowl, and the fox happily scampered back into his hole. He was probably her fox for life now. Tyghan filled their goblets, and they both ate—and drank. He had ordered her favorites. A mellow red wine from the north country, braised boar shanks, warm buttered rolls, stuffed figs, raspberry cream tarts. Like the fire, it seemed to be a welcome distraction for her. He kept her goblet full and watched her shoulders loosen and warmth return to her cheeks.

Sometimes everyone needed a break from their thoughts, but when she set her last shank bone on her plate and sat back, staring at the hearth and crackling logs, he knew her mind had circled back to the same thought: Her mother had ordered him to kill her. Even he was shocked and still reeling from that moment, and the risk he had taken. He was a fool to have put any hope in Maire caring for her daughter.

"She's gone," Bristol said. "The mother I knew is gone, just like my father warned." The emptiness of her tone gripped Tyghan, and he wished he had a remedy for her anguish. "For me, it's like she's died all over again," she went on. "The first time I was angry, but this time . . . This is different. It feels like I've stopped existing too. She gave birth to me. On a dark and stormy night. She always laughed about that, like I had to make an overly dramatic entrance. After thirty-two hours, she'd remind me, like she was as proud of my endurance as her own. And now, in her mind, I'm no one. That story, that life—it's gone. When there are no memories left of you, do you even exist?" She turned to him, her eyes bright again. "Kiss me, Tyghan. Kiss me like you will never forget me. Please don't ever forget me."

Tyghan gently tucked her hair behind her ear, and with a single finger, he slowly lifted her chin. His lips grazed hers, so lightly they barely touched, and yet it was a sunrise, a sunset, the lifetime he wanted with her. He pulled her closer, and her head rested on his shoulder, sinking into him like she was anchored again. He calmed the blaze in the hearth and summoned the shadows around them like a blanket, and she fell asleep in his arms.

Forget her? Never. She was sewn into his soul.

CHAPTER 8

Cat dropped the heavy cardboard box into the back of the van and went back to the house for another. She and Harper were moving into an apartment in town. They could afford that now. In addition to the windfall that came from their father's painting, the money from the da Vinci and Escher sketches had come in, and thanks to Sonja's wise negotiating, it was a fortune. After a lifetime of living out of duffle bags, they now had whole boxes' worth of possessions, and yet their lives didn't seem any fuller. There was a hole. There would always be a hole until Bristol returned.

Cat and Harper passed each other several times on the old creaking porch as they loaded boxes. Harper was not happy about the move, but the apartment was far more practical and safer. With Cat commuting long hours to the music institute now—they had welcomed her back—she didn't want to worry about Harper riding her bike back and forth along deserted country roads to school. Especially not the one where their father had died—or at least disappeared. Enough people had disappeared from Cat's life. She wouldn't lose Harper too.

"Hey, don't look so glum," she said, ruffling Harper's hair as she dropped another box into the van. "There's a pool at the new place. And the library is only a block away. You're going to love it."

"Yeah." Harper sighed. "I just worry. What if she comes back and we're not here? What if—"

Cat looped her arm around Harper's shoulder. "Come on." She walked her to the mudroom where the portal had once been. "Look. She is not going to miss that note, or the card. With all the tape you used to fix them to the washing machine, they're not going anywhere."

They stared at the cheery envelope that Harper had illustrated months ago with balloons and a birthday cake for Bristol's twenty-second birthday. Blocking most of the floor in the mudroom in front of the washing machine was the gift they had planned to surprise Bristol with before she left unexpectedly. It was a new bike to replace her rusted one. It had shiny baby blue fenders and a basket filled with a new hoodie. The bike was secondhand, but they had saved like crazy to buy it for her.

"I promise you, Harper, we will never touch this house or that bike until she returns. It will always be here for her."

"Did you know, Cat? Tell me. Did you know what they were?"

What they were. Cat had shed so many tears over what had transpired, she didn't think she had any more, but she felt her eyes welling, still feeling the guilt. Would it ever go away?

She had already told Harper what she knew. But maybe sometimes the truth had to be revisited more than once, especially when so much of your life had been a lie.

"I swear, I didn't think Daddy was telling the truth. Would you have believed him? After Mother died, he wasn't the same. You know that. When he called me at school with this wild story about Elphame and leaving to find Mother, I thought he had finally lost it. And when he warned me about Bristol and her birthmark, I was certain he had. He said I should know in case anything happened to him. When he died, or I thought he had, I was as grief-stricken as everyone else and forgot about his wild stories. They didn't seem important then."

Harper nodded and looked down as if ashamed. "I went to the library and got a book of spells. I tried a few, but nothing happened."

"We're not fairies, Harp."

"But Mother was. That has to be where Bri got it from."

Their dead mother. It was possible Bri got it from her, but now they would never know. These past months they had tried to put the pieces together. They were still trying to unravel their past. At least they had each other. But who did Bristol have to help her? Cat's throat swelled.

"She'll manage," Harper said, as if she could read Cat's thoughts. "Those were the last words she said to me so I wouldn't worry: *You know me. I always manage.*"

But Bristol's last spoken words to Cat were the ones she would always hear. *How could you not tell me? I trusted you. Get away from me. Get the hell away.*

CHAPTER 9

Kierus trudged through the forest. It was a miracle he had made it this far. He had thought his quest to find Maire was over in the barn, when he was surrounded by Kasta and the other knights, but then he felt something tight around his waist, and he was flying through complete darkness. A nightjump. He landed hard in the arms of a woman. He barely had time to take a breath before she was doing another nightjump, and then another.

"There," she said on their last landing. "This should keep you out of their reach long enough to escape. Go, Mr. Keats, preferably home, like Bristol asked, but I doubt that you'll listen to me either."

"Who are you?" he asked.

"A friend of Bristol's. I'm only doing this because of her concern for you. That's all you need to know." She refused to tell him more. He eyed her suspiciously, because Bristol hadn't ever been the friend-making type. She turned and ran into the woods, leaping into the air and transforming into a large white lion just before she disappeared into the shadows. A shape-shifter.

Whoever she was, he was grateful to her—but she was right. He wasn't going home.

Fritz was there, watching over Cat and Harper, keeping the wards fresh over the doors and windows. Fritz was faithful. He would keep them safe.

Kierus reached the narrow river and navigated along its edge for several miles. The languid, smooth surface reflected the leafy greens and yellows above. Drooping limbs reached down, nearly touching the river. *Like curious fingers.* That was how Maire described it. He felt it in his bones—he was getting close. And then he saw it, peeking out of the trees as he rounded a bend.

The old water mill was broken and tufts of moss grew in its wooden wells. It creaked back and forth in small increments, the only proof that there was a current at all. Abandoned, peaceful, isolated. No wonder Maire loved to go there. The cottage alongside the mill appeared sturdy enough, but the window shutters were askew, like crooked spectacles on a nose.

Kierus climbed the steps. The wooden porch moaned under his weight. As soon as he eased open the door and stepped into the cottage, heat sprang to his temples. *Her loom.* It was perched in the middle of the room, as regal and important as a queen's throne, but the weft, a good ten inches of already finished blanket, was frosted with a thick layer of dust. The warp just behind it sagged, rotten yarn dangling loose. The loom was as abandoned as the rest of the mill. Maire hadn't been here since her return to Elphame. Was that Kormick's punishment, or had she forgotten this place? Had she forgotten him and their daughters?

He stepped closer. On the floor, neatly placed near the treadles, was a pair of soft leather slippers, the kind she liked to wear when working the loom. He knelt and clutched the dusty shoes to his chest, resisting the ache in his throat. *Maire. My love.* He stood quickly, refusing to let misery overtake him. He was a warrior, the wonder of Danu. He would not lose this battle. He threw the slippers across the room, choosing the anger inside him instead of the loss.

"This is not over," he said between clenched teeth.

He paced the room. Now he would have to go deep into Fomoria. It was the only way to find Maire. *How do you think you're going to bring her home? Knock on Kormick's door and ask to speak to her?* He had never heard that mocking tone in Bristol's voice before, at least not directed at him. The complete scorn. She had always believed in him.

Bristol knows what you did to her.

Tyghan's condemnation hit him anew. He swallowed, his rage subsiding. He remembered the exact moment when he and Maire placed the tick on Bristol's tender skin. She was only seven months old. Angus had retrieved the tick for them from the High Witch's workshop of monstrosities. They'd had no choice. She was already exploring her abilities, and the scent of her magic was beginning to attract unwanted attention. A group of redcaps had circled her stroller at a seaside bazaar a full hour after she had levitated a trinket, the magic still clinging to her skin.

He and Maire probably should have removed the tick long ago, but, after so many years, it just became a part of who the Keats family was. It made it easier for Bristol, they told themselves, if her magic was suppressed.

I'm not your Brije.

But she would always be his and Maire's Brije, their *little goddess*. And one day she would understand the hard choices they had to make. She would remember how much they loved her more than she remembered what they had done. She would know that they were the best parents they knew how to be.

A creak pierced the room, and his gaze shot toward the door. Outside, a breeze stirred the trees, and he thought it was only the old broken mill rustling in the current, but in the next instant he felt something cold at his throat. Steel.

"This time, you won't be making any sudden exits."

He recognized the voice. It was colder than the long blade pressed against his neck.

Melizan.

"Let's go, traitor," she said. "We have some special accommodations waiting just for you back at the palace."

CHAPTER 10

Tyghan quietly eased open Bristol's door. It was still dark, and he was hoping not to wake her. He had slipped out well before dawn to check with the watch commander on the status of the skies and borders. It had been two days since the botched rescue, and the city continued to be surprisingly still. Morning rose quiet and calm. It didn't bring him the ease that it should have. Something in his gut was still wary. Maybe it was just the sight of Bristol's bloody neck that he couldn't shake.

When he stepped into her room, he heard water running. She was already awake. He went to the bath chamber and found her in the shower, water falling from above like warm rain. She seemed strengthened by a good night's rest. Her eyes were shut as she lazily soaked in the streams of water, her long hair clinging to her skin. She sponged her neck where the bandage had been. There was no sign of injury from the cut he had inflicted, and relief flooded his lungs. More feelings surged lower in him as the sponge skimmed her breasts.

"You could have slept longer," he said.

Her eyes opened, and a seductive smile curled her lips. "Join me?"

He leaned back against the wall and crossed his arms. "I'm enjoying the view from here."

She shrugged and continued washing herself, but more leisurely, guiding the sponge down the length of her leg, then back up again along her inner thigh. When the sponge reached her abdomen, she squeezed it, and soap bubbles glided over her skin. His groin ached.

She looked sideways at him, her gaze lowering to his crotch, where a bulge strained against the fabric.

"Yes," she said, "I can see you're enjoying the view."

He tugged his shirt free from his trousers and pulled it over his head, throwing it to the floor. Her attention sharpened. He slowed when it came to his trousers, knowing she was eager too.

"Just giving you due notice," he said, undoing the first button of his fly, "if I come in there with you, you'll be the one begging for mercy. Unlike the other night when you controlled everything, I'll be the one in charge this time. And this time I won't be silent. I have a lot to say. Like how much I want to fuck you."

Water dripped from her lashes. "Sounds interesting. I'm all ears."

He undid the next button, his eagerness already on display. Her teeth scraped her lower lip. He popped the last button, and his trousers dropped to his ankles. He kicked them loose, and her chest rose in a deep, shivering breath. In three strides, he was in the basin with her, taking the sponge from her hand, pressing against her back. She was trapped between him and the marble wall, his mouth tucked near her cheek.

"I will always be at your mercy, Bri," he whispered. "Forever, I'm yours. But right now, you are mine, and I plan to own every inch of you." His hand slid down across the slickness of her belly, and his fingers raked through the thick patch of hair below, his middle finger sliding between her legs. She moaned, and her hips pressed forward against his hand. She swelled beneath his touch, and he stroked her as his lips skimmed her shoulder.

"This time there will be words. You'll tell me that you want me to fuck you. I want you to scream it. And I want to know every other way you want me to touch you. I want you breathless and weak and begging me for more. But most of all, I want you to tell me that you love me, because I cannot breathe without you."

She groaned his name, and he turned her to face him. "I love you," she whispered, plaintive, leaving no doubt between them. His insides twisted with heat, and his mouth came down on hers, his tongue parting her lips. It wasn't just his erection that throbbed, but every part of him, from skin to soul. He wanted to give himself wholly and fully to her, and protect her from anything that could ever harm her again.

Everything about her, from the sound of her voice to the smoldering in her eyes, set him on fire. She dropped down, the shower still raining down on them, and she took him into her mouth, her tongue teasing, her lips tightening around him. His breath shuddered; his head swam. As his thighs tightened, his control waned, and he dropped to the floor in front of her. He grabbed her wrists and pushed her beneath him. Water rained down on his back, shielding her, and her eyes were golden pools looking into his. "I'm not done with you," he said.

Between heavy breaths she whispered, "You should know, Tyghan Trénallis, I will never beg you for mercy, because I never want you to stop."

"Be careful what you wish for."

"Bragging again?"

"Aspiring. And I usually get the things I aspire to."

His lips skimmed her neck, her shoulder, skating down to her breasts. She tasted of summer, and plums, and sweet cream. His tongue circled her nipple, and his teeth gently grazed the tender flesh. Her moans filled him with madness, his blood burning, his heart hammering. He resisted plunging into her right that moment, wanting to draw out her pleasure. He explored the silk of her skin, her ribs, her belly, lower still, until his mouth was between her legs. Her breath came harder, a delirium in her moans, and in seconds she was pleading with him. "Tyghan, wait. I'm already—wait." Her breaths came in short gasps, and her hips rocked forward, pushing toward him. He didn't wait, and neither did she. He brought her slowly and mercilessly to a crescendo, her muscles tense, convulsing, her moans ragged, until it seemed she wasn't breathing at all. He was so hard he thought he might come just by listening to her. Her crescendo finally peaked, her flesh throbbing in his mouth, and when it subsided, she blew out a long, quivering breath.

"Again?" he whispered.

She nodded.

🔑

Tyghan was true to his word and owned every inch of her with abandon, and Bristol lost herself in the thrill of his passion—and her own. They had moved from the shower to her marble dressing table, to the thick rug on the floor of her dressing area. He pressed into her from behind, his hands gripping her hips, but then he lifted her upright against him, one hand caressing her breast, the other stroking between her legs, like he wanted every part of her at once. This time they came at the same furious moment, an exquisite tangle of breaths and elation.

They finally ended up on her bed, their arms spread, their skin damp, their breathing shallow, exhausted. "Uncle," he whispered. She smiled that he knew the phrase.

"So you're only a demigod after all," she teased.

"A humbled braggart who has learned his lesson."

She laughed. After three intense rounds of lovemaking, she was getting a little sore in the nether regions and was glad he needed to rest. His enthusiasm was appreciated, but so was respite, and savoring the enormous afterglow. Not just the glow of sex, but the words. They were mostly hard to utter in the course of lovemaking, but they were as intense as the incredible spasms that left her breathless. *Love, need, want, adore, love, love, love.* She felt it with every touch, word, and move between them, a yearning that reached into her marrow.

"Do you believe in destiny?" she asked.

Tyghan's hand slid across the bed and clasped hers. "I believe we make our own destiny."

"But what were the chances of us ever meeting?"

"A million chances happen every day. The difference is what we make of them. We can let them slip past us, or we can turn a chance into something that lasts forever."

It struck her how similar his words were to the ones her mother loved to repeat. *I saw a once-in-a-lifetime chance*, she would say about meeting Bristol's father, *and didn't let it slip past me*. Her stomach bobbed, thinking how ephemeral a chance was, how easily one could slip past. "I didn't like you at first, you know?"

A soft chuckle lifted his chest. "I noticed. I thought you were going to punch me."

"Our beginning didn't look too promising."

"Maybe endings are more important than beginnings."

Maybe so, she thought. Beginnings were made of hope, but endings were made of stubbornness and determination.

Still, she liked the idea of destiny, that they were meant to be together, that chance couldn't step in the way. "You are my destiny, Tyghan."

"And you are mine, Bristol Keats."

Tyghan had dozed for minutes, maybe an hour, he wasn't sure, every muscle spent and satisfied, his hand still laced with hers, when his rumbling stomach woke him. It was past the breakfast hour, and he had just expended considerable energy. "Hungry?" he asked.

"Starved," Bristol answered dreamily.

"Let's go down to the kitchens. I'll make you something. Anything."

She sat upright. "One of those big, fluffy pancakes like you made at the farm?"

"It's yours."

They dressed and raced down to the palace kitchens, where dozens of cooks were already preparing food for the day. They were a wonder to watch, creating cakes that were works of art for the evening festivities, and seasoning meat with pinches of herbs as thoughtfully as a painter applies strokes of paint to a canvas. Everyone was so immersed in their tasks, they barely noticed the couple enter the kitchen, but when Tyghan grabbed a frying pan from a rack, heads turned and the chefs welcomed the king and his guest.

But before the butter had even melted in Tyghan's pan or an egg was cracked, Ivy rushed in, her wings fluttering in a state of urgency. "There's been a delivery at the front gates. It's a package for you."

"Take it to Eris or the throne room. I'll tend to it later—"

"I'm afraid you need to come now," she said. "It's from the Dark-land monster."

By the time Tyghan and Bristol reached the palace gates, there was a crowd of knights waiting for him, their weapons drawn. Archers stood ready, arrows nocked, bows taut. Hollis and Julia were just arriving, the other recruits not far behind. Even Cully was there, fresh from Madame Chastain's infirmary, readying an arrow. Olivia and Esmee tested the air around a wooden chest for magic, their hands raised, ready for battle.

"It appears clean," Esmee said with some hesitation. Olivia nodded to confirm, but kept her hands poised to deflect a potential attack.

Eris stepped forward. "I'll take care of—"

Tyghan waved him away. "I've got it," he said, eyeing the large chest. Bristol looked over his shoulder as Tyghan knelt and undid the latch. He carefully eased opened the lid. On top of a red velvet cloth was a folded piece of paper. Tyghan lifted the note and unfolded it. In beautiful scrolled lettering was a message:

*Send my daughter to the base of Queen's Cliff by midday. Alone.
I will meet with her <u>today</u>, or by tomorrow the next head delivered
to your palace will be your brother's.*

Tyghan crumpled the note in his fist. "Clear the area."

"No," Kasta said from behind. "We all need to see what the monster has delivered."

Quin rumbled agreement. "Her deeds can't be kept hidden."

Tyghan stood and grabbed a fistful of the velvet cloth, lifting the contents. The weight inside the cloth shifted, and the promised head tumbled out onto the ground.

For a brief moment there was shocked silence, as everyone stared at the severed head with bloodstained flowing white hair. A head with graceful curved horns, and beautiful blue eyes that stared sightless into the sky.

Glennis.

There were seconds of confusion, then cries of disbelief. Cully turned, his hands squeezing his head. Eris's face drained to a sickly pallor.

Bristol stumbled, turning away, falling into someone's arms. Julia's. When she looked back, Tyghan had already covered the head with the cloth.

"I'm going," Bristol said. "And I'm going alone."

CHAPTER 11

Eris watched from a distance as Tyghan and Bristol argued at the entrance to the barn. They were all still reeling from Glennis's death, but there was no time to grieve. Decisions had to be made. Time was short. Maybe the arguing gave Tyghan and Bristol a reprieve from the horror. Though it was really only Tyghan who argued. He demanded and commanded. But he was losing. Miss Keats was unwavering, and her logic was sound. She had to go. She was the only one who could. Cael's life depended on it, and no one doubted Maire was true to her word. No one cut off heads, then issued an ultimatum as an empty gesture. The question was, what did Maire intend to do with her daughter?

The recruits huddled nearby, exchanging their own whispers and solutions. Avery openly wept, and Rose repeatedly shook her head, as if she couldn't believe what had happened. Glennis had been beloved among the recruits, always the most encouraging officer. She had been beloved among her fellow officers as well. Cully leaned against the paddock fence with his eyes closed, still struggling to compose himself.

Kasta's gaze was fixed on Tyghan as he and Bristol argued. "Should we step in?" she wondered aloud.

Several noncommittal grumbles answered.

Eris sighed, wanting to step in himself. But hard decisions were part of a king's job, and Tyghan had to make one. "Not yet."

"Miss Keats is doing quite well on her own," Dahlia added.

And she was. In the face of her mother's dangerous demand, Bristol was strangely steady. Or maybe *compelled* was a better word. Her resolve to go had come swiftly, taking them all by surprise. Eris wondered what was going on inside her head. Deftly disguised terror? Guilt? Revenge? But he suspected it was more than that. Kasta had told them everything that transpired at Queen's Cliff, including Maire's order to kill her own daughter. Eris was certain that played into Bristol's rushed decision to go.

"Perhaps she's in denial that her mother actually beheaded Glennis?" Dahlia suggested.

"Maire did it, all right," Quin answered.

Dalagorn agreed, and they mulled over fit retributions as Tyghan and Bristol wrestled over her decision.

Maire's demand was perplexing. She wanted to *meet with her*. For what purpose? To take her daughter prisoner? To remove any possibility of Bristol helping them? To confirm that she actually was her daughter and not a trick? What role was Kormick playing in this? Why hadn't the note come from him? And threatening to kill Cael? He was Kormick's leverage, to keep Tyghan from even attempting to take the throne. What kind of trickery was he up to now? Why would he even allow—

Unless Maire was acting on her own, without his knowledge? The questions and conclusions came in a flurry as Eris, Dahlia, and the others waited from afar. There wasn't time to convene in the rotunda to properly evaluate their options, as Eris would have preferred. He hated rushed decisions.

He leaned close to Dahlia. "If something happens to her, we have no hope of closing the Abyss door."

Dahlia's lips pursed as if weighing some other thought. "Removing the tick may kill her anyway, and there is still no certainty she will be successful in closing the door. But we know with certainty, Cael will die if she doesn't go. Let's just hope that when Maire meets with Miss Keats, she is more mother than monster."

Hope. It was not something Dahlia turned to. Hope had no formula or magic spell. There were no chapters in the vast library of grimoires that included it. She was High Witch, after all. Her sights were always set on reliable outcomes, tried and true spells, developing wards that could trip up armies and mists that could blind them. In her position, it was who she had to be. And now she was placing hope in the Darkland monster? Everything about their world seemed upside down, and Eris wondered if it would ever be aright again.

Tyghan turned, irritated by the tug on his arm. "In case you hadn't noticed, Quin, you're about as welcome as a rash right now. I'm busy."

Quin nodded. "I know. But you need to let her go, Your Majesty."

Quin never used his formal title, and Tyghan knew it was a reminder that he needed to make a king's decision, not a lover's. His oath bound him to use every possible opportunity to save his brother—the rightful king—and this was a chance. He turned back to Bristol. If she were anyone else, they wouldn't be having this conversation at all. He would stop wasting precious minutes arguing and be preparing her to leave instead. But she wasn't anyone else, and he was afraid she would never return, at least not alive.

He stared at her. The details. Her eyes. The firm set of her mouth. Her decision was made.

"She's my mother, Tyghan. She won't hurt me."

There was no changing her mind. She was going. Not just for Cael or Danu, but for herself. Maybe mostly for herself. Just as he had been plagued by demons, she had a demon of her own: a history with her mother he didn't fully understand. But neither did Bristol. The encounter with her mother at Queen's Cliff had unmoored her. Bristol had finally seen the Maire that the rest of them knew, not the mother but the monster. Something inside her was floating loose and wild, and she needed to secure it again. But at what cost? Maire had brutally murdered Glennis and made a heartless show of delivering her head.

"I'll go with you," he said, desperate to find a compromise.

"The king of Danu? Are you crazy? You'll only put us both at risk if you do. She said *alone*. Not to mention, you'd be too great a prize not to capture. I'd be worrying more about you than myself. Dammit, Tyghan, don't make this harder for me."

But he wanted to make it harder for her. He wanted more time to think. Except Maire had robbed him of time too. "If anything happens—" He already felt himself breaking his promise to Bristol. No arrow would be spared when it came to Maire. She was a dead woman. *Dead*.

"*She won't hurt me*," Bristol repeated more earnestly.

Kasta stepped forward. "Listen to her, Tygh. Maire let her go last time. She will again. Her fellow recruits will accompany her as far as the Mistriven border and wait for her there. It's not that far from the base of Queen's Cliff. They're all well trained, and so is she, plus there is a strong bond between them. They're good together. Quin and I will take it from here."

Instead of letting her go, Tyghan pulled Bristol into his arms. He buried his face in her hair. "Come back to me, Bri," he whispered. "Promise me you'll come back."

Her lips were warm against his cheek. "I promise. I'll come back to you."

He shifted his hold and brought his lips to hers, his mouth hovering against their softness, pressing a seal to her promise.

"Tyghan," she whispered against them when his grip remained tight. He let go.

Quin and Kasta wasted no time whisking her away to the barn, where Reuben was waiting to outfit her, the recruits, and their horses with every possible amulet and ward, in case there was an ambush along the way. Tyghan started to follow, but Melizan appeared and intercepted him.

"Whoa," she said, putting her arm out to stop him. "There's another urgent matter that you need to address." She and Cosette stood shoulder to shoulder, their faces flushed. Their clothes were soiled, their boots muddy, and their hair windswept like they had just come from a battle.

"Where the hell have you been?" he asked.

Melizan glanced at Eris, who had just joined them, and she nodded, some secret message passing between them.

"What's going on—"

"They've been away on important kingdom business," Eris said. "We'll explain as we walk."

CHAPTER 12

*S*end *my daughter.*

In the face of horror, Bristol clung to those words. *My daughter.* Those two words reduced Bristol to a small child lost in a marketplace, hoping to be gathered up in her mother's arms. *My mother remembers.* Or did she? Bristol had no right to be hopeful, not after what she had done to Glennis.

She's my mother. She won't hurt me.

There were things people said to those they loved, little lies to ease their worries, lies so they could move forward, unafraid. Like the ones she told Harper and Cat. *I will bring Father home soon.* Soon was long past. Maybe that was why Cat had conspired in the lie about what Bristol really was, to make it easier. She had known that Bristol was at least part fae, but she never said a word. To keep the peace. Ignore the elephant in the room. Look away, because whatever it was, it was too big for them. *Look away*—the message ingrained in them from childhood.

Bristol felt the warmth of Tyghan's lips at her temple, heard his quiet plea, *come back to me.* And she had promised that she would, but promises were made of smoke, maybes, and luck. It was easy to make them. Far harder to keep them.

In truth, Bristol wasn't certain what would happen to her. Leanna Keats was her mother, but this Maire, she was a woman Bristol didn't know.

The horses stamped on the trail, eager to keep moving.

"We can go farther," Rose said, her eyes glistening with tears. "No one will know if we've crossed the border."

Bristol shook her head. "She'll know. Stick to the plan, Rose."

"I could shape-shift. Follow you from above." Rose's voice wobbled. "You can't trust her, Bristol. She's a monster."

The word stung, like Rose had struck her. *Monster*. She saw it shake the others too. Julia winced. Avery looked down at her saddle. Fear shone in all their faces. Fear for her.

Bristol didn't argue. How could she? Maire had shot Cully and then delivered Glennis's severed head to the palace gates. But Maire was not her mother.

"Her name is Leanna Keats," she said to Rose. "She likes orange soda pop, powdered doughnuts, and lambswool is her favorite yarn for weaving." It sounded like a rebuke. She didn't mean for it to be. She just wanted them to know that her mother hadn't always been who she was now. Or maybe Bristol just needed to remember that herself. "Breath by breath, everyone changes, and not always by choice. None of us know who we might be a year from now."

Rose didn't reply, but Julia nodded, and her gaze locked tight onto Bristol's. "You're going to be all right," she said. Julia knew about little lies too. They had to move forward.

"But don't waste time," Sashka added. "Get out quickly. Let her say her piece, then tell her you have to go."

Avery hedged closer. "If she doesn't let you—"

"I know what to do." Bristol and August were fortified with the strongest wards that could render them both invisible and at least give them a good head start before Maire and her wizards could expose her and take chase. And August was fast, faster than any horse in the kingdom, maybe in all of Elphame.

Hollis sidled close to Rose, as if to block her from following. "Be safe, my friend," she said to Bristol. "We'll be here for you."

And Bristol knew they would be, even to their own peril, and that only made the weight in her chest heavier.

CHAPTER 13

Tyghan pressed one hand against the vault door, leaning in, thinking, the dark of the narrow stone hallway swallowing him up. His thoughts skipped unevenly between then and now. He contemplated what he would say, what he would do. But at this point, what was left to say? He felt cold inside. Dead. Vengeful.

He had sent everyone else away. They understood. This was more than a king addressing a prisoner. He fingered the hilt of the demon blade sheathed at his side. He hadn't removed it from its locked cabinet since the first day it was placed there after his stabbing, but after Eris told him the news, it was the first thing he retrieved. The second thing was a bottle of whiskey. He gripped its smooth neck in his other hand.

It was only a little stab. His chest seized with something wild and lost as he remembered Kierus's words. His jaw clenched, trying to contain the storm swirling inside him, and then he turned and opened the door. Sconces on either side of the entrance flickered dimly, leaving much of the room in shadow. A single votive burned on a small table in the room, illuminating the prisoner sitting just behind it. He was shackled to his chair, and a thick collar was secure around his neck to prevent any magic from within or without.

His eyes cut into Tyghan, defiant, challenging, in spite of his circumstances, as if he were still the acclaimed hero of Danu.

Tyghan walked closer, pulling two small shot glasses from his vest and setting them down on the table.

"A last drink for the condemned?" Kierus asked.

Tyghan shrugged. "We have a few minutes to kill. Why not?"

"And a last meal? Is that coming too?"

"It can be arranged if that's what you want."

Kierus swallowed, then shook his head. "A drink is enough."

Tyghan sat down opposite him and pulled the stopper from the whiskey. He filled both shots. "This used to be your favorite."

Kierus lifted his glass and sipped, a low, approving rumble rolling from his chest. "They don't make whiskey like this in the mortal world."

"If I'd had your address, I would have sent you some."

Kierus smiled. "I'm sure you would have. Next time."

Tyghan didn't reply, the charade of friendship already wearing on him. This wasn't a game he wanted to play, and yet he didn't want to move forward either. He wanted something he couldn't have, something that didn't exist anymore. "Who helped you get a note to Bristol inside the palace?" he finally asked.

"Come on, brother, you know I can't tell you that."

"Even if they're a traitor to the Crown?"

Kierus's dark eyes drilled into him, scrutinizing, superior. Older. "Is that all you are now, Tyghan? A crown? Aren't you a man anymore?"

Tyghan ignored the taunt. "A knight's oath used to mean something to you."

"A friend's oath. That's what you mean. Isn't that what this is all about?"

The ache that had plagued him all these months swelled, tearing at his insides, but instead of the pent-up words he had planned, he only poured more whiskey for them both. Carefully. He worked hard to keep his hand steady, to not spill a drop, in spite of the tremor shaking beneath his ribs. Kierus had over twenty years to get past his betrayal. For Tyghan it had only been a few months. His wound was still fresh.

Kierus leaned forward, his hands protectively cupping the shot glass, and a flood of words poured out. "I know what I did was wrong. Is that what you want to hear from me? That I know? But what if *every* choice I had was wrong? That day . . . it haunted me. I relived it over and over, trying to think of all the ways I could have done something different. Things I could have said, done. Begged harder? Begged more? But I knew you, Tygh. I knew you too well. I used to finish your sentences, and you mine. You know that's true. And that day—" He shook his head, as though the memory was fresh and alive in his head. Like it was making something inside him tear in half too. "That day, I looked into your eyes. The resolve, I saw it. It was already done in your mind. I saw the knight in *me*, inside *you*. I knew what you had to do, the oath you had to honor. I didn't know how I was going to stop you, and I only had a split second to decide."

"You decided wrong."

Kierus leaned back, his eyes darkening. "Really?" he said, his superior air returning. He wasn't ready to back down from his choices. "I've had a life now, Tygh. The life I always wanted. My art. A woman I loved and who loved me. Three beautiful daughters. What about them? What about *Bristol*? Do you think she's a mistake?"

Tyghan's fist tightened. He would not discuss Bristol with him. "Any thief can sow a field of wheat. That doesn't pardon him from what he stole."

"What have *you* stolen? Her trust? She thinks you love her. Or are you only using her to get at me?"

Tyghan shook his head. "I won't discuss Bristol."

Kierus's chains rattled as he strained against them, his fist pounding the table. "She's my daughter, dammit! I have a right to know!"

"You abandoned her. Don't talk to me about rights. This is not about me and Bristol. It's about you and what you did!"

"Who made me the Butcher of Celwyth? Your brother? Sloan? You? All the knights who lifted me up on their shoulders? Praising my kills. I was the amusing mortal who exceeded everyone's expectations. As long as I was doing these things for you, I was your hero."

That much was true. He had been the charming hero, quick of tongue, who delivered his lethal blows with finesse. His fellow knights brought back stories of his exploits.

Tyghan shrugged. "All knights do their share of killing to defend the kingdom. You weren't special in that regard."

"But what if I never wanted to be that person at all? What if I wanted to be something else? Someone else. That's all I wanted. A second chance. That's what Maire wanted too."

"And you got it. You've had twenty-three more years than you deserved. Your time is up on that second chance."

"So I'm going to die."

"No, Kierus . . . you're not."

His lips parted, his imputed sentence sinking in. He was still enough of a knight to feel the disgrace, the humiliation. "The worst of the worst? Is that really what I am?"

"The council passed sentence. You committed regicide."

The color at his temples surged. "But you're still alive!"

"It was your intent. And other good knights died searching for you." Tyghan called out a few names, knights Kierus had known.

His gaze faltered at each mention, but when Tyghan finished, Kierus quickly countered, "And how many died looking for Cael because of his recklessness? He was betrothed, and he snuck off to fuck his mistress. Are their deaths on him? What sentence does he face? Don't play with your words. This is about you."

"Then let it be about me."

"Don't do this, Tyghan. For Bristol's sake. She will never forgive you."

"She'll never know."

Kierus's head sank into his hands, and he stared down at the table. Tyghan knew he was only regrouping, thinking of more arguments or, more likely, a way to disarm him. Kierus never gave up. But when he looked back at Tyghan, his words were quiet, pleading, leading in a new direction. "Don't kill Maire. I'm begging you, Tyghan. I would get down on my knees if I wasn't chained to this chair. Kill me. Do whatever you want to me. Put my head on a pike and parade it around Elphame. But Maire, she doesn't deserve this."

Tyghan pushed his drink aside. Veins rose in his neck. "Glennis is *dead*. Her head was delivered to the palace gates this morning. A gift from your wife. Don't tell me what she deserves."

"Because she knows you have Bristol. She's scared, dammit! She is terrified."

Tyghan stood, his head pounding. "I don't give a shit that she's terrified! Neither does Glennis! She will never feel anything in this world again!" He pulled the demon blade from its sheath and stabbed it into the table, a hair's breadth from Kierus's hand. "This is my mercy to you. My only mercy. I was going to stab you with it before you began your sentence. *Just a little stab*." He pulled the blade free from the table and returned it to its sheath. "But I remembered that you were once my friend, and I wouldn't do that to my worst enemy."

Kasta was waiting for Tyghan when he emerged from the vault. As First Officer, it was her job to carry out the sentence. She was ready, eager even, so he kept his orders brief. He needed to get out of there, get away. The vault was airless. His lungs ached.

"Take care of it quickly. One month. That will be his full sentence."

She balked, as if she hadn't heard him correctly. "A month? You mean a thousand years. That's what Judge's Walk always is. It's what the council ordered."

"One month," he repeated. "In that length of time, this conflict will be settled, and he can quietly go on with his life."

"*Let him go?* Have you completely lost your senses?"

"I'm the king, and I have the power to commute a sentence."

"No you don't, not after a full council vote!" she argued. "Once his punishment is entered into the record—"

"Delay the entry."

"But if they find out—"

"They won't. *No one* else is to know, not even Eris. The council ignored his summons to rescind the order. One month is what Kierus took from me. That's what I'm taking back from him."

"He took more than a month from you. You're still not whole. You might never be. Not to mention, he stole the trust of an entire company of knights, including me. You can't—"

"Take care of it, Kasta, and don't instruct me again on what I can or cannot do. Remember your place."

She looked at him like he had struck her. Her shoulders pulled back. "You're risking *everything*. Why are you doing this?"

Because Bristol loves Kierus. Because he's her father. Because he was once my friend, he thought. His throat swelled, and he only answered, "Because I'm king and I can."

He walked away quickly, muttering some excuse. The hallway to his chamber seemed to lengthen to miles, every step growing more un-bearable. *What if every choice I had was wrong?* When he finally reached his room, he slammed his door behind him and fell back against it, his breaths uneven, and he swiped the sting from his eyes.

CHAPTER 14

Kill the creature. She means nothing to me.

Which woman would Bristol be meeting at the base of Queen's Cliff? Her mother, who had protected her and whispered desperate spells into her ear, or the monster who served the king of Fomoria? Was this all an elaborate trap to capture Bristol—a trap that had cost Glennis her life? Was Kormick behind it? *Of course he was. My mother is not a murderer. Kormick controls her. He uses her fear.*

Bristol wasn't immune to fear. It was a heavy stone sitting in her gut, but rage crawled over her skin too, multiplying with each mile like an infection.

Glennis's sightless blue eyes burned bright in Bristol's mind. Glennis, now forever the watchful knight, scanning a sky she would never see again. Bristol would be Glennis's eyes now. Bristol would be her teeth and nails and fire.

She and August crossed over Balor Pass, quickly approaching the base of Queen's Cliff, a flat span of sand along the shore that gleamed in the noon sun.

Stay clear of the water. There's merkind there that will pull you under.
Stay invisible until you get your bearings.
Circle first. Look for a trap.

Don't dismount from August.

Be ready to flee. Go low. They'll expect you to go high.

No. Follow your instincts. Always follow your instincts.

The advice the officers piled on her could only take her so far. They all knew, any trap laid would likely be sure and complete. A deathtrap. This was either a real meeting meant to appease Maire and keep Cael's head attached to his shoulders, or it was meant to capture Bristol—and odds were, it was the latter.

Come back to me, Bri. Promise me.

The thought of her mother or Kormick trying to thwart her return only made her rage burn brighter. She would return, and it wouldn't be with her head in a chest.

She circled the beach again, wary.

The sandy base of Queen's Cliff only stretched for about two hundred yards. It was deceptively as beautiful as the cliffs of Étretat, though Bristol was certain Monet had never painted these, nor had any other painter who might have skipped into Elphame on sabbatical—or by accident. No matter how beautiful, this was not a place to set up a canvas and linger, not if you valued your life. *Get out quickly.* But how quick was quick enough?

The beach at the bottom of the cliff was deserted. Bristol eyed the widest section in the middle, maybe thirty yards deep, that would give her the greatest distance from the shore and the merkind dwelling in the water.

"Down," she whispered to August. He shed his invisibility, and Bristol pushed back the hood of her cloak to shed hers, and they descended. August's hooves kicked up white sand and stone as he slowed and bellowed his misgivings.

Not far from the shore, a silver tail flipped out of the water and disappeared again. The creatures already knew she was there.

There was no sign of her mother, but Bristol sensed a presence, a feeling of being watched. Maybe it wasn't a learned habit after all, but a suppressed fae skill she was born with?

Against advice she slid from August's saddle.

"I came alone as ordered," she called into the emptiness. "No hidden weapons. You have nothing to fear from me."

The small sound of ripples lapping at the shore was the only reply.

She scanned the beach one way and then another, and called out again, "I know you're there. More games?"

Though she really wasn't certain at all. The air was heavy with the sea, salty and sticky on her cheeks. She considered returning to August's back, but then, in a niche at the base of the cliff, a mist grew, and from it, a figure materialized.

Maire. Leanna. Her mother. Or whoever she was today.

Maire, Bristol thought. *For today she needs to be Maire. A stranger.*

The flutter in Bristol's chest accelerated to a sickening thump. Maire was perched on a smooth boulder like it was her throne, an elegant raven gown hugging her svelte form. Her copper hair was done up in multiple graceful braids that twisted across her head and around . . . her horns. Horns that Bristol would never get used to. She had seen them on a hundred different creatures and fae, but horns did not belong on her mother. Bristol's gaze dropped from the golden horns to her mother's jade eyes. They were inscrutable.

"No games," Maire finally answered. "I just wanted a moment to get a quiet look."

"And Kormick?" Bristol asked, eyeing the surrounding beach. "He's still hiding?"

Maire laughed, her eyes sparking. "Kormick? He never comes here. It's too primitive for his taste. Not to mention, he can't stand that worthless bag of bones that he's holding up top. He can't wait to be rid of him."

Worthless. Cael. The way she said *rid* didn't sound at all like *release*. It sounded permanent.

"Only my trusted guards are here with me," Maire continued. "They're waiting at the fortress and won't come down here unless I summon them."

Bristol had known this reunion with her mother would be different from that with her father, but it was colder than she expected. There was no temptation to run into her mother's arms. No tears. No hugging or soft endearments. Even as her mother continued to study Bristol from afar, her body language was as chilly as frost.

"Finally convinced it's me?"

Maire rose to her feet. "I know my own daughter when I see her."

"You didn't seem to when you ordered Tyghan to slit my throat."

"Elphame is full of tricks. I know now."

"And yet—" Bristol scrutinized Maire with an equally dissecting gaze. "I don't know my own mother when I see her. I don't know who you are at all. You're a stranger to me."

Maire's chin lifted slightly like Bristol had struck her, a crack in her steely composure. Her thumb grazed her finger, her old habit coming to life, and a thin veil circled around her until she was glamoured into Leanna Keats, a woman without horns, her hair loose down her back. She wore cheap drawstring trousers and a loose tee that slipped off one shoulder. Her feet were bare.

Bristol resisted the flinch of her stomach. "You needn't have bothered," she said, keeping her tone just as cool as her mother's. "A little glamour doesn't change what's inside. You're still the woman who murdered Glennis."

Her mother smiled, and her perfectly arched brows rose higher, as if amused. "Murder? Is that how they're painting this?" Her smile faded, and her voice went sharp and deadly, the voice Bristol had heard at their disastrous first encounter. "They kill one of my trusted guards? They snatch my daughter from her home and hold her hostage, and I am supposed to do nothing? That was an act of war, and Glennis was a casualty of that war like any other."

Her mother nudged a step closer, and Bristol took a step back, mindful of the shore behind her. They moved in half steps as they spoke, equidistant, in a circle, like wrestlers in a match, contemplating each other's moves.

"I'm not a hostage, Mother. Tyghan and I—"

Maire cursed. "I knew it. You leaned into that knife." Bristol searched for a denial, but her mother was already hurling another question at her. "You're sleeping with him, aren't you? It's in your voice when you say his name."

Bristol stared, shocked at how she could glean that from just a few words. Did her mother have more motherly instincts than Bristol gave her credit for? Or did Bristol's tone actually change when she said Tyghan's name? Was Bristol so inextricably tied to him already, that she couldn't even think his name without it showing in her face?

"He's the one who dragged you here?"

"No. I came here of my own free will."

"Nonsense," Maire replied. "You didn't even know about this world. Your father and I made certain—"

"I know about it now. I know more secrets than you think." She stared at her mother, trying to imagine her placing an ugly tick on her own baby's back all those years ago. Instead, she shared a different secret. "I know what your uncles did to you."

The revelation had the desired effect, but Bristol found no joy in it. The ugliness of the secret left Maire speechless. Years of anguish were alive inside her again, and she stared at Bristol like she had betrayed her with something as lethal as a demon blade.

"Father told me," Bristol added. "I came here to find him. I made a deal with Danu in return for their help."

Maire sucked in a breath at last, her cool reserve fully shattered. "Your father? Your father is *here*?"

For a brief moment, Bristol saw a glimpse of her mother, the woman she used to be. "That's right," she answered. "He thought you were coming back, and when you didn't—"

"He's a dreamer!" She scowled, the hardness restored. "He always was."

"He said you promised to come back—"

"I said I'd *try*! It was the only way I could get him to let me go. Try! I didn't promise."

"So you lied to him."

"I did what was necessary."

"You should have known he would follow. You're his whole world. He was devastated when you left. We had to sell off all of his paintings to survive, but he refused to sell his sketches of you. You were his muse. His everything. You always were. He was miserable and lost and couldn't go on without you. And now he's here to save you."

"I don't need saving!" her mother hissed, swiping her fingers across her temple. Her steps became erratic, turning one way, then another. "Damn you, Logan," she whispered under her breath. "Damn you."

Her anger toward him was real. A sharp pang pierced Bristol, like she had lost something else she had always believed in—her parents' enduring love for each other. "You always said he was the love of your life."

"Leanna Keats said those things, and that woman no longer exists, if she ever did. She was an illusion, a life I tried to live for over twenty years."

"Are you saying you never loved Daddy?"

She recoiled at a truth she couldn't face. "Where is he?" she demanded.

"I'm the only one who knows where he is. I haven't told anyone. I need to know he'll be safe."

"*Tell me.*"

Bristol hesitated. Her mother's face was lined with rage. Maybe she really was finished with him. *Only I can reach her.* Was her father right, or was that his delusional optimism? He would be destroyed without her either way. Bristol had no choice but to take a chance and trust in her long-held beliefs about their love for each other.

"He's at the cottage on the Runic River where you keep your loom. He's waiting for you to come to him."

Maire's head wobbled slightly, like she was disoriented. "He's going to ruin everything."

"Ruin what? Your plan to rule Elphame?"

"To give my family a future! Kormick came to Bowskeep and

warned me that Danu was closing in on our trail. Who do you think we were running from for all those years? But Danu only wanted me, not any of you. I couldn't do it anymore. I couldn't do it to my family. When I returned to Elphame, their pursuit was over. They know exactly where I am now. I made that clear to them as soon as I returned. I've sacrificed everything to save you, and now your father is ruining—"

"He's not ruining anything, Mother. Kormick is. He was the one hunting us down. *He* wants your power. He's using you and your fear to take control of Elphame."

"Kormick? Using me?" She paced, biting her lower lip. Now she looked like Leanna Keats, the one who grew restless, bottled up tight like a forbidden potion, weighing silent strategies, simmering herbs on the back of the stove, the mother always ready to move on. To run. And Bristol thought maybe that was exactly what she was about to do.

"You can't—"

"Quiet!" Maire whirled around abruptly and glared at Bristol. Her glamour faded, her horns and formal gown returning. Her eyes held the cold edge of winter, cutting through Bristol, her power and beauty frightening. "Let me tell you something, dear daughter who thinks she knows everything about this world—and me." Her lip lifted in disgust. "You *think* you know. I'll spare you the uglier details, but after my parents were murdered, my uncles moved in and claimed their house—and me. I was twelve the first time they chained me to a post out in the yard. It was punishment for an endless list of offenses, for not jumping fast enough at their orders, for not sweeping the floor clean enough, for weeping when I missed my parents, but mostly for creating portals to other parts of the Darkland Forest to escape from them and their vilest demands. My problem was I didn't escape far enough. The forest was all I knew. They always found me and chained me again—if not in the yard, in the house. They did this when I was fourteen." She motioned to her silver hand. "They thought if they chopped it off, it would end my magic. It didn't.

"We lived off a tiny road in the forest, a dark byway. The only ones who used it were those going somewhere they shouldn't, which is probably why they ignored me. For two long years, I watched lords

and ladies pass by on the lane in their golden carriages, their voices tin-
kling from their windows like cut glass raised in a toast, their laughter and chatter far more important than my cries. And when nobles
weren't passing by in their carriages, they passed by on great white
steeds with their fine cloaks billowing out behind them like wings,
indifferent to my state. That's what I prayed for every day, wings to
deliver me from my misery. But those wings didn't come. If anyone
did take notice of the ragged girl in the yard, my uncles explained it
away with a multitude of excuses. I was possessed by a demon, they
said. Or it was to protect me from flinging myself off a bluff. I finally
stopped calling out to those passing by, because they wouldn't look
my way. My screams flew past them like I was one of the chickens
squawking from the henhouse."

Her pupils became furious pinpoints. "The only one, *the only one*,
who ever bothered to stop and inquire at any length about me was
Kormick, the king of Fomoria. He alone cared about the crazed girl
chained in the yard. He gave my uncles a great deal of gold to let me
go, and he took me to his home in Fomoria. He gave me food, clothing, a warm bed, a new right hand . . . and my own servants. He gave
me a lot of things no one else ever did. Time. Education. Understanding. Power. He gave me the wings I so desperately needed. If that's
using me, give me more of it."

"And revenge? He gave you that too?"

"*Yes*," she answered. "Maybe that was the best thing he gave me.
For that I owe him everything."

Her answer was crisp and practiced. A memory she clutched so
tightly, no others could wedge their way in. But Bristol needed a wedge,
one that would make her mother remember other things that had once
mattered to her more, and Bristol delivered it.

"Then why would you leave Kormick in the first place? Why not stay?
Had he shackled you with a different kind of chain, one that grew too
short? Did he limit your choices? You were allowed to take as many lovers
as you wished, weren't you? As long as you didn't take just one? As long
as you didn't fall in love? And then you betrayed him because you *did* fall

in love. You left him when you promised not to. Is that the deal you and Kormick have? You're not allowed to be devoted to anyone but him?"

Maire faltered, her bright eyes turning the color of a dark forest—a color Bristol had seen before. *Come away, child.* Desperate for Bristol to stop challenging her. To listen to her. *Come away.*

This truth stabbed too close to her mother's heart. She had escaped one kind of prison, only to walk into another. A prison that gave her the power to kill, the power to unleash legions of demons, to exact revenge and instill terror, but not the freedom to love.

Her head cocked slightly to the side, like a painful memory had wormed its way into her head. "No," Maire said, rubbing her temples. "No, it's not—I—" She searched for words that wouldn't come. Words and thoughts that Kormick had buried.

Her gaze whipped back around to Bristol. "You're going home. Now. You don't belong here. The Danu Nation will not destroy what I have created. You're going back to Harper and Catalina, and the three of you are going to run. You'll keep moving the way we taught you. You will have a life that is not under anyone's thumb."

She spun toward the towering cliff behind her, her palm raised in concentration like she was pushing against it. Light glittered around her eyes, traveled down her shoulder to her arm and then down to her hand. A swirling ball of silver light hovered just in front of her palm. Bristol watched awestruck as the sparkling light lengthened until it reached the wall, then spread out, rippling like gushing water. Maire mumbled words, and Bristol heard *the meadow, the old green barn, the split oak tree, the windmill.* Coordinates. Bristol knew the exact place her mother was describing—a place on the outskirts of Bowskeep. At the sound of those words, the silver light spread out along the cliff wall, and Maire's arm shook. Her pale cheeks warmed with color. The light grew to the size of a barn door, and as Maire dropped her arm back to her side, it vanished. She picked up a stone and tossed it toward the cliff. It disappeared through the rock, and a green meadow briefly appeared. "There," she said. "It leads to Bowskeep. Go back to your sisters."

Bristol stared at the door. Her mother had created an entirely new portal in less than a minute? It didn't take days to construct, then, as the historical records claimed.

Only the strongest of bloodmarked can open the Abyss. Or close it.

How powerful was Leanna Keats? Far more powerful than Bristol had imagined. It had taken Bristol several tries to close the one portal just outside Timbercrest, and even approaching the Abyss portal had left her hand badly blistered. And she still hadn't been able to create one. Her mother had done it with ease.

"Now," her mother ordered, pointing at the door.

When Bristol didn't move, Maire pounced on her, her fingers wrapping around Bristol's wrist like an iron bracelet, and she started dragging her toward the portal.

"No!" Bristol yelled, realizing her intent. "Let go!" She had read accounts of what happened to mortals who went back through a portal to their own world without a timemark. They could lose years, decades, or even centuries. One man even turned to dust the minute his feet touched back on mortal ground. She struggled fiercely against her mother's grip, digging her boots into the sand, twisting her arm until she broke free, just inches from the portal opening. She scrambled back, her heart hammering. "What's the matter with you?" she screamed. "I'm not fully fae! I'm half mortal! If I go through that wall, I could end up decades or centuries away from Harper and Cat."

Her mother's mouth fell open. "You don't have a timemark?"

"Not here!" Bristol shouted. "They gave me one, but it's back at the palace. It—"

It's back at the palace.

A thought uncoiled beneath her ribs, dark and cunning.

"They're keeping it there. They'll only give it back to me once I fulfill my end of our bargain."

"You made a bargain?" Maire shook her head and growled. "Never make deals with the lower gods! What did you promise them?"

"To help them protect Danu. They thought I might have your powers. Unfortunately, they've discovered that I don't, so now I must give them something else of value."

"Like what?"

"I don't know. Right now, it's basic servitude, but they want something important, something big and worthy of their help. Something like . . ." Bristol shrugged. "Maybe something like Cael—"

Maire instantly balked. "*No*," she answered. "Kormick is using him to keep Danu in line. They are prideful and arrogant and refuse to acknowledge his right to reign."

"*His* right? Isn't it the Stone of Destiny that chooses the rightful heir to the throne?"

"The Stone will choose Kormick."

Because he was forcing that decision through threat, but that was a different argument.

"You already said that Kormick never comes here," Bristol said instead. "He wouldn't even know if you gave Cael to me. And together, you already lead an unbeatable army. What difference does Cael really make to him?"

Maire's brow knotted. "Because after Fomoria, Danu is the most powerful kingdom in Elphame, and the other kingdoms follow their lead. Without Danu's compliance, it will be a far messier transition. Kormick prefers for his coronation to go down in history as a grand celebration, not as a bloody massacre. What good is becoming king if all your subjects die in the process?"

"Danu doesn't want a massacre either, Mother. Yes they are prideful and arrogant—what kingdom isn't? But they're not fools. They know they have no chance against Fomoria's army of the dead. Kormick has made that clear to them. Don't you think they'd be attacking Fomoria right now if they thought they could win? They only want their king returned, a small token of pride tossed back to them. And if I was the one who gave them that, I'm certain they'd give me my timemark— and more. I could leave. I could take Father and go back to Cat and Harper. *Home.*"

Maire's face lost all expression, like she was doubling down on her final decision. "No," she said quietly. "Cael is one of those kings who ignored my screams. His carriage slowed when I cried out, but then he continued on because rescuing a filthy peasant girl was too much bother." Her lashes fluttered. "Cael's also the one who shamed your father in the middle of the throne room for wanting to return to his art. If not for Cael, both of our lives would have turned out differently. That man deserves a worse end than this. He will get that worse end."

A worse end like her uncles? She and Kormick never intended to let him go. Was that the only goal that consumed her now? To make everyone in Elphame pay, including those who got in her way, like Glennis? Like Cully, who she regretted not killing? Her scarves and loom were forgotten. Had her hunger for revenge erased her family too? She had already given Bristol two firm nos, but there had been a slight tremor, a sign that she was more than cold stone inside. A sign that Kormick couldn't steal every last piece of Leanna Keats. She studied her mother, trying to find some way to reach her. Trying to find—

Slow down, Brije, watch, listen. Her father's long-ago advice crept into her head. *In order to win over a crowd, you have to watch them, understand them. Search their eyes. Every one of them has dreams. Speak to their dreams, and you will win them over.*

Somewhere buried deep inside, her mother still had dreams, even if they were hidden beneath mountains of blood and hate and goldtipped horns. Even if she had traded them away for revenge, and a false sense of safety and power. Those dreams still lurked somewhere. Kormick had made the ultimate sale. Bristol had to best him. She had to make the best sale of her life.

"You're right, Mother, he does deserve worse, but is his worse end more important to you than your family? More important than me getting back home to Harper and Cat? Is Cael really worth that? Doesn't Kormick allow you to make any decisions? Wouldn't this be a good one? Let's talk. Give me something, and I will give you something back."

CHAPTER 15

There!" Rose shouted. "She's coming!"

The others strained to see where Rose pointed, their vision not as sharp as her hawkish gaze, but a few seconds later, Bristol came into view for them too. They heaved a collective sigh.

"Thank the gods," Hollis said, but then angled her head, puzzled. "Why is she riding so slowly?"

"Should we ride to meet her?" Avery asked, even though they had been ordered not to cross the border.

Julia urged her horse a few paces forward, puzzled by Bristol's slow pace too. Her palm curled around the hilt of her sword. Her insides hummed, ready to shape-shift.

"What's that behind her?" Sashka asked.

Bristol was cast in shadow by the surrounding trees, and they all squinted, trying to make out the dark blur.

"It's a person!" Rose answered.

Questions came in rapid fire after that.

"Is it a trap?"

"Are they holding her hostage?"

"Can you see a weapon?"

"What's our plan?"

"Should we go—"

"Wait." Julia rode a few lengths to the side to get another view, as eager as the rest to disobey orders. "No," she called to the others, finally getting a good glimpse of the unexpected passenger. "Hold your positions." She breathed out with relief, wondering how on earth Bristol had managed this, and then, with the next breath, worried what it might have cost her.

🔑

Da Vinci. The name clouded Bristol's thoughts, pressing down like a heavy sky on a windless day. *Da Vinci.* Her father's find of the century. Anyone's find of the century. But did he really *find* it, as he claimed, or was it a deal that cost him something? Something dear. Did he have to sell part of his soul to get it?

That's how Bristol felt now. Like a gash had sliced through her middle, her insides torn away. Like she had traded part of her soul for the deal of the century. And that deal rode behind her now, a deal more valuable to the twelve kingdoms of Elphame than any da Vinci.

I promise.

I promise if you give me Cael, I will go home.

I'll take Father with me, and we'll go back to Cat and Harper.

Today. But you have to give me something now. I won't get another chance.

She sold it to her mother. Sold it like there was no tomorrow. Every word curdled in her stomach as she said it, like she was using a Keats strategy against her own mother. And it worked. She sold her mother a dream.

Bristol felt the slight shift of hands at her waist. "Make a move for my knife, and I'll throw you off my horse."

"My brother's horse. You think I don't know that? Did you . . . kill him? No one else rides this beast."

Cael's words were slurred like he was drunk. Or maybe slightly delirious. He was so weak he could barely hold on to her. She wasn't too concerned about him grabbing her knife out of its sheath. A quick jabbing elbow would send him tumbling. As it was, she had to proceed at a snail's pace so he wouldn't fall off. He already had once, which cost him a split lip, and getting him back up on August was no small feat. She couldn't levitate something that big. Cheese puffs were her forte, not large men. And he was large—like Tyghan—though at this point, thin. His cheeks were hollowed out, and he barely resembled his robust portrait in the foyer of the palace.

He still wore the collar that prevented him from using magic, so he was useless in that regard too. Her mother had refused to remove it, saying it would give his sorcerers something to occupy their time. Bristol teetered between sympathy for his pathetic state and complete loathing for who he was and what he had done. His lack of empathy for her mother was fire inside her, like the burning goblin brew that made her choke. How different all of their lives might have been if he had been the one who stopped to help her mother instead of Kormick. And if her father could have pursued his art instead of being laughed out of—

"You didn't answer me. How did you get his horse?"

His inane mumblings were driving her mad. "I already told you—"

"I don't believe a word from your lying mouth. Another trick, that's all I see, and that monster has had an endless supply of them. A real Danu knight would have respect for me as their sovereign. They wouldn't—"

"Shut up!" she ordered, sick of his arrogance. "I don't have a shred of respect for you at all. You're a game piece on a board, and not even a useful one at that, and I am removing you from play to make our other moves easier. That's *it*. There, does that clear things up for you?" God, why did she end with a question when she didn't want him to say one more word?

By the mercy of one of their many gods, he remained silent.

For a full minute.

"Why do you hate me?" he asked. His words were still weak but clear, like he had carefully composed them.

"It doesn't matter," she answered. "All that matters is I'm taking you home." He didn't know she was Maire's daughter, and it was best to leave it that way.

"It matters when the first face I've seen in months doesn't belong to the enemy. Or are you?"

She wished he were still delirious. Maybe the fresh air was shaking his brain alive again. She didn't answer, hoping he would grow foggy once more.

Cael sighed. "Fine. Have it your way. Don't speak to me. But thank you, *if* you're truly rescuing me."

If.

It was a steady beat in her head. *If. If only.*

"I hate you because when Maire was chained to a post in her yard, you rode past without helping her. If you had only shown her the smallest bit of compassion—"

He grunted. "So she fed that story to you too? She shoved it in my face so many times I lost count."

"And yet I don't hear an ounce of remorse in your tone."

"Remorse? I was barely thirteen. I was a sudden orphan and a newly crowned king. I don't even remember seeing her. If we passed by, I was probably being schooled by a squad of tutors on my way to a kingdom that I was expected to impress."

"Even a thirteen-year-old can hear screams," she said.

"Through the jostle of a team of horses pulling a carriage over an uneven forest trail? You haven't ridden in many carriages, have you? I told you, I don't even remember her."

So very convenient, Bristol thought. The bitterness inside her doubled. "Then what about my—what about Kierus? You weren't a boy when he came to you asking for leave to study art. You humiliated him. You laughed him out of the throne room."

"What difference would that make to you?"

"You asked why I hate you. Decisions have repercussions. Real people have to live with them. Yours have affected all of Elphame. If he had pursued his art—"

"Are you mad? You're saying laughing at Kierus gave him just cause to betray Danu? I laughed him out of the throne room numerous times. He was always coming up with some new scheme. Art was just another one of his crazy—"

"My father loved his art! After his family, it was his passion! It wasn't a scheme!"

A schism ruptured the air. Bristol's ears echoed with the temporary silence. She realized her misstep too late.

"Your father?" Cael finally said. "Then that means—"

In her fury, she didn't care what he thought, but in the next second, she felt something sharp at her jugular. "I knew this was a trick," Cael whispered close to her ear.

He had either rapidly regained his strength or he wasn't as weak as he had pretended to be—and she had fallen for it. His breath was hot against her neck, his free hand tight and strong around her waist, his broad chest snug to her back. "Now who will be throwing whom from the horse? Or maybe I should do something else—"

Cael sucked in a fast breath as he jerked Bristol tighter against him.

"I wouldn't, Your Majesty." Julia's voice was slow and buttery as she lifted her veil of invisibility. "If you kill her, you'll be killing Elphame's last chance for survival. And if you make the slightest move, that sword you feel at your spine will immediately sever it, because this woman matters more than you do."

Julia sat tall and regal on her horse in front of them. Sashka and Rose flanked her, just as magnificent—and deadly. Avery and Hollis materialized behind Bristol and Cael, their faces enraged, Avery poking Cael's back with her sword, eager to carry out Julia's threat.

"Lower it. *Now*," Julia ordered again, her tone making it clear that there wouldn't be another warning.

Cael lowered the knife and tossed it to the ground.

Sashka hissed and levitated the knife, guiding it to her hand, then shot the king a stinging glare. "Ingrate," she said. "Last time we rescue you."

CHAPTER 16

"What are you staring at?"

Maire faced the window, stone-still, her eyes unsee-ing. Kormick had noticed her empty gazes more often in these last few days. What was she thinking? She never shared, but he couldn't afford for her to fall apart at this point. She had, many times before, but he always managed to put her back together again, and she loved him for it. At least in her own way. He would remind her of her strength, her power, and, more covertly, that he had been her savior. He *was* her savior. He had saved her when no one else would.

"Nothing," she answered. "Just looking."

He stepped up, standing behind her, his hand on her shoulder. He looked out at the vista of Fomoria, the foreboding rocky crags, the lush forests, the wild realm he ruled, vast in its reach but limited in its offerings—at least for someone like her, who had partaken of all the sights and pleasures of the mortal world. He kissed her bare shoulder. He wanted to give her everything they both deserved—the power they had been denied. That power was within their grasp now.

"Is it a mortal lover you miss? I can bring you one. Or many."

She stiffened under his touch, silent in her answer, but then reached up, caressing his hand on her shoulder. "I lack for nothing. I am done with mortal lovers." She turned to face him and added, "But I think some time at my loom would do me good."

"I'll arrange an escort."

"The cottage is remote and long abandoned. My personal guards are enough."

CHAPTER 17

There were a hundred other things he should have been doing, but instead Tyghan poured himself a drink and stared out his window at the skies, watching for Bristol, and then down at the path that led to Judge's Walk, watching for Kasta. Waiting. Waiting for the whole world to stop. Or to move faster. To make sense, if that was even possible.

Let him go? Have you completely lost your senses?

He probably had.

I've had a life now, Tygh. Three beautiful daughters. What about Bristol? Do you think she's a mistake?

Nothing about Bristol was a mistake. He couldn't reconcile the two opposing facts: Kierus had brutally betrayed him, but had also given him the most perfect thing in his life.

He stole the trust of an entire company of knights.

Kasta's arguments were sound. The betrayal had devastated them all. Had he made a mistake? He'd been shaken by Kierus's pleas. Had he succumbed to Kierus's golden tongue? To the deep-rooted feelings of friendship that he couldn't put behind him? He touched his side. They weren't friends anymore, and he still had the scar as proof. Was meeting with Kierus face-to-face his biggest mistake of all?

Tyghan eyed the mouthful of amber whiskey left in his glass. Kierus's favorite. The whiskey they used to drink together. *I saw the knight in me, inside you. I knew what you had to do.* And now, Tyghan had done what he needed to do. Kierus was out of the picture for one month so he couldn't go fuck things up again, and when this was all over, he could quietly return to his old life in the mortal world without the council ever knowing. Bristol would have her father back, and Tyghan wouldn't have to think about him ever again. He just needed to keep this all quiet for a few more weeks, which was no easy task. He swigged the brew back and had just poured himself another when there was a knock. He ran to his door and threw it open. It was Melizan.

"Is there news? Is she back?"

Melizan shook her head. "No. Nothing yet." She walked past him to the sideboard where his glass sat next to the whiskey bottle and poured herself one too. "You met with Kierus?"

He nodded. "A little while ago."

She brought his glass over to him. "How did it go?"

As badly as anyone would expect, Tyghan thought. *Worse.* "Not well," he answered. "We only met for a few minutes, long enough for a drink. No one else is to know that we have him, not even the council."

"Good idea. If the council starts celebrating his capture and word gets back to Maire, we may have a whole new wave of beheadings."

He didn't tell Melizan about the abbreviated sentence. When he told Kasta that no one else was to know, he meant everyone. It was one more thing that would create an uproar, and with the clock ticking, he had no time for chaos.

"Kasta is taking care of the sentence."

"As she should," Melizan answered. "It's the First Officer's job, and you've wasted enough time on him." She wrinkled her nose in distaste. "Besides, I've heard the process is quite gruesome."

"More gruesome than enduring the torture of a demon blade?"

She shook her head. "No. Nothing is worse than that. For two months I watched a strong, stubborn knight reduced to a weak, tormented—"

Tyghan put his hand up in a stopping motion. "I don't need to hear."

She sighed. "For you, this torture will never be over, brother. We just watched you suffer through it again last week. It will always be lurking. He deserves what he's getting. Don't agonize over this."

This.

Don't do this, Tyghan. For Bristol's sake. She will never forgive you.

"Let's talk about something else," he said, turning back toward the window.

"Happily. I actually came to discuss another matter. I've asked Cosette to marry me."

A fist tightened in his chest. It was the last thing he expected her to say. He spun to face her. "*What*—"

"We plan to wed before the Choosing Ceremony."

Now it seemed it was Melizan who had lost her mind. He rubbed the back of his neck. Now? Of all times? "What's the rush?"

"There's a very good chance we're all going to end up dead. If we do, Cosette and I would like to walk hand in hand into Paradise. We want you to perform the binding ritual."

Tyghan shook his head in disbelief. He didn't need this right now. "When did you get so sentimental?"

"When I met Cosette. It's called *love*. I thought you had become acquainted with it—"

"Don't bring me into this. There isn't time for a wedding now. After—"

"Is your objection to the timing or to who I'm marrying? Not that she needs to, but hasn't Cosette proven herself to you by now?"

Tyghan sighed. "Yes. She has. But—"

"There are no buts, Tyghan. Yes, she is merkind. Yes, she still has family in the waters of Fomoria. But she is not them, not any more than Bristol is Maire."

His stomach clenched at the comparison. "I know," he said. "I know that, but the preparation—"

"The whole ritual takes fifteen minutes. Less than the length of a meal. And I presume you still plan to eat before we meet Kormick in battle. I'd like my brother to do the binding, but if you're too busy, I'll find someone else."

Her gaze rested on his, steady as stone, like she had already prepared herself for a clash with him. Was he just used to going to battle with her? Had it become habit? But there was something else in her eyes too, something he couldn't ignore. Joy? He wasn't sure, but something hopeful shimmered in them, something that was not like Melizan at all. Now that her decision was made, had she suddenly embraced the whole idea of *caring too deeply* that she had rejected only weeks ago? This meant more to her than he had thought possible.

"Brother—"

"All right," he answered. "I'll do it." A wedding. Another thing to add to his list.

"Thank you," she said softly.

He grudgingly stepped forward and kissed her cheek. "Congratulations to you both. I suppose it will be good to have something to celebrate for a change."

A puff of air escaped through her teeth. "Look at you. Now who's being sentimental?" She gave his cheek a peck and walked to the door. "I'll let you know when," she chirped over her shoulder.

"Don't tell Eris," he called after her, but she had already slammed the door.

Eris and Ivy would turn fifteen minutes into an all-day affair.

CHAPTER 18

The guards secured the struggling and cursing prisoner to the towering column, a cloth sack covering his head. A chain shackled his wrists around its circumference, and his cheek pressed into the cold marble as he threatened the four junior knights from the garrison.

"Leave us," Kasta ordered when they were done. The rest she could do on her own, and there were things that still needed to be said—without others listening.

"But our orders were—"

"My orders are from the king, and I'm your senior officer," Kasta answered. "I said leave *now* and speak of this to no one."

They shuffled back a few steps and retreated, not just because she was their senior officer but because there was something wild in her expression.

Kasta turned and faced Kierus. He was quiet now, the only sound his labored breaths. She stepped forward and yanked the sack from his head. A strand of hair hung over his brow, a strand she might have once smoothed back with her fingers. His dark eyes drilled into hers, eyes that had always made her weak. Even now, they wrenched something inside her.

"You can't do this, Kasta," he pleaded. "You can't. We have too much—"

"Stop!" she ordered. "I let you go once, Kierus. I let you go, and you betrayed me."

"I didn't tell anyone what you did. No one knows—"

She shook her head. "You still don't understand! I disobeyed orders! You didn't leave as you promised. I trusted you, and you turned around and stabbed Tygh. You made me complicit. It may as well have been me who plunged that knife in his gut. Can't you see that?"

"I swear we were about to leave. But—"

"I've had to live with my decision. It eats away at me. *Every single day*. I loved you, Kierus. I loved you so much that I let you go. I wanted you to be happy, even if you couldn't be happy with me."

He winced at the truth that he could never bring himself to say. "I always cared about you, Kasta. You know that. What we had together was good. It just wasn't the same as—"

"As with her." Her eyes welled. "I could have been a monster. Is that how your tastes run, Kierus?"

"Please, Kasta, these are Tyghan's orders. Not yours. Don't do this."

She smiled and a puddle in her eye spilled over, trickling down her cheek. "Because of Bristol, he took mercy on you and only ordered a month of imprisonment. It could cost him his crown."

Kierus's mouth opened, his misery replaced with surprise.

"But Judge's Walk is always a thousand years. It gives the worst of the worst time to contemplate their choices. It's what the council ordered, and it's what I'll give you. I'm fixing the terrible mistake I made, right now."

Kierus strained against the chains, his wrists bleeding as he screamed at her. "No! Kasta! I beg you! You can't do this! Please!"

She pulled the dropper from the bottle and put four drops on the column and whispered, "*Eda laespi mil fidan*. He is yours for a thousand years."

The drops began smoking, spreading over the column toward

Kierus, like the liquid was tracking his scent. When the first drop reached his arm, his skin began cracking, turning to stone the same color as the column. It spread up his arm to his shoulder, toward his face. A hoarse sound jumped from this throat as he struggled to get away.

The other columns down the line shivered and whined, waking from their stupors, sensing that another soul was being added to their ranks, reminding them of their own crimes and despair. A dark magic crackled between them, searching for power they no longer had.

Kasta watched as Kierus twisted and screamed in a futile attempt to evade the creeping curse, until his screams were finally muffled by the stone inching up his neck, and the column slowly absorbed his body. The agonized sounds stopped as his head was pulled into the column along with everything else, except for the chains around his wrists.

They dropped to the ground with a loud clatter, and then there was only silence and the tick of time inside Kasta's head. The time she had wasted. The time Tyghan had lost. The time Kierus had stolen from them all. The time he would now give back, always remembering his last moments with her.

"Now I will be your monster," she whispered.

CHAPTER 19

C lear the portico! Everyone!" Eris ordered. Hollis had ridden only a minute ahead of the others, with news of Bristol's impending arrival and a warning to empty the area of everyone except guards and knights.

"Now!" Hollis shouted, sending servants and gentry scurrying for shelter in the darkest and farthest reaches of the palace, afraid of another attack. Archers poured onto the grounds, taking positions.

Seconds later, Bristol and the other recruits materialized in the sky. As soon as they landed near the front steps where carriages would normally drop off passengers, commotion descended, officers rushing to see who they had brought back. Seeing that the grounds were clear, the recruits began untying the many knots securing the mysterious "prisoner" to August's back like he was a lumpy sack of potatoes. That's what many of the guards and archers were already murmuring, *a prisoner*. Quin, Cully, Eris, and Dalagorn demanded answers.

"What's this—"

"Who—"

"Where—"

"Is he dead?"

"Very much alive," Bristol answered, still focused on the ropes, which had become frustratingly more secure. Cael was slung belly down over August's back, his long hair covering his face, his hands filthy, his clothes in rags, quite unrecognizable from the portrait hanging in the main hall. She and Hollis had tied him to the saddle in order to give August free rein and ride at a higher speed. Cael may have had a burst of energy when he pulled the knife on her, but he still wobbled when they attempted to resume their journey. Tying him to August's back was the only way to get him home without the trip taking days, and Bristol, in a few hours, had already had more than enough of Cael. His riding position might have caused a cracked rib or two, *but oh well*, she thought. She'd leave the ribs for Esmee and Olivia to deal with. The knots were tedious, pulled tighter by Cael's jostling weight.

"Step back," Avery said. "I'll take care of it."

She circled August, her hands sweeping the air as she spoke to the fibers in the rope, her kinship with plants making the ropes wiggle and come to life. They followed her commands, unraveling swiftly before falling to the ground.

Cael moaned and rubbed his wrists.

"Get ready to catch him," Bristol said to the knights who were facing his backside. "His Majesty is weak."

"His w-*what*?" Eris rasped, choking on his words.

Bristol gave Cael's shoulders a firm shove, and he slipped off August, tumbling back into Quin's and Cully's arms, his legs noodles below him, bending and twisting until he got his footing.

"Let me go!" he ordered, still swaying.

"Your Majesty?" Eris said, his eyes wide with horror. He looked back at Bristol. "What—How—"

"I made a bargain with my mother."

"See! It's a trick! She's the monster's daughter! Kill the bitch!" Cael's hand shot up, pointing first at Bristol, then circling to the other recruits, his finger poking the air like he was hitting each one of them in the chest. "Seize them! All of them! Kill them! Do something!"

"But, Your Majesty," Eris said, "it appears they just rescued you. Are you certain—"

"They threatened to kill me! Regicide! They pushed a sword into my back. Execute them! Especially that one," he said, pointing at Bristol. "Kill her! Why aren't any of you following my orders? Get this damn collar off me!" he shouted, pulling at the ward around his neck. "I'll take care of them myself!"

And then he fainted.

Dalagorn caught the king, scooping him into his arms. Eris turned back to Bristol for answers. She blinked slowly. "In the last two days, I've had a knife held to my throat twice—both times by the Trénallis brothers. I am done for the day. *Done*. He's all yours. Keep him under wraps. Kormick doesn't know we have him, and he's not likely to find out. It's best to leave it that way."

Bristol turned, and Sashka looped an arm through hers as they walked away. The other recruits followed, leaving Eris and the knights to deal with their returned king.

"What bargain did you make?" Eris called after her.

A bad one, Bristol thought, but she only shook her head in answer.

CHAPTER 20

The waiting was killing Tyghan. He strapped on his sword, centering it on his back, and lashed out with his hand, for no reason at all. Magic flew from his fingertips like shimmering darts, shattering a vase. It didn't ease the energy straining inside him. What had he been thinking? It was madness to let Bristol leave to meet a monster who had just beheaded his officer. He was going after her, even if he had promised not to follow.

He cursed under his breath and threw open his door. Eris was there, his hand raised to knock. "She's back." Eris was breathless as he explained. "They've just returned. Bristol's completely fine—not a scratch on her—and has gone with her friends to the dining pavilion."

Tyghan doubted there was anything else that Eris could say that would keep him from flying to Bristol's side, from holding her until it hurt, but he was wrong. When he added who she had brought back with her, Tyghan didn't believe it.

Cael? Impossible.

Eris assured him it was true. Bristol had made a bargain with her mother.

"The even better news is that Kormick doesn't know, and we must keep it that way. But we still have a problem."

Tyghan recognized Eris's sigh. It was always provoked by some boneheaded thing his brother had done. "Well?"

"Your brother has demanded that Bristol and the other recruits be executed."

🔑

"He's resting now," Madame Chastain said when Tyghan and Eris entered Cael's outer chambers. She paused, noting Tyghan's and Eris's identical scowls, the angry dimple in the exact same place on their left cheeks, and wondered how no one else had ever noticed. The older Tyghan got, the more the similarities surfaced. "His lucidity comes and goes," she explained. "Olivia, Esmee, and I have done every cleansing spell we know, but we don't dare remove the collar yet. He is . . . unstable."

Unstable? Tyghan thought. That was an understatement. If Cael was ordering Bristol's execution, he was within an inch of his own. Tyghan took a step toward Cael's bedchamber. "I'll speak to him—"

"He's still sleeping. I wouldn't—"

And then there was a crash. Cursing.

Get out! Everyone! Out!

Are you all idiots?

I can piss on my own!

And bathe myself!

Three servants streamed out of Cael's bedchamber, including his groomer with a foamy razor still in hand.

"I guess he's not sleeping anymore," Tyghan said as he headed for the chamber door to knock some sense into his brother's hard skull.

Tyghan hadn't been in the king's bedchamber since before Cael was taken. It was triple the size of his own quarters, lavishly appointed, and in perfect order—except for a rumpled bed, an overturned tray on the floor, and a broken bowl beside it. There was no sign of his brother.

"Cael?" Tyghan called.

"I thought I told everyone—"

Cael emerged from his bath chamber, buttoning his trousers, and stopped short when he spotted Tyghan. Maybe it was the enormity of the room that made him look even more shrunken than he was. Fragile. He had easily lost forty pounds. It aged him. Or maybe it was the expression on his face. Dark smudges hung beneath his eyes like moons, and his light brown hair reached past his shoulders in tangled strings. He noted the long scar on Cael's neck half-hidden by the collar that thwarted his magic, and a smaller scar on his chin, perhaps acquired during his abduction—wounds Kormick's wizards never bothered to heal. Tyghan's ire cooled.

"Brother," Cael said, his voice husky. "It's you. It's really you." And then he collapsed onto the floor beside the fragmented bowl. Tyghan crossed the room, lifted him in his arms, and carried him to his bed.

Madame Chastain entered with Eris and they stepped up to the bed. She looked down at Cael and sighed. "This is how it's been going. He's weak, but in true Cael form, he overexerts himself and then passes out."

"Why did he order Bristol and the recruits executed?" Tyghan asked. "Is he completely demented? Doesn't he know that Bristol rescued him?"

"He thinks it's a trick," Eris answered. "That's what he was screaming out on the portico when he arrived. Apparently on the ride back he held a knife to Bristol's throat and when—"

"He *what*?"

"He was riding behind her on August and held her at knifepoint. His explanation was rambling and muddled, but he knows she's Maire's daughter. On Julia's orders, Avery held a sword to his back to get him to release Bristol. Now he wants them all dead."

Tyghan turned and slammed his hand against the wall. Cael had been back less than an hour, and already he wanted to kill his brother. He whipped back to face Eris. "You're sure Bristol's all right?"

"Disgusted, but completely fine," Eris assured him, "but there is one other thing." Eris glanced warily at Cael and lowered his voice. "He doesn't know yet that you've been crowned the interim king. He thinks he's still ruling Danu."

Tyghan hissed, already anticipating Cael's reaction. "Then the sooner we disabuse him of that notion, the better. He needs to be updated on a few other things as well." Tyghan surveyed the room and spotted a tall vase of flowers on a table. He grabbed it, tossing aside the flowers, and threw the remaining water in his brother's face. Cael sputtered to life, bolting upright. He cursed, shouting orders, but just as fast, Tyghan pinned him back against his pillow. "Listen to me, brother, and listen carefully—"

"Get off me! What is the matter with you? I could have you—"

"Shut up! For once in your life, shut up and listen." Tyghan's update turned into a tirade that didn't allow Cael any time to protest. "I am interim king now, by order of the council." He went on to cover everything that had transpired since Cael snuck out to meet his mistress, from the lives lost, to the ground gained, like the recruits who had just helped rescue him, including the one who was bloodmarked, so Danu could close the door to the Abyss.

"It is seventeen short days until the ceremony. We have a chance now," Tyghan went on, "a real chance, unless you screw it up. There is no magic within the inner circle of the ring to help you. You have to rely on your own strength. All you have to do is relax and regain your health—so when the time comes, you can step up on the Stone of Destiny and take control of Elphame. Twelve kingdoms want you on that throne, though only the gods know why—"

"Because I'm nice. They like me. I converse and laugh with them. I attend their parties. They're afraid of you."

"I don't give two fucks about your parties and who they like. I care about you showing up to the ceremony. That's it. Get better by then. That's *all* you have to do. My officers and I will handle the rest. And until you get your senses about you and compose a worthy apology to Bristol for nearly slitting her throat, you will not be leaving this room. Do you understand?"

"An apology? To the daughter of that monster—"

Tyghan's hand clamped around Cael's neck. "*Don't*. Don't say another word. Or I will do something I'll regret. And you'll regret it even more."

"How dare you talk to me this way. I am not just your brother, I am your king."

His voice wobbled, his eyes sunken, and Tyghan briefly saw his twelve-year-old brother about to be crowned king—the boy wiping tears from his cheeks with the sleeve of his royal coat. The boy Tyghan had forgotten, and Cael had probably forgotten too. The boy who never wanted to be king.

Cael reached out and gripped Tyghan's hand. "I think it was her, you know, my betrothed, who betrayed me. She knew about my indiscretions. It was never a love match. She knew that from the start. We agreed."

There were rumors of Cael's escapades, and his betrothed certainly had motive, but Tyghan was skeptical. "How would she know where you were in the middle of the forest?"

Cael shook his head miserably. "I don't know. I suppose the betrothal is off now?"

Tyghan only nodded. Cael was still delusional. He didn't want to tell him that his betrothed had moved on in a heartbeat. She was married with a child on the way. He squeezed Cael's shoulder. "Rest, brother. That is your only job right now."

He stepped over to where Eris and Madame Chastain waited. "Remove the collar. It might be part of the reason he's unstable. But be prepared to put on another if he becomes erratic. No one is to enter these chambers without my permission. His return must be kept quiet. I'll send guards to relieve you."

"Where will you be?"

"The dining pavilion."

He needed to see Bristol. Hold her. Know that she really was back. And he needed to find out just what this so-called *bargain* was that she had made with her mother.

He couldn't feel good about it, even if it meant his brother was free.

Nothing Maire contrived could ever end well.

On that much he and his brother agreed. There was a trick in this somewhere.

CHAPTER 21

The thump of the basket against Hollis's hip matched her gait. Bristol gripped a wine flask in each hand, as did Avery. Julia, Rose, and Sashka carried trays loaded with meats, cheeses, and treats. They had raided the pavilion tables and were taking their feast to a secluded plaza behind the palace, overlooking the Bay of Mirrors, a small shimmering inlet, home to dubious creatures. It was always quiet and empty there, and that was what they all needed—a little less of Elphame for a few hours. Glennis's death weighed on them. And facing execution didn't exactly brighten spirits.

As they walked, Bristol noticed the sizable notch in Hollis's ear. Esmee said it was always trickier healing a shape-shifter. That part of Hollis was gone forever, deep in the belly of the wretched hound that had bitten it off, but it didn't seem to bother her. At least for now. Her mind was elsewhere. "A funeral and a wedding. Strange, isn't it?" Hollis mused.

"Strange how?" Bristol asked.

"How life goes on. Grief and happiness walking side by side. Sometimes that seems impossible."

"My grandmother always said that news came in threes," Rose chimed in, "the good, the bad, and the questionable."

"Questionable?" Hollis asked.

"The kind of news you're not sure about yet. It could be good or bad." If news came in threes, Bristol wondered what questionable news might be headed their way.

"When is the wedding?" Julia asked. "Did Ivy say?"

Hollis shook her head, unsure. "No. But before the Choosing Ceremony."

"And the funeral?"

"Late tomorrow," Bristol answered. "Sunset, I think she said. Glennis had no one else, so the funeral will be here. The officers were her family."

"What's a Danu funeral like?" Avery asked.

None of them knew. Not even Julia. "But it's apparently intensely personal," she said. "Only family and close friends participate."

Which was why they never saw Liam's funeral. His body had been returned to his family in Greymarch. Bristol had only been to two funerals in her life—her parents'. Funerals for people who weren't really dead. The urns with their "ashes" still sat on a shelf in her father's workshop. She wondered what was really in them. Fireplace ashes? A bag of beans? A lifetime of lies? The urns were sealed, and she had never looked inside. Who would? Her father knew that. Paper cuts. They still sliced into her skin unexpectedly. All the things at her fingertips she never saw or knew. In a twisted way, that pain was a comfort too—proof that her father was not only crafty but devious when it came to survival. It quieted the persistent worry still nesting in her gut.

"Should we go?" Rose asked. "Do you think we're considered close friends?"

Bristol shrugged. "I don't know, but I'm going."

"I am too," Julia said.

In seconds, it was settled: They were all going.

"What about weddings?" Sashka wondered aloud. "Do you think they're the same as ones in the mortal world?" No one knew that either. But they all thought it was odd that Melizan and Cosette would choose to get married now with so much going on.

The day after the funeral, everyone would be back to drills and preparation. Bristol's temples pounded. Almost everyone. She would be occupied with another matter—one she hadn't told anyone about yet. Removal
of the tick. And now there was also the matter of Cael's return—and the
complication of her bargain with her mother and her promise to leave
Elphame. But no one knew about that yet either. At least not the details.

You give me your word, Bristol? Your promise?

A well-crafted wince. A tilt of the head. *Of course, Mother. Going
back is all I ever wanted.*

And without that prince.

The careful slow pull of her brows. An extra beat. A serious nod of
the head. Everything her own parents had taught her. *Yes, without him,
of course. There's not that much between us anyway.*

Bristol could still see her mother, eyes glistening, vacillating between mother and monster, between nightmares and dreams.

A nudge.

A pause.

A grimace.

Bristol did what she had to do, but she felt the twitch and pull of
every manipulation.

Isn't our family worth more than him?

She made the sale and got Cael back, and now anyone could step
up on the Stone of Destiny without it costing Cael his life. Anyone. It
didn't have to be Cael. Maybe it shouldn't be.

"Ahhhh," Julia sighed as if she had just slipped into a warm bath.
They had arrived at the quiet plaza with the beautiful view of the sea.
"Peace at last."

Sashka tweaked her head to the side, catching the hint of a siren
song wafting on the breeze. "Tempting. Almost makes you want to go
for a swim."

"Tempting you is their job, and they're good at it," Julia said. "But
go for a swim, and it will be your last."

"Fish food," Avery confirmed.

Bristol was tempted too. The siren song was strong, piercing the senses like an arrow, like so many of the enticements of Elphame—so much of it beautiful, so much of it deadly. Right then, swimming seemed like the most perfectly logical thing to do. Let the water and waves drown out the world she was trying to escape. But Bristol didn't want any swim to be her last. She had goals that didn't include being dinner for bottom dwellers.

They laid their feast on the table and dug in, passing plates and flasks and baskets of bread. Bristol's heart floated as she watched them effortlessly working together, the easy comradery. She loved them all and wondered again about chances, the slim probability of them all ending up here from so many far-flung places, and the even greater odds of failure during that first week. Yet here they all were, still together. She remembered Tyghan's words: *A million chances happen every day. The difference is what we make of them.* These friends took a chance on her and on each other. They had reached out and cheered one another on from day one. Without them, Bristol wouldn't still be here. She likely wouldn't even be alive. The clatter of dishes, the splash of wine in glasses, the hush of the tide pushing and pulling at the rocks on the shore far below them, their relaxed chatter, it was the music they all needed.

"Good thing Old Noodle Legs didn't nick you today," Sashka said, "or we really *would* be guilty of regicide!"

"A very good thing," Julia echoed.

"Old Noodle Legs isn't that old," Rose said. "Thirty, tops."

"Thirty-one," Avery corrected. "I checked."

"Hmm," Hollis said. "Already checking out the king?"

Avery hissed, like he was the last person she would ever check out.

Bristol poured herself a goblet of velvety red wine and quickly downed it, determined to push thoughts of Cael and bargains from her mind, to enjoy this time with her friends, to make every complication disappear if only for one evening. Was that too much to ask? But thoughts were hard to turn off.

That prince. She poured herself another glass. *Without him*. It was a blatant lie. Leaving Tyghan was unthinkable. She still wasn't sure how she had convinced her mother she was only using him, but Bristol had risen to the challenge, her inflection disdainful, her timing perfection. Maybe when you were afraid and desperate, lying was elevated to an art. If so, Bristol had become a master artist.

Julia lifted her glass in a toast. "It's a feast fit for knights."

"Which we practically are after today's feat!" Rose said, clinking her glass with the others.

Avery jumped to her feet, her fist waving high above her head like it held a weapon, and proclaimed, "Every one of us should be presented with a ruby-adorned sword!"

"Hear, hear!" Hollis called. "Ruby swords all around!"

Sashka laughed, imitating Julia's order to Cael. "*Lower it. Now!*"

"His face!" Rose squealed. "It was priceless."

"Best moment since we got here," Avery agreed.

They all laughed, recounting the antics they had to go through to tie Cael to August's back—his noodle legs, threats, and the weak orders he kept spouting.

"What a prize. Do you think he's always so disagreeable?" Avery asked.

Julia's glass hummed as she ran her finger along its rim. "Well, he was imprisoned for months under harsh conditions. He may have lost a lot of perspective and trust during that time."

"And weight," Hollis added. "Did they even feed him? He was so gaunt. I get grouchy as a bear when I haven't eaten."

Rose grimaced. "I bet he had to scavenge for roaches and rats. Maybe he does deserve some pity—"

"Except that he wants us all executed," Sashka reminded her.

This was met with a flurry of snorts and curses.

An evil glint lit Rose's dark eyes. "I'd like to see him try."

"Who knows what might have happened if you all hadn't been there," Bristol said. "I was never so happy to see anyone in my life."

Avery's brows pulled together. "How did he know Maire was your mother?"

"A slip. I mentioned my father, and he put two and two together."

"It shouldn't matter who your parents are," Sashka said. "You saved his fucking neck."

"Yes, she did."

The voice came out of nowhere, and they all jumped and turned.

CHAPTER 22

Tyghan stepped out of the shadows, flushed and breathless. He was speechless for a long graceless moment when they startled and stared. He felt like he had intruded on a private party. Which he had.

"I'm sorry to interrupt. I've been looking all over for you, and I—" His eyes froze on Bristol, and in a few fast steps, he crossed the plaza and pulled her from her seat into his arms, his trajectory unstoppable, like his heart would stop beating if he couldn't hold her immediately. "Bristol," he whispered into her hair. "I was worried." One arm circled her waist and the other rubbed her back, trying to take in every inch of her—or maybe reassure himself that there was no wound from his brother's knife.

"It's okay, Tyghan," she whispered. "I'm here."

"I just needed to see for myself that you were all right." He eased his grip and, forgetting they had an audience, kissed her, long and deep.

"Oh please, you two," Sashka moaned. "Get a room."

Tyghan released her and whispered to Bristol, "A room?"

"I'll explain later," she answered.

"We were just discussing you, Your Majesty," Hollis interjected, lounging sideways, one leg slung over the arm of the chair, a large goblet sloshing precariously in her hand. "And how after today, we all deserve ruby-studded stords."

"Swords," Rose corrected.

"And the title of knight," Avery boldly added.

The others concurred with affirming hoots.

"And a special squad title," Julia said.

"Like *elite*?" Hollis replied. They all fell into limp laughter.

Tyghan stared at them, surprised. He guessed the empty flasks on the table had something to do with their loosened tongues. He regained his composure, moving from worried lover to the much easier role of stern Knight Commander. He slowly scrutinized each one, his icy gaze resting first on Avery, and circling until he came back to Sashka, who seemed to sober under his stare.

Then he nodded. "I agree. You've earned that much and more. I'll have Cully attend to it immediately. You'll have your swords and titles by tomorrow."

There was a brief moment of stunned silence, and then a round of cheers.

"And you'll also get an apology from my brother. As you might imagine, he's not well after all he's been through. I've had a talk with him, and he's remorseful. There will be no executions." He turned toward Bristol. "He's especially sorry for holding a knife to your throat when he should have showered you with gratitude."

Bristol's chin angled to the side, and a suspicious brow rose. "He said all that, huh?"

"Maybe I'm paraphrasing a bit."

"What you mean is, you threatened to knock out his teeth if he didn't apologize."

Tyghan shifted feet. "Probably more like that."

"Works for us," Hollis said. "An apology from the king! Or whatever he is now!"

Whatever he is, Bristol thought. *Good question.* Another complication to add to the pile. Who was really king? Tyghan or Cael? But the others were already moving past it and toasting.

Tyghan turned to Bristol. "Can we walk?"

She saw it in his eyes. *The bargain*. He knew about it. Eris always reported everything, and Bristol had made the mistake of telling him. "Yes," she answered. "Let's walk." There were even more urgent things he needed to know, and he wasn't going to like any of them. Not any more than she did.

CHAPTER 23

Get it off! Now! You heard Tyghan!" Cael pulled at the collar like all it took was brute strength to remove it. "An apology? There will be no apology! Why aren't you—"

"Your Majesty, please," Eris said. "Calm down. We think there could be dark magic in the amulets. We have to approach this carefully, so you don't suffer lethal consequences."

Dahlia and Eris exchanged a knowing look over Cael's head. They were stalling, but the warning worked, and Cael stopped pulling. "Do something," he said pitifully. "I can't stand this on me for one more minute."

"Of course. But after all this time, removing it might be painful," Dahlia said. "With your permission, I suggest a potion to ease the pain." She knew Cael was fond of potions of many kinds, and he readily agreed. She administered a sweet, potent one, and within seconds he fell into a deep sleep.

Eris heaved out a relieved breath, while Dahlia removed the collar and sniffed at the ease with which it fell into her hands. "Only petty magic. I expected more of Fomoria," she said with contempt, and dropped it in her bag for safekeeping.

"How long will he be out?" Eris asked.

"Not long enough. Though I could always give him more—"

"No. We have to address this sooner or later."

"Then let's go with later." Dahlia went to the sideboard and poured them each a generous portion of another kind of potion—Cael's favorite sherry.

They sat on the sofa opposite the king's bed and watched him sleep, enjoying the few minutes of peace.

Dahlia sighed. "You know we can't allow him to resume power yet. He's still unstable. He'll ruin everything."

Eris's head bobbed in agreement. "I know. But he's a good ruler at times. He wisely defers all matters of security to Tyghan. And when he's in the throne room, he makes fair decisions."

"And yet he is so rarely there. Any kind of invitation lures him away."

"His mother always said he was impulsive," Eris mused, taking a long sip of his sherry. "She called him her little ram, always running headlong into anything that caught his attention. Tyghan should have been king. I think she knew it too, but Tyghan was still so young. And then things spun out of control."

They fell quiet for a moment, both of them reflecting on that dark time that was filled with so much uncertainty and despair, those years before the two of them became confidantes and lovers. Dahlia knew nearly everything about his early life now, details spilling out over time in bits and pieces.

She leaned closer to Eris, cupping the goblet, the sherry warming in her hand. "What was she like, the queen?"

"You knew her."

"Not well. Not the way . . . you did. I wasn't High Witch yet."

A low sound rumbled in Eris's throat, recalling those difficult years. "She was kind. Sensitive. Intelligent. She loved small animals, from mice to bumblebees. She never harmed anything. But she was broken after Cael's father died. He was her third husband to die suddenly, and the rumors were cruel. Her inner court tried to protect her from them, but you know the gossip. To quell the talk, her counselor sent off a marriage proposal to a lord who had shown interest once. At the same time, I was broken in my own way after my wife's death, and my banishment from the Elphame court—"

"Dismissal," Dahlia corrected, as she always did. It was a chapter of his life that had been carefully concealed, but he had shared with her from the beginning of their relationship.

Eris shrugged. "Call it what you will, but it felt like banishment. I had nowhere to go, and I came home. It wasn't exactly a love affair. We had both suffered staggering losses, and for a few months, we took comfort in each other. That was all. Comfort. Her counselor reminded us more than once that he expected a response to the proposal any day. It was a subtle warning not to carry our consoling to a more permanent level. I was a nobody with a tainted history if anyone went digging, and was shamed by my dismissal. And then Lord Jannison, whom she had never met, accepted her marriage proposal, and I slipped into the background. Tyghan was born eight months later. A bit on the small side, so no one questioned it. Lord Jannison never said anything. Neither did I. And the queen was happy again. That was what we all wanted for her."

"Will you ever tell him?"

"Tell him what? Even I don't know for sure." He felt the pull of the lie. He had known from the moment he held the newborn Tyghan in his arms. When those tiny dark eyes peered straight into his soul. Eris wanted everything for him, including the solid name and reputation that Lord Jannison could provide.

Dahlia scoffed at his answer. "You know. So do I. The evidence is there. Between his mother and you—that's where his power comes from. Jannison was a very good man, but he could barely kindle a fire with a match. And Tyghan's build, his curiosity, his expressions, even his temper—they come from you."

Eris didn't like to be reminded of his temper. He had carefully excised that part of his past. "I'm a different man now than I was then."

"You may rigidly follow the rules now, but you're still the same man. You just keep it hidden."

"Tyghan's mother gave me a second chance when no one else would. She trusted me."

"Which you deserved. If not for you, this whole kingdom would have crumbled after she left. He should know, Eris."

"For what purpose?"

"You're his *father*."

"His father is the man who raised him as his own."

"Yes, for the first seven years of his life. But you've been there and guided him for the last twenty."

Eris drank back the last of his sherry. "His mother chose not to tell him. Neither will I."

"He was too young to understand then. He would now."

They both startled when Cael grunted some gibberish.

Dahlia checked him to be sure he was still sleeping. She shook her head. "Shouting orders even in his dreams."

Cael. The enduring problem of a boy forced to be king before he was ready.

Dahlia returned to his side on the sofa and sighed. "I'm sorry that I've made you complicit with Cael."

"It was my fault. Every day you had to listen to me complain as he flaunted every rule."

She poured him more of Cael's precious sherry. "It wasn't your complaints, Eris. You know how I feel about cheating. I shouldn't have told his betrothed where he was going when she asked."

Eris was silent. It was true. Dahlia had committed a major breach in revealing the king's destination to the angry young woman, but still, something told him it hadn't been her. Cael's betrothed didn't have the expertise nor the ability to inform Fomoria of Cael's precise location. *No*, Eris's instincts told him, *it was someone else*—someone far more powerful, with a stronger motivation. Cael's philandering was old news.

He put his hand on Dahlia's thigh. "It wasn't your slip. I'm certain of it. Put it out of your mind."

CHAPTER 24

Bristol and Tyghan walked along a path that bordered the sea, on their way to the sacred groves. Giant ferns hugged the cliffs, and tiny fern sprites danced on the curled fronds, making them bounce like they were alive. Bristol had suggested going to the groves, saying she would share news with him there.

"Or maybe we could go for a swim? That might be fun."

Tyghan wondered how much she'd had to drink. "But—"

"I miss our talks, Tyghan. You have no idea how much I miss them. The way we used to talk at the end of the day when we met beneath the hazel trees. The groves are where we began. Where we shared things with each other—spiders and laundromats and secret dances. Where there was a mysterious burn on my skin—and that burn was *you*. I miss the distant music like we were miles from the rest of the world . . . and I miss worrying about bruises and scrapes instead of—" Her eyes briefly squeezed shut. "I thought life was challenging then, but I had no idea how much more complicated it could become. I wish we could have just one night of peaceful ignorance."

"I took you away from your friends and your rest. I'm sorry. But the bargain you made. I need to know—"

"I'll tell you. I promise. Once we reach the hazel grove. For now, please—" She swallowed. "Let's just hold hands as the moon rises and watch the stars come out as we walk."

Stars? He couldn't see stars. He could only see Glennis's lifeless stare entwined with the threat that Maire still posed, and a murky bargain that must have come at great cost to Bristol for Maire to let Cael go. Cael was Kormick's greatest prize. Most of the time he avoided the subject of Maire around Bristol at all costs, his hatred of her too great, but now . . .

"I have to know at least this: Did she hurt you?"

Bristol grimaced. "No."

Maybe not physically, but Tyghan knew she was hurting. He could almost see the lump in her throat. Just days ago he had shouted at Quin, *How much more can one person take?* And now more had been thrown at her. Facing a ruthless enemy was one thing, but facing an enemy that was your own mother was another. He wished he could turn back time, retrace his steps so she never—

He caught himself. No. The past choices made, for good or bad, had brought them to this point. He loved Bristol too much to wish her out of existence. He tried to think of something else to talk about, to give her those few peaceful minutes she deserved, but his mind was mired in all the grim things they still faced. His inability to conjure a few simple, distracting words infuriated him. He dug deeper, pushing aside his own worries, searching for something, anything that would put her at ease. *Art.* She loved art.

"Did I tell you that the other piece of art you demanded was delivered to your sisters?"

She grinned. "The Escher piece? Yes, you did. Weeks ago."

"Oh. Right." But there was another question he had mused about at length and had never asked. Something he still wanted to know. "I always wondered about that first sketch you chose. The one with the dragon and lion."

That piqued her interest. "Wondered what?"

"What made you choose that particular one? From the moment you saw it, you seemed set on having it."

She smiled. "Ah, that notorious moment we first met? How could I forget? When you were invisible and spying on me? In close proximity, I might add."

She was smiling, and that was all he needed, a small measure of success. "That was my plan all along, you know? To make it memorable."

"Of course it was your plan. Just which parts of me were you secretly checking out?"

His brows rose and a devious grin pulled at the corner of his mouth. "Every part."

Her smile turned as devious as his. "I knew it."

"I especially checked out your hands, which were about to steal the da Vinci."

She scoffed. "My hands? Ha. I felt the burn of your eyes more in this vicinity." She brushed a finger across her breasts. "But I do confess, I was planning a heist. Want to arrest me?"

He swung her around, so her back was to his chest, his hand sliding up her bare throat. He kissed her behind the ear. "Absolutely," he whispered. "But first, answer my question before I forget the topic entirely and arrest you right here on this path." He swung her back around to his side and blew out a dramatic breath.

She laughed. More success.

"What was so special about that sketch?" he repeated.

She purred like it was a delicious memory. "Everything," she answered as they resumed their walk. "Everything made me choose that sketch. Two beautiful, fierce animals fighting? What's not to love? That dragon, it mesmerized me. Every delicate line. And you can't be certain which one will win—or which will die. There's a hidden story in every stroke. I was fascinated the first time I came across it in a dusty little shop in Austin that sold reproductions. It's a brilliant, bloodthirsty battle in the middle of other half-finished sketches, like da Vinci was only drawing it for himself, like he was capturing something right in the heat of the moment. It was so alive and real. To me, anyway. And the surrounding sketches—the smiling faces—that's so much like real life. Everyone going about their business, oblivious to the turmoil around them. Even when da Vinci improvised, it was a testament to his genius."

"The title of the sketch is *Dragon Strikes Down Lion*. Doesn't that hint at who wins?"

She shook her head. "Artists don't title sketches. That title was the creation of a curator or auctioneer who only assumed the dragon would win. That doesn't mean it did."

"Do you want to know who won?"

She stopped walking and faced him. "Wait. What are you saying? That it wasn't from da Vinci's imagination?"

He shook his head. "There were several patronage pieces he created from memory when he returned to your world, but the original that you received was created here in the city, just outside a pub. An argument erupted between shape-shifters. Da Vinci happened to be in the wrong place at the right time. He ended up with a gash that nearly ended him because he was more interested in capturing the moment than getting out of the way. The winner was—"

She turned away, her hands lifted in a stopping motion. "No," she said. "Don't tell me. I don't want to know."

"But—"

She whipped around to face him again. "*No*, Tyghan. That sketch is dear to me. It holds memories. Good ones. In that Austin shop, my father pointed out its significant features, and my mother . . ." She winced, hesitating. "My mother praised its masterful energy and the intrinsic questions it raised. Where? How? Why? It was an admiration we shared that day and many times afterward. It's one of my warmest memories of the three of us. Sometimes it doesn't matter who wins. I don't want its meaning to change, for it to become something it hadn't been before." She hugged her arms and added, "For better or worse, there are some illusions I want to keep. Everyone needs something to hold on to, even if it's a lie."

His success was short-lived. Their light conversation had taken a sudden dark turn. He should have known that discussions about

Kierus and Maire couldn't end in any other way. He pulled Bristol into his arms and held her because he didn't know what else to do. "Please," he finally whispered. "Tell me what bargain you made with her to get Cael back. Tell me if there's something I need to do."

She pulled away, and her silence only made the worry in him twist tighter. "I promised her that I would leave today. That I knew where my father was and that I would take him with me and return to Bowskeep and my sisters. Without you. That was the condition. That I'd leave you behind and have nothing to do with you ever again."

Tyghan couldn't speak. He was floating somewhere outside himself, afraid if he moved she might disappear right that moment. *Leave him?* That was the condition? Maire knew exactly how to destroy him.

Bristol grabbed his arms. "I lied, Tyghan. It was a lie. I would never leave you. Not forever. But I lied to her like I've never lied before. I used her dreams against her the same way Kormick uses her fears. I twisted every word into something she couldn't resist. A lost dream come true, like we would all live happily ever after in Bowskeep. At the time it seemed right, but now it feels dirty instead of victorious. And that's not even the worst of it. There's more."

More? Tyghan braced himself. How much more could there be?

"The historical records are wrong. Madame Chastain is wrong. It doesn't take days to open a portal—at least not for my mother. She opened one right in front of me in less than a minute. With very little effort. We don't have the time we thought we did." Her gaze shot up, locking on his. "She's powerful, Tyghan. More powerful than any of us knew. Far more powerful than me. I have to be there at the Choosing Ceremony going head-to-head with her. I may have to seal the Abyss again and again, because she can reopen it as many times as I close it— that is, *if* I can close it." Her teeth scraped her lower lip. "I've already sent a message to the Lumessa asking her to remove the tick as soon as she possibly can. We can't wait any longer, hoping my powers will somehow materialize. It's not a chance we can take. There's no more time."

The tick.

The tick he had forced from his mind.

And the faint scales that continued to spread across her back. The scales she didn't know about yet.

He was going to lose her. One way or another, he was going to lose her.

"No. We'll figure out something else. We'll—"

"I don't have just one family to worry about anymore. I have two. My family in the mortal world, and the family I've made here. My decision is made. It's the only way."

CHAPTER 25

G ood work, Cully," Tyghan said. "Especially on such short notice."

He walked around the table in Lir Rotunda examining
the six hilts, each studded with three small rubies—the mark of first-
year knights. They also had the rare addition of a blue diamond, recognition for exceptional service. Their beautifully crafted silver scabbards
lay beside them.

Cully lifted the smallest sword, Rose's, testing its weight, which
Tyghan still hadn't bothered to do. "And yet you don't seem pleased."

"What? Of course I'm pleased," he answered. Following Cully's
lead, he lifted another sword, turning it in the light and admiring its
craftsmanship. He set it down and went on to the next. "Just . . . a lot
on my mind."

"The funeral?"

A loud clock ticked in Tyghan's head. *Today. Today after the funeral.*
He had immediately sent another message to the Lumessa last night,
demanding a meeting with her before she met with Bristol. Neither
the Lumessa nor the Sisters had replied. Yet. Would he be forced to go
pound on the impenetrable doors of Celwyth Hall? And fend off her
wolves? The fact that he was king meant nothing to them.

So yes, besides the funeral, Bristol's pending tick removal and memories of the last dismal attempt to remove it, keeping his brother under wraps, Maire's newly discovered ease at opening portals, and the Choosing Ceremony—*oh gods, and now a wedding*—his mind was a constant blur of motion.

And Kierus. Kierus always loomed in his thoughts. When he saw Kasta that morning, she only nodded to indicate it was done. One month for Kierus would be an eternity, but it would also keep him out of reach of the council. They would never know he was released. No one would know but him and Kasta.

Tyghan understood now why Bristol had begged for a single evening of stars and peace—such a small request, and he hadn't given it to her. He wanted to beg the gods for one himself now.

But instead, he only nodded at Cully, truly looking at his face for the first time. Grief still rimmed his eyelids. It was Glennis who had taken him under her wing when he joined the squad. He was only eighteen then, and Glennis would pinch his cheek and call him their fresh-faced buckling. "Glennis's gear is gathered?" Tyghan asked. "And her sword?"

Cully paused, swallowing hard. "Yes, and the site prepared. I still—"

"I'll take care of the rest. Why don't you go find Ivy and see if she needs help with anything."

His face brightened. "Yes, I'll do that right away—"

The rotunda door swung open, slamming against the wall, and Sloan vaulted through it like a prodded bull. Sloan was the last person he wanted to see. Except for garrison meetings he had mostly managed to avoid Cael's former First Officer. Apparently Tyghan's luck had run out. "Why wasn't I immediately informed about the king's return?" Sloan shouted. "And why am I barred from his room? This is unacceptable, and I demand answers!"

Tyghan's hackles rose. He would not tangle with Sloan today, not with so many other things to attend to. "Stand down, Sloan, and go about your duties. I don't have time for your antics. You'll get your answers when I decide." Tyghan turned his attention back to the swords, but felt a hand grab his shoulder, roughly yanking him back around.

"You will *make* time."

Tyghan looked from his partially torn sleeve to Sloan's dark eyes that seethed with pent-up rage. "Go ahead. Take a swing," Tyghan goaded him. "No weapons. No magic. That's what you've wanted to do for months, isn't it?"

Cully stepped forward to stop them. "Don't. Not—"

But Sloan was already swinging. He clipped Tyghan in the jaw, sending him crashing back onto a chair, but Tyghan immediately rebounded, returning a blow to Sloan's ribs. When Sloan doubled forward, Tyghan propelled him backward with a direct hit to his chin.

Cully lost track of the swings, punches, and curses from there. They were a swirling cloud of rage and fists, old grievances suddenly pushed to the forefront. But when they both finally staggered back, catching their breath, Tyghan had a bloody lip and Sloan a bloody nose.

Sloan bent over, his hands braced on his thighs, his chest heaving. "I am Cael's First Officer, and you are no longer king. He's back, and I should have been informed."

Tyghan wiped his bloody mouth. "Your arrogance is astounding. Are you so desperate to be First Officer again that you don't care if Cael is fit to rule? Just as long as you regain your former status? Is that all that matters to you? To be clear, I am *still* king, and I will be until further notice."

"You swore to relinquish the crown when he returned."

"I already told you, he's not fit. But I'll tell you what, Sloan, even with our differences, I recognize that you're a skilled knight and useful to Danu. I will lift the ban to his quarters for you only. Go see Cael. Have a nice *long* visit with him. And if, in all your ambitious wisdom, you still think he should be back on the throne, I'll relinquish my crown. Now get out of my sight. Or shall we go another round?"

"Stop!" Cully yelled, and stepped between them. "Now is not the time to settle your past squabbles! What's the matter with you two?

One of our own has fallen and is waiting to be sent into Paradise. Her burial is only hours away. Stuff it for now! No one has time to be healing your broken faces!" He turned and stormed out.

Tyghan stared at the open door. *Stuff it?* A phrase he learned from the recruits?

He turned toward Sloan, and their gazes locked once again. Had they both just been reprimanded by a junior officer?

Sloan left, still seething, no doubt on his way to see Cael. Tyghan turned, looking at the large empty room, the gleaming swords still on the table, and at the overturned chair beside it. He returned it to its feet, but one of the legs was broken, and it wobbled unsteadily.

Cully was right. Now was not the time.

He lifted one of the swords, turning it in the light. There wasn't time for the usual ceremonies either. He sheathed it in its scabbard and did the same with the other swords before gathering them up and leaving to distribute them. The new knights should all be fully suited for Glennis. She helped get them to this point.

CHAPTER 26

The tray bobbed in the servant's hands, tea spilling from the pot and soaking the lace napkin beneath it. That, and the rattling teacups, drew the attention of two passing hobs who didn't recognize the urisk, but his glare effectively silenced their questions.

He worked to keep his hands steady. The more he faded into the background, the better. Perhaps he should have just used an invisibility cloak, but he had to gain access to Bristol's room in the quietest manner possible. He couldn't just barge his way in. She might put up a fight. Tea and sweet biscuits, on the other hand, were always a welcome gift. It hadn't been easy to find out which room belonged to her, but he managed to pry it from a sprite in the garden for the price of a sugar cube. Of all the rooms in the whole sprawling palace, Bristol's was conveniently close to Tyghan's. He wasn't surprised.

Reggie curled on the chaise next to Bristol. She had given her fox a name after learning from Tyghan that he was a real fox from a real forest somewhere in Elphame. Woven from the mind's eye of the artist, some clever creatures, like Reggie, managed to breach the veil of the artist's imagination, burrowing into the carpet that was the artist's canvas. *Freeloader*, Tyghan had called him. Bristol thought he deserved

a more dignified name, like Reggie. He nudged her hand—not for
food but for more scratches behind his tufted red ears. He had adopted
Bristol, and maybe she had adopted him too, both of them adapting to
a foreign world. She brushed her hand over his soft fur, and he nuzzled
closer. Angus was amusing, but their ferret had never been a cuddler,
and she had never had any other pets. She liked the comfort of this
creature who had barged into her life, and she mused about getting
Harper a dog when she got home. Or could she bring Reggie?

"I need to finish getting ready," she warned him, gently easing his
sleepy head aside. She went to the bath chamber, tidying up her towels
and bath balms, and spotted her pills, which she hadn't put away the night
before. She may have told Tyghan she was the goddess of birth control,
but Harper was the brilliant one who made it so. She still had three weeks
of pills left, just enough to hold her over until she got home. She remembered when Harper frantically brought them to her, trying to think of
everything she might need for her trip to faerie. She smiled. The sardines
and rock-hard raisins had been tossed long ago—the aspirin too, since it
was no longer effective on her—but it was nice having her own familiar
toothbrush with the swirl of blue and white bristles. She saw Harper every time she used it. It was pretty much all she had from home now, except
for her old jeans and tank top stuffed on the top shelf of the wardrobe.

She began brushing her hair and had just swept it over her shoulder to braid when she heard a knock. She wasn't expecting anyone,
and had agreed to meet her fellow recruits at the barn for the short
walk to the funeral site. But then she remembered the message she had
sent. Maybe this was a reply from the Lumessa? She eagerly opened
the door, but it was only a hunched servant with a tray, a urisk she
had never seen before. Reggie scurried away and hid in his burrow,
transforming from full-bodied back into art. He was always shy with
visitors—he only recently warmed up to Tyghan—but he was usually
bold with servants bearing trays of food.

"My lunch was already delivered this afternoon," she said.

"This one was ordered by the king." He brushed past her toward
the table, the dishes rattling unsteadily in his hands.

"Tyghan ordered this?" she asked as he set the tray down.

"No," he answered. "The real king of Danu ordered it. King Cael Trénallis." As he turned, his hunched back straightened, and his haunches and horns disappeared, along with the rest of his glamour. It was Cael, standing taller and stronger than he had yesterday—and far more imposing in the confines of her room.

Bristol reached for her knife.

"I'm only here to apologize," he said.

"Gaining entry disguised as a urisk?"

"I've been told that my return to Danu must be kept quiet, and with palace gossips—" He raised his brows. "I'm forced to be discreet. I'm only here to express my regret for my behavior yesterday."

"Under threat from Tyghan?"

He chuckled. "You know him well. Yes, he provided inspired prompting that included wrapping his hands around my throat. But I do wish to apologize on my own initiative as well. Really, I am not a total boor. You need to understand that yesterday, after months of only savage brutes for company, I responded in kind."

"As I understand it, you've always been a demanding pain in the ass."

He smiled. "Ah. That came from my brother too, no doubt. He's right. I am a pain in the ass. And I demand a lot of him. Sometimes probably too much. The thing is, there is no manual on how a king should behave, especially when the role is foisted on you when you're only twelve. I didn't have a parent to study. I'm not making excuses, but early on, you learn that shouting covers a lot of ignorance and insecurities. May I?" he asked, lifting the teapot.

Bristol eyed the pot and the two teacups. *He came for tea?* She cautiously nodded. "Does Tyghan know you're here?"

He shrugged. "I don't know. By now, perhaps. He's busy with duties. But as I mentioned, he bade me to take care of this matter."

He poured them each a cup and added a cube of sugar to the deep pink brew, then motioned to her chair. She sat opposite him at the small table, always aware of how far her hand was from the hilt of her knife.

Or if need be, with the flick of her fingers, she could set his hair on fire. Though she was leery of summoning even the smallest spark now, after her disastrous results with her bathtub and singed ceiling. It seemed she had developed an unreliable kinship with fire.

She noted that Cael had been groomed since yesterday, his hair freshly cut and his face clean-shaven, hardly looking like the same man at all. He bore the same strong Trénallis jawline and searing eyes, though his were a deep brown. The split lip he had acquired on the ride back was gone, and the dark smudges beneath his eyes had nearly faded. The scars on his chin and neck were gone too. Madame Chastain had apparently been hard at work restoring his health and appearance, but he still had weight and strength to regain. She noticed his hand tremble as he lifted the small teapot.

He took a sip of the floral tea, looking over the rim of his cup at her. His eyes were warm and arresting, unlike the bloodshot, unfocused ones from yesterday. His gaze moved to her untouched tea. "It's not poisoned. I promise."

"You did order my execution."

He reached across the table and took her cup, taking a healthy sip, then returned it to her saucer. "Again, I was not myself then." He sighed. "I might not be myself for some time to come, at least according to the High Witch. Having been isolated with a collar around my neck for so long left me with the impulsive mouth of a clod, but it's important that I thank you for rescuing me—at great risk to yourself. I'm sorry I didn't recognize that immediately. Fear and anger have ruled my small world for months now. I've lost all perspective. But I want you to know that what I told you yesterday about your mother is true. I never heard or saw her in any of my travels, especially not when I was twelve. I didn't even know of her existence until years later, when the attacks began. That much I swear is true. I tried to tell her that whenever she visited, but she wouldn't listen."

"She visited you often?"

He nodded. "Kormick only came to Queen's Cliff twice the whole time I was there, but she came regularly, maybe once a week. I lost track of the days in that dirty cell, but she always asked me how it felt to be trapped and know that no one was coming to rescue me. She'd watch me, waiting for me to break. Some days I thought I would. Nothing I said could appease her. I don't know what your mother has been through or how much is a conjuring of her own imagination, but I was not part of it."

He took another slow sip of his tea, his eyes studying her again. Bristol's tea remained untouched.

"But your father . . . What you said about me laughing him out of the throne room, I'm afraid, is true, and for that I'm sorry. I'm not sure why I did it—selfishness, I suppose. Your father was a good knight—no, he was a *great* knight. And considering he was mortal, he was a wonder. That's what everyone called him, the wonder of Danu, and I didn't want to lose him. I knew Tyghan wouldn't want to lose him either." He reached out, plucking another cube of sugar from the bowl, and stirred it into his tea, staring at a few loose leaves swirling on top. "Tyghan was closer to Kierus than he was to me."

She heard a thread of regret in his voice, but then he perked back up, looking at her again.

"I really did think art was a passing fancy for your father. Who would want to leave such a revered position behind?" He rose, and she did at the same time, watchful of his higher advantage, but he only walked over to a painting hanging on her wall. He examined the serene pastoral scene. "I understand it was art that brought you to Danu in the first place."

"How would you know that?"

"The Royal Counselor and High Witch told me what transpired during my absence. A da Vinci, I believe. Ironic, don't you think, that art is what took Kierus away from Danu, but also what brought his daughter back?" His finger ran along the frame of the painting. "Although your motives were more mercenary than creative."

Bristol's spine stiffened.

He turned, his eyes inching over her in a leisurely, familiar fashion. He took a step closer. "I can see why Tyghan is smitten with you.

You're as alluring as your mother. But his interest surprises me too, considering who you are. He's usually more cautious. One thing I have to ask . . . Did you cast a spell over him?"

Her fingers twitched, brushing her knife's leather scabbard, a warning for him not to step closer. "You've twisted it around, I'm afraid. He's the one who cast a spell on me. You need to work on your delivery, Your Majesty. Your apology had a convincing start but a weak finish."

He shook his head. "I've insulted you. I'm a clumsy oaf. Again, I'm very sorry. I had no intention of inferring—"

"I'd stop while you're ahead. As my parents—both of whom I know you greatly admire—always told me, read the room, and read it again before you open your mouth."

He nodded, a hint of a grin pulling at the corners of his mouth. "I am king of Danu. Soon to be king of Elphame," he said, as if trying to remind her of her place. "But noted. In spite of my blunders, you and I are going to be friends, Bristol Keats."

And with that, he slowly hunched over, his glamour back in place, and shuffled out the door.

CHAPTER 27

"Wait here."

"But it's been a long time since—"

"If you hear me scream, you'll know there's a problem. I will go in alone."

They didn't argue further. Maire's escort of guards knew the routine, even if it had been a while. No one entered her cottage without her permission. It was her sanctuary. A place where her mind both fogged and cleared. An in-between place where she was outside herself, where time ceased to exist. Where she was still a girl watching her mother spin, watching her father stir the stew over the fire, where she was a child playing beside the hearth with dolls made of yarn and felted sheep's wool.

When she told Kierus about the abandoned cottage, she never thought either of them would see it again, much less return to it. The Runic River was long and twisted, and the cottage dark and dull—easy to miss, which was why she had chosen it. Had he actually been able to find his way there? But Kierus was aptly named the wonder of Danu. That was what drew her to him in the first place. She recalled another cottage, the one where they first met, his invitation impossible to refuse. She had known his intent, but she was good at killing too, and he was a challenge she couldn't resist. But she had underestimated his golden tongue, his eagerness that disarmed her, and when it was over, his fingers still strumming her arms like . . .

If anyone could find this cottage, Kierus could.

She climbed the gentle slope up to the old mill, still broken and creaking in the current. The peace here was hypnotic. Maybe that was why she told Kierus about it. Peace. They had always chased after it.

When she reached the porch, she spied a smudged footprint of dried mud on the first step. Her heart sped up. Kierus's boot? She sensed his presence all over the porch. She was certain of it. She walked up the steps and drew in a deep breath before giving the door a gentle nudge. It squeaked on its hinges. Light streamed in from the opposite window, illuminating her loom in the center of the room, but nothing more. She stepped inside, her gaze sweeping the dark corners of the cottage and then the open loft. Nothing. But then she spotted more footprints on the dusty floor. Smaller boots. *Bristol.* She had come, just as she promised. She had gathered up her father and taken him back home. She kept their bargain. *That is good*, Maire told herself. But nothing inside her felt good. *It's done. Over. He can't ruin anything again*, she repeated to herself.

And then she spotted her leather slippers, the ones she always placed on the floor beside the treadle, flung across the room. Maire felt the burn of Kierus's anger, and something inside her choked. She pressed her palm to her mouth, but then caught herself. *He's angry. He's gone. He'll never come back. Just as I wanted.*

But when she walked over to her loom, something shot out of her, something just as angry, and her fist came down, shattering the wooden crossbar. Rotted yarn rained to the floor.

"Now it is done. There is no going back."

CHAPTER 28

Awall of tears surrounded the glade, held back by will and denial. Tears were a finality, an acceptance, and no one present had reached a place of acceptance. But beneath the strained silence, an undercurrent of music floated on the breeze, weaving into throats thick with grief, into warriors, witches, knights, and nobles, and every creature, winged or horned. A crescendo rose in their hearts—this was not an ending.

It was not a small affair. Hundreds dotted the hilltop meadow overlooking the western sea. They circled the shallow vault that still awaited the final sealing stones. Important kings had been ushered into Paradise with fewer witnesses. Glennis was not just esteemed among knights, but loved.

Eris stood beside the cradle of rocks that held her remains. Wildflowers that should have been woven through her hair instead circled the cloth that encased her head. He recited the revered laws of the gods and sang their promises, every word memorized, a library of knowledge flowing from his tongue. He spoke each word with tenderness and respect, recounting noble quests, valor, and higher causes, and the history they shared. Flesh rose on arms, and broken hearts swelled, but when his voice wavered and he had to look down for a moment, Bristol's own resolve faltered. Glennis was dead, and by her mother's hand. Among the mourners, Bristol felt out of place on the glade, a weed in a garden.

She and the other recruits stood together, some distance back, fully suited in their best tunics and jackets, their newly granted swords bearing the cherished gems of knighthood sheathed on their backs. Before they left the barn for the funeral, Tyghan and Kasta had hastily presented them, lightly tapping their shoulders. *And with this sword, I also grant you the title of knight.* Rose and Avery had wept.

They weren't weeping now. They stood as tall and silent as all the other knights from the garrison, there to honor their fallen comrade.

When Eris finished the recitations, he motioned to the officers of Glennis's squad to step forward with the items that would accompany her into Paradise. Kasta went first, tucking two silver goblets and a cask of honeysuckle wine beside Glennis. Quin laid a golden torc and a handful of jeweled hair combs beside her, saying, "You'll have time to wear these now."

The awkwardness of placing these items beside the small wrapped head only emphasized the brutality of Glennis's death. Dalagorn was next, with a chest belt holding three small knives. He lowered his massive bulk to one knee, his own belts and hardware jingling, and gently set it beside her, as though her remains were as fragile as a butterfly. His thick ogre lips twisted. "Swift travels, my friend."

Eris nodded to Tyghan, and he unsheathed a sword on his back. Glennis's sword. Tyghan held it across both of his open palms in a reverent position as he walked toward the grave. Bristol watched his face, the clench of his jaw as he struggled for control, his effort to be the best Knight Commander he could be to honor this beloved knight. The gem-encrusted hilt glittered in the sun, a dozen cut stones that marked her years of bravery and loyalty. He knelt beside the vault and laid her sword next to the other treasures that would accompany her to the otherworld. "Go to your deserved rest, Officer Dervy." He swallowed. "Prepare the halls for the rest of us." He bowed his head closer and whispered a few more words to her that no one else could hear, then returned to stand beside the other officers.

Cully was last, carrying a shallow earthen pot with a lid. His steps were halting, and when he reached the stones that held her, he fell roughly to his knees. His shoulders shook as he carefully laid down the pot. "Leek pie," he said. "Your fa-favorite." His cracking voice almost undid Bristol, but as he rose to his feet again, his face became suddenly fierce. "This is not the end!" he shouted, and raised his fist to the air. "It's only the beginning!"

A hail of shouts called back to him, fists raised in unity. The chorus echoed over the hills, his fellow officers joining in, but as the shouts finally calmed, Cully realized he had broken protocol and delayed the final benediction for Glennis. He returned his fist to his side and went to stand with his fellow officers.

Eris turned to the west and the setting sun and called upon the great gods, Danu, Dagda, Brigid, Lugh, and more, to smooth the waters of her route and prepare the halls of Paradise for a grand feast with leek pie and honeysuckle wine. With that, a strong breeze whipped up, whistling over the glade as if the gods had answered his call. Eris turned back to Glennis. "Through the mists and over the golden waters to where the sun sets, your final rest awaits. Remember those of us who will follow."

And it was done. The sealing stones were set on the vault and mounds of dirt piled atop, until it was part of the earth, where in a season, grass would reclaim the mound and heal the scars.

In solemn silence, everyone began to depart. But then Bristol heard a sound. Strangely out of place in this stoic company, but familiar. *Weeping*. She turned, scanning the meadow, but saw no one sobbing. The sound of grief shouldn't have stood out, not at a funeral, but somehow it did. Bristol shook it off and left with her friends, saying quiet goodbyes as each turned toward their own hallways and rooms. When Bristol got to her own, she was surprised to find a posy of flowers hanging from her door handle. Was this a Danu tradition after a funeral? But on closer inspection, she gasped. They were wildflowers tied up with rough sisal twine—like the kind Willow used to leave on doors in Bowskeep. And there was golden yarrow in the bouquet, the exact same flowers that filled the fields near her father's memorial. Was it possible Willow had come to Elphame? Bristol spun, looking in both directions down her hallway. "Willow?" she called softly, but there was no answer.

Only a fae tradition, she thought. Willow was a world away. But then she remembered the weeping as she left the funeral.

CHAPTER 29

Maire.

Maire.

Would she hear him calling? Would she know he had come for her?

Kierus strained against the confines of the stone. At times he thought he felt it give, but it was never enough.

He had failed his wife. Failed his daughters. He had to get out, but how?

A thousand years. He had already lost his concept of time. One night felt like ten, one day, a hundred. A blink of his eyes started his day all over again. It seemed a thousand years had already passed, but he was sure he was just at the beginning of his sentence. He had to be. He couldn't accept anything else. He began to live for things like a bird chirping, the sound of rain. *Footsteps.* He prayed to the gods for footsteps.

Today, he heard horns. Three long bellows of a carnyx. A funeral. Someone was dead.

No matter how hard he strained, he couldn't get closer. Sometimes he thought trying was more torturous that giving in, giving up, but he had never done that before. He wasn't that far gone yet. He tried again.

Bri, he screamed. If anyone could hear him, she would. But she didn't come either.

And then an unwelcome voice stirred in his head. *This used to be your favorite*.

It wasn't the angry words that tore apart his insides but the quieter ones. Words that made memories flood back. What he had lost. His bond with Tyghan. The grief that always followed him and spilled over into his art.

You decided wrong.

Never. Not in regard to Maire and his daughters.

But it hurt to see the terrible pain in Tyghan's eyes and know he had put it there. If he had only had more time, if only he could have found another way to stop him and the army of knights from hunting Maire down, he would have. This is what he was condemned to think about for a thousand years.

He pushed against the stone, pounded, called out, determined to break free. The wonder of Danu never gave up.

CHAPTER 30

Muscled gray clouds rolled in from the sea, shrouding Badbe Garrison in darkness, and thunder rolled overhead. Fat raindrops pelted the officers as they arrived, and cadets rushed forward to take their horses to the stable. Tyghan and the other officers ran for the meeting chambers, still dressed in their formal attire from the funeral. As they began shedding coats and taking their places at the long table, Dalagorn squinted at Tyghan. "What's this?" he asked, motioning under his eye. "You got a shiner?"

Tyghan reached up, touching his cheekbone, and winced. He sighed as he pulled out a chair and sat down. He had healed his bloody lip and two swollen knuckles before the funeral, but some bruises took longer to surface. He had missed the one under his eye.

Quin whistled with admiration. "It's a beauty. All the colors of the rainbow."

Melizan wrinkled her nose. "All the wrong colors."

"Sloan and I got into it," Tyghan explained. "He heard Cael was back and wondered why I was still in charge."

A voice from the doorway responded. "But we've come to a temporary agreement."

They all turned. It was Sloan, just entering the room with more officers behind him. He had a matching shiner on the opposite eye. "I think His Majesty may need a little more time to regain his . . ." He searched for a diplomatic word.

"Faculties?" Tyghan offered.

Sloan took a seat opposite Tyghan at the long meeting table. "As you stated, he's still disoriented by his harsh imprisonment."

Tyghan chuckled inside. *Disoriented?* Cael was delusional. But he knew the admission was not an easy one for Sloan. "Then I guess I should have had you meet with him right from the start, so we could have avoided our earlier"—Tyghan rubbed the healed knuckles of his fist—"discussion. My mistake."

Sloan nodded in reluctant agreement, because he and Tyghan rarely agreed on anything. "He was fixated on the topic of executions," he added, but then quickly moved on. "What's the agenda?"

Before Tyghan could answer, Badbe Commander Maddox arrived with her chief strategist, Officer Ailes, who would help direct the sky fighters. Two cadets followed on their heels, depositing bowls of hot spiced nuts, platters of fruit and cheese, and baskets of seasoned breads around the table. Dalagorn grunted with satisfaction. "The messengers you requested will be right along," Maddox said. "More food is on the way. And ale. I think it's going to be a long night."

It was unusual to have an officers' meeting this late in the evening and at the garrison, but these were not usual times. With Cael's stealth rescue suddenly accomplished, they were in a new position to bring select kingdoms they could trust into their confidence—and get more troop support. Knowing Danu had achieved the impossible—snatching Cael from Kormick's grasp—would instill more hope in the kingdoms than they'd had in months.

Though Tyghan now had news that could extinguish their hope all over again. He hadn't even shared it with his own officers yet. He knew where their questions would lead—to Bristol. Eventually everything led to her. He'd wait as long as he could before bringing it up.

The first order of business was composing messages to two kingdoms—ones that had been on the cusp of committing forces at Beltane Eve. Handpicked knights memorized the carefully worded message—it couldn't be trusted to pen—and then were sent off to the kingdoms of Bleakwood and Silverwing.

> *The king fondly remembers his discussions with you at*
> *Beltane Eve and your admiration of his elite squad. He*
> *wants you to know that the weeks since then have been*
> *unusually prosperous for the nation of Danu. A fruitful*
> *harvest is in their sights.*
>
> *The king looks forward to seeing you at the Choosing*
> *Ceremony, but you are always welcome to visit him at*
> *his palace before that.*

If this message worked to push the two kingdoms to a decision, they could expect as many as three thousand additional troops backing up Danu, Greymarch, and Eideris, bringing their totals to twenty-three thousand. One problem they faced was that no one knew how many Fomorian warriors they would still have to contend with once the restless dead were eliminated from the equation. Estimates were fifteen to twenty thousand, but it was only a guess.

Six hours later, they were still barricaded in the chambers, hashing out plans, poring over terrain maps, and naming regiment leaders. When they began discussing the ceremony itself, Tyghan interjected. "New protocol—we'll be bringing forty witnesses. Maybe double that."

Kasta's eyebrows flew up. "Is that wise? You want to antagonize Kormick before we even get started? He laid it out clearly. Only twenty witnesses allowed per kingdom."

"Forget Kormick's plans," Tyghan said. "Here's mine. Once the Abyss door is closed and we're only going up against the Fomorian army, I still have twenty thousand troops to move into place, which will be no easy task. I want Kormick to concentrate on small trespasses instead of looking for the big ones. Let him think we're pounding our chests because we're desperate. He's going to have teams watching for advancements from all directions. This will divert his attention, and possibly minimize it."

Melizan nodded. "He's not going to slaughter us because we can't count."

"Agree," Sloan said. "It will likely make the fool snicker. He'll find it amusing. Twenty or forty won't make a difference facing the restless dead."

Dalagorn blew out a long, bothered breath but said, "Agree."

"Another thing we need to address," Tyghan continued, "is that once Cael appears as a contender for the Stone of Destiny, all hell will break loose. Kormick will have Maire summon the restless dead—"

"But by then Keats will have the Abyss door closed, correct?" Ailes asked.

"Unfortunately, there's been a new development," Tyghan answered. This was the part that had to be delivered carefully. "It would appear the historical records are inaccurate, at least in regard to Maire. Her power is greater than we thought." He told them what Bristol had witnessed, Maire opening a portal in less than a minute—not the days or even hours they had anticipated. If Bristol shut it, Maire would likely reopen the Abyss door right there in the valley. Bristol would need to be present to possibly close the door, over and over again.

"Not if Maire is in our sights," Commander Maddox offered.

"Which she never has been," Quin noted. "Kormick keeps her well protected."

"Wards, warriors, amulets, she has it all," Kasta agreed.

Ailes sat forward in his seat. "But if she is vulnerable—"

"No," Tyghan said. "We promised Bristol not to kill Maire. We'll rely on her thwarting her mother's efforts."

A disgruntled rumble rolled from Dalagorn's chest. "It took Keats five tries and almost an hour to close the Timbercrest door. Time won't be on our side."

"But if Keats had more power . . ." Quin's fingers strummed the table. "Where are we on that tick?"

That was the question that had been circling like a ravenous buzzard for weeks. Tyghan had come to a decision about it, but he had to talk to Bristol first, to tell her things she had to know, things that would only make her choice harder. "There are risks in removing it. I should have more information to share with you tomorrow. Until then, nothing has changed."

Tyghan moved on, asking Maddox for a squad to hide and protect Cael until the last minute at the ceremony. Everyone weighed in on the logistics of that crucial moment except Cully. Tyghan noted that he had remained silent throughout the discussions. "Any thoughts, Cully?"

"How do we know that Kormick doesn't know about Cael?" he answered. "Maybe our ignorance is what he finds amusing. He's probably planning a retaliation right now while we're all huddled here like frightened mice."

The room went silent. *Frightened mice?* It was a hurled accusation more than it was a comment. Everyone waited for Tyghan to respond.

Tyghan briefly angled his head to the side, taking a moment before he spoke. He forced calm into his voice. "We know, because Bristol assured us that he doesn't know. It was the deal she made with her mother."

Cully snickered. "Based on what her mother told her? Because we all certainly know that Maire is trustworthy."

The pulse of the room raced. Tyghan's chest rose in a measured breath. "What are you saying, Cully?"

"I'm saying that Bristol is gullible. And biased. Her parents lied to her for her whole life, and she fell for it."

Tyghan's head pounded as he struggled to keep himself composed. He reminded himself that Cully was still shaken by Glennis's death. Bitterness clouded his judgment and loosened his tongue. But every knight in that room had endured the unjust deaths of fellow knights. Bristol gullible and biased? Was Cully's memory so short?

Tyghan cleared his throat, his words as precise as one of Cully's arrows. "Yesterday, Bristol gave up something dear to her. For us. Do you understand that? She has risked her life, faced her own mother, who ordered me to slit her throat, and then leaned into my knife until she bled to convince her mother that my threat was real. And then two days later, she went back on her own, not knowing what kind of trap she was headed into, and fed her mother lies. Does that sound like someone who is gullible or biased? She made promises to Maire she never intended to keep. Promises about keeping her family safe. Bristol *manipulated* her. Do you think that was easy for her? She has a family, Cully. A family she loves, regardless of what we think of them. Bristol has survived this world with astounding skill, and only a few weeks ago at Beltane Eve—another time she risked her life for us—you were calling her fucking brilliant. Do you want to reevaluate your opinion of her or be dismissed from this detail entirely?"

Silence choked the room, everyone frozen in place. Waiting. Cully finally shook his head. "You're right. I misspoke. I'm sorry."

Tyghan bit back his anger while Cully sullenly looked into his lap. The room remained airless, the equilibrium lost. The rift and threat of dismissal had stolen their thoughts, and Tyghan couldn't muster one more word to his lips. Seconds ticked by.

"And speaking of weddings." Cosette spoke up cheerily. "Did you all hear that Melizan and I set a date?"

Dalagorn was quick to chuckle, and Quin nudged Cully's shoulder, forcing a smile, and the rift was buried beneath the congratulations that ensued. Air filled the room again, everyone eager to recover the balance they thrived on as a team, the balance they desperately needed, and in that moment, Tyghan almost loved Cosette.

His sister's eyes met his, and he nodded. Cosette was skilled and knew how to save a lot of situations.

Now he regretted complaining about the wedding at all. It was just what they needed. Something to balance the tension that was eating them all alive.

CHAPTER 31

A soft breeze swept through Bristol's open window, gently billowing the sheer curtains into ghostly companions. Shadows danced on the ceiling, and an occasional rumble of thunder made Bristol smile. How quickly everyone scrambled to escape summer storms, while she had always loved them. She and her sisters would rush outside to dance in summer downpours and catch the drops on their tongues, the warm water mysterious and sweet. It was one of those things that was even more magical if shared with someone else. She wondered if it was raining in Bowskeep too. *Are Cat and Harper outside, dancing together in the rain?* A pang of longing pinched in her chest. The rumbles grew fainter. Soon the storm would be gone.

She rolled to her back and stretched, feeling the emptiness of the bed. It was well after midnight, and she couldn't sleep. Tyghan would sometimes skim her temples or shoulders with his fingers when she couldn't sleep, to release her tense energies, as he called it—fae shorthand for a massage. It always worked, helping her to let go of the day and fall asleep. He used it on himself too—which explained how he slept like the living dead. But he wasn't here now, and the night stretched on forever. A single candle burned low in the corner. She wondered if he was still entrenched in meetings at the garrison. She missed the warmth of his body beside her, the sound of his slumbering breaths, the stretch of his arm reaching out for her, even in his sleep.

For hours, her mind had jumped from one thought to the next. There was still no word from Jasmine about removing her tick, though Ivy assured Bristol the message had been delivered. She knew Jasmine's health was delicate, but she would go to Celwyth Hall in the morning herself to make sure the Sisters understood the urgency of her request. There could be no more waiting. She had to be as powerful as her mother if this whole thing was going to work.

She turned on her side, eyeing Anastasia's encyclopedia on the nightstand, remembering the unexpected entry she had found in it. She had been looking for more information about ticks in the chapter on fairy animals and legends when, for the first time, she found a mention of the Danu Nation, a legend about a prince turning a queen into a frog. Most of the legends seemed to be about scorned or star-crossed lovers, and a ridiculous number of the stories involved flies. Strangely, she hadn't seen a single fly since she arrived here, but she had seen numerous frogs, holding court on giant lily pads like kings and queens on thrones.

She had skimmed the rest of the chapter in the encyclopedia and found nothing on ticks. They were, perhaps, a more shameful secret of Elphame—the creation of vermin to steal magic—and not worthy of inclusion. Anastasia's book was a whimsical one, after all, a guide to customs and fantastical creatures, not the airing of dirty laundry. Or was it? Bristol had never read any other informational books about Faerieland, so she had nothing to compare it to. Was it completely fictional? Anastasia had certainly gotten some things wrong—like about fae not being able to lie. Just like mortals, they were quite accomplished at it. But other things seemed too precise—like the mention of the Danu Nation or her descriptions of the gossiping and idle gentry. And a door. *The universe opened a door for me, and who was I to look away?* Did she stumble upon a portal? Those details made it seem as if Anastasia had actually been to Elphame. It would have been decades ago, since the copyright on the inside page was 1940. Or maybe Anastasia was simply regurgitating old myths from other sources. Fairies had certainly been around for a long time.

Bristol also searched the encyclopedia for funeral and flower traditions, still wondering about the posy left at her door. All she found was a general tradition of leaving flowers on doorsteps and windowsills to ward off evil and illness, or maybe just bring a smile. She remembered the loose petals Deek and his fellow sprites often left on her windowsill. But the spray of flowers tied up with sisal? That had Willow's fingerprints all over it. As Bristol tossed and turned, she alternated between certainty that it was Willow, and certainty it was only a fae tradition. Sisal twine, after all, was as common as field grass.

But then there was the weeping she had heard. And Willow always came to funerals. Except her father's funeral—because she knew he wasn't dead. Was she here looking for him too?

♟

Tyghan opened the door gently. He pulled off his coat, boots, and then shirt, trying to be quiet.

"I'm awake," he heard through the darkness.

"The storm?"

"No. I just couldn't sleep."

He was relieved because he wasn't tired. He was too wound up and wanted to talk. He fell back on the bed beside her, half-dressed.

"You can't exhaust yourself," she warned. "It was only a few nights ago that I—"

"I'm not tired," he said. "But you're right. I'll be careful. I know I can't expect you to sing me through another night of demon visits."

She rolled over, slipping her arm across his ribs, her cheek against his arm. "Tyghan Trénallis, I would sing you through a thousand nights. I would sing you through as many nights as it took to keep you with me."

He squeezed her hand, his fingers memorizing her touch, the softness of her skin, the feel of her knuckles beneath his thumb. Each little bump, small, but everything. *A thousand nights*. That's what he wanted. That was all he wanted.

His chest grew tighter, like Dalagorn was sitting on it, and he forced himself to rise, shifting on the bed to look down at her. The single lit candle in the corner of the room had burned to a nub, barely illuminating her head on the pillow, but even in the dark, every inch of her was perfect. *Tell her, Tyghan. Get it over with*. He flicked his finger, lighting two more candles on the candelabra so he could see her face clearly.

"Bri, I have to talk to you."

He tried to say it casually, but she immediately pushed herself upright. "Something's wrong."

"No," he answered. "I mean, yes. But it's not something we can't figure out together."

"You're scaring me, Tyghan." She searched his face.

"I went to Celwyth Hall today and met with the Sisters. I ordered them to ignore your message until I spoke to you. I said they had to wait at least a few more days to remove the tick, so you could really think about it."

She pulled her hand from his. "I don't need more time. It's my choice—"

"Yes," he said. "It is your choice. But you need to know all the facts. There's something about the tick I've been holding back."

She rolled off the other side of the bed and stood, her fingers raking through her hair. "Okay. Say it. Just say it."

He circled around the bed and grabbed her hands—the hands she always kept glamoured. "Show me," he whispered.

She released the glamour, and the sharp blue nailbeds appeared. "Does it have to do with these?"

He nodded. "Other changes have surfaced. Ones you haven't seen."

Confusion creased the corners of her eyes. "Where? I haven't seen any—"

"Your back."

She paled. "Why didn't you tell me before?"

"It was just after Madame Chastain stabbed the tick on your shoulder. I didn't know what the changes meant—I still don't know—and you were so happy about closing the portal and—" He paused, taking a breath. "I didn't want to worry you about something that might mean nothing."

"But?"

"The markings have spread."

"Markings," she repeated, and her hand went to her middle, like she was going to be sick. "What kind of markings?"

It was better that she saw for herself. There was no way to say *scales* that wouldn't panic her. "Do you want to see them?"

She nodded, but as he stepped up to her floor mirror, she whirled around, her thin gown billowing out behind her. "Wait," she said. "Not yet. I need a minute. Maybe a few minutes." Her pupils were pinpoints even in the dim light. He could almost hear her pulse racing.

"Or a week, or as long as you need," he said. "I don't know what the markings mean, but I remember what you said in the throne room, about profound changes, and not wanting to turn into something else. This has to be your decision." *Something else?* He silently cursed himself for his poor choice of words. But was there any good way to say it?

Her brows pulled together, her tone suddenly angry. "Why can't they figure this out?" she asked. "It shouldn't be that difficult. With all their magic and libraries and powerful witches and wizards, why don't the Sisters know?"

"Because they've never encountered anything like this before," he answered. "Because your parents' bloodlines are unknown to them. Because you're equal parts fae and mortal, and that makes you a mystery."

An unexpected laugh rippled through her chest. "Looks like I won't be sleeping tonight." The faint roll of thunder floated through the room. Her eyes glistened. "And now the storm is gone. I should have gone outside when I had the chance."

He studied her uncertainly, wondering what a passing storm had to do with anything. The despair in her eyes overwhelmed him. "I can make it rain for you."

She looked away, as if embarrassed. "No, it wouldn't be the same. It's the miracle of catching the moment."

He was desperate to do anything for her. "What about swimming? You wanted to do that last night. I can take you. And I know a secret place where it always rains."

"A secret place?" She shook her head. "It's late, Tyghan. It's not important—"

He turned her to face him. "I want to, Bri. Please, let me give you swimming and rain and the night of peace you wanted. Let me take you there."

CHAPTER 32

S loshy mud sucked at their boots, and the forest smelled like
rain. The pungent scent of drenched pine and the lusty breath
of warm, wet earth rose up to meet them. Other than putting on
boots, they hadn't bothered to change. Bristol was still in her thin gown,
the hem now spattered with mud, and Tyghan still bare-chested. He
said clothes were not important because they wouldn't be running into
anyone where they were going, and now, walking along this dark path,
she believed him.

She wondered at his impulsive offer. It seemed maybe he needed
this as much as she did. A rare brokenness lined his face when he
told her about the markings. In the midst of his mountain of other
problems, he was worried about her. But his concern also made her
breath catch. How bad was it? Yes, maybe they both needed time to
think. Walking this steep, dark trail with him was the reprieve she
craved.

The rain had stopped, and there were no other sounds besides water searching for a river to fill or a root to nourish—no bird songs,
no rustling animals. They had veered off the path that led to Thistle
Lookout, and it made Bristol feel like she had stepped into a new world
and left behind the worries of the old one. Her shoulders relaxed, and
her breaths deepened into a smooth, unconscious rhythm—until they

reached a forested cliff and Tyghan told her how they would proceed with the rest of their journey.

"A nightjump? Have you lost your mind?"

"Two nightjumps, actually. It's the only way. That's why this place is a secret."

"Then it can remain a secret. The last time I nightjumped, I couldn't breathe."

He circled his arms around her, pulling her hips snug against his. "The last time you weren't with me. This time you'll breathe, I promise."

"Two nightjumps?"

"Trust me, Bri." And he lowered his mouth to hers.

She felt her weight drop away, her feet no longer anchored to the earth. She was a feather on a current, turning in the air with him, his arms secure around her. Warmth enveloped her like a balmy storm. He was her storm. His tongue gently skimmed her teeth, his breaths becoming her own. He tasted of cloves and ale, and she breathed in deeply, feeling the spiciness roll through her mouth, her lungs, even through her veins, every part of her growing lighter. She breathed him in, and it was like they were their own planet spinning through a galaxy, the stars parting as they swept past. And then, too soon, she felt her feet touching a firm surface again. Their mouths parted, and he smiled. "Nightjump one is done. Can you handle one more?"

She cupped his face and brought his mouth to hers in answer.

The second time they landed, she heard the quiet rush of rain, and when the moon peeked out from the clouds, she saw they were at the bottom of a deep gorge. Above them, a waterfall emptied into a small lake.

"This way," Tyghan said, taking her hand. He led her across a mossy shore to the thin edge of the waterfall, and then they stepped down, knee-deep in water, and waded through the cascading falls before rising again on the other side. It was pitch-black, but Tyghan roused a flame in his palm, and the walls and water around them came alive. They were in a large sandy cave behind the waterfall. Water dripping from the ceiling reflected the flame and turned the cave into a sparkling sky.

"It's not exactly rain, but—"

"It's perfection." Bristol quickly yanked off her wet boots and dug her toes into the golden sand, circling the cave in childlike awe. The remnant of a mostly burned log in the back of the cave was evidence that Tyghan had been here before. With a gentle flick of one hand, the fire in his palm flew to the log and set it aflame, making even more light sparkle around her. She stared, mesmerized by the backside of the waterfall. "How on earth did you ever find this place?"

He smiled. "It was an accident, actually, one that cost me a few bruises and an impressive knot on the head."

"That *is* impressive. We all know how hardheaded you are."

"Says the pot to the kettle?"

"Maybe so." She laughed. "When did this amazing discovery happen?"

He shrugged. "It was a long time ago. I was only seven."

She was impressed all over again, wondering how a small child could find such a distant place. "Tell me more."

His expression turned somber as he walked along the back of the cave, gathering up dried branches for the fire, and she knew she was entering tender territory. "It was the day of my father's funeral," he said.

Very tender, she thought, and she was grateful he no longer deflected painful questions. He had changed. *You made me want to share my life with you.*

And he did, sharing one of the most painful days of his childhood. "When the rites were over, Eris took my hand in his and led me away. My mother and brother were walking just ahead of us, and he told me I would need to be strong for my mother now. I remember turning and burying my face in his robes, and holding on to him. I was terrified." Tyghan stopped at the back of the cave, looking nowhere in particular, maybe seeing the frightened child he had once been. "I was certain I could never be strong enough. Eris put his hand on my head, like he was protecting me from the world, and said, *But on the days you can't be strong, I'll be strong for you.*"

Bristol's throat twisted, seeing Tyghan's loss in a whole new light, and seeing Eris in a new way too, a man not only juggling the duties of a transitioning kingdom, but considering the needs of a broken family as well. "Was he?" she asked. "Strong for you?"

Tyghan nodded. "More times than I can count." He added the dry branches to the glowing embers on the log, and it flamed up. "But at the time I was still afraid and overwhelmed and wanted to disappear, and then, just like that, I did my first nightjump." A small laugh lifted his chest. "It didn't go well. I didn't know what the hell I was doing or where I was going, just that I wanted to get away from it all. I'm lucky I didn't kill myself. I missed the first landing and bounced down the side of the mountain until I ended up here. I lay on the beach nursing my wounds, but even as my head throbbed, I felt a powerful calmness. It's such a small canyon, a small lake, but it was all mine. In a single day I fell in love with this place, and determined to get better at nightjumps."

"Well, you succeeded with that," she agreed, remembering the feeling of floating in his arms. "This has been your secret sanctuary ever since?"

He nodded. "I've never shared it with anyone, but now it's yours too."

"Hmm, could be bad news. I don't do nightjumps."

"I guess I'll always have to be your personal guide, then." He stood and began unbuttoning his trousers. "Ready for a swim?"

"It's safe in the lake?"

"Empty. The only creature you have to worry about is me."

More buttons.

"Then I have a lot to worry about."

His trousers fell to his ankles, and he stepped out of them. Firelight licked over every exquisite, sculpted muscle he possessed. Heat kindled low in her gut. She remembered the first time she stumbled upon him, half-naked in his room, and her useless admonishment to herself to *look away*. Now she brazenly drank in every inch.

Her first assessment of him still stood—the planes, the sinew, the hard cut of deltoids meeting biceps, the tight ripples of his abs, even his calves were carved to perfection. Except now his long, jagged scar didn't seem like a flaw but a victory. Michelangelo wouldn't reject an imperfect piece of marble if he saw Tyghan. His flaws, inside and out, were what she loved, what made him perfect, a hard-won version of himself that was a work of art.

This time of course, there was no towel covering his middle. He let her assess him, standing perfectly still—except for one part of him that was quickly growing. She was caressing him with her eyes, and it appeared that was enough.

She felt the heat of his eyes on her too. She glanced down. Apparently, it wasn't just her gaze causing things to grow. Her gown was wet from going through the waterfall, and the thin fabric clung to her like skin. Her chilled nipples eagerly peeked through.

"You can join me whenever you're ready," he said. And with a few steps, he dove, disappearing through the waterfall.

CHAPTER 33

Tyghan treaded water in the middle of the lake. He glanced down and sighed, though nothing was visible beneath the dark water. "Down boy," he whispered, lamenting that his near instant erection would make Bristol think he only lured her here for his own "devious" passions—though she never objected to his passion before. Except tonight he wanted to make it all about her, giving her what she wanted, what she needed. But damn, he ignited every time he was near her.

He swam the short length of the lake, maybe thirty yards, his shoulders swaying in rhythm with each lap, his arms gliding through the water, neither cold nor warm, the perfect balance that made him feel free and unbound to the world.

I fell in love with this place.

That was why he brought her here. A childlike hope that it would be enough to buoy her for what was to come. After his mother left, he sometimes thought that if he had only brought her here, shared this place with her, the powerful calm of it might have helped her to stay. It was a game he had tortured himself with for months after she was gone. If he had loved her more, if he had been stronger, if he had shared—

It was a childish thought, and one Eris set straight immediately. *This was not about you or anything you could have done. Your mother loved you more than life itself. She left to save you.* Tyghan asked him if there was truly a curse, as his mother claimed. Even Eris didn't know. *She was deeply broken*, he told him. *Sometimes fear is the most powerful curse of all.* Eris encouraged him to concentrate on being the best Knight Commander Danu had ever known. *Safeguard the kingdom your mother loved.*

It was a message that was sealed into him. Whenever he lost his way, he always returned to that. Maybe that goal had saved him even more than the secret place. Or maybe it was Eris who had saved him all along.

Safeguard the kingdom. That should have been his only thought. But it wasn't. It hadn't been for a long time. He had to safeguard Bristol too. He had to make those two goals become one.

He did another lap, and another. The storm clouds had moved on, and a crescent moon shimmered on the surface of the water, lighting his way. The soothing sound of his strokes slicing through the surface, the balmy air, the sheer joy on Bristol's face when she saw the cave dripping with light, drained away his thoughts and cares. That was how it had always been, this place. The only thing that made it better was now he had someone to share it with. Midway in the lake, he stopped and treaded water, turning to face the cave. What was she doing behind the waterfall? Still soaking in the wonder? He didn't want to rush her but—

"*Hey!*" Bristol startled him, breaking the surface a few feet away like a triumphant breaching fish. Her chin and lashes dripped with water.

"You swam all that way underwater?"

"Motel swimming pools," she said, laughing. "One of the greatest luxuries of my childhood. My sisters and I would swim in them for hours. I got pretty good at holding my breath. But here . . . here I don't feel the need to breathe at all. It's like this place is breathing for me."

She disappeared beneath the water again and resurfaced in his arms, sliding close, her gown shed and her skin like silk against his.

Her mouth skimmed the bristle of his chin, nipping at his jawline, her breaths warm against his wet skin. "Thank you for this," she whispered, "but I don't want you to worry about me, Tyghan. I'm a knight now, remember?"

For twelve full hours. "Got it, Keats," he answered, and brought his mouth to hers, their tongues barely touching, caressing, a delicate signal passing between them but with a message that was as deep as the ocean. *I love you.*

Bristol leaned back into the circle of Tyghan's arms. He locked them gently beneath her breasts and she lazily rested her head on his shoulder. "Take me for a tour of your lake."

They floated together, Tyghan's legs gently moving them along, gliding like there was no hurry, no tomorrow, no up, no down, only the gentle sounds of the falling water and them—exploring the secret place and each other. The shoreline, the fig trees, his finger skimming her lips, her mouth closing around it. The mossy banks, the passion flowers, her hand pressed to his chest, letting his heartbeat become her own. His mouth breathing air into hers when they dipped beneath the surface, the music she heard in her head, as languid as his thumb strumming the knots of her spine. Gravity gave up its laws to them; the stars pressed closer, curious at this new center of the universe.

Yearnings. Dreams. The past. The future. Time folded over on itself.

They circled the lake again, because one time wasn't enough, the thin moon sinking lower in the sky. The climbing clematis, the giant oak, his teeth dragging across her shoulder, his knees spreading her legs, her nails scraping over his back, their words few.

They stumbled onto the bank, the moss a velvet cushion beneath their backs, the heel of his palm stroking her while his fingers pushed inside her, every touchpoint aching with pleasure, her muscles loosening and tightening all at once. Her pelvis rocked forward against his touch.

Their mouths met over and over again, as they gripped each other and the ground for purchase, because they needed more, because there were never enough ways to know each other. Bristol lifted her knees, her legs circling around his back, to let him in deeper, his arms straddling her shoulders, looking down at her, memorizing her face as he pushed in. Slow. Slow. Torturously slow. Pulling out just as slow, memorizing the feel of her. But then pushing back faster, harder. Pounding, deeper, his breaths shuddering, his eyes narrowing, her hips lifting higher. "Look at me," he said, "look at me." And then harder, the glorious ache between her legs building, her back arching, the throb exploding, his eyes a thousand blue splinters flashing in her vision, his gaze still sinking into hers as his thrusts came harder, the hoarse moans, and finally his head thrown back, coming undone, coming into her. And even when he reached a crashing height, it wasn't over. He still pushed, his throbs receding like a slow tide, his moans softening.

Finally, he pulled out, and fell back beside her, panting. "You're going to kill me one day, Bristol Keats."

She smiled. "But what a way to go?"

The frog croaked, hoping to disturb the amorous couple. It had little effect. He hadn't always been a frog, and still had vague memories of walking on two legs before a curse changed all that. It wasn't so bad being a frog, at least not here, but he didn't like sharing his paradise with others. They needed to move on. He croaked again, louder, to no avail, their whispers and laughter cutting into his tiny frog heart, reminding him of lost love and bad choices. He hopped off into the shadows, trying to ease the pain in his warty chest and to convince himself that life as a frog was preferable to a broken heart.

Bristol stared into the sky, smiling at the croaking somewhere in the darkness.

"There *are* creatures here," she whispered.

"None that can ever harm you."

Rivers of heat warmed her. The way he said it, like a declaration, a vow, a warrior at her side poised to slay any threat. Her fingers inched across the mossy blanket, searching for his hand, her palm pressing onto his knuckles, the peace of the stars settling into her bones. All of this only two nightjumps away. Nightjumps she nearly rejected, but courage and trust turned them into something beautiful, into the best decision she ever made.

"I'm ready," she whispered.

"To go back?"

"To see the markings."

Tyghan stood behind her, knee-deep in the water, angling his palm between her back and the waterfall, focusing the light of the moon and stars onto it like a reflective mirror. "You don't have to do this," he said for the second time. We can—"

"I do, Tyghan. Not just for all of you. But for me too."

"All right." He took a deep breath. "Ready?"

Her chest fluttered with a lifetime of warnings drilled into her by her parents. *Look away. Run. This truth is too big for you. Too dangerous. Some things you don't need to know.*

But running never made the problem go away. It just delayed the inevitable, giving it more power. She couldn't go back to the illusion of a ladybug birthmark. She didn't want to. Whatever she had to face, she had to face it now. And somehow that decision was freeing, a giddiness overtaking her, like when she made the decision to return to the Willoughby Inn and strike a deal with the fae. She was taking back a portion of power.

"I'm ready," she said. "Show me."

The image in the waterfall rippled, trying to focus. Tyghan blew out an even breath like *he* was trying to focus. Maybe this was harder for him than it was for her. He had already had time to think about what the markings meant—and maybe he feared the worst.

This would be the first time she had seen the tick since the day it was revealed to her in Madame Chastain's treatment room all those weeks ago. Its hideous dark shadow loomed in her memory again, and queasiness lifted her stomach like she was plunging down a roller coaster. She swallowed, refusing to be dissuaded.

She heard Tyghan's strained breaths behind her and the air grew heavier, sound turning to syrup, and everything seemed to slow—including the waterfall. It shimmered now, like a glassy sheet of water, and she could almost feel the sweat on Tyghan's brow as he commanded the elements around them, drawing in the shadows, directing the light, a reluctant demigod revealing one of the things he couldn't control—who or what she was.

Her blurred back came into view, sharpening breath by breath, until the image was as crystal clear as her dressing room mirror. The first thing she noticed was the dim shadow of the tick at the small of her back, barely visible now, like it had burrowed deeper into her so no one could find it. The dimness made it less horrific. But then her gaze rose.

She stared, trying to discern what it was, and she became a child again, looking at her mother in a motel bathroom and seeing something that didn't make sense. But this time she didn't scream and run. Skirting the edges of her shoulder blades were golden marks, diamond shapes, and trailing down her spine was a line of more diamonds. They almost looked like—

Her stomach lurched.

Scales.

She worked to steady her voice. "Have you felt them?"

"Yes," Tyghan whispered, the single syllable apologetic, like he was invading some deep personal moment. "They feel soft like your skin now, but the ridges are growing more pronounced."

Ridges. Every word stole a piece of her, leaving her numb. She forced in another breath.

Hubris, she thought, *fucking hubris,* to think she could face this without the world tilting beneath her feet. She stared for a long while at the scales trailing down her back like tears, trying to imagine them as something else. Anything else. A rash. Even an illusion. She flexed her shoulder blades, and the marks shimmered in the light, moving

THE LAST WISH OF BRISTOL KEATS

together like armor. Her stomach tumbled again. This much had surfaced just by pricking the tick. Once it was removed entirely—

"What will I become?" she asked, her voice flat, like it belonged to someone else. "A fish? A mermaid? Something halfway between?"

"I don't know."

His voice broke something inside her, something that was still trying to be strong, and her thoughts went into freefall. What if the changes weren't only on the outside? What if—

"Will I remember who I was?" And then another thought before he could answer. "Will I remember you, Tyghan? Will I remember that I love you?"

His hands fell to his sides, the waterfall rushing once more, the image of scales vanishing, and he turned her around to face him. His expression was as determined and desperate as when he had faced down Braegor in the maze. "Yes," he answered, "yes, you will," and he pulled her into his arms, whispering against her temple. "And if you don't remember me, I will dance with you in the moon shadows every night for the rest of my days, until you fall in love with me again."

CHAPTER 34

It was a sight to see, and it never ceased to inspire and sober Tyghan. He stilled, like a stalled wind changing course, taking in the rolling terrain of Badbe Garrison and the thousands of knights moving in unison. The low, haunting bellow of the carnyx carried for miles, vibrating through flesh and bone. The rumble of the six-foot trumpets sounded like the warning of a fearsome beast approaching. The beast that was the Danu army. The faster notes were just as mysterious and menacing, messages that couldn't be deciphered by the enemy but guided the troops. Tyghan watched Quin and other officers on the rise just below him stop at the sounds that could hollow out a heart.

The regiments moved in mesmerizing precision, their steps like an ancient dance, no matter the weapons or magics they bore. Shields interlocked in unison, spears lifted, swords poised, and arrows nocked on bowstrings. Mounted lancers, swordsmen, and archers streamed into the air above them like hawks set on prey. Summoners poised to call on their kinships with fire, water, and wind. There were no wasted moves, and heeding the trumpets' call, they pivoted in perfected harmony. North. South. East. West. The synchronized heft of their movement thumped in the air like a hand on a drum.

It made Tyghan's chest ache in a way it never had before. No matter how perfect and prepared they were, some would still die.

"Magnificent, isn't it?" Kasta said, coming to stand beside him. "It's a sight I'll never tire of." She drew in a deep, satisfied breath. "I knew from the first time I saw these maneuvers, I was meant to be a knight." She nudged Tyghan's shoulder with her own. "You too, right?"

Tyghan nodded, but his attention had returned to Bristol, wondering what she thought. She'd been hard to read ever since they got back to her room last night. Or maybe her manner just surprised him. She seemed calm. Too calm. The first thing she had done was sit down and write a letter to her sisters. Her expression changed as she wrote it, her lips pursing in concentration, her brows rising as she reread it, crossing something out and adding something else, then a crease between her brows before she called for a servant to deliver it to Eris in the middle of the night. *Urgent?* he had asked. *No, just an update*, she answered. After they went to bed to get a few precious hours of sleep, she curled into his arms. *Do you want to talk?* he had whispered. She only said, *I'm all right. Let's sleep*.

He thought maybe she just needed time to absorb what she saw, but in the morning, as they dressed, she still didn't speak about it, like she had completely accepted the idea—or was completely avoiding it. Should he have told her sooner? Or had he made a mistake by telling her at all? *Are you all right?* he asked, too many times, until she finally forbid him from asking again. And then she produced another letter she had written during the night and gave it to the hob who delivered their breakfast trays. It was a message for the Lumessa. The scales hadn't deterred her: She still wanted the tick removed as soon as possible.

That morning, when he stepped forward to address the waiting troops, he grabbed her hand and pulled her to the crest with him. With only two weeks until the ceremony, he wanted to be sure everyone saw her at his side. When he proclaimed the strength of the Danu army, he

lifted Bristol's hand with his, holding it aloft, shouting the accolades of
the gods. With the delivery of Glennis's head on the palace steps, Bristol's parentage was now a matter of record, and he wanted to present a
unified and powerful image to the troops to dispel any lingering doubts
about her loyalties—especially after Cully's remarks the night before.
There was no room for doubt. She was not Maire or Kierus. The troops
had responded with thunderous cheers.

Bristol now stood on the rise just below him, along with her squad,
being instructed on the complexities of the horns' messages. While
technically they wouldn't be part of the regiments, they still had to
know who was where and who was approaching, so they could respond
accordingly. Assuming all this came down to the worst-case scenario of
a battle, instead of the best-case scenario—with the Abyss permanently
closed and Kormick forfeiting his claim. That was probably as likely as
Tyghan sprouting a tail.

Kasta's next words sent his thoughts barreling in a different direction.
"I saw Melizan and Cosette this morning before maneuvers, whispering
plans. What's the rush with this wedding, now of all times? I'm surprised
you agreed to it."

He wiped a line of sweat from his hairline, not wanting to get into
it with Kasta. They'd been more at odds these past few weeks than
they had ever been before. It was the tension, he told himself. Everyone had been pushed too hard for too long. "It's only a fifteen-minute
ceremony," he answered, "and it will make my sister happy."

She snorted. "Fifteen minutes." A long pause followed, her mouth
twisting like she was trying to swallow rotten meat. "Okay. Good
enough."

The dripping disapproval in those few words snapped something in
him. He shook his head, fighting with his thoughts, but they spilled out
anyway. "We're ready, Kasta. We've been training nonstop for months.
We're as ready as we will ever be. We can't just prepare to fight. Sometimes we have to prepare to live too. We have to remember what we're
fighting *and* living for."

Her gaze darted sideways at him, like it had been a personal admonishment. "Just so you know, I still have dreams, Tygh," she finally said. "I've just learned to put them on hold. Priorities, remember?" She set off down the hill to the officers gathered below, his reply abandoned on his tongue.

Maybe you shouldn't put them on hold.

Maneuvers ended at noon. Bristol's squad gathered their gear, including their new swords, all of them walking just a little bit taller as they headed for the garrison pavilion to eat before returning for afternoon assignments. When they noticed Hollis lagging behind, talking with Quin, they slowed.

"Should we wait for her?" Rose asked.

Avery set her gear down, the alert crown of leaves and twigs on her head settling in for rest too. "Wars are won on full stomachs, or something like that. We should wait."

"Agree," Julia said. "And Hollis has more the appetite of a lion than a mouse. She'll be along soon, I'm sure."

Bristol set her gear down too. "But she also has an appetite for Quin. I think he wins over her stomach."

"She spent last night in his room," Rose whispered, like it was a big secret.

"Where have you been?" Sashka hooted. "She's spent the last three nights with him!"

Rose laughed. "I know! I wasn't sure if anyone else did! I guess they're officially an item now."

Julia chuckled. "I think they've been an item since Quin snatched her from the jaws of a snapping hound and put her in his pocket for safekeeping."

They all turned and watched the partially camouflaged couple in the shade of a tree. Quin held Hollis's hand to his lips.

"Aren't they cute?" Avery swooned. "Wynn and I were never that cute together. He didn't believe in PDA."

"Shit," Sashka said. "PDA is what I live for. To be publicly adored!"

Avery gave Sashka a playful elbow in the ribs. "Says the person who told the king to get a room when he kissed Bristol."

"That was more than PDA. Did you see his hands? I thought he was about to—"

"*Okay*," Bristol said. "Point made."

They all laughed, but Rose reached out and touched Bristol's arm. "I'm so glad you and the king reconciled and are together again—after that whole mess with your father. I was so worried."

Avery nodded. "I think we all were. Even Olivia and Esmee said they were worried."

Bristol was confused. "Worried about what?"

"That it was over and so was the plan," Rose said.

Julia spoke up to clarify. "The Knight Commander is the only one capable of leading the Danu army and uniting the kingdoms against Kormick, and you're the only one who can stop your mother. For a time, the future was shaky."

"With you two at war, the other war looked grimmer," Avery added.

"You heard the troops this morning," Rose said. "The cheers and excitement. Seeing the king lift your hand in his made all the difference. They feel powerful again. A little confidence goes a long way."

Bristol knew what Rose really meant. *Trust*. A little *trust* goes a long way.

She remembered when Tyghan was afraid to trust her, afraid to dance with her, afraid to love her, but then he took a chance, and in front of the glaring lords and ladies, and the powerful council members eyeing her at Sun Court, he made a grand gesture—he asked her to dance in front of them all. He showed them that he trusted her. Things changed after that. The whispers and sideways glances mostly stopped. He believed in her, and so they did too. She never considered the risk he took. How they might not just reject her but him too, a new king just beginning to garner trust and power. He risked throwing it all away. How fragile their efforts were on so many levels.

Today was another grand gesture, confirming to the throngs that he believed in her. If their Knight Commander could trust her, so could they. Otherwise, she was still only the monster's daughter.

She surveyed her squad, her friends. They had believed in her from day one, before she had even earned their trust, looping her arms in theirs, cheering her on when she failed at every magic spell she attempted, before they even knew that their dreams depended on her. And even when she and Tyghan had their terrible argument, her friends remained steady and true. Especially Julia, not pushing Bristol to any one decision, but supporting, healing her, and leaving her to make her own choices.

"I'm sorry I worried you all," she told them now.

"Hey, they fucked you over," Sashka said, "but they came around. We all make mistakes, right?"

Bristol nodded. "And you can all rest assured that Tyghan and I are completely committed to each other. One argument can't end us."

Avery grinned. "Yeah, we kind of got that."

Hollis rushed up to meet them. "Sorry to keep you all waiting. I just needed to talk to—"

"Ohhh, we don't need to hear the details," Sashka said, making kissing sounds.

"Speak for yourself. I want the details!" Avery snapped, and they all laughed.

Easy. Comfortable. It was the best feeling, Bristol thought, having these women as friends, sisters of another kind. When the time came, she would ask them to be there when the Lumessa removed the tick, to help her accept whatever she might become. And to comfort Tyghan too.

He had asked her so many times that morning if she was all right, it was clear he wasn't all right. She wasn't happy about the scales, but it didn't change anything. Acquiring all of her power was a necessity, not an option. That was all she concentrated on—what was necessary— like paying an electric bill. She had to whittle it down to something small like that or she might implode. She smiled. Life lessons from Bowskeep.

They had only gone a few more steps when they were intercepted by a shout. "Hold up!" It was Tyghan, with Quin and Dalagorn on his heels.

"What now?" Julia whispered as they approached.

Hollis groaned and rubbed her stomach.

"We were about to go eat," Julia called back.

Tyghan stopped in front of them. "I just wanted to remind you about dinner with Cael tonight in the Winterwood Palace. Formal attire."

Some low-grade moans were swallowed. Knights, especially brand-spanking-new ones, weren't supposed to complain.

"One other thing. I've spoken with my officers, and we've realized that in these past months, you've had very little free time."

Hollis snorted. "As in none?"

"Zzzip," Avery concurred.

Sashka formed her thumb and finger into a big zero and punched the air with it.

"Unless you count evening festivities," Julia said, "which we were *required* to attend."

Tyghan cleared his throat, eyeing Sashka's big zero still hanging in the air. "Your point is made and so is mine. From now until the Choosing Ceremony, your afternoons will be free."

Bristol let out a disbelieving laugh. "Who are you, and what have you done with the real Knight Commander?"

Tyghan's eyes narrowed, but a grin lifted the corners of his mouth. "I promise you, morning drills will be twice as brutal to make up for it."

"Whew, what a relief," Bristol answered. "I'd really miss that full array of cuts and bruises."

"Then you have nothing to be worried about."

"And this starts today?" Julia asked.

"Right now," Tyghan confirmed. "And another matter—"

"Oh, here it comes," Bristol moaned. "The other shoe."

"Being a full-fledged knight comes with a salary." He nodded to Da-lagorn, who pulled six small pouches from his vest, handing one to each of them.

"You'll find gold and silver coins inside. Don't spend them all in one place. It will be a month before you get another."

They all quickly calculated the days until the Choosing Ceremony and made a unanimous decision. "We'll spend it all today," Julia said.

"Now, quick," Bristol said, glancing over her shoulder, "let's all get out of here before the real Knight Commander shows up. But you," she said, grabbing Tyghan by his weapons belt and yanking him closer, "you I'd like to catch up with later."

Tyghan leaned over and kissed her. "You can count on it, soldier."

CHAPTER 35

The teapots trembled, and their lids rattled with unease. They
knew something was brewing and it wasn't tea.

"Quiet!" Camille ordered. Her nerves were already on edge
without the porcelain pots adding to her distress. "Let us think! When
did those wretched things become sentient?"

"Last century, I think," Izzy replied, "probably from spending too
many decades crowded between four brilliant witches as they drank tea
and discussed kingdom woes."

"Not so brilliant, or we wouldn't be in this pickle," Adela commented.

The lids settled at Camille's harsh order, but the spouts huffed out
two last puffs of steam.

Izzy buttered her crumpet and sighed. "They usually hold their
tongues."

"Sisters, shhh," Jasmine said softly, her fingers crumpling the letter
in her palm. "I have a decision to make. I need your counsel. She still
wants it removed immediately."

"As you said, there's only one way," Adela replied, unable to say it
aloud: *Stop her heart for good*. "It would be a mercy. And we do have
our blood oaths to consider. Her kind—"

"She is our kind too!" Camille argued. "And pooh on oaths."

Camille's blasphemy swept through the room like a stinging gust.

Adela brushed a tired hand over her brow. "Then just what is your solution, Camille? Chain her and deliver her to the northern islands, where she will die a slow and cruel death? I have witnessed—"

"Absolutely not! Don't forget Elphame *needs* her. Would it be better that we all starve when Kormick takes control of the cauldron?"

"Yes, Elphame needs her," Izzy said, "but once the kingdoms have what they want, they will still chain her and take her to the northern isles anyway."

"Only if they find out."

If. It circled in their minds, Jasmine's most of all. Hiding the truth? It might solve one problem, but another still remained.

"I have an idea," Camille said.

The Sisters were silent, leaning in, the teapots shifting, the candle at the center of the table wavering. Camille told them her plan.

Adela groaned. "Tell her another lie? And a thinly veiled one at that. That's what the poor girl has lived with all her life. And what if she doesn't listen to us?"

"She will. Trust me," Camille said.

"And how long before it's found out? It's just a matter of time—"

"She plans to return to the mortal world. She'll be gone in a few weeks. She will never shift, and no one will ever know."

Jasmine shook her head, contemplating the lie and the risk. She finally rose, wincing as she pressed her hand against her back. "I've made my decision." And with that, she left the Sisters to their tea and misery, and went to her study to write her reply to Bristol. She would do what she had to do and not make the others complicit. This was her burden to bear alone. Hiding one of Bristol's kind was a high crime.

And then she worked out a backup plan, in case stopping Bristol's heart wasn't enough to persuade a tick that was drunk with power.

CHAPTER 36

Perched high atop Lugh Bridge on one of the premier balconies were six newcomers. They had to have connections to get such a plum vantage point—not to mention, much gold. The Cailleach Café came with a hefty price. A few fingers discreetly pointed.

Up there . . .

Who do you suppose . . .

Rich nobles . . .

Not from around here . . .

One observer in particular took note. She recognized the woman in the middle. They'd had some brief words, and there had been numerous inquiries about her. Money could be made in infinite ways. Information was a commodity just like a bolt of silk.

⚷

"Look at that view," Rose crooned. "I could stay up here forever."

"Mmm," Hollis agreed, then motioned to the end of the table. "Pass down more of those prickly purple things, would you?"

Sashka reached for the platter. "Those are—"

"I don't want to know what they are. I just want to eat more in ignorant bliss."

A few seconds later, their server brought them yet another platter to share. They had ordered the Queen's Sampler, which seemed to include every delicious thing on the menu. Most of it was finger food, and Bristol felt like she was back at Sal's on a Friday night, dishing up platters of garlic knots and bruschetta. It was a delightful, leisurely way to eat as they took in the sights—and those were abundant and entertaining. Jugglers; shape-shifters; colorful gowns that drew gasps; a merkind, fresh from the river, her hair dripping down her bare body, as she bargained with a merchant for a hair bauble; a team of miniature blue horses from Amisterre; a cloud of river sprites making teamwork of stealing a thimble-size pastry from a bakery. It seemed a minute didn't pass before one of their group was saying, *Look over there!*

Bristol spotted Mae making her way down the center of the bridge like she owned it, but as Street Mother, Mae seemed to think she owned the whole city. Maybe she did. Bristol remembered passing over this bridge on her first day in Elphame—how the sights had fascinated and overwhelmed her. The grand towers, homes, and gardens teetering on top of one another, jammed together like a jeweled puzzle, and the many filigreed balconies filled with all manner of fae, sipping their precious drinks and observing the chaotic crowds below.

Now she was one of those fae, watching from above, sipping her own mysterious smoky drink, mostly unafraid of Mae now. Across the bridge from them on a lower balcony, a brightly dressed faun plucked out a tune on a fiddle, the notes bouncing in the air in time with the bustle below. She looked over at Rose, whose cheeks were practically glowing.

"Is this what it's like being a hawk?" Bristol asked. "Taking everything in at once?"

"Yes," Rose answered dreamily, "but even better, because you're soaring far above it all, completely weightless and apart. It's hard to describe how heady it is."

"How old were you the first time you shifted?" Julia asked.

"Only four. It was an accident. My parents panicked because they couldn't get me to change back. We were in a small flat in Hampstead at the time, and I darted through the rooms, batting into walls and furniture—but they didn't dare open a door. They finally found a sorcerer in the city who guided me back to human form."

"That's so young!" Julia said. "I didn't even know I could shift until I was thirty, and didn't master it until I was forty. How about you, Hollis? When was your first time?"

Hollis shrugged sheepishly. "A year ago?"

There was a burst of surprised reactions.

"I mean, I knew I could before that. I had partially turned for years, a furry ear here, a long tail there. Whiskers. But I was terrified to fully change, afraid I'd never be able to change back." She explained that her mother passed when she was in college, and she only knew a handful of fae in Seattle, none of them shape-shifters, so she had no one to ask for guidance. "There was a little fae bookstore in town—just a back room, really—so I read everything I could about shifting, and finally took a chance in the safe confines of my apartment. It was exhilarating. But I never did it in public until I came here."

"Really? I never would have guessed!" Sashka said. "You do it so gracefully. Those cute little turns and hops."

"What does it feel like to be something else?" Avery asked. "Do you still feel like yourself?" The questions made Bristol's heart race, but when Hollis began answering, she found herself leaning in, not wanting to miss a word.

"No," Hollis answered. "You don't feel like yourself at all. First of all, every part of you moves so differently. Every muscle. Every twitch. Even your tongue feels odd inside your mouth. And your senses are different too. I can't see as well, but my whiskers tell me everywhere I need to turn. And scent! Gods! I can tell exactly how many minutes a loaf of bread has been out of the oven, and how far away a ripe strawberry is. But I can smell the bad things too, like danger and fear, and sometimes, I think, death that hasn't even arrived yet. It's a cold, dank smell."

"But do you think the same?" Bristol asked. "Do you remember *who* you are?"

"Yes, mostly, but you don't want to. You want to fully sink into who and what you are, to feel the fur on your belly, and the tap of your tiny claws on the earth. The feel of your tail sliding behind you, adding a strange balance you've never felt before. When you change, something calls to you to forget your other self, and only live in the moment of who you are in that place and time. At least, that's how it is for me."

Julia nodded. "It's seductive, the incredible power you feel, the new instincts that overtake you. Once, when we were visiting the Kalahari, I changed for two full months and nearly forgot who I used to be. My aunt had to coax me back."

"Yes," Rose agreed. "The power and freedom enchant you, but probably no less than returning to human form enchants you again. I guess balance is the key, like playing a piece on the piano, performing the melody with one hand and the accompaniment with the other. You need both hands."

"Beautifully expressed, Rose," Julia said.

"Yes, beautiful," Hollis agreed.

But Bristol's mind was dwelling on other words, Jasmine's words: *profound changes*. There was nothing beautiful in the way she said them. Instead, her words were thick with warning.

The server arrived with a final platter, filled with the prettiest chocolate meringue rose cookies dusted with shimmering sugar flakes. Hollis groaned, holding her stomach, but the cookie roses were too enticing, and they all took one.

"I'm never going to be able to eat dinner tonight," Avery complained, licking sugar from her fingers.

Sashka moaned. "I forgot about dinner with the ingrate. And we can't be late, or he might go into another meltdown."

"Yes, the sooner we get it over with, the better," Julia said.

"I'm kind of looking forward to watching him grovel," Hollis mused. "This could be fun."

Avery scoffed. "It's only an apology. *Sorry*. One word. That won't take much groveling."

"Unless we drag it out," Rose replied, her eyes full of mischief.

Julia laughed, and put her hand to her ear, pretending she was talking to Cael. "What's that, Your Majesty? I can't hear you. Say it again? A little louder! Preferably on your knees."

Sashka clapped her hands. "I am so doing that."

Bristol was actually looking forward to the apology too. Maybe this time Cael would have more finesse than with his last botched attempt, when he accused her of casting a spell on Tyghan, but she thought about what he said too: *Fear and anger have ruled my small world for months now*. Maybe she shouldn't judge him based on his first day of freedom.

The hunched shopkeeper hummed cheerfully as she wrapped Bristol's purchase, her gnarled hands surprisingly nimble. She had teeth as sharp as Mae's, but her voice was sweet, almost childlike, with a disposition to match. When she smiled, her pointed fangs sparkled in a friendly way, if that was possible. Bristol had learned not to assume anything about appearances in the fae world. "You'll love it," the old woman said. "No shenanigans with this one! Just sweet notes."

What kind of shenanigans could a tiny flute stir up? Bristol wondered, but only replied, "Good to know."

The woman wrapped Bristol's purchase, her gnarled hands surprisingly nimble. She tied some sisal string around the floral paper before handing the package over. *Sisal*, Bristol thought. *It is common here.* A few brass horns up on the wall wheezed as Bristol tucked the package in her bag, apparently disappointed that Bristol hadn't chosen them. Maybe they were the ones more prone to shenanigans? "Thank you," Bristol said. "I know my sister will love it."

The squad had separated after lunch to shop on their own, since time was short before they had to be back at the palace, and Bristol had gone searching for gifts for her sisters. This small music shop had immediately caught her eye.

Besides being an immensely talented singer, Cat had never met an instrument she couldn't play. Give her a day with just about anything— piano, guitar, harp—and Cat could pluck out at least a few tunes. She was remarkable in that way. Bristol smiled, remembering how she would even tap out songs with half-filled drinking glasses and a spoon. Maybe this beautiful little flute would help make up for all the time Bristol had been gone, though a present wasn't really necessary. For all her worrying and ranting, Cat was quick to forgive. She never held a grudge.

"Bring your sister back with you next time," the shopkeeper called after Bristol as she left. "I will give her the full tour."

Bristol smiled. "I'll try." She mused on that thought as she walked out the door. Maybe one day she really could bring her sisters here, once Elphame was in a safer, more settled state. She would never dare bring them now.

She had gotten Harper a gift too—a book to make up for the one Harper had to shuck like an ear of corn to pass through the portal. This new one was definitely not a weeded book from the library's twenty-five-cent bin. It was bound in hand-tooled leather, with gilded edges. It outlined the history of each kingdom in Elphame and their unique features. Harper would love it. Hopefully it would earn Bristol best big sister status forever. Regret tugged inside her. She missed her sisters and wished she hadn't closed the tiny portal from Tyghan's study to their mudroom. Just seeing a glimpse of them for a few minutes would lift her heart, but it might also gut her with guilt, especially if Cat started in. For now, letters would have to do. It wouldn't be much longer until she was home with them—and hopefully with her parents too. *Patience*, she told herself. *It will be worth the wait.*

With two gifts secured, Bristol set out to find something for Melizan and Cosette's wedding day, though she had no clue what that might be. Eventually, she found herself walking down a narrow winding street of curiosities. One shop carried nothing but beautiful jeweled insect brooches—beetles, butterflies, and scorpions. However fascinating, they were not Melizan and Cosette's style. Another merchant only sold mirrors—hand, wall, and freestanding, all of which had eerie phantom eyes within them that stared back at Bristol. She didn't linger there for long. Last, she came upon a little store that sold small, beautiful knives—finally something the newlywed knights might appreciate. She picked one up to study a bronze hilt fashioned in the shape of a dragon, a true work of art. It might be perfect. "Hello?" she called, looking for the shopkeeper. Silence was the only reply, so she tried again, walking toward the back of the dim shop.

"Hello? Is there—"

Something slammed into her, and light exploded behind her eyes.

CHAPTER 37

Bristol fell onto a table and heard the tear of fabric and the crash of glass. Before she could scream, the room went dark and icy. She gasped for air that wasn't there, and then there was another slam—this time harder, into a rough wall that scraped her skin. She sucked in a deep breath, struggling to get her bearings. Musty air filled her lungs. Her arm throbbed. A body pressed close, pinning her against the wall behind her, strong hands clamped around her wrists.

A voice split the air. *"Where is he?"*

The voice was lightning shooting through her. "Get off me, you ass!" she shouted.

His hands clamped tighter, her burning wrists feeling like they might snap. *"Where is he?"* he demanded again, pressing harder against her, pain shooting through her shoulder.

She already recognized the voice, but as her eyes adjusted to the dark, she saw Mick's angry face looming in front of hers.

"Get off me," she repeated through clenched teeth.

He eased his grip on her wrists, but his hips still pinned her to the wall. "If you answer me, I will."

"Are you stalking me? What's wrong with you? Every time I come to the city, you pounce on me?"

"I'm here more often than you think. This city was once ruled by my ancestors. I have friends here."

With a slight tilt of his head, he made the shadows roll back, and a candle on a table sparked to life. Dim light slithered across the room. Timbers crossed the dark ceiling above her, and darker rugs covered the floor. She felt a cold draft but couldn't see any windows or even a door. It was sparsely furnished, with only a small table and a bed—an enclosed basement that only someone able to nightjump could reach. Mick was her only way back out.

"Friends? Or do you mean spies who keep you abreast of interesting visitors like me?"

"You're avoiding my question."

"Where is who?" she asked, but she knew, of course, who he was burning to find. What was important was staying a step ahead of him.

"My prisoner, Cael. Don't lie to me. I'll know if you're lying."

Not if she was good at it. And she was. All lies were about making them true. Owning them. Making the stakes your own.

"Sweet fuck, Mick. You've got to be kidding me. You've lost him?"

He eased his grip on her wrists, and she yanked free. "He escaped."

"*Escaped?* How? To where?"

"I don't know. A guard found his cell empty. That's why I'm here. This is the first place he would run."

She shook her head in disbelief. "If he's out in the wilds, he's *dead*. Tyghan's made it clear how helpless his brother is. If he finds out you lost him . . ." She blew out an angry breath, like this was the biggest botched deal she had ever heard of. "How did you screw this up, Mick? It's simple. You kidnap a king. You give him back. Easy. Cael's the only thing keeping Tyghan's anger in check. If he finds out his brother has become wolf food—"

"Why would you care?"

"Because I don't want to be caught in the middle of a major testosterone blowup between you two idiots. I have plans of my own. I've got one last lead to follow next week in Bogshollow before I go home.

An ogre is meeting me there. Only five days before I'm out of here for good! I made a promise—"

Mick suddenly leaned close to her, breathing in deep, pressing her shoulder back to the wall. "I smell magic on you." It was an accusation.

She pivoted without missing a beat. "Of course you do. I've been here for way too long. I've learned a few things. I can almost levitate an apple across a room now. If only I could master invisibility, I could manage to stay out of your annoying hands."

"Levitation? That's all?"

"What do you expect from me, Mick? Summoning your gods? I'm afraid apples are the best I can do. I'm a fucking mortal who would rather be home delivering pizzas, but instead, I'm stuck here, searching for my father."

Mick sighed, his finger slowly tracing a line up her arm. "Same old Bristol. You'll never listen, will you? Trénallis is leading you on. I already told you, your father's dead."

Her eyes welled—for the theater.

She paused—for the timing.

But her throat swelled all on its own, the real ache taking her by surprise. The worry for her father never went away. She looked down, trying to shake the feeling. "Stop. Please don't tell me one more time that my father is dead. I promised my sisters I'd bring him back, and I'm still empty-handed."

He lifted her chin with the crook of a finger. "You're chasing a ghost, Bristol. Take them home a trinket instead. A shiny bauble. They'll forget him soon enough."

He reached up and brushed his thumb along her lashes, and the puddles in her eyes tumbled down her cheeks. She didn't know what was a game and what was real anymore. He leaned in, brushing her cheekbone with his lips. Her heart slowed. Sound and movement became muffled, like she was being pulled into a cocoon. The tension in her muscles drained away. Something was happening. Something that—

"I want you to know," he whispered, "that I didn't use you when I was in Bowskeep. I went there to find out what my enemies were up to, because they're always up to something. I cared about you. I truly did."

No, she thought, *no*. But his words were soothing, and he sounded sincere, like he had so many times when they met after hours at Sal's, holding her, rubbing her back like he could rub everything that ached inside her away, mending all that was broken, kissing her like she was the center of the universe. During those two weeks in Bowskeep, he had showered her with his golden words, and she had thought they had something together. But there had always been a niggle in her gut, warning her that something was off. But his touch, his kisses, they were the balm that silenced the niggle, at least for a while. She felt that same balm spreading through her now, telling her to give in to it. Let it heal the pain. Let *him* heal the pain.

"Can I kiss you, Bristol? Just once more, for old times' sake?" he asked, his lips hovering closer.

She pushed back against the feeling. "Why, Mick? So you can prove your kisses are better than his? So you can make me believe that you really care about me?"

"Both of those things, and so I can show you how sorry I am for leaving without a goodbye. You deserved that much. A kiss goodbye, that's all . . ."

Before she could refuse, he brought his lips to hers, and those weeks in Bowskeep flooded back to her, the stolen moments they shared, the fear that was drowned out, the inexplicable balance she felt, like she wasn't going to fall off the edge of the world anymore. Mick's cocoon, that was what she was being pulled into. But she didn't want to be there. She wanted to push him away. Except the worry was melting away. His tongue circled hers, and the heat inside her said yes, but the distant warning—

A part of her remembering, a voice trying to break through a surface she couldn't see.

"Doesn't this place remind you of Sal's storeroom?" he whispered. "But instead of a couch, here we have a bed." His hand slid up her side, brushing her breast. "Once more for old times'—"

No. A steady faraway beat trying to rise.

Not this. Not ever.

She shoved him away. "No, Mick! Nothing ever for old times' sake! You take care of your business, and I'll take care of mine. But never touch me again! Do you understand? I don't need your sick brand of magic swaying me, or your false promises. My will is my own, and you will not bend it, not ever again."

A confident grin tipped the corner of his mouth. "I'm offended, Bristol. You underestimate me." He grabbed her hand, pulling her to him, and her world went dark again.

CHAPTER 38

Winterwood was a palace within a palace. It was believed to have been built by the daughter of winter, but no one knew with certainty, for it was made during a blizzard, and when the long, furious storm finally calmed, it was there, fully finished, sparkling with the snowy mortar of winter. It was there that the first queen of Danu was born. Over the millennia it had grown, inching outward century after century, but it always remained the warm heart at the center of the sprawling palace, the safe haven in times of storms, whatever kind they might be.

Because of its status as the inner sanctum of the palace, Winterwood was chosen as the best place to host a dinner for a king who was still presumed to be a prisoner of Fomoria. A tucked-away place of safety—and secrecy.

Tyghan was the first to arrive, other than Ivy, who had just come from checking on the menu in the kitchen. "Come see the dining room," she said, leading the way.

Even Tyghan, who was not easily impressed, had to pause and admire it. Ivy had brought the outside in. Moss and ferns lined the table, with gleaming dishes and silver nestled among them. Glass candlesticks rose halfway to the ceiling, flickering like stars above. Garlands of wildflowers fell from the backs of the chairs, and in each corner of the room, a forest of birches rose up and disappeared into the ceiling. He had vague memories of such extravagant tables when he was a child—before his parents died.

"The chef and I worked together on this," Ivy said proudly. "Beautiful, no?"

Tyghan nodded. "Very." He imagined Bristol's eyes lighting up when she saw it. And if this didn't pull the grumpiness out of Cael, nothing would. "Ivy, I've been thinking. About Melizan's wedding."

"The binding ritual? Yes, I have it on the schedule. Day after tomorrow. Fifteen minutes, correct?"

"Maybe a little longer than that. Some food and drink for whoever shows up? And could you throw in a special thing or two to make it more of a celebration?"

A wide grin lit Ivy's face. "Wise move, Your Majesty. I'll take care of it."

"And when do you think there will be another wedding?" he asked.

She coyly tweaked her head to the side. "Are you trying to tell me about one I should add to the schedule?"

"No! No. I was talking about you and Cully."

She frowned, twisting her hands in front of her, and finally sighed. "I'm pixie, he's elven. You know my parents."

"I do. But you're a grown woman, Ivy. Is their permission really necessary?"

"In their world, it is, but—" She smiled, and a small laugh escaped through her lips. "No, actually. It's not." She turned and left to consult with the chef, her wings fluttering behind her as she went.

Julia and Hollis were the first guests to arrive, waved past the guards by Esmee, who was approving all the guests for the small dinner party. They swept into the grand salon, their fancy shoes tapping on the red marble floor. Tyghan turned at the sound of their footsteps, and Julia couldn't help but register the surprise on his face.

"You did say it was formal?" she said, hesitantly.

"Yes. Of course," Tyghan answered. "You both look very nice. I guess I won't be able to demand any laps."

"Probably not," Julia replied, noting he was getting better at light conversation, *entirely thanks to Bristol*. She and Hollis both took a shameless spin, showing off their last-minute finds of the day. Julia was dressed in a black and silver striped taffeta gown that whispered in the nicest way as she walked. Hollis wore a slinky pink gown that matched her hair perfectly, and a black satin cape shimmered on her shoulders.

"Can I get you both something to drink?" Tyghan asked.

Hollis shot Julia a sideways glance. *The king is serving us?* Julia noticed the lack of servants, no doubt being kept to a minimum because of Cael. The fewer who knew he was back, the better. Julia kept her request simple. "Some Bordeaux, if you have it?"

"And I'll have a Pink Lady with a twist of lime," Hollis said. Tyghan looked at her blankly, and she laughed. "Just kidding. I'll have the same as Julia."

He poured and handed them their drinks, glancing toward the foyer. "The others are coming along?"

"Don't worry, Bristol will be here," Hollis said. "A little late, maybe—she had a long shopping list. But you'll only be stuck with us for a few minutes."

He smiled sheepishly and lifted his glass. "Cheers, ladies."

Julia remembered the last time she was in Winterwood with Tyghan. He had skulked in the corner, barely able to contain his worry for Bristol after her throat had been cut. He had become fiercely protective of her since that encounter. *We are completely committed to each other*. Julia hoped Bristol was right. Love was fierce, but also fragile. It could be destroyed in infinite ways. She thought of her own lost loves, the sorrowful tugs that still wove through her heart. Even the strongest lion was at the mercy of a hunter.

Footsteps clamored through the foyer as Sashka, Avery, and Rose stampeded in, laughing and twirling in their splashy gowns. They said quick hellos and waved Tyghan off, helping themselves to the bar.

Tyghan glanced again at the foyer.

"Remember, Your Majesty," Julia said softly, "Bristol is always last to show at evening festivities."

"Am I that obvious?"

"In some matters, yes." She motioned to the sofas. "Shall we sit while we wait for the others?"

Avery and Rose immediately began sharing stories from their day in the city: the troll they spotted on the banks just below the bridge, the winding streets they discovered, their shopping steals.

Tyghan perked up. "You stole merchandise?"

"*No*," Sashka said, like he hadn't been listening. "Steals are deals."

"Then why not just call them deals?"

"You don't go shopping much, do you?" Rose said, and went on to tell him about a gift she got for Melizan and Cosette's wedding. The conversation took off without him as the others shared their finds.

Tyghan finally intervened. "Gifts aren't usually part of a binding ritual."

"Well, they are where we come from!"

He leaned back, curiosity sparking in his eyes as he took a sip of his whiskey. "What are some other mortal wedding traditions?"

They eagerly supplied him with a long list, from proposals on bended knee, to rings and thrown bouquets. Seeing his confusion, Hollis added, "And of course the taller of the couple is required to give the other a back rub every day for the rest of their lives."

"Interesting," he replied, guessing he was being played. "I've never heard of these things. I'll have to ask Quin if he knows about those back rubs. I hear he's seeing someone taller than him."

Avery spat her mouthful of drink into her glass as she broke into laughter. They all laughed, enjoying the company of their usually stern Knight Commander, engaged and relaxed. But it didn't last. More footsteps sounded in the foyer, and Tyghan turned, expectant.

It was Cael, who was slowly shedding his veil of invisibility.

A small *oh* escaped from Rose's lips, and Julia squeezed her hand to keep her from saying more.

Cael was barely the same man they had tied to the back of August just days ago. Julia was sure his royal coat was adding bulk to his thin frame, but his cheeks had color back in them and his light brown hair was attractively trimmed and groomed. His chestnut eyes were bright and focused—on them. And the collar that had prevented his magic was gone.

Hollis rose to her feet, not out of respect but so the knife tucked in her cape was more accessible. Julia had no weapon on her, but her magic was fully tuned and sharp now, ready to respond. Her lioness claws itched for release.

Tyghan watched the squad follow Hollis's example, rising to their feet one by one. But they stood more like a silent, united wall than subjects offering respect, and he wondered if this forced apology had been a good idea after all. He stood too, ready to intervene if necessary.

Cael offered a slight bow of his head. "Good evening, ladies, but please, don't get up. I'm the one who should rise in your presence." He looked down for a few seconds as if distressed before continuing. "Our first meeting was unfortunate, and I would like to make this one better. But proper introductions first. I am your humble and indebted servant, Cael Trénallis."

He immediately proceeded to greet each of the dinner guests, respectfully lifting their hands in turn as he bowed his head, working his way down the line with phrases like *my purest pleasure*, *at your service*, *with humblest gratitude*.

When he finished, Tyghan let out a relieved breath. His brother had his charm on full display. He only hoped it would last. After introductions, Cael stepped back and offered a heartfelt apology. "Again, I sincerely apologize for my appalling behavior. There was no excuse for it, except that I was dreadfully jaded and disoriented after my long imprisonment. Thank you for risking your lives on a sour curd like me. I will forever be indebted to you."

The squad was speechless for a moment. Avery's mouth hung open, and a furrow lined Hollis's brow. But Julia's eyes narrowed, and her cat pupils contracted. "We're honored to serve the Danu Nation, and accept your apology, Your Highness."

Your Highness. Testing him. Julia knew royal protocols. Tyghan saw Cael's shoulders pull back at the slight. Though he was not the official king of Danu at the moment, Eris and Madame Chastain had continued to call him Your Majesty as a way to soften the blow and avoid further conflict.

But Cael made no correction. He only nodded and said, "The Danu Nation thanks you all for your service."

Julia nodded. Cael apparently passed the test—at least this one.

The dining room doors opened, and Ivy invited them in. Sashka whistled at the magical opulence, and the others craned their heads in all directions as they took their seats, whispering like they were in an enchanted forest. Cael smiled and nodded toward Ivy, approving the table settings and décor. But as he took his seat, Tyghan hesitated and glanced once more toward the foyer.

Cael noticed the empty seat. "It seems we're missing one of our guests. Where's Bristol?"

"A few minutes late is all," Tyghan said. "Ivy, could you send someone to check on her?" But as Ivy headed for the door, they all heard a rapid rush of footsteps.

It was Bristol at last. She barreled into the dining room, breathless, and with a sudden stop she braced herself at the end the table. "I'm sorry I'm late."

She hadn't changed. Her dress was torn, and her hair was a wild swirl of tangles. A dark smudge of dirt ran across her cheek, and a shopping bag still dangled from her arm.

Tyghan stood, his chair screeching out behind him. "What happened? Where have you been?"

Between labored breaths, she said, "I was with Kormick."

CHAPTER 39

Bristol looked around the table, everyone in their finery, their mouths hanging open like gaping fish. This was supposed to be a formal dinner, but she hadn't had time to change. Should she apologize? She was too shaken to sort out the small from the big things. Her skin still crawled from the feeling of Mick's hands all over her. She had been certain she was going to die when he nightjumped again and she was trapped in that netherworld. Her lungs were on the edge of collapse when she finally felt fresh air on her face and found herself back in the knife shop, able to suck in hoarse breaths again. Mick had to hold her up until the dizziness was gone. Changing for a formal dinner was the last thing on her mind when she finally made it back to the palace.

Tyghan was frozen in place, his eyes bright and wild. "You were with Kormick?"

"Yes, in town. He found me when I was in a little shop. One minute I was looking at a knife, and the next I was in some kind of cellar with no way out. A nightjump." She paused, her breath shuddering. "Mick knows that Cael escaped. He's looking for him. But I turned it back on him, saying I had no idea where he was and accused him of making a stupid mistake, letting Cael get away."

Bristol heard herself going on and on in a long rattling breath, trying to remember every word that was said—except for the parts when

Mick talked about their relationship and what he wanted to do with her in the cellar bed. "I played up my anger, and I think he bought my story. He took me back to the shop and let me go. He's going to search the wilds for a dead body."

"What about—"

Cael cut in before Tyghan could finish. "Mick? Kormick has a pet name? And he came to you of all people?" His eyes narrowed as he leaned forward in his chair. "Just how do you know *Mick*?"

The sickening innuendo in his tone punched the air, and Bristol's veins went molten. She thought Mick had pushed her to the edge, but Cael shoved her over it. She'd had enough.

She took a step toward him, and Cael saw the threat. He stood to meet her. "In spite of what my brother may have said about me being helpless, I am quite capable, and I should warn you, I have full control of my powers again. I asked a simple question, that's all, how you are on such friendly terms with a king who is trying to destroy us."

Tyghan waved his hand. "Cael, stay out of this and sit down."

But Bristol stepped closer, her hands trembling. "An affair! I had an affair with him. Is that what you want to hear? One that I deeply regret, almost as much as I regret saving your ass."

Cael's hands went up in defense. "I meant nothing salacious by it, I promise. I was surprised, that's all. Please, sit down. Join us. Someone pour her a drink."

A flurry of words and activity rushed in to fill the awkwardness, but Bristol only heard it as a dull roar. She looked down at her soiled, torn dress. *Tonight is formal. Dress in your best.* "I need to go change." A way out. A place to breathe.

"No, no," Cael said. "Please—"

But Bristol was already bolting for the door, Tyghan on her heels.

🔑

"Slow down," Tyghan said, keeping his voice calm as he trailed behind her. "It's not a race. You've been through a scare. We'll get you cleaned up, and I'll have dinner brought to the room."

Her paced picked up. "No. I just need to get out of these clothes, and then we'll go back."

"*Bristol*." Tyghan grabbed her arm. "Slow down. Are you all right?"

"I'm fine. A few scrapes. That's all." Her steps slowed, and she looked sideways at him. "I overreacted, didn't I?"

He winced. "Maybe a little. Cael's been away for months and is hearing all this news for the first time. Remember when you saw Kormick in the Timbercrest ballroom for the first time? How shocked you were? How you felt?"

"You're right," she said. "I just—" She finally stopped walking and faced him. "We kissed, Tyghan."

His jaw clenched. "Kormick? He kissed you?"

She shook her head. "No. *We* kissed. I kissed him back." She reached out, like she was dizzy, and braced herself against the wall. "I understand now what he's doing to my mother. He did it to me when we were in Bowskeep, and then again, just now in that cellar. I heard the warning in my head, my instincts were there and ready to act, but then a strange warmth flooded into me. It drowned out my fears, my logic. He muffled every worry in my head."

Tyghan nodded as if he understood what Kormick had done. "He can flood your head with energies from his own body, ones that drown out your own thoughts. The effect is short-lived, but can last long enough to gain favor or information."

"Like a drug? Is that something only a demigod can do?"

He nodded.

Her eyes drilled into him, her pupils pinpoints. "Can you do that?"

"I don't know. I've never tried. It's against the statutes of Elphame. The mind and will are sacred."

She rubbed her temple. "I'm still foggy. Though that might be from the nightjump. I nearly suffocated. It was long, like he was trying to punish me. He took me back to the gift shop and warned me to leave like I promised, or there would be consequences."

Tyghan's brow furrowed. "Like you promised?"

She explained about her concocted story of wanting to get out of

Elphame but needing to follow one last lead in Bogshollow—an ogre who claimed to know something about her father. "So after five days, I'll have to lie low too."

By the time they got to her room, her fogginess was gone, which made her stress ease. While she washed her face, Tyghan pulled a fresh dress from her wardrobe—the aqua dress she was wearing when, in front of everyone at the palace, he had asked her to dance. The dress that had fallen unceremoniously to the floor the first night they had made love.

"This one acceptable?" he asked.

"My favorite," she answered. "Always will be."

His eyes gently creased. "Mine too."

As she dressed, he noted the shopping bag she had tossed onto her chaise. "Find any steals?"

"Steals?"

"That's what I'm told you call shopping deals."

She laughed. "You've been talking to Avery and Rose." She turned so he could weave the laces on the back of her dress. "Yes, as matter of fact, I did—a lovely little flute for my sister Cat. I still need to find a wedding gift for Melizan and Cosette."

"That's all they were talking about tonight—the wedding. What do you think about it?"

"I think the timing is unexpected," she said. "*Swift* might be a better word. But they're clearly in love, so why not?"

"Right. Why not?" He pulled the laces tighter.

"Hey, easy back there."

"Sorry." He let the laces out a bit, and kissed her shoulder. "They were telling me about marriage traditions in the mortal world while we waited for you. There are some strange ones—throwing flowers and taking showers."

Bristol laughed. "Giving showers," she corrected him.

He tied off her laces and turned her to face him. "And traditions like getting down on one knee."

There was something in his face, an earnestness that hadn't been there seconds ago. "I'm not sure exactly how it's done but maybe—"

"No, Tyghan. No." She backed away, shaking her head, but he held on to her hands.

"Why not? You said it yourself. We clearly love each other."

"Yes. We do." She took a step closer. "I love you, Tyghan. More than I can even explain. Sometimes it almost hurts, how much I love you. But Melizan and Cosette are rushing their wedding along because they think they might die. And that is fine for them. But that's not how I want to marry you. I want to marry because we have a lifetime ahead of us. Because we're going to build something together, have adventures and babies and dreams together. I want to marry you, Tyghan, not because we're going to die but because we're going to live."

His eyes turned dark. "Things happen that we can't predict, Bristol. People die in battles like these."

"Then you better not die, Your Majesty. I don't plan to."

He nodded, his teeth scraping over his lower lip. "All right," he finally said, then fell to one knee. "Bristol Keats. I don't want to marry you today, or tomorrow, or even next week, but when this is all over, I want you to be my wife. And I want to be your husband. Because I want to share dreams and adventures and babies and pizza with you. In the meantime, I'll study up on the proper way to ask you to marry me so I get it exactly right, because I want you to know I would do anything for you."

His unproposal twisted her heart in two. She cupped his face between her hands. *Yes, we are going to have a long life together.* Some things she felt to her core. Tyghan was her destiny.

♟

Music vibrated in the air when they returned to the dining room. It was Rose, playing the piano in the corner. Bristol had almost forgotten that Rose was an acclaimed concert pianist. Her fingers danced effortlessly over the keys, and a serene smile lit her face, her chin tilted to one side, as if she was soaring along with every note, a current of air elevating her to someplace far away. The piece was "Für Elise," at times very simple, and other times quite complicated. Just like life.

Everyone was transfixed, and Bristol and Tyghan slipped quietly into their seats. Cael angled a silent apologetic nod toward Bristol, and she offered one in return.

Bristol's breath stilled as she watched Rose. It was like she was seeing two sides of her at once—the soft-spoken young woman and the majestic hawk—both sides coming together in a beautiful way. Finally, her fingers slowed, her hands rising dramatically from the keys, and she played the last few notes. Then she bowed her head in the silence, like she was honoring the composer.

Cael was the first to rise to his feet, as they all applauded her.

Rose shyly accepted everyone's praise and joined them at the table just as servers descended on the room with the delayed dinner.

But then Ivy hurried in. She went straight to Bristol and handed her a sealed envelope. "I'm told it's urgent."

Dishes stopped rattling. Chatter quieted.

Bristol tore open the message and read it.

"Well?" Tyghan said.

"It's from the Lumessa. She's ready to see me. Now."

CHAPTER 40

Celwyth Hall hadn't heard so many voices since Kierus brought his little friends over to rollick through secret passages as they played their hiding games. Kayana liked those games. She sometimes played with them, but that was decades ago. Now these walls were accustomed to the quiet murmurs of ancient witches. Kayana sat alert, her nose sniffing the air, her haunches taut, ready to leap at any threat. She bared her sharp canines now and then, just as a reminder she was watching them. She didn't like the visitors. Powerful fae. It wasn't safe. The Sisters were usually more cautious. Kayana growled. The dozen knights congregated in the foyer glanced her way.

Jasmine snapped her fingers. "Kayana."

The wolf lay down, but she was still ready to leap.

Jasmine eyed Tyghan and Bristol at the end of the hall, whispering their goodbyes, and looked back at Madame Chastain. "Can't he move this along?"

"He's afraid, Jasmine," the High Witch answered. "Surely you can understand that? They're in love."

"Love. It never should have happened."

"What?" Madame Chastain huffed. "Who can decide who they'll fall in love with?"

"Obviously you can't—it's happened enough times—but I was referring to Kierus and Maire. That never should have happened. If he had pursued his art, he never would have met her."

"I seem to recall he loved the knighthood too. No one forced him into it. Are you still blaming Cael for that?"

"He pushed Kierus into that role. *His amazing mortal,* he used to call him. Kierus was a feather in Cael's insecure cap for a long time. How unfortunate that Cael is back. I didn't think he'd survive. You must be disappointed too."

It was not like Jasmine to speak so bluntly—bordering on traitorous. If she was fishing for agreement, she wouldn't get it from Dahlia. "He was the queen's son. Heir to the throne. I did the best I could with him, as was my duty."

"Really, Dahlia, you think I don't know whom you'd prefer to see ruling? Whom *Eris* would prefer to see on the throne permanently?"

Dahlia didn't reply. She always wondered how much Jasmine knew, but wasn't overly surprised by her comment. Jasmine was still the High Witch when Eris returned to Danu from the Elphame court, and he *comforted* the queen in her sorrows. And Jasmine surely noted Tyghan's early arrival into this world by a full month, though she had never said a word about it before. Discretion was part of the High Witch's job too.

Jasmine sighed. "It seems we were both raising sons who weren't our own at the same time. I discovered a new part of myself during that period, the lines I would cross and the lengths I would go to, to save that boy. But there comes a time when we can't save them from themselves, no? Some things are out of our hands."

Dread pooled in Dahlia's chest. "What lines have you crossed, Jasmine?"

"I think you know. When Kierus went missing, I thought he was dead. And I blamed Cael."

Dahlia remembered the turmoil that gripped them all during that time. It was right after Cael was snatched from a forest trail that Jasmine's health took a sudden turn. An impossible thought gripped

Dahlia. A High Witch crossing a line came with consequences. "What did you do?"

Jasmine looked down the hallway at Bristol, squinting like she was searching for a palatable answer. Instead, she avoided the question. "And this girl. I don't know how to save her. Except by crossing a line again. Saving something that should never be."

"That is why your health is failing?"

Jasmine shrugged. "A lifetime of crossing small lines. The trespasses, they add up. That's the purpose of a High Witch's blood vow, isn't it? To ensure that we never skirt the laws of the gods or a nation? Sign that thick tome of Danu statutes and seal it with our own blood as proof that we believe in every word? That we'll uphold every law within, even at peril to ourselves and those we love?" Her pale eyes locked onto Dahlia's. "No one else is held to such a high standard. Not like you and me. It is both an honor and a burden, especially when our belief is tested. And with the role in my hands for over six centuries, I was tested more than most. And now I've burdened you with this, too, a truth you cannot unknow."

Dahlia nodded. But it was a truth she didn't want to know. *Jasmine*. It was the highly honored Lumessa who had betrayed Cael. And then a new dread crept into her, a dread that felt something like death. She studied her predecessor. *The trespasses, they add up*.

Jasmine glanced back at Bristol and Tyghan, still saying their good-byes. "It's time," she said with finality, but had only taken a few steps down the hallway when she turned back to Dahlia. "My son tried to kill the one you and Eris so dutifully raised, and that is something I deeply regret." She smiled, looking again like the beautiful, serene woman Dahlia had always known, the woman filled with centuries of wisdom. "Sometimes desperation makes villains of us all."

CHAPTER 41

T he ceiling loomed over Bristol in all its painted glory, sweeping scenes telling stories of the ages. Paintings of goddesses and
gods arriving on a shore shrouded in mist were surrounded
by scenes of them planting, harvesting, swimming in lakes, dancing
in forests, making love beneath the stars, and fighting great battles.
The scenes were vast and vivid, and reminded her of the ceiling of the
Sistine Chapel, except these were painted in a more sensual style, with
lush landscapes and innuendo in the shadows. Something Fragonard
might have painted—and maybe he actually had, since other artists had
visited Danu. She was absorbed by the scenes, and perhaps that was the
point, a distraction for those about to receive treatment. This room was
nothing like Madame Chastain's plain stone-walled treatment rooms.
The Sisters had already given her a potion to put her out, but her chest
still thumped out of time, like drunken sprites had taken up residence.

Please don't let me die, she thought. Harper and Cat needed her.

She blew out a steadying breath and turned her head to study another painting. Art had always been something that could transport
her from her immediate circumstances. She imagined the artist creating it, mixing paints, pondering his or her own circumstances and the
world that inspired the art. She imagined the whole story behind the
painting—just as she wondered about her father's paintings and his

expressions as he worked on them. Some things he would share, but some things he kept locked inside. She knew what some of those hidden things were now.

The painting above her now was of a beautiful goddess with shimmering copper hair and a windswept gown that blended in with the sea and sky. Her beautifully rendered hand reached out to help a bedraggled woman cross a great expanse of water. At first Bristol thought it was a rescue scene, but then it hit her. *Paradise. This is a death scene.* The goddess was helping the woman cross the threshold to the otherworld.

Bristol gasped and sat up. She didn't want to view someone dying as she went under. "Shouldn't I be on my stomach?" she asked. "To make it easier to get the tick out?"

Camille and Izzy eased her back down. "Don't worry, dear. We'll roll you over once you're asleep. You'll be more comfortable this way for now." Camille brushed a wisp of hair from Bristol's brow. "All will be well. Now let the potion do its work."

Adela had only put three drops of an icy substance on her tongue, but Bristol finally felt her limbs getting heavier, the sleeping potion taking effect. They had already explained the procedure to her—an untried one, but they thought it would work. Since they could only safely stop her heart for three minutes, they prepared her by having her breathe in various potions deeply, and then they used another to slow her body down to simulate the process of dying to give them more time. The tick would notice her body slowing down and start preparing for its exit. Once the tick showed signs of loosening its grip, they would stop her heart to force its departure.

That's right, let the potion do its work.

The ceiling grew blurry. The Sisters' voices became a distant warble. And then . . .

Footsteps echo. Her father's steps. She walks down a long hallway, trying to catch up with him, passing paintings of the masters. She calls to him, "Daddy, stop, you're missing it all, come and see. Fragonard, O'Keeffe . . ." But he just keeps walking until she can't see him anymore, the footsteps dwindling until the echo is gone. "He's lost," she tells the docent. "Help me find him. Please. He's lost."

"My father is lost!"

"Deeper," Jasmine said sharply. "She's not deep enough yet. Another drop."

Adela slipped a hand beneath Bristol's head. "Open your mouth."

Bristol felt an icy drop on her tongue, and then another, and another.

"Enough," Camille ordered. "No more!"

"It's the only way," Jasmine said.

Bristol shivered, her tongue, her body, everything cold. *Dark. Wind. The rush of water. Brigid. Her hand outstretched to Bristol. "Are you coming or staying?" the goddess asks. "I don't know," Bristol answers.*

🔑

The Sisters rolled Bristol's limp body over and exposed her back. The tick's shadow wriggled uncertainly beneath Bristol's skin, edging in one direction and then another.

Jasmine shook her head. "He's thinking about it. As far as he's concerned, she's dying." The tip of a single leg emerged near Bristol's spine, a bristled dark splotch against her perfect skin. Even for the Sisters, who had seen centuries of horrors, it was a sickening sight.

"How could Kierus do this to his own child?" Camille lamented.

"He didn't know it would come to this," Izzy said. And silently they all accepted that answer because it was what they wanted to believe.

Another leg tip emerged out of her side just below her ribs, but then the tick stopped, still clinging to its host, twenty-two years of feeding off her too much to give up.

"Come on, you bastard," Adela whispered.

It stalled, refusing to move.

"It's time," Jasmine said and stepped closer. The Sisters moved in with their hands hovering over Bristol to amplify the spell that would stop her heart, but only Jasmine said it aloud: "*Daeskah callonai.*"

Bristol's chest stilled. No more beats, no more breaths. They set the timepiece. Three minutes.

And they waited, time suddenly racing by too fast.

Yet the tick didn't move.

"Come on," Camille whispered desperately.

Still nothing, with only seconds left before Bristol would die.

There was only one last thing Jasmine could do. Something she hadn't even shared with the Sisters. "Step back," Jasmine ordered. "Now!"

CHAPTER 42

Eris burst through the front doors of Celwyth Hall, clad only in trousers and a half-buttoned wrinkled shirt, his official robes left behind in his rush. "Where is—" His eyes landed on Dahlia, and she glanced to where Tyghan sat alone in the parlor, his long legs stretched out in front of him, staring blankly out the window at a midnight sky.

In a few steps, Eris reached Dahlia, and she said quietly, "Miss Keats is in with the Sisters. It's been over an hour. We're still awaiting word." Dahlia's normally even demeanor cracked, her lips pursing, like something painful had almost escaped them. "Jasmine told me outright that she might die."

"Why aren't you in there too?"

"The Lumessa refused to have anyone else but her and the Sisters in the room. There was no arguing."

"Why?" Eris asked.

Dahlia shrugged. She didn't know, but Jasmine's last words to her made her uneasy. What desperate choice was she contemplating?

Eris angled his head toward Tyghan. "How is he doing?"

She sighed. "Not well, I suspect. He wouldn't talk to me. He says he needs to be alone. To think. He's barely moved a finger. But he needs to talk to someone—someone who is *more* than an advisor. The girl may die, Eris." She tilted her head toward Tyghan in that way she had so many times over the years, that tilt that said, *Tell him*, but it had never swayed Eris. Some things were buried in the past, and it was too late to dig them up. It wasn't even his right to dig them up. That didn't mean his heart wasn't torn. It always had been.

Eris walked into the parlor. Tyghan glanced up and waved him away, but Eris continued walking and stopped in front of him, blocking his empty stare out the window.

Tyghan's gaze slowly rose to meet Eris's. "As Avery would say, I need space."

"Waiting is a hard business," Eris replied. "Especially when you're waiting to hear news about someone you love. I know what it's like."

"But there is still no cure for waiting, is there? Time always wins."

Eris noted the flatness of Tyghan's voice, and yet his fingers fisted and unfisted, like he was preparing to smash them through something. The sight transported Eris back twenty-seven years to when the queen had lost her third husband. She had been listless for weeks—except for the rhythm of her hand kneading the corner of a pillow in her lap. Eris had impulsively pulled her to her feet and into the garden for fresh air. They had even danced. He had grossly overstepped his bounds in that moment, but she was glad for it. They both were.

"You don't need space," Eris told Tyghan now. "You need to expend some energy." He walked over to a rack on the wall that held several ancient collectible swords. He grabbed two. "I don't think Jasmine will mind." He tossed one to Tyghan, who jumped up and caught it, his training kicking in against his will.

Eris turned his own sword, examining it, and adjusted his grip. "Not exactly the best balance for me, but let's go out to the rooftop garden and spar a bit. No magic, just—"

"What? No," Tyghan said. "Me spar with *you*?"

"Afraid? It would do you good. I promise to be gentle." Eris was already walking out the door to the garden that glowed with the soft light of lanterns. Tyghan grumbled and reluctantly followed.

"Ready?" Eris asked.

Tyghan refused to lift his sword. "You've never used a sword in your life. What's this all about? I don't need distracting." He started to turn away, and Eris swung.

Tyghan's razor instincts blocked Eris's powerful blow before the reality had even sunk in. *Eris is swinging a sword like he knows how to use it.* Tyghan stumbled back a few steps, bewildered. "Where did *that* come from?"

"The usual places."

"Do you practice alone?"

Eris advanced, offering gentler thrusts and skilled cuts, the beats of their blades falling into a rhythm. "I haven't lifted a weapon in almost three decades, but some things you never forget. I once served in the Elphame court. For nine years I was First Officer to Queen Lilias."

"*You*, a First Officer?" Tyghan laughed. "You've always been a counselor. Only a counselor. What are you really—"

In a quick move, Eris swung, knocking Tyghan's sword from his hand, and then pressed the edge of his own blade to Tyghan's neck. "You're good, but I'm better. Never underestimate the value of age and experience." Eris lowered his sword, his point made.

Tyghan stared, silent and listening.

"I gave nine years of impeccable service to the queen of Elphame," Eris continued, "but then one day, after my wife became violently ill and died in my arms, I attacked an esteemed member of the queen's court. I thought he was responsible for her death, but I was wrong. As a result, I spent a month in custody, then was banished from court."

"What do you mean, you attacked him? Physically?"

"I gathered every molecule of energy in the room into my hand and slammed him into a wall. Then jumped him, pressing a sword across his throat so he couldn't breathe, with every intention of killing him. I watched him gasp for air, the way my wife gasped in her final moments. It took three guards to pull me off."

Tyghan shook his head, trying to absorb Eris's words. "How did your wife die?"

"She had secretly consulted with the man I attacked. He was the court alchemist, and he gave her a potion to help her conceive. I learned later she was only supposed to take one drop per day on her tongue, but after two months with no success, she swallowed the whole bottle."

Eris heard himself going on, telling Tyghan more than he intended, about his service at the Elphame court, his wife who was desperate for a child, her last words to him, his grief, and the shame of his expulsion. Somehow it was easier to tell Tyghan about his sordid past than to tell him the biggest secret he had ever kept in his life. Whatever relationship he and Tyghan had, he didn't want it destroyed by the truth. If Tyghan rejected him, it would be more than he could bear. Still, he heard the words *tell him* and saw the insistent tilt of Dahlia's head. *He deserves to know.*

Tyghan studied Eris, like he was looking at a stranger. "How did I not know any of this about you?"

Eris saw the traits in Tyghan's expression that he had been noting for twenty-six years, things he had always forced himself to ignore, like the dimple in his left cheek when he smiled, the scowl wrinkling his brow when he was angry, and the things Dahlia had noted too. *His power, his build, his curiosity, even his temper, they come from you.* Only his mother's black hair and striking blue eyes managed to obscure the other half of his lineage.

"I found ways to bury my past," Eris answered, "but there are a lot of things I should have told you. Long ago."

Tyghan angled his head to the side. "Like?"

A storm surged in Eris's chest. Four words. Four words tore through him, *I am your father.* Words he had always imagined saying. But in the past, he couldn't.

"Eris?" Tyghan prompted. But Eris saw Tyghan's mother looking back at him. *It's all right, Eris. It's time. Tell him.* Eris had loved her. He'd been afraid to admit that too.

"When I returned to Danu, your mother was grieving. So was I.

We were both . . . broken. We became friends as we healed together. Sometimes we even danced to chase away the grief, and over time, she and I—"

The door to the garden flew open and Quin exploded through it, his eyes wide and expectant. "She's awake, and she's screaming for you!"

CHAPTER 43

Tyghan!"

Bristol's arms thrashed through the air. She gulped in ragged breaths, the air burning in her lungs, her eyes stinging,
everything too bright. Someone was trying to push her arms down,
pushing on her shoulders. "Tyghan—"

"He's coming, dear. We called for him."

"Shhh. It's all right. You are all right."

Camille came into view. "You're waking up. That's all. Coming out
of it is always a bit startling," Izzy said.

Bristol looked at her hands. A sharp blue nail bed on her index
finger was still there. Despair engulfed her. "It didn't work. I still have
the tick."

"No, no," Izzy said, "the tick is gone. That small sign is all that's
left. We call it a vestige. It will fade too, just like the others."

"Vestige of what?"

Camille stroked her hand. "You're a shape-shifter, darling, that's
all. A vestige is a reminder of that. Like Julia's vertical cat pupils."

"A shape-shifter?"

"Yes, you have two forms to your nature."

"And the scales?"

"Gone. The tick made the magic inside you unstable. You were navigating a shaky line between your human state and your other one. But now your magic is restored, and that shaky line is gone, along with the tick. Isn't that great news? The greedy fool gave you up at the very last second."

But Bristol was still caught up on the words *vestige* and *shape-shifter*. They were thick on her tongue. "What is my other state?"

The Sisters exchanged a glance and deferred to Jasmine. She stepped closer, resting her hand on Bristol's arm. "We don't know, and you don't have to know either. You never have to change. In fact, we don't recommend it. It takes great effort, and when some fae try to change at this point in life, they can get stuck in their other form. Some can never change back. They can forget their old lives."

"It has happened," Adela said.

Bristol eyed Adela. There was something in her tone. Something grim that—

"But there is no need to ever change," Camille joined in, her plump cheeks flushed. "With the tick gone, your powers as a bloodmarked are fully restored. You have everything you need, just as you are! We only tell you in case you ever feel any inclination, an intense burning here"—she drew a line down Bristol's sternum—"that you ignore it. That's all you have to do."

Bristol nodded hesitantly, still trying to absorb their words. She didn't want to change. Not ever. She wanted to go home to her sisters looking as she always had, with no scales, no claws, and whatever else might have appeared, like fins, maybe even something that condemned her to live in the ocean. She only wanted to be who she always was. One fingernail? Even if it didn't fade, it was nothing. She could deal with it. She sat up and eased her legs over the side of the treatment table. "May I have a mirror?" she asked. She had to be sure. She had to see with her own eyes that the tick was really gone.

Adela brought two mirrors, one for behind and one for Bristol to hold, and Camille opened her gown so she could view her whole back. Bristol swallowed, taking a moment to soak it in. Her back was smooth. The scales were gone. But more importantly, the ugly beast beneath her skin that had fed on her magic ever since she was a baby was gone too. She bent over, clutching her stomach, and sobbed.

🔑

Tyghan heard the cries as he approached the treatment room, and clammy sweat sprang to his face. He threw the door open, slamming it against the wall, and saw Bristol doubled over, crying. Gods, she was alive but—

"What's wrong?" he yelled to Jasmine as he ran to Bristol and searched for injuries.

"It's gone," Bristol told him, relieved sobs still pouring out of her. "It's finally gone."

Tyghan looked to Jasmine for confirmation.

She nodded.

"Side effects?" he asked. There was a moment's hesitation.

"None," Jasmine answered. "Her powers are fully restored. She should be able to close portals with ease now. And open them. As to whether her power equals her mother's, that remains to be discovered. Keep her quiet for the rest of the day. Food and sleep, that's all she needs."

Tyghan drew in a full breath. Power and no side effects. It couldn't have gone better. He understood Bristol's relieved sobs. At the same time, he noted the extreme fatigue in Jasmine's face and the droop of her shoulders. Her lips were ghostly white. Whatever she had done to remove the tick, it had taken something out of her.

He thanked the Sisters, but held Jasmine's gaze a little longer. There had been friction between them over these past months, suspicion and accusations, but growing up, he had always been welcomed within these walls. Endless times, Jasmine had hugged both him and Kierus in one fierce grip and warned them there would be consequences if there was any more breakage. But there never were consequences. Instead, following their childish mayhem, there was usually a treat in the kitchen for them. Only after Kierus stabbed Tyghan and fled did their relationship become strained. Tyghan never stopped to think that Jasmine had probably been as devastated by the turn of events as he was, her loyalties tested. Caught between her heart and her duty.

"Be on your way now," Adela said briskly as she guided Tyghan and Bristol toward the door. "As you can see, the Lumessa needs to rest."

When they were gone and the door was closed, Jasmine said, "Arrange for transport to Mount Nola first thing in the morning."

But as Jasmine turned away, she collapsed to the floor, a shadow beneath her skin creeping up her neck.

The Sisters ran to her aid, Adela tucking a pillow beneath Jasmine's head. "Now," Izzy cried. "We have to take her to Mount Nola tonight."

But Camille knew Jasmine would never make the trip to Mount Nola. She likely wouldn't even make it to a new moon. Jasmine knew that when she laid her bare chest across the tick to save Bristol. Only the more powerful blood of a Lumessa was enough to persuade the tick to let go.

🔖

They lay in the dark, Tyghan tracing circles on Bristol's arm, both of them feeling everything anew, every breath, every swipe of their legs across the sheets, every whispering word, like they had both received a second chance at life, a life together.

She remembers me.

I remember him.

Both of their thoughts swirled around what they had not lost. Each other.

His hand skimmed her shoulder, smooth, the scales gone. She told him about the shape-shifter buried deep inside her, the one she never had to be. Would never be. It would take great effort to change, and at this point the Sisters recommended she never try.

What kind of shape-shifter?

The Sisters didn't know, and it didn't matter. She would always be just Bristol.

"Don't tell anyone," she whispered. "No one needs to know. The tick is gone. I am fully bloodmarked now. That is all that matters."

But the Sisters did know, Tyghan thought. He saw it in their eyes. They had lied. But maybe that didn't matter either. He had what mattered in his arms.

CHAPTER 44

Spirits soared. For the last five days, drills and maneuvers had been in full swing at Badbe Garrison training grounds. Hope was renewed. Danu had a bloodmarked—a powerful one.

"It's astonishing," Esmee said. Tiny birds as elated as she was flitted in and out of her bird's nest of hair.

"Beyond our hopes," Olivia agreed, and clasped her hands in front of her.

They'd been watching Bristol practice for the last hour and commenting on her newfound powers.

Olivia shook her head. "The poor thing. How frustrating it must have been for her to memorize all the spells we threw at her and get no results. Look at her now."

Esmee, Olivia, and Reuben sat beneath a canopy, observing maneuvers and taking notes, looking for holes in security and spells they might prescribe to remedy them. But it was Bristol who kept drawing their attention.

"Marvelous," Reuben replied dryly. While he understood everyone's elation, a larger part of him still wished Bristol was gone, that she had followed his advice and left Elphame for good. It was not likely now that she would ever leave.

"Look at that!" Esmee exclaimed. "She twisted that flame around the kindling like it was a ribbon on a package."

"Perfection," Olivia said. "I think she has a kinship with fire."

Esmee clapped. "Our lessons weren't for nothing after all."

Reuben heaved a sigh.

Olivia rolled her dark eyes. "What, Reuben? Just say it."

He shrugged his bony shoulders. "All is not flowers and sunshine, you know?"

"But neither is it—"

"She'll be hunted. If she isn't already. From this day forward, every kingdom in Elphame will want to control her, at least until another bloodmarked is found. There are Kormicks all over this land. One will eventually get her. She's too great a prize for them to resist."

Esmee clucked her tongue, annoyed with his doom and gloom. "She has all of us and Tyghan to protect her. She'll be safe."

Reuben only nodded. "A bird in a cage. Going back to her old life will be impossible."

Bristol had never been so exhausted in her life, but it was in the very best way. She'd had no idea that magic could be so tiring. Like everything else, it came with a cost, but it was worth it. She had been opening portals and closing them from one end of the palace grounds to the other, each effort taking less time. Exhilaration fueled her. She was surprised at how free she felt. Like a final shadow of the past had been shed.

All those weeks of faking magic, knowing she was a fraud, were gone. The shame was gone. She was confident she could close the Abyss door now—again and again if necessary. It might cost her a few blisters, but she would close it, and she'd make sure it stayed closed.

There could be a happy ending after all, she thought. For once in her life, it wasn't too much to hope for. Her promise to Harper and Cat seemed more certain. She pictured her father, hiding somewhere out in the wilds, strategizing, scheming, still concocting an impossible rescue plan, one man against all of Fomoria.

Hold on, Daddy. Stay put. Stay hidden just a little bit longer. This is almost over. I will take you home. Bristol knew he didn't want her help. He only wanted her to return home. But this time, he would get her help whether he wanted it or not.

And I will take Mother home too.

Her heart tugged. Another promise. Had her sisters received the letter yet? Her mother had never asked or wanted to be the monster of Elphame. Tender moments with her mother had resurfaced in these past days. Bristol remembered the warm colorful scarves her mother wove for her daughters, the summer nights she lay in a meadow with them all lined up like sausages as she pointed out the stars, the way she would recite poetry as she brushed their hair, adding sound effects to make them laugh. The good memories had been buried beneath Bristol's mountain of anger when her mother left so suddenly without word. It had been a cruel rejection Bristol couldn't accept, especially as her father fell apart. But now she knew why she had left. Her father said she did it for them.

She had no choice. She sacrificed everything to keep us safe. She vowed her daughters' lives would be different from hers.

Leanna Keats would get her life back too. And Kormick would pay for what he had done. That was Bristol's vow.

She checked her nails. It had become a habit, just to make sure nothing had surfaced. Her nails were only creamy, with pale moons. She looked forward to the day when she would stop thinking about it altogether. *Don't tell anyone.* It was a shameful whisper to Tyghan, and she wished she hadn't said it at all. It made her think of her childhood, the whispers that made her ashamed. *Pack up, ease out, don't cause a stir.* The secrets grew in her imagination, secrets that became monsters. She was done with monsters. She wouldn't live this way. She would never think of it again.

Bristol reached out, tendrils of light flying up her arms and through her hair, her lashes sparking with magic and the buzz of power humming in her chest. "*Abiendubra,*" she whispered as she closed her fist. And without a drop of sweat, without fear, without hesitation—success: The portal to the sacred groves that she had just opened was gone. A handful of onlookers applauded.

But then she felt a presence at her back, eyes watching her. Very specific eyes. She turned to find Tyghan studying her, his mind brewing with some question. Officers milled around him, absorbed in their own conversations. Tyghan had been in meetings all morning with the monarchs of Bleakwood and Silverwing, but had popped in with the officers when he could to check on maneuvers. He left the group and walked closer now that he had her attention. "I have a question for you, soldier."

"Yes?" she said, drawing out the word seductively.

A smile lit his eyes. He was ready to play her game, but then he cleared his throat, knowing they had an audience, and got back to business. "How big can you make one of those portals?"

She had been so focused on opening them so she could practice shutting them that she hadn't really experimented with the size. "I don't know. Let's see."

She started to raise her arm, and he grabbed it. "Wait. This time I want you to open one to a place farther away. Timbercrest. Where you closed your first one. Think you can do that?"

She needed coordinates—a specific spot in mind. Her mind tumbled back to the ride through the predawn forest, the purple sky, the silhouettes of trees, and she nodded to herself, seeing the exact spot in her mind. "I'll try." Big and far—another challenge. She lifted her arm, her palm facing upward, as she concentrated. A ball of silver light hovered in front of it. "The glade. The brook. The stand of alder trees," she whispered. The silver light jumped and spread outward in a line. *Wider*, Bristol thought when it reached a width of a few yards. *Wider*. As the watery light spread, Bristol's arm shook, like she was holding a heavy weight. *Wider*. Sweat sprang to her brow. *Wider*.

By now, a crowd had gathered.

"That's enough, Bri," Tyghan said. "Your arm—"

Wider.

"Bri—"

She dropped her arm, the energy released. The light slowly dissipated until the portal couldn't be seen. Far and wide, just as Tyghan had asked.

He stepped up to where the light had been and tossed a rock. The spot lit up again briefly, illuminating a massive entrance to the glade in Timbercrest.

"Holy loving shitcakes," Sashka mumbled.

"Concur," Cully said.

Quin stared, his eyes wide. "I've never seen one that big."

"None of us have," Kasta replied.

Bristol glanced at Tyghan and shrugged playfully, trying to act like it was no big deal, but giddiness bubbled inside her. She was just as awed as everyone watching. "Is that what you had in mind?"

Tyghan's mouth circled into an O. "I think I need to test this," he finally said. He called for August and settled into his saddle, circling and positioning himself in front of the portal.

"What? Wait," Bristol said, concern rapidly deflating her awe. "You're going to go through it? It won't light up from the other end! How will you find—"

"Now!" Tyghan shouted, and August bolted forward. The portal lit up as they sailed through it, and then they were swallowed whole. Light, man, and beast. Gone.

The silence was jolting. The officers, even Commander Maddox and Officer Ailes, moved closer, peering at the place where the portal had been, as shocked as Bristol. She stared, uncertain what to do. Terror clutched her. What if he didn't come back? Her knees weakened. What if she got the coordinates wrong? What if—

And then the portal lit up again. Tyghan and August raced through it, the Timbercrest glade visible behind them, and they leapt back onto the training grounds.

A round of cheers went up, but Bristol's heart still hammered against her ribs. Tyghan slid from his saddle and officers closed in, clasping hands overhead, ecstatic. Bristol remained planted where she was, still trying to catch up with her own emotions. Tyghan noticed, and in a few long strides, was beside her. Instead of offering him similar congratulations, she shoved both of her hands into his shoulders. "What do you think you were doing? You could have—"

Tyghan laughed and grabbed her before she could shove him again. "Have more faith in yourself," he said. "Don't you realize what this means? I don't have to worry about moving twenty thousand troops into place on the day of the ceremony. With portals of this size, whole regiments can jump straight from the garrison to the valley. Fomoria won't know what hit them." When she still just stared at him, he added, "This is huge, Bristol. You can smile."

Her initial fright subsided, and the news sank in. *Huge*. A small laugh finally shook her chest, and she threw her arms around his neck. "But don't ever do something like that again, without warning me first."

"Got it. But before we experiment any more—" He grabbed her hand and began dragging her to the supply hut. "We need a little talk." As soon as he closed the door behind them, he began kissing her and pulling his jacket off at the same time. Talk? His zeal resulted in a shovel and two shields crashing to the floor. "Ignore it," he said.

Bristol laughed between kisses. "Everyone's out there waiting."

"Ten minutes max, I promise," he said.

She scoffed. "You better count on fifteen," she said as she shed her tunic and he snapped her bra free. In seconds, his trousers dropped to his ankles.

"What is this?" she asked, both amused and aroused by his eagerness. "Celebration sex?"

"Could be," he said as his mouth slid down her throat. "How many kinds of sex are there?"

"Oh, I'm guessing a hundred at least."

"Then we better pick up the pace, Keats."

CHAPTER 45

Knights surrounded August near the watering trough, reveling in his performance, and August soaked it in. They acknowledged the king's small role too, but it was August who had done all the magnificent running and leaping.

They praised the feat and patted August on his hindquarters. *Rather undignified*, he thought, but they were celebrating, and he could understand that—though he'd much prefer a good brushing down, or better yet, a juicy red apple. The reds were his favorites.

But then their attention was drawn away by six royal destriers just arriving at the Badbe stables, being delivered by Master Woodhouse. One for each of the new arrivals. Now that they were officially knights, they would no longer be using borrowed horses but would have their own Royal Tuatha de horses. Not quite as grand as August, but horses like himself only came along once in a lifetime. Still, these destriers weren't a shabby lot, and skilled in their own ways, but the new knights gushed over them like they were made of spring clover. This was only an initial meeting, though. Above all, the horses had to be pleased with the prospects first, as it should be.

Even though she wasn't royalty, he would miss the one named Breeze, or was it Bri? She appreciated him in ways most commoners didn't. He was about to join the newcomers, but it was then that August spotted the shadow lurking nearby. An odd shadow, unanchored to any object, and he immediately knew it was trouble. He reared on his back legs and charged. The shadow couldn't get away from him. August reared back, again and again, trampling it beneath his massive hooves, and the knights around him shouted, calling for August's master, the king.

♟

Tyghan was just putting his last boot back on when the shouts rang out. He and Bristol rushed out of the supply hut, and his eyes first darted to the sky, but then he saw knights circled around something. They ran to the group and saw a shadow at its center, barely rippling over the rough earth, slower to transform than other shadows he had encountered. But the changes were proof it was dying. Death was the only escape from the torturous limbo existence inflicted by hyagen claws.

"August trampled it," Kasta said, but she had her sword drawn, in case the shadow made a run for it—or had to be put out of its misery.

Every knight held their breath, waiting. It was an anguish none of them would ever get used to, seeing the hapless victims used as spies. Would it be a knight one of them knew?

Slowly the edges of the shadow took form, a soft doeskin boot, a green tunic, until it wasn't a knight lying there at all, but a boy gasping for breath, his freckled face dirty and taut with alarm.

"Who are you, boy?" Tyghan asked gently.

But the boy only coughed, blood trickling from his mouth, his eyes wildly glancing back and forth between the knights hovering over him. Bristol dropped to her knees and brushed a curly red lock from the boy's eyes. "Samuel? Samuel of Rookswood?"

He nodded, tears trickling from his eyes. Between labored breaths he answered, "Yes, my lady. Where am I? What happened?"

Tyghan knelt beside him. "You're at Badbe Garrison. I have to ask you, Samuel, are there more coming?"

"More what?" he gasped. "What's happened to me? Am I in trouble?"

Tyghan had seen a lot of brutal deaths, but this— His eyes stung, then blurred. Samuel was only a boy, snatched from a farmhouse roof, too young to even understand where he was or what he was supposed to be looking for. The claws of the hyagen had stripped him of his humanity, just as his father had feared, throwing Samuel into the limbo existence of a shadow where he became the eyes of the enemy. To see one of his fellow knights reduced to this was gutting, but to see a child— Tyghan swallowed, remembering the sobbing father's plea in the throne room. *He's a good boy. Ease his passage.* He reached down and held the boy's hand. "No, Samuel, you're not in trouble. In fact . . . your father is very proud of you. He told me himself." But Tyghan also remembered the father's request, *Make his end quick.*

The boy coughed and choked, but managed a weak smile. "My father?"

Tyghan nodded. "Yes. He told me how much he loved you. And even now, the gods are smiling upon you, ready to welcome you into Paradise. Your work here is finished. You can rest now. Is that what you want?"

The boy's face clouded, his chin dimpling as he tried to be brave. "Yes, sir, please. I don't want to go back to—" The boy couldn't even finish, because he didn't understand the dark world where he had been.

Yes, please. Tyghan struggled to smile at the small plea, not wanting Samuel's last glimpse of this world to be one of tears. "You have brought your family honor. Go to your deserved peace, young Samuel of Rookswood."

Quin gently slid a knife between Samuel's ribs into his heart, and the boy took his last tortured breath, the glistening fear in his eyes finally gone.

There were coughs, heavy drawn breaths, seasoned knights struggling to hold back anger and grief for a boy they didn't even know. Tyghan's throat ached as he scooped Samuel's limp body into his arms. He carried him to an empty wagon and covered him with a blanket, then rested his hand on the boy's chest to be certain he was dead. His voice cracked more than once as he told the driver to take the body to the infirmary to be properly cleaned and wrapped before it was returned to the boy's parents, and then he heard shuffling behind him. He cleared his throat and turned.

His officers were waiting for orders. He was glad for something to focus on, something he could control. "Kasta, set a high alert. Quin, dispatch platoons to the border to watch the skies. The rest of you, search the immediate area. It's not likely from his position that the boy saw anything more than the water trough, especially with wards in place, but we can't be certain. If they did see anything, they will be on their way. Keats, you come with me. And your squad. We have coordinates to mark."

Tyghan turned to August last, stroking his neck, words caught on his tongue again, but August understood his touch and softly whickered in reply.

The stretch of time that followed was grim. Tyghan paced silently like a hungry wolf, eyeing the hills, the sky, and then stopping abruptly to drill the squad at length that Bristol was never to be left alone. Ever. If he wasn't with her, at least two of them would be. At all times. It was a reprimand where none was needed. Rose cried into her hands.

Tears never moved Tyghan in drills, but today he backed off, raking his hand through his hair, and headed into the hills without a word.

"I think he needs a moment," Avery said softly.

Bristol agreed. She knew he didn't walk off because of Rose's tears, any more than her tears were because of his orders. No one could get over what they had just witnessed in only a few minutes. Not even the Knight Commander, who had encountered countless deaths in battle.

Bristol settled herself on a bench that overlooked a distant paddock and after ten minutes said, "You all go back. I'll wait here for him."

Julia shook her head. "You heard our orders. We can't leave you alone."

"Those weren't orders. That was pure frustration." Bristol scanned the garrison grounds bustling with activity with over a dozen knights at any time within earshot. "Besides, do I look alone to you? I'll wait here for him. He might be a while, and you all have plenty to do—like find out which horse is going to be yours."

"You two are a perfect match, you know?" Hollis said. "Whenever one of you is down, the other is there to hold them up."

Bristol wasn't sure she was doing anything at all except waiting. Maybe that was all she had to offer—being there for him when he returned. Believing in him even when he struggled to believe in himself. Samuel's death weighed on him. Every death weighed on him.

Rose pursed her lips, still looking weepy, and nodded. "You're strong together. It's what we all need right now. Especially after this."

She hugged Bristol, and the squad left.

Bristol stared in the direction Tyghan had set off. He was no longer in her sights, heading into the hills in his effort to quash his feelings. She understood his frustration—and guilt. It gnawed at her now.

When they encountered the dying Samuel, instead of focusing only on him, her mind had jumped to her sisters—more innocents. Earlier that day, as she opened and shut portals with ease, she'd had a smug and dangerous thought. Why not open a portal to Bowskeep? One that went straight to her front yard? She wasn't sure she could even do it—a portal that went all the way from one world to another. But she imagined it anyway, going through the portal, walking up the porch steps, and knocking on the door, and then seeing Cat's and Harper's surprise when they flung it open. She would spend time with them, just an hour or two, to reassure them and make sure they were well, and then she'd go back through the portal to Danu, filled with the joy of seeing them. It would hold her over until she got home. She had almost made up her mind to retrieve her timemark and try and do it, but on seeing Samuel, the risk instantly crystalized. Samuel was a complete innocent, snatched from the safety of his own home and plunged into a netherworld by monsters. The fear in his eyes had gutted her. It was impossible not to think of Harper and Cat. The distance between this world and theirs now seemed like a treasured safety zone. A sacred distance. Yet she could have led someone directly to their front door and put them at risk, only to satisfy her own wants. There was no lock and key she could put on a portal—anyone could pass through it, even monsters. The infinite power she had been feeling instantly vanished. Waiting a couple more weeks to see her sisters now seemed like nothing.

The sun was setting, a glowing ball settling between the crook of two hills, when Bristol and Tyghan finished marking the fourth coordinate. Each designated spot had distinct surroundings that Bristol memorized, plus an added rock with a symbol to differentiate it for the troops who would pass through the portals: a sun, a star, a crescent moon, and this last one, a needle—the eye of Danu that was the symbol of power granted to the daughters of Brigid. The power that Bristol now possessed.

She watched Tyghan staring at the rock bearing the needle, wondering what he was thinking. They had hardly talked since his return—he only wanted to get down to work. Now he was swathed, like everything else, in the pink glow of the sunset, like Lugh, the sun god himself, was trying to heal him with his magical light.

"Another coordinate?" she asked.

"That's enough," he answered quietly. He looked up at her and shook his head. "I'm sorry. I shouldn't have walked off—" He sighed, still wrestling with his words.

"You don't have to explain, Tyghan. We're all struggling. Especially with the death of a child."

His voice changed then, thick with despair. "I am king and Knight Commander, and I can't even protect innocents, much less all the troops under my command. While I was gone, I was thinking about what you asked me once—if I was a demigod. I am nothing. I am less than nothing if I can't protect a child like Samuel."

"All of us are given powers, Tyghan, from small to great. I've read your histories. Every great god from Dagda to Lugh had their failures and losses. You're doing everything in your power. There is only so much one person—or demigod—can control. You can't carry guilt about this. Take time to breathe and then get angry as fuck and move forward."

He offered a grim smile. "You sound more like the Knight Commander than I do."

"You can't be Knight Commander twenty-four hours a day. You have to let your guard down sometimes. It's okay to let others see you hurting."

He shook his head. "That's not a lesson I was taught."

"But it's never too late to learn."

He pulled her into his arms, his face tucked in her hair. He smelled of meadow grass, sweat, and endless sorrow.

She stroked his back. "We'll get through this."

He nodded and held her tighter.

They walked back to where August waited for them, and Bristol reminded him, "Tomorrow is the wedding. Something positive. Maybe that's the reset we all need."

Tyghan's head dropped, like another weight had hit him. *The wedding.*

He started to groan but then remembered his words to Kasta. *Sometimes we have to remember what we're living for.*

And Melizan's wedding was one of those things.

Kormick would not beat the life from them before the battle even began.

CHAPTER 46

Sprites swooped through the air, drunk with excitement and the heady scent of the flowers that were strung from one end of Sun Court to the highest reaches of Sky Pavilion. Garlands were everywhere. Even the normally dark and somber Jasper Court radiated with heavy swags of lavender peonies.

When Melizan arrived at Sun Court and saw the extravaganza, she screeched.

"What have you done, Ivy? I promised my brother it would be fifteen minutes! That's all!"

Ivy laughed. "Don't worry. This was his idea. He told me to do it up big. He wanted it to be special for you. His words."

"No, you must have misunderstood. That's impossible. I'm talking about Tyghan."

Ivy patted her on the shoulder. "I know. He had a change of heart. Trust me. And he ordered food and drink for everyone—and everyone *is* coming."

Melizan was struck silent, maybe for the first time in her life. Bristol had to be responsible for this change in him. Or had he been drunk when he came up with the idea? She scanned the grounds, the chairs set up for the binding ritual, the arbors of flowers, the flowing silk canopies, the dozens of banquet tables awaiting food—enough to feed the entire palace and half the city. Musicians were setting up on four different plazas. It was like the commencement for Beltane festivities.

"You're *sure* about this?" Melizan asked again.

"Absolutely. Straight out of his mouth."

Cully came up behind Ivy and openly slipped his arm around her. "I can vouch for that. More or less."

Melizan blinked at the usually restrained couple. A lot of things had changed.

She felt a new sensation overtaking her, an annoying giddiness. She wasn't feeling like herself at all. She soaked in all the elaborate preparations. *Cosette will love this*, she thought. *She might even cry.* And now her own eyes were feeling misty. What had her brother done? Was she even ready for this?

"Shouldn't you be changing?" Cully asked. "The schedule says it starts in an hour."

Melizan looked down at her clothes—her plainest tunic and trousers, slightly dirty from maneuvers that morning. Minutes ago, these clothes had seemed fine, but now they were out of the question. She ran to her room.

Tyghan took the sheet of parchment from Eris. "Thank you. I want to make sure I say everything, and include all the right words. I didn't have time to compose my own."

"Understandable," Eris answered.

"Are you coming to the ritual?"

"I'll stop by as a witness. Don't forget the contract for them to sign." He pushed it across his desk.

Tyghan picked it up, noting Eris's quiet demeanor. "The other night you were telling me how close you and my mother were—that you comforted her. I appreciate that. Thank you. I'm sorry you didn't get to finish your story."

Eris's brow furrowed. "Another time."

"Were you at her binding ceremony to my father?"

"I performed it. It was a rather hasty affair, and the kingdom counselor was away, so I stepped in."

"Hasty? Why?"

"Your mother was eager. That's all."

Tyghan waved the parchment. "Did you perform it with these words?"

"Yes. Those words."

Tyghan had never seen Eris so tight-lipped. He studied him for a moment, wanting to prod him a little more, but he didn't have the time. Still, he stopped at the door of Eris's study and looked back. The counselor's gaze was locked on his.

"You saved these words for all these years? Why?"

"Because I spent quite some time composing them. As you've already noted, it's important to get all the words just right."

CHAPTER 47

This time Bristol caught Willow in the act. She was heading back to her room to change for the wedding when she spotted her hooking a posy of flowers on her door latch. Willow turned and saw her.

Bristol froze, then put her hand out in a stopping motion. She eased closer. "Please, Willow. Don't disappear. I need to talk to you."

Willow looked the same as she had that last day in Bowskeep. Her long, tangled hair trailed behind her. She was gaunt, dark circles beneath eyes that were still bloodshot, but this time tears streamed down her face.

"Are you all right?" Bristol asked.

"No!" Willow shouted, her voice bouncing off the walls. "He's missing! Your father is still missing!"

Bristol's heart pounded. She wasn't sure if it was safe to approach Willow. What was she capable of? In Bowskeep, she had always been meek and soft-spoken. Now she sounded angry and disoriented. But Bristol had questions. How was Willow wrapped up with her father? She had to know. She stepped closer. "Why are you always stalking my father? Who is he to you?"

"I saved him. When he was a baby toddling in a meadow, I saved him from a wolf. I snatched him before the beast could."

Bristol's lips parted. "*You?* You were the fairy who took him from the mortal world?"

"Yes. I was the one who found him. I brought him home to keep him safe," she said in one long, sobbing breath. "He was *my* baby, and they took him from me. It was Reuben's idea, but then he made me give him to the queen."

At the mention of Reuben's name, Bristol could barely think. "What does he have to do with this?"

Tears dripped from Willow's chin. "Nothing now. He is cruel, that one. He tore my heart out. But even when the baby wasn't mine anymore, I still watched out for him and the wolves." She sobbed into her hands.

"My father's not missing, Willow. And trows didn't take him. He's somewhere here in Elphame. He came here on his own to find my mother."

Willow shook her head, her expression changing. Her tone went from tearful to angry. "You're wrong. If I can't find him, he isn't here. He's nowhere. *Nowhere.*"

Bristol hesitated, afraid to ask. "Are you saying you think he's dead?"

"No one dies here in Elphame. They just change."

And that was what Willow began to do. Change. The edges around her softened, dissolving like they had the last time she made a quick departure.

"No!" Bristol said. She still had questions, and reached out to stop her, wrapping her hand around Willow's bony wrist. A bright light flashed from Willow's arm, and Bristol flew back through the air, slamming to the floor and sliding down the hallway, catching a brief glimpse of Willow before she vanished again.

Bristol lay there, stunned, her shoulder aching, but as soon as her head cleared, she had one thought: Reuben. He would be at the wedding. This conversation wasn't over.

Before she could get to her feet, footsteps pounded in the hallway, and hands slipped beneath her arms, lifting her. "What happened?"

It was Cael.

"What are you doing here?" she asked as she got her footing.

"I came to escort you to the wedding."

"Like that?" she said, noting he wasn't in disguise.

"I shed my glamour when I ran to you. Are you all right?" he asked, one hand rubbing her shoulder like she was injured.

She nudged him away. "I'm fine. Just a little tumble. You can go on to the wedding without me. I still need to change."

He grabbed her hand, stroking it with his thumb. "I could help you?" he said. "If you'd like help, that is." He glanced at her chamber door. "I could come inside with you and—"

She yanked her hand away. "Are you hitting on me?"

"Hitting? No, of course not!" he said with offense. "I would never raise a hand to you! I'm just trying to prove to you I am not the demanding pain in the ass that you once called me. I'm trying to show you I can be helpful too. I can be pleasant, if you give me the chance."

She eyed him carefully, wondering if she had overreacted again. Was he as clueless as he appeared, or was it an act? If it was an act, he was nailing it.

"My mistake," she finally said. "I will see you at the wedding, Cael. Goodbye." She went into her room to change, and bolted the door behind her.

CHAPTER 48

When Melizan arrived in her chamber, she found it filled with merkind—at least a dozen of Cosette's relatives from the river. Puddles shimmered on the marble floor.

They fluttered and fussed around Cosette, who sat on the chaise as they rubbed scented balms into her skin, slipped bracelets made of shells and pearls onto her wrists, and laced delicate pink flowers through her emerald hair. Their laughter and chatter stopped when they spotted Melizan.

Cosette looked up at her with worried eyes. "I hope it's all right. They all wanted to come."

Merkind at the wedding. A lot of them. What would Tyghan think?

But Cosette was so beautiful, so happy—

"Of course it's all right. Your family should be here."

She hoped. This whole thing was twisting her stomach tighter by the minute, but then Cosette smiled like Melizan had just given her the greatest wedding gift of all. Her aunts and mother turned toward her, smiling too, and looked like they were about to pounce on Melizan with a merciless hug. "I have to go now," she said quickly, feeling strangely breathless. "I'm going to go change, and I'll meet you at Sun Court."

"I hope these flowers aren't too much?" Cosette said, motioning to her hair.

Gods, no.

"They're perfect, my love. Trust me."

She hurried to her bath chamber, eager to get out of there as fast as possible.

She was doing this. She was really doing this. The one thing she said she would never do: care too much.

⚷

"Where's Ivy?" Tyghan shouted when he reached the top of the grand staircase and got his first glimpse of Sun Court and the plazas around it. "What is all this?"

Quin whistled, his hand skimming the back of his freshly shaved head. "Looks like more than fifteen minutes to me."

Sun Court was filled with *chairs*. Guests were already filling them.

"And get an eyeful of Jasper Court," Dalagorn said, pointing in the other direction.

Their normally dark tucked-away court was now bright with silky ribbons and puffy purple flowers.

Tyghan shut his eyes and pinched the bridge of his nose. "Ivy!" he yelled.

She promptly appeared, her wings beating with happiness. "Like it?" she asked. "Just what you ordered."

"I said a special *thing or two*."

"That's what this is. And food and drink. The celebration you asked for."

"A celebration? This is a fucking coronation! I have meetings this afternoon—"

"No you don't. I moved them for you. I knew that—"

"You *what*?" It was one week until the Choosing Ceremony! He was about to throttle Ivy, or send her to the infirmary because she had certainly gone mad. "I told you—"

"Tyghan!"

He turned. It was Melizan, her eyes glassy, as she descended on them, half running, her blue gown billowing behind her.

"What's wrong?" he asked.

"Nothing," she said. And then she hugged him. Or gripped him like she was about to fall off a ledge. He wasn't sure. She spoke into his ear so the others couldn't hear. "I didn't expect this of you, brother. I didn't even know how much it meant to me until I saw it. Ivy told me it was all your idea. Coming from you, this means everything. Thank you. Cosette and I will never forget it." He looked at Ivy over Melizan's shoulder, and she smiled.

Melizan stepped back. "I do have to warn you about one thing, though. There will be merkind at the ritual. A lot of them."

Tyghan stood behind the short, draped pedestal that held the binding ribbon. A large part of him still fumed, but Melizan's joy, and Ivy's knowing smile, managed to keep his tongue in check. He tried to remind himself this was the break and celebration everyone needed, especially after yesterday.

His sister anxiously watched the grand staircase for Cosette. She was late. "Do you think she's changed her mind?" Melizan whispered.

"She'll be here," he said, not to reassure her but because he knew Cosette was fully committed to Melizan. She had been proving that for months—it just took Tyghan a while to catch on.

His gaze jumped to the guests sitting in the front row. *That*, he still couldn't quite accept. Their hair dripped with water from the river, and their damp clothes clung to their skin. Merkind. Since he had time to kill, he counted them. *Fourteen*. All one cousin away from being Fomorian. But Bristol's words tempered him. *There is only so much one person can control.*

Sitting just behind them was Cael, today glamoured as elven, sleek red hair falling to his waist. He insisted on coming to witness his sister's binding ritual, and Tyghan could hardly deny him that, so he consented, but that was before he knew the wedding would be turned into a spectacle. And, of course, lords, ladies, and council members were there too, still skittish about any violation of protocol. What could possibly go wrong? And then he noted the monarchs of Bleakwood and Silverwing being escorted to seats. He was about to throw his hands up in the air. As long as they were here for meetings, why not? *Ivy.* He hoped there were no more surprises. He searched for Bristol but hadn't spotted her among the guests yet. *Always the last to arrive*, he thought.

Melizan gasped and Tyghan followed her gaze. Cosette stood at the top of the grand staircase, wearing a sleek pale pink gown that hugged her curves. Her emerald hair, which was usually tied back for her duties as a knight, flowed down her shoulders past her waist and was woven with pink flowers that matched her gown. A murmur rolled through the court. She was breathtaking. But then Tyghan flinched. *Gods*, she was trailed by still more merkind, like they were some kind of marriage committee following her down the stairs. He forced a smile so he wouldn't groan.

♟

Eris stood with Dahlia at the perimeter of Sun Court, witnessing the proceedings. He noted the fully outfitted knights with swords on their backs flooding the surrounding courts and overlooks, ready for battle, but more likely, ready to valiantly protect this celebration. Melizan was one of their own, as was Cosette. Fomoria would not steal this moment.

The décor and trimmings were excessive, as was the attendance, but Tyghan never missed a beat, rising to the occasion for his sister. When the binding began, he wound the ribbon around the couple's hands as he recited the words that Eris had given him. Words he had written so long ago, for Tyghan's parents.

"... and there is no greater gift that one can give to another than the gift of their heart, their love, their commitment, their promise to always be there for the other, to bring comfort to one another in the hardest of times, to understand the value of silence, but also, the grasping of hands and dancing in gardens when your partner needs to be lifted."

Tyghan slowed with each word, and his gaze finally rose to meet Eris's. *Dancing in gardens?*

Eris looked away. Had he really said those things back then? Had he been so blatantly transparent? Apparently so. He sighed. He should have at least changed the words for Tyghan.

"It's all right," Dahlia whispered.

Eris slipped his hand into hers, but she discreetly pulled away. "Not here," she said.

The patience that Eris usually reached for wasn't there this time, and the tug in his chest wasn't love.

When Bristol slipped into her seat at Sun Court, she methodically scanned the guests, looking for a scowling alchemist in a fancy robe, but she couldn't spot Reuben anywhere—at least from her vantage point. A lord with a ridiculously large-feathered hat obscured a whole section of the court. She was still disturbed by Willow's visit and the distress she saw in her eyes. *He's nowhere.* What did that mean?

But as Tyghan began to speak, Reuben and Willow disappeared from her thoughts. She watched Melizan and Cosette looking into each other's eyes, appearing so oddly fragile. Not like themselves at all. Bristol's heart swelled. They were laying everything on the line for each other, *publicly*, and with each word Tyghan spoke, their hard exteriors fell away. They were no longer two fierce knights but two people fiercely in love. And as Tyghan talked about love and comfort and commitment, Bristol's thoughts turned to his unproposal to her. *When this is all over, I want you to be my wife. And I want to be your husband.* Her stomach bobbed like it was loose in a sea. How she regretted saying no now, regretted putting it off for the ideal moment, because there was no such thing as the perfect moment. She wished she could tear a ribbon from her dress right now and tie it to Tyghan's hand and her own and declare her love publicly, so everyone would know. *Yes, I want to be your wife!* But now was not the time. This was Melizan and Cosette's moment. Bristol consoled herself that it wasn't a missed chance. Not yet. There was still time.

"And so," Tyghan continued, "as we are all present here to witness the binding of your hands and your hearts, I ask that you publicly state your commitment to each other."

"I bind my heart and life to you, Melizan."

"And I bind mine to you, Cosette."

Tyghan lifted their bound hands above their heads and called out, "And these witnesses say . . ."

A loud cheer of affirmations reverberated through the court.

"It is done," Tyghan concluded.

Melizan and Cosette kissed, and just like that, they were married. Bound in this life and the next in only fifteen minutes as promised— but the celebrations were only beginning.

Tyghan kissed them each on the cheek, had them sign their marriage contract, and then stepped back as Cosette's relatives moved in, piling flower chains on Melizan, welcoming her to the family. Then they moved in on Tyghan, too, clearly unaware that Melizan's brother was not the daisy-chain type. But Bristol watched him take it in stride, thanking them, wearing lopsided flower crowns on his head.

Sashka came up beside her, eyeing Tyghan. "Who is that guy?" she asked.

Bristol laughed. "Not sure, but he's mine. All mine."

With the palace grounds overflowing with guests, music, and laughter, no one noticed Kasta's absence from the ceremony.

She sat on the marble corridor of Judge's Walk, leaning back against a column, the light of the stars and moon shimmering on the surface of her full wineglass. "Do you hear that, Kierus?" she asked. "The music? It's a wedding. Melizan's, actually. Yes, even Melizan, who swore she would never commit to one person, is getting married. I suppose Bristol and Tyghan will be next. They're very close, you know? Think of it, your daughter marrying the man you stabbed. No doubt you'll be able to hear their wedding from here too.

"Oops," she said, when she poured more wine and it sloshed over the side, spilling onto the tile. "I'd share some with you, but I guess that's not possible. But can you smell it, Kierus? Can you imagine the sweetness of a sip? I just want you to know what you're missing. What you could have had."

CHAPTER 49

Where are you going?" Bristol asked when Tyghan got out of bed. "It's still dark."

"Go back to sleep," he whispered as he got dressed. "Ivy kindly canceled my meetings yesterday without telling me and moved them to dawn this morning."

Bristol groaned. "It *was* a magical wedding. Don't be too hard on her."

"I'll find an appropriate way to make her suffer. See you at the valley midday." He kissed Bristol's forehead, but as soon as he left, she forced herself out of bed too.

She never did spot Reuben last night, and she was hoping to catch him this morning before he slipped from her grasp again.

The sprawling wings of the palace housed nearly all the nobles, gentry, sorcerers, and workers who lived there. There were a few large manors on the grounds too, where more lords and ladies lived. And there were several isolated cottages. Reuben lived in one of those, which didn't surprise Bristol. He wasn't the sociable type, even if he liked to show off his fancy robes at parties.

Bristol hurried down the narrow trail in the predawn light. She had to meet her squad at the stables midmorning, and she wasn't sure how long this would take. As she walked, she pondered Reuben's role in all this—although knowing what part he played wouldn't change a thing. It couldn't turn back time and deliver her father into the arms of his parents. It couldn't erase the years of running, the familiar fear that gripped her every time her parents rushed to pack and leave one town for another. Knowing couldn't change anything about the past, but it might give her more of the answers she came here for in the first place. Like *why?* Answers she could share with her sisters to patch up the holes in their lives. Knowing might also explain why Reuben hated her so much. *He is cruel, that one.* That part didn't surprise Bristol, and she was prepared to defend herself. With the tick gone, she had a new proficiency with fire. She could twist and direct it with pinpoint accuracy. Olivia called it a kinship. Esmee called it masterful. Reuben never commented, perhaps fearing he would suffer far more than a singed robe if she attacked him.

Maybe most of all, confronting him would put him on notice that she had something on him—his involvement in the abduction of her father. It might be leverage if she should need his help, or might at least wipe that perpetual smug scowl off his face. *Go home, Miss Keats. You don't belong here.* His words were still a kick in her gut, even after all this time.

She arrived at the humble little cottage. The windows were shuttered, but smoke rose from the chimney. He was up. She pounded on the chipped painted door. His home was not as meticulous as he was.

"*Go away!*" A string of mumbled threats followed, noting the time and idiocy of the early intrusion.

She pounded again. "I'm not going away!"

More curses, the sound of something clanking to the floor, then the door swung open, an enraged Reuben staring at her, his normally sleek hair in frizzy disarray. "Have you lost your pitifully small mind?" he said between gritted teeth.

"We need to talk. About Willow." She pushed her way past him, and glanced around, eyeing other escapes in case she needed one. It was a cramped cottage, an unmade bed pushed up against one wall, a stove on the opposite one. Almost a hovel. No other doors, and not what she expected.

When she turned to face him, she saw that the mention of Willow's name had punched the bluster out of him. He was silent now, but his face was a chiseled nightmare, like a gargoyle in a graveyard. But then his sunken cheeks began to flush. He blinked, his crow-like eyes flashing in the firelight.

"Coffee?" he finally said. "I was just about to pour some."

If he was trying to shock her, he achieved his goal. She couldn't think of a more unlikely response, but then she realized, *he* was the one who was in shock. He didn't know what else to say. The name Willow had completely stymied him. Master Reuben didn't look like a master of anything at the moment.

He walked to the stove and lifted two mugs from hooks on the wall behind it. He stared at their shimmering surfaces long after he filled them with coffee, then finally picked them up and brought them to the small table in front of the fireplace. Bristol hesitated, but took a seat opposite him.

"You found Willow?" he said in an uncertain voice.

"No," Bristol answered, "she found me. She told me about your role in my father's abduction."

"She's here? Is she well?"

Well? He was asking after her well-being? Like Bristol had simply run into an old friend? No, she was not well. And neither was Bristol. "She is crazed, Reuben! She's rambling about my father and not being able to find him. She called you cruel and said taking my father from the mortal world was *your* idea. I didn't come here for coffee, Reuben. I came for answers, and I want them now! How are you involved with Willow?"

His thin lips pressed together, and he nodded. His smug scowl was long gone—instead, he looked like a scarecrow with the stuffing pulled out of him. He couldn't seem to focus.

"*Everything*, Reuben," she said to nudge him.

"Willow," he finally said, like he was confirming they were on the same topic. He heaved out a slow breath. "Willow is the biggest regret of my life. I could never make it right. I figured this day would come eventually. No one knew her name. No one but me. She was my secret."

Bristol stared at the transformed Reuben, no longer the arrogant master alchemist with sharp words and haughty stares, but someone else confessing the biggest secret of his life.

"Back then—during the time period you mentioned—our relationship was new. She lived in a little shanty in the woods. It wasn't much to look at, but it was magical." His dark eyes lit up with the memory. "*She* was magical. I'd steal away for days at a time, between my studies at the university, to be with her. She was wild, and playful, and she completely entranced me. I led two separate lives back then—my strict internship under the High Witch, and my untamed days with Willow. I loved her." He squinted at the memory. "But, as I discovered, I didn't love her more than my ambitions. One day she asked me to stay and not go back to the university. She wanted me to stay for good. *We could have a baby*, she said. *Wouldn't a baby be nice, Reuben? We could be a family. We could make this little place bigger*. That was when I made my greatest mistake. I tried to let her down gently, to tell her it was impossible, that I had a different future in front of me, but I said it all wrong. *Yes, a baby would be nice*, I told her, *but* . . . She never heard the but, or what came after. I should have known. Willow was carefree and impulsive, everything that I wasn't. That's what I loved about her. She was the light to my darkness."

Bristol sipped the last of her coffee, but Reuben's remained untouched. He said when he returned two days later, he heard squalling coming from the shanty. Willow was rocking a baby, trying to calm it. She had happily explained how she found the baby in a meadow, and that she came along just in time because surely a wolf would have eaten him. *See what a good mother I am already?* she told him.

"I was horrified and told her she had to take him back, immediately. I raised my voice. I yelled at her for the first time in our relationship. She was distraught by my reaction and only remembered a meadow—a mortal meadow. I tried to help her retrace her steps but soon realized it was hopeless. Willow only lived in the happy moments of life. She couldn't navigate the sad ones. That was when I told her she had to take him to the queen herself. She did as I ordered, but said I had destroyed her. She hated me after that and never returned to her shanty. She escaped to the mortal world, which was probably for the best. Unfortunately, the baby's parents were never found, and he was given over to the Sisters to raise him. I always carried guilt about it, wishing I would have been harder with Willow from the start, no mincing of words and trying to placate her, but my wishes were worthless. So as the baby grew, I did everything I could to help him, but slyly, because I was still shamed by my mistakes with Willow. I knew how difficult it would be for him growing up in a fae world, so over the years I made sure he had the finest amulets to amplify his skills and to protect him. And far later, I helped Kierus when he wanted to leave Elphame once and for all."

As he spoke, the breath in Bristol's lungs thinned, like she had stepped into an alternate world. A world where Reuben was an ally? "*You* helped my father?"

"Many times, though he proved himself quite capable, his tongue as much a weapon as anything else. He could disarm others without magic. But when I did help him, I thought that maybe it was a way to redeem Willow—and myself, especially when I helped him return to the mortal world at last. I understand he was happy there for many years. He had the life he wanted, his art, his wife, his family, you. I helped him in ways I shouldn't have. I was the one who planted Fritz's bloody cloak so he could escape with your father. And I provided a distraction so Fritz could slip into Celwyth and access Jasmine's art collection when Kierus needed funds."

Bristol didn't know of any person in her father's life named Fritz. If he came with her father to the mortal world, she never saw him. "Who is this Fritz person?" she asked.

"The doorward of Celwyth Hall. But you probably knew him in his other form, as Angus. Not many knew he was a shape-shifter. He preferred it that way."

Bristol showed no emotion. She didn't feel like a surprised novice anymore, but a jaded veteran of this world. Still, anger curdled in her stomach at the lies she never saw. Angus was a shape-shifter. The family's long-lived ferret who always managed to disappear at convenient times. He *had* been listening to them all those years. And he didn't take crumpled letters from the trash to shred the paper. He read them.

"Fritz told me about you," Reuben said. "May the great gods save me, I never wanted you to come here. Except for a few artists who stick close to the conservatory, things rarely end well for mortals in this world. Even da Vinci suffered a gash that nearly disemboweled him when he ventured too far. Elphame is a dangerous world that's often difficult to escape once you're here, especially if you become someone of particular worth. That's why I told you to go home, Miss Keats. Before you or anyone else discovered your value."

Value. A chill trickled down her spine. She was the only known bloodmarked in Elphame besides her mother. The thought had lurked in her mind, cloudy and unformed, but now she saw the danger of it, fully formed in Reuben's eyes. There was a threat in being needed by the wrong people. Her mother was proof of that. But Bristol had the means to leave whenever she wanted to. Her timemark was safely hidden away.

"That's also why I put your father's note in your room," he continued. "I thought if I couldn't convince you to leave, surely he could. He had the golden tongue that I was not blessed with, but clearly you were immune to his pleadings too."

"He came to you with the note?"

"No. It was Mae who passed it on to me. She was the go-between for a trow who knew of my involvement with Willow. He requires a favor of me from time to time for his silence, though that time I was happy to oblige."

Bristol hissed out a breath. "Mae told me she hated trows."

"She does, but she'll do anything for a coin."

Anything? Bristol remembered the cloaked mercenary guide who led her to her father at the barn, always rubbing his fingers together, requiring coin for the smallest bit of information. His identity was carefully disguised. A glamoured Mae? Bristol sighed. She had been duped by a master. Mae would probably be the first to calculate Bristol's value. "That's why you ordered me to leave, to spare me?"

"Why else? Some mistakes I can never fix. That only leaves me to mitigate the mistakes about to happen. You're a prize, Miss Keats, and at risk."

"I can take care of myself, Reuben."

"No doubt. You are your father's daughter. But be judicious with your risks. During my early days with Willow, I thought I owned the world. Now I can see I was only hanging on to its edge all along."

Be judicious now? Bristol could almost laugh. She'd been reckless ever since she decided to stop running from unseen monsters and return to the Willoughby Inn. Now wasn't the time to put on the brakes. "Willow said my father was nowhere. Does that mean he's dead?"

Reuben's brow wrinkled. "I don't know. It probably means he's out of her reach, but I don't know if that is a good or a bad thing."

"Neither do I," Bristol said, "but the last thing my father needs right now is an unstable fairy exposing where he's hiding."

Reuben tapped his knuckle to his chin, thinking. "Agreed. I'll go to her shanty today. I visit there every few years—my own pilgrimage of sorts—even though it's mostly been reclaimed by the woods now. Without Willow, its magic is gone." He sighed wistfully. "Chances are slim that she'd be there, but I'm due for a visit anyway."

"Thank you," Bristol said quietly, then added, "I'm sorry about burning your robe."

A pensive smile pulled at his mouth. "It was my least favorite."

She stood to leave, and Reuben reached out and touched her arm. "He was a good man, at least as good as any man can be."

♟

Bristol leaned against the cottage door after she closed it behind her, still thinking about Reuben and his long-ago life, one she never would have dreamed existed. A life he still grieved for, like it had all happened yesterday.

Of everyone in court, she had hated Reuben most of all, and with good reason—but she had also understood him the least. He had offered her a stiff, shallow mask, and she had assumed only more of the same lay beneath it. Was it possible to know anyone at all? *Reuben, a broken man?* Impossible. A man trying to redeem himself by making it hard for Bristol to stay in Elphame? A man who regretted his fateful mincing of words and now spent a lifetime firing them out like bullets instead?

She tried to imagine Reuben and Willow living in a forest shanty, entrenched in a steamy affair. Reuben, a stuffy, ambitious scholar enamored with a quirky free spirit who only lived in the moment, star-crossed lovers who had been perfect for each other—at least in his faded, bejeweled memory.

Maybe that was why he understood her father so well.

He was a good man. A good man forced to become a hated one instead.

CHAPTER 50

Sonja walked from her gallery to Cat and Harper's new apartment in the heart of the village, a small, secure complex that gave Sonja less to worry about. They were wealthy young women now, and Sonja and their attorney had tried to keep their new status as quiet as possible. Sonja still had concerns over their sister's disappearance, but there was no evidence of foul play, and Bristol was a capable and clever adult. More than capable, apparently. She looked at the letter in her hand. It was addressed to the house on Oak Leaf Lane, which was why it had been forwarded to the gallery. She had compared the handwriting on the front of the letter to the script on the consignment papers Bristol had filled out for her father's painting. The handwriting matched. She was alive, but Sonja still wondered about all the secrecy.

Faerie.

Sonja smiled and shook her head at the Sisters' half-hearted answers about Bristol's whereabouts. Perhaps there were stranger explanations. She remembered when Bristol came to her at the gallery, intent on getting the money she needed. *A sketch by Leonardo da Vinci. Someone wants to give it to me*. Sonja had laughed. A slightly nervous laugh. But then on the heels of Bristol's disappearance, the da Vinci sketch actually came, then the Escher sketch, finally followed by the offer for Mr. Keats's painting. Everything had checked out, and the commissions brought a windfall to the gallery, but Sonja still carried some unease about it. She just wished she knew with certainty that Bristol was all right.

She walked up to the apartment complex gate and punched in the security number, and when the girls didn't answer the door, she tucked the letter in their mailbox, hoping it contained good news from Bristol.

Hurry home. We got another letter, Harper texted.

Leaving. Be there in 30. Don't open til i get there.

Harper didn't have to say who the letter was from. There was a shorthand of knowing between them. Only one person was worthy of an urgent text to hurry home.

In twenty-eight minutes, Cat burst through the door.

Harper stood in the hallway waiting, the letter in her hands.

Cat dropped her purse and keys in the entry and took the letter from Harper, her finger grazing the handwriting. Bristol's handwriting. Her eyes welled.

The sisters immediately settled onto the couch beside each other.

Dear Cat and Harper,

I'm sorry I closed the portal. I wish I hadn't done that. I miss you two terribly. Cat, I know I told you in my last letter that I was sorry for my harsh words to you. I still wish I could take those words back. If I had a magic spell to wash them away, I would. I know now, it wouldn't have mattered what you told me, I wouldn't have believed you because this world didn't yet exist for us—until now. In the end, none of it really matters. I think I was meant to come here. I have a purpose.

It may not have been my first choice for a little getaway, but life deals us curves, right? This was some curve, but us Keats girls have always been good at navigating those. I'm embracing new challenges here daily, and those challenges include change. There may be more changes in me by the time I see you—more than blue nails. I hope not, but again, we can't choose every road we're destined to travel—and we've been down a lifetime of roads together. I'll deal with it, just like you always do. That's something we learned together.

Now I have something else to tell you. Are you sitting down? (Don't roll your eyes, Cat.) Because you really should be sitting down when you read these next words. I'll give you a moment.

You too, Harper. I know we've kept so much from you in the past. (Pretty lame because you were all over it.). But Cat and I were only trying to protect you, trying to give you a more normal childhood than what we had, but you're old enough and smart enough—probably smarter than both of us—that you can handle this now.

I'm glad you're both sitting now because what I'm about to say will be a lot for you to absorb.

Daddy is alive. I found him. He is as strong and healthy as ever. And still as stubborn as a brick wall. We had a long talk, but he refused to come home with me because he is still trying to find Mother.

That's right. Mother. <u>She is alive</u>. He knew it all along. Mother is healthy and well too. I know this is especially shocking, but it's true. I don't know what's in the urns out in the workshop, but it's not their ashes.

Mother is different now—she is fully fae. All of our lives she used glamour to hide who she was (Harper, explain to Cat what glamour is). Mother is afraid to leave this world—she's under a spell of sorts—but I'm confident that will change soon once we confront the man who brought her here. Don't worry, I won't be confronting him alone—a lot of powerful fae will be with me, including the leader here that I mentioned to you earlier. We have grown close (yes, read between the lines). This will all happen in just a couple of weeks, and then I'm bringing them both home to you. That's why this has all taken so long. Just like our world, this world is complicated and has its problems too.

So I hope this good (but shocking) news makes the wait worth it and that you aren't angry with me for being away for so long. As you can see, I have a good reason. (Oh! And besides Mother and Father, I have some cool fae gifts for you too. I think you'll love them. BTW, did you get decent phones?) I wish more than anything that I was there with you, but it won't be much longer now. While I'm gone I hope you're putting down the deepest roots ever, because we are never going to have to run again. Take care of each other until then, and please always know, I love you both more than anything.

Your adoring sister,

Bri

Cat's chest shook. She kissed her index finger and pressed it to Bri's name. "I love you too, sis."

Harper put her arm around Cat, and they both stared at the letter, reading it again and again, reading between all the lines that Bristol hadn't intended, noting every place where she inserted cheerful remarks or breezed past events to lessen the gravity of it all.

Curves. Challenges. Confront. Powerful. Afraid. Complicated. Problems. Deal with it. Those were the words that glared at them between the lines.

They discussed the improbability of it all, that the fae world really existed, that both of their parents were still alive. It seemed too much to hope for. But Bristol said it was all so, and they trusted her.

"What is glamour?" Cat finally asked.

"It's faking appearances."

Cat chewed on the corner of her lip, thinking. "Then maybe we're fae after all," she said. "That might be the truest part of our lives." She stood and pulled Harper to her feet too. "Our sister will be home soon, I do believe that much. Let's get the old house cleaned up, so she's not coming home to a dusty mess."

CHAPTER 51

Tyghan's meetings ended early, and he had been on his way to Bristol's room when Eris intercepted him.

It arrived. The two words still reverberated in his head. Eris said them in passing, making Tyghan's other thoughts scatter.

It's large, Eris had told him. *That's why it took so long to transport. It's in your room.*

His footsteps slowed as he walked toward his chamber, reluctance building inside him. *It's only a fucking painting*, he told himself. But he hadn't thought it through. He didn't count on the effect that it might have on him.

When he entered his chambers, he spotted the velvet-draped painting in a hallway, leaning against a wall. He eyed it for a long while before pulling the cloth free.

He sat in front of it now, sipping a glass of goblin whiskey that burned his throat, and stared at Kierus's last piece of art.

Tempest #44.

Forty-four times Kierus had painted that scene. And still, forty-four times hadn't been enough.

Tyghan had bought the painting anonymously, wanting to provide quick additional funds for the Keats sisters to ease Bristol's worry. But he also bought it because he was curious. The gallery owner had been suspicious at the five million he offered—far more than she was asking—but then gladly accepted it on the sisters' behalf. Tyghan would have paid any price.

The pamphlet that accompanied the painting lay on the floor. He had already read it, but it was unnecessary. It talked about things like paint, style, and technique. Not pain, betrayals, and regrets. Tyghan saw the real story, what Kierus had seen—the story beneath thick layers of paint. He saw it in every stroke.

A forest.

A dark swirling sky.

The haze of dusk.

A tired and worried prince finally spotting horse tracks. He had dismounted from August and left him behind to quietly follow the narrow trail of hoofprints. Desperate to find his friend. To save him.

And then he came to a clearing—and a cottage.

That was when he spotted Kierus coming out the cottage door, alive. Relief had flooded Tyghan's chest, but he immediately knew that something was wrong. Kierus had an expression of panic on his face, and then someone else appeared in the doorway behind him, the Darkland monster, the terror of Elphame. He knew it was her by the descriptions he had heard. That was when Tyghan drew his sword with one hand and prepared to summon magic with the other.

Kierus, still a trusted friend as far as Tyghan knew, rushed over to him, rattling off nonsense about being in love.

And then the monster, a beauty with only a blanket draped around her, stepped out onto the porch and called, *Get it over with, Kierus. We have to go.*

Kierus's voice grew louder, more earnest, angry. *You have to leave. Please, Tygh. I'm going with her. Walk away like you never found me. Walk away.*

Tyghan couldn't do it. He was certain Kierus was enchanted, and Tyghan still wanted to save his best friend and take him home. Instead, they argued. Tyghan ordered him to step aside, but Kierus became a wall. He became someone else pushing back against him. And then he seemed to embrace Tyghan, pulling him close.

That was when Tyghan felt a hot sting in his side. The rough tug of a blade, one way and then another. The vicious upward lift to make sure the job was done. And then Kierus left. He walked away without looking back. The surprise hit Tyghan before the pain. But when the pain hit, he couldn't breathe. He pulled the blade free, and clutched his side, still in disbelief. Hot blood trickled between his fingers, and his legs gave way. He dropped to his knees, his head swimming, unable to call out, *Kierus, come back*.

The pain overtook him then, but didn't offer him the mercy of passing out. He writhed in the mud, wishing for death. At some point, August found him and went for help. The last thing Tyghan remembered was Dalagorn cursing as he lifted him from the mud.

The colors were all there in the painting, the dark swirl of their lives spinning out of control, a storm that could never be calmed. Even the crimson that marked the severing of their friendship. Demons would always haunt Tyghan, but another kind of demon possessed Kierus.

That day . . . it haunted me. I relived it over and over.

Forty-four times.

Tyghan finished his brew and wrestled the painting up the stairs, hiding it in his study with his other nightmares. He didn't want Bristol to see it.

CHAPTER 52

E ris swept into Dahlia's chambers, and after two shallow niceties, she asked, "When are you going to tell him?"

"I tried. As you know, we were interrupted and—"

"So you try again. You can't keep putting it off."

Eris spun, not trying to hide his frustration. "Why do you care, Dahlia? Really, I'm wondering, *why* do you care? You keep everything so bottled up. Who are you to say anything to me about what I do or don't say?"

She looked at him, her head angling slightly to the side, unaccustomed to being talked to so carelessly. "What brought all this on?"

"The wedding. When you pulled your hand away from mine."

"Yesterday? That's what's consuming you? It wasn't the time or place."

"When Tyghan was ill this last time, you sat next to me on the couch and laid your head on my shoulder—in front of Quin and Melizan. In front of everyone. I thought that was a step, a new beginning, that we were finally moving forward in our relationship. That it meant—"

"We were in his private quarters and everything was bleak and looking hopeless. I—"

"So the only time you can publicly show me affection is when you're feeling hopeless?" He threw his hands up. "At least I know I serve some useful purpose for you. I don't know what your past husbands and lovers did to make you so cynical about love, Dahlia, but I am not them. If you can't see that after eight years, maybe I am not the right man for you."

He turned to the dresser and began opening drawers.

"What are you doing?"

"I won't keep paying for the sins of your past lovers. We need some time apart."

"Eris, you're being ridiculous."

He turned to face her again. "Really? Do you realize, you have never once told me that you love me? I love you, Dahlia, but I need more, and if you can't give it to me, it is best to part ways now. I won't be sleeping here anymore." He slammed two drawers and opened a third, rummaging through it. "Whatever you're holding on to, it's time to let it go. If you won't even give yourself a second chance, how can I expect one?" He slammed the third drawer and turned.

Dahlia's eyes were stone, her lips pulled tight. "I've burned through too many chances, Eris. Far more than two. And now, finally . . . what you and I have is perfect. It has been for years. I don't want to lose it. I don't want to break the magic between us."

"Love is not magic, Dahlia. It is not a spell in one of your grimoires. I am a man, and I don't need what's in a book. I need what's in your heart, but if you'd rather dwell on your past failures, so be it." He glanced down at the belongings in his hands. "Look at this, eight years of sneaking into your room when no one's looking, and all I have to show for it is a razor, a hairbrush, and two wrinkled shirts." He shook his head and walked out.

CHAPTER 53

The barn bustled with stable hands preparing horses for the Choosing Ceremony. "This way," Master Woodhouse said as he walked Bristol out to the meadow where her horse waited. It had been two days since they first "met" the horses at Badbe Garrison. The rest of her squad had already been matched with their horses and waited nearby.

"There she is. Her name is Zandra, and she has chosen you," Master Woodhouse declared with pride.

Bristol eyed the beautiful horse. She was magnificent, her long white mane shimmering in the sun, but Zandra was reluctant to approach, despite Master Woodhouse beckoning her over. Bristol didn't feel chosen. More like the last person to be picked for the team. Bristol was all that was left, and now Zandra was stuck with her.

She was smaller than the other horses, and standoffish. She finally approached when Master Woodhouse clucked his tongue in a disapproving manner. An arm's length away, she stopped and sniffed.

"I don't blame you, Zandra," Bristol said. "I'm not much to look at. But look at you—you're a queen. Shall we make the best of it? I thank you for your service, and I'll try not to shame you."

Zandra's fierce eyes met Bristol's, the same fire deep in her pupils as with all the Tuatha de steeds. The regal horse stared, in challenge or curiosity, Bristol wasn't sure. She circled Bristol, sizing her up, and then she bowed, allowing Bristol onto her back.

"See?" Master Woodhouse said. "She was waiting for you. And don't let her size fool you. She's the fastest of the bunch."

Bristol's squad was within earshot, and two of their horses whinnied in protest.

Zandra's ears twitched in agreement with the stable master. She had spotted the one called Bristol two days earlier at the garrison. She was curious about her, but it was the king who had chosen Zandra for the woman, a mortal of no particular renown. Not a royal. Zandra was insulted at first—Tuatha de steeds usually chose their own riders. The king put Zandra through the paces. He was very exacting in what he expected, and apparently Zandra's performance pleased him. August had been overly nosy about the whole thing, but it was none of his business. In the end, Zandra thought the king chose well. She would have chosen Bristol on her own, and she liked her already—humble, respectful, and calling Zandra a queen was a nice touch. *Fastest of the bunch.* August would be stewing all day when he heard about that. And she would make sure he did.

"Now, you all get acquainted and go," Master Woodhouse said.

They were headed to the rim of the valley surrounding the Stone of Destiny to map out coordinates on the other end, and to bond with their new horses. On the day of the ceremony, both man and beast had to work in unison. It would not be the day to get acquainted.

"That's it? Go?" Hollis asked.

"No special training? Just go?" Avery added softly, her timid side resurfacing.

Master Woodhouse frowned. "Of course. You've already had your horse training, and these majestic creatures have all had their fae training. Nothing more to teach any of you now. Fae and horse just need to fall into the same rhythm—listen to the magic pulsing in each other's veins."

Avery turned quietly to the others. "I think I need a little more time to find the magic."

254 MARY E. PEARSON

"We're not in a rush," Julia said.

Bristol patted Zandra's neck. "You don't mind waiting a few minutes, do you, Queen?"

As they waited, Julia pulled Bristol aside. "Tyghan did a fine job yesterday," she said.

"The binding ritual?" Bristol replied. "Yes, he—"

Julia laughed. "That too. But he was exceptional at holding his tongue when he saw the guests in the first row. I saw him eyeing them."

Bristol smiled. "Yes, astonishing. He even danced with most of them. Cosette was floating. It was the best gift he could have given her."

"I heard Cosette call him brother," Julia said, still laughing. "He choked on his drink but recovered quickly."

"He's coming around in many ways. What about that guest in the second row? What did you think of him?"

Julia's brows pulled together, trying to recall.

Bristol stepped closer. "Cael," she whispered. "The long-haired elven that no one knew. If anyone had tried to see under his glamour . . ."

Julia rolled her eyes. "Oh, *him*. Yes, I wondered. Though no one would be expecting Cael at his sister's wedding. Officially, he's still a prisoner. And he still doesn't really match his completely perfect portrait. But he probably never did."

"I question his judgment, Julia. I'm wondering if he's even fit to—"

"Shhh," Julia said gently, glancing around at the nearby stable hands. She moved closer to Bristol. "I've had my doubts too."

They talked about alternatives, keeping their voices low. Julia laughed when Bristol suggested strapping him to her horse again and giving him back to Fomoria.

She winked. "But they might not take him back. Tyghan seems like the best choice to me, but the Stone will do the choosing," Julia concluded before they rode into the sky for the valley.

Maybe, Bristol thought, still mulling over their slightly traitorous conversation, but she knew Tyghan had no interest in ruling Elphame—only if it was necessary—so he likely wouldn't step up at all. But who else cared about Elphame as much as he did?

"Take it all in," she heard Julia say to Sashka and Rose as they soared above the landscape that was such a bright lush green, the color needed its own name. "Never take it for granted. It's the beautiful jewel that we're risking our necks for."

Bristol looked down, knowing the beautiful jewel Julia spoke of was not just the landscape but centuries of history, the rich world that gave birth to her own.

She recalled Julia's great-aunt foretelling that Julia would have an important role to play in Elphame one day. That day had come. Julia could have simply retired comfortably from the university and still be enjoying the wonders of Paris and her espresso and cinnamon palmier at her favorite local bistro. Instead, she was here, with them. Risking her neck.

And Bristol was grateful. Julia would make a perfect ruler of Elphame.

CHAPTER 54

The old spriggan shook his head, looking out at the valley, his wrinkled eyelids drooping. "It's been a long time," he said, his voice wistful.

Certain traditions were an elusive element of the Choosing Ceremony that Tyghan still needed to understand. The fae who started them were long dead in this world. The living who carried on the traditions had only history and hearsay to guide them. Especially when it came to the Choosing Ceremony. Since it happened just once every hundred years, neither Tyghan nor any of his officers had ever witnessed one. Most of those in Danu hadn't. But there was one fae, Shane of Dubrick, an old spriggan knight retired from service, who had witnessed three. He had been invited on their fact-finding expedition—a last-minute mission. Now that Bristol could open massive portals, some strategies had changed as to how they would advance their troops. Logistics needed to be nailed down.

"The Choosing always happens when the sun's at its highest," Shane told them. "But normally, monarchs, challengers, and their entourages show up the day before for the Parley of Royals. It's a chance to size up the opposition, share meals, and let tempers and ambitions cool. It's the Stone that chooses, of course, but reducing the competition is the goal.

The fewer who step past the Mother Ring onto the sacred grounds, the better your chances are of being chosen."

They stared at the tall double row of standing stones, pitted and aged by time, almost like crooked teeth protecting the Stone of Destiny at the center. That was Kormick's goal—to ensure no one stepped past the inner ring of stones except him. He would be the only choice by default.

"Sometimes everyone agrees on a clear choice," the old spriggan continued, "and they go home happy and with full stomachs. Other times not. That's when blood is shed."

Shane squinted as he scanned the valley. Weathered leaves on his shoulders crumbed in the breeze. "Nothing has changed here," he said with mild surprise. "My first ceremony was bloody, three stubborn fools vying for the crown, but it was an unassuming cobbler who stepped up and was granted cauldron and crown by the Stone—just like that." He cackled. "That sure punched the piss out of the rest. They went home with wounds in their sides and their tails between their legs."

The officers laughed uneasily, hoping there would be no tails between their own legs—or spears in their sides. Tyghan pressed the knight, needing to know more. "What about the kingdoms that came? Where did their entourages set up for the parleys in the past?" he asked. "Can you still remember?"

Shane pointed his crooked finger, circling the valley. "Always on the rim where they could see everything. Colorful little cities popped up overnight, fanciful tents shining in the sun like jewels, with their kingdom banners raised high and flapping in the wind. It was a sight to behold. Proud and hopeful moments for everyone. But many came with no interest in claiming the crown at all. The ceremony was a once-in-a-century affair, not to be missed. Nobles who had no business being there tagged along too. It gave them bragging rights to history."

"What about Fomoria? Was there a certain place they set up?" Tyghan asked.

Shane rubbed his bristled chin, thinking. "Most who made the journey tended to set up in a direct line from their kingdoms—easy to retreat that way—so Fomoria would have set up right about . . ." He raised his arm and pointed to a spot just east of a stand of oak trees. "There. Yes, just above that steep rocky region, that was it. I remember their black and silver banners."

"And Danu?"

"That one's easy. I helped set the tentpoles. Right there." He pointed to the opposite side of the valley, which was exactly what Tyghan hoped. "Only six days left," Shane said. "Think you've got this one? Need an extra hand?"

Tyghan grasped Shane's forearm and thanked him. "You've given more than your share of service, my friend." Junior knights escorted the old knight back to his farm, and Tyghan and his officers invoked their veils of invisibility and set to work, riding the rim.

"Archers up there," Cully said. "And there. With the sun high and in Fomoria's eyes, these would be the best places to join the fray."

Tyghan agreed. This time there would be no marking the landscape—only memorizing it. Four points of entry for the garrison troops, high above the valley.

Quin, Dalagorn, and Kasta eagerly weighed in. *Sky fighters here and here. Shield guards there. Spear platoons here. Sorcerers and ward casters interspersed. Greymarch forces can come in here and Eideris here.*

Tyghan heard the fervor renewed in his officers' voices. Despite all the death his knights had witnessed, they still weren't immune to its horror, and seeing Samuel, an innocent, so cruelly taken, had invigorated their hatred of everything that was Fomorian. Maire's name was never said, especially not in Bristol's presence, but it always simmered beneath the surface.

The plan hinged, however, on Bristol eliminating the restless dead from the equation. And now they had little doubt that she could make that happen.

"Bloodmarked," Dalagorn said under his breath. "Damn if we didn't get lucky."

"And she's on our side," Cully added. "I'm sorry for what I said about her at the garrison—"

Tyghan shook his head. "You were grieving, Cully. It's behind us."

"What about those blue nails of hers?" Quin asked. "I thought maybe she had another kind of fae in her. What happened with those?"

"It was nothing," Tyghan replied, the practiced answer ready on his tongue. "According to the Sisters, it was only unstable magic inside her."

Quin hissed. "Miserable tick."

Only unstable magic. It was what Tyghan wanted to believe, but the worry he had seen in Jasmine's eyes continued to circle his mind. Worry for what?

"All done here?" Dalagorn said. "Horses need grazing."

What he meant was that he was hungry, and they returned to the valley floor to await Bristol's squad—and so Dalagorn could quiet his ogre-size stomach.

Tyghan stood beside August, searching through his pack. Master Woodhouse always wrapped up light provisions for them before they left on a journey of any length. Kasta was not far away, doing the same. Tyghan pulled two apples from his pack and gave one to August, who whickered his appreciation before trotting off to graze with the other horses. Tyghan bit into his own apple, then turned to Kasta. "Where were you last night?" he asked. "I didn't see you at the wedding."

She was already sitting on the grass with a handful of fresh figs. "I was there," she answered. "Mostly staying in the shadows. You know me, that's where I like to be, just like you."

Tyghan got the gentle jab. Kasta was still irked at him, like he had strayed too far from the rules—and he had. First his affair with Bristol, then Kierus's shortened sentence, and then Melizan's wedding on the eve of war. Not to mention his cold words to her: *Remember your place.* He and Kasta weren't only king and subject, they were close friends and fellow knights. They grew up together, and they'd never been this out of step before. He couldn't regret the things he had done, but he didn't want it to be this way between them either. They had too much history.

He took another bite of his apple and sat down on a rock, not far away, trying to think of some sort of order to give her. Something that showed his trust. Work always seemed to brighten her, and for Kasta, the harder the better.

"I need you to do something for me," he said, "and it has to be done quickly. Handpick twenty knights at the garrison to be our extra witnesses at the parley. Outfit them as nobles—shallow and curious. Every detail matters. They must be able to play the roles believably—but be skilled and useful too, when the time comes. We can't be everywhere. They'll be our on-the-ground eyes and help direct incoming regiments through portals. I know it's short notice and you already have a lot—"

"Done," Kasta answered. And she did brighten, her eyes glowing with anticipation. He really did need the job done quickly and done well by someone he trusted, but seeing his old friend sitting across from him, instead of a distant one, was something he needed too.

When Bristol and the others arrived, most of Tyghan's instructions were for her fellow squad members. "She'll be concentrating on closing the Abyss portal, possibly multiple times if Maire reopens it, and she won't be able to watch for threats. You'll be her constant eyes, ears, and shield."

"That's something we already do for each other," Rose said.

"But this time you'll have no cover, and possibly be hundreds of feet in the air on the backs of horses. We don't know where Maire might reopen it."

Bristol cringed as they spoke about her mother. "*If* she reopens it," she said, but heard the weakness of her reply and the uncomfortable silence that followed. She wished she hadn't said it. She sounded so needy, so in denial. She wasn't. Like them, she knew exactly who Maire was. The problem was, she also remembered who Leanna Keats had been.

"Of course. If she reopens it," Tyghan said, easing the tension.

They took to the air, taking their positions around Bristol, and tackled their task with vigor as Tyghan tried to break through from every angle. They managed to block all his attempts.

"That was too easy," Hollis said, rolling her eyes.

And then they did a second round with Tyghan—and Cully, Quin, Dalagorn, and Kasta—attacking them from all sides.

Sweat was broken that time. Hollis suffered a bruised chin, but she was valiant, protecting Bristol's back with her life.

When they landed in the valley again, Tyghan nodded. "Better than I expected."

"Why do you always have such low expectations of us?" Sashka asked.

"Just the opposite, Sashka," he replied. "I have the very highest expectations. When you exceed them, I am happily surprised."

The squad glowed. The Knight Commander did not offer empty praise. If he said it, he meant it. They were ready.

"And now," Tyghan said, taking Bristol's hand, "I need to show you the coordinates on this end." These were the places the garrison portals would open, sending thousands of knights to defend Elphame. The opening of the portals would happen at the last possible moment, so no one and nothing could stumble through it, alerting Fomoria that something was amiss. It also required extra concentration on Bristol's part, riding high above the valley to set the coordinates in her mind's eye. She used rock ledges, stands of oak, and ravines along the valley rim to mark coordinates high above them. From there, the knights would swarm from the skies to subdue Fomoria. She closed her eyes for moment, sealing the places into her memory, her heart fluttering. It was sinking in. She wasn't going to war only against Fomoria but against her mother too.

"Isn't she a beauty?' Bristol said when they returned to the stables. She scratched Zandra's soft muzzle, and the horse flicked her tail in appreciation.

"I thought you two would be a good match," Tyghan replied, handing off August's reins to a stable hand. "Where were you this morning?" he asked as they walked out of the barn. "My meeting ended early, and my punishment of Ivy was brief, so I was back before—"

"Punishment? You didn't—"

"No," Tyghan answered regretfully. "Instead, I thanked her and gave her the afternoon off, but I had a few choice words stored in my head."

"So the wedding swayed you?"

He sighed. "I've never seen Melizan smiling for a full minute, much less a whole evening. And I danced with almost all of Cosette's relatives. Even the wet ones. They were actually all . . ." He shrugged. "Pleasant. They might even turn out to be helpful allies."

Bristol's brows pulled together. "Oh, what a disappointment that must have been."

His arms circled around her. "There's nothing I hate more than admitting I'm wrong."

"Obviously. You do it so rarely."

Tyghan scowled and scooped her up, carrying her toward the water trough. "Is that so?"

She screamed and laughed, trying to wriggle free as he held her over it. "Don't you dare!" she ordered.

He spun around and set her down on the ground again. "See? I'm very compliant." He kissed her, his mouth hungry, but quickly, a frustrated rumble grew in his chest, and he pulled away. "Unfortunately, the rest will have to wait for later."

"Another meeting?"

He nodded. "And I'm late." He told her briefly about the docket and the special assignment he gave Kasta. The last days before the Choosing Ceremony were packed with endless details, and new ones kept cropping up. "But I'll walk with you as far as the rotunda." They took off in brisk strides. "Whatever you did this morning, I hope it at least included a leisurely breakfast."

"Not exactly," she said, "I had an encounter with Willow yesterday, so this morning I went to ask Reuben about her."

Tyghan's long strides came to an abrupt halt. "Willow was here? You saw her and didn't mention it?"

Bristol looped her arm through his and kept walking, pulling him along. "When? I found her outside my room right before the wedding.

Was I supposed to tell you as you performed the wedding ritual? And then this morning, you left so early, I was barely coherent."

"What did she want?"

"She was leaving flowers on my door, and when I intercepted her, she became agitated and said that she couldn't find my father anywhere. I guess she's been looking for him ever since he disappeared from Bowskeep. She mentioned Reuben, and after that, she disappeared. I saw her for less than a minute."

"What does Reuben have to do with Willow?"

She could hear the ire rising in Tyghan's voice, like he was ready to tear every bit of information out of Reuben himself. Fae, even the good ones, didn't like secrets.

"Nothing anymore, but years ago, Reuben and Willow had an affair. Who would've guessed?"

Tyghan was shocked silent for a moment. "*Reuben?* Are you certain you heard right?"

"Willow implied it, and he confirmed it. I never would have guessed that he had a secret like that. He told me he hadn't seen her in decades."

"I still don't understand why Willow is obsessed with your father."

Bristol hesitated. "She still worries about him because she was the fairy who stole him from the mortal world."

She was glad that Tyghan was in a rush. He mumbled a few disbelieving words but didn't belabor the subject, only asking her to stay away from Willow. "She sounds unstable and possibly dangerous." Bristol couldn't disagree, remembering how easily Willow had flung her down her hallway. Though it had seemed more like a frightened response than a deliberate action. How different she had been from the quiet, quirky woman who wandered the streets of Bowskeep.

She touched his arm as he turned to leave. "Tyghan—" She hesitated. "I know my father isn't a subject that you like to talk about, but I can't help worrying about him now. Willow's distress worries me. What if she knows something? What if he's been captured by Kormick—or worse? He was so adamant about finding my mother."

She noted the momentary clenching of his jaw. *Yes, a subject he hated*. But then he put his hands on her shoulders. "Stop. I don't want you to worry about your father. Understand? I'm certain he's safe."

Her heart sped. "You know something?"

He quickly put the brakes on her hope. "No. I don't know anything. But I do know your father isn't stupid enough to walk straight into Kormick's hands."

"Not stupid, but maybe desperate enough. He's done desperate things before."

He stared at her, a storm rising in his eyes. They never talked about what her father had done to him after their last bitter argument. All of their words had been so vicious, all of them right, and all of them wrong. It remained a dilemma with no sure answer except to avoid thinking about.

"He won't do anything desperate this time," he answered, his voice barely a whisper.

She slid into his arms, her cheek pressed to his shoulder. "Thank you. Thank you for believing in him, at least in some small way. I know it's not easy for you. Even if it may not be true, I needed to hear it, that someone else thinks he's safe too."

"We'll talk more later," he said, then kissed her and left.

CHAPTER 55

W ell, at least you're not the last one here," Madame Chastain announced. "Kasta and Melizan still haven't arrived."

Tyghan scanned the large round table. In addition to the officers and Eris, Esmee, and Olivia, there were unexpected guests—Lady Barrington and Lord Csorba. "Kasta's not coming. I gave her urgent business to attend to. Melizan is probably on her way."

He eyed Barrington and Csorba. "Look who's here. But you couldn't bother to show up when I urgently asked for a council vote."

Lady Barrington offered a patronizing shake of her head. "Getting a unanimous council vote on such short notice is an impossible feat. You're a young and unrealistic ruler, Your Majesty."

"And yet, as Knight Commander, you put me in charge of sharp lethal objects."

Lord Csorba scowled. "Warring and ruling are two different skills."

"You may leave now," Tyghan said, already done with their nonsense. "This meeting is for senior council members and officers only."

"I told them," Madame Chastain said, "but they refused to leave."

"We won't take up much of your time," Lord Csorba said. "But we have urgent business too. We received a report that your charge is indeed fully bloodmarked."

"That is privileged information."

"As well we know," Lady Barrington piped up, "and that is our point exactly. This information needs to be carefully guarded, but we've seen her freely flitting about the palace grounds. Considering her singular and vital role in our future, we find that to be unwise."

"We think guards should be placed at her door," Csorba continued, "and a collar to control her magic would be a prudent security measure."

"She is an ally, not a prisoner."

"She's an asset. One too great to be careless with. She could provide us with advantages for centuries to come. And we do have to consider that she has certain loyalties to our enemies."

Veins rose at Tyghan's temples. "Get out," he growled. "Get out before I rip out your tongues as an additional security measure."

Lord Csorba jumped to his feet. "You will not be king much longer."

"We know Cael is here," Lady Barrington added as a warning. "He came to see us just a short while ago."

Tyghan struggled to contain his fury without breaking any bones. "Guards!" he shouted. "Escort these council members to their quarters. They are not to see *anyone* until I give further orders. Not even a servant. And see that Reuben applies a collar to both of them. Gag and hood them in the meantime so they don't disturb anyone."

"What? Have you gone mad?" Lady Barrington yelled.

Lord Csorba raised a hand to summon magic, but Tyghan was faster, gathering a stream of bright energy into his hand that slammed the lord across the room, sending him tumbling to the floor. He rose to his feet, sputtering and disheveled. "You've gone too far this time!"

"You haven't begun to see how far I will go to protect our *asset*. You picked the wrong battle this time, Csorba."

Everyone was stunned into silence as the guards escorted them out.

Quin finally broke the silence. "That was the best fucking thing I've seen all day."

CHAPTER 56

Bristol came to a fork in the trail and was uncertain which way to go. She was making her way back from Reuben's cottage after a fruitless attempt to see if he had learned anything from Willow. He hadn't been there, but her burning desire for more information had subsided. *I'm certain he's safe.* Maybe that was all she needed—someone to believe in the same thing she did, in the resourcefulness of her father. The wonder of Danu. Willow had shaken her belief, but Tyghan had strengthened it.

Now she headed for the dining pavilion. She had missed her midday meal and was starving. She had hoped to find a shortcut straight to Sun Court but then stopped, studying her unfamiliar surroundings. The palace had infinite pathways, and she had never traveled this one. But she could still see the spire of Sky Pavilion and used that as a beacon. One way or another, she would get there. She rounded a curve and came to a place she recognized. Judge's Walk. She hadn't passed through it since Cully first led her down the path.

She paused, talking stock of her surroundings. "Perfect," she whispered, knowing the way from there, but inside she didn't feel so perfect. She viewed the wide corridor more cautiously this time. *The worst of the worst,* Cully called them. *By the time their sentence is over, they beg for death.* She tried to recall where Pengary's column was. He had given her a scare the last time she traveled this way. Cully had told her if you pressed an ear to the stone, you could hear the prisoner's heartbeat. The silent ones were still empty. But Bristol had no intention of putting her ear to any column, so she would simply move quickly down the center of the walkway and hope she didn't wake any of them. Thankfully, Cully said it was rare that they roused and pushed against their prison walls.

Partway across, she spotted a wine bottle near the base of a column. An offering for the condemned? But the bottle was empty. Someone had enjoyed it, but not anyone within the monoliths. *They can see but never touch, smell but never taste*. She couldn't imagine the agony of that limbo existence, not unlike what Samuel went through as an unanchored shadow. He, like Liam, welcomed death when it was offered. She carefully stepped wide around the empty bottle, but then a terrible keening split the air. The scream of anguish quivered through her bones. *Pengary*, she assumed as she ducked to escape his giant muzzle and sharp teeth. But it wasn't a dragon's head straining toward her. She blinked, unable to move. It was a man. A man who looked like her father.

What was she seeing? Her head pounded.

The marble mouth struggled to move. *Reeeeeeeeeeee.*

A man. He was the color of pale veined marble, like a tortured sculpture. But the deep-set eyes, the strong brow, the square jaw. The determination twisting across his face. He was trying to say her name. *Bri.*

She choked back a scream.

He struggled to say one more word. *Kasssss tuh.*

And then he was gone, yanked back into the column. Bristol stared. Her hands trembled. She hugged herself, trying to stop shaking.

Her father, in a pillar of marble? The worst of the worst? They had hunted him down and sentenced him to this without telling her?

Kasta. He wanted her to go to Kasta.

CHAPTER 57

K asta pored over the roster on her desk, making a few last notes. She knew every one of the knights personally. They came from five different regiments and had a variety of deadly skills, but the one skill they all had in common was that they were loquacious. They were the ones who told stories around campfires while on patrol. At the parley, each could play a chatty lord or lady with ease, while they fingered a weapon beneath their silk and satin ruffles, or summoned magic with their tongues as they laughed.

Tyghan would be pleased. She knew he was trying to mend the rift between them. That was what she wanted too. To go back to the way it had always been between them. Easy, relaxed, trusting. She reviewed the list one last time because she was his First Officer, not just a position of prestige but one that demanded perfection. She wanted to be that officer again, in every way. If she hurried, she would be able to deliver it to him at the rotunda before the meeting was over. Once approved, the outfitting of these lords and ladies could be finalized. An army of tailors were on standby to provide last-minute alterations to wardrobes that had already been chosen. Kormick would indeed laugh at the extra witnesses and what he perceived as Tyghan's weak show of power. He would find her crew shallow and amusing. Until he didn't.

She lit a candle on her desk. The sun was low in the sky, and her room was growing dim.

And then she heard an urgent knock.

🔑

When Kasta opened the door, Bristol stared at her, panting for a few empty seconds.

"What's going on?" Kasta asked, motioning her inside. "Your face is as bright as an apple. Did you run here?"

Bristol leaned on the back of a chair across from the desk, her fingers digging into the leather. Her breaths grew steadier as she took in the study, the neatly arranged bookshelves, the stacks of parchment on Kasta's desk. She nodded. "Yes, I ran."

"I'm busy," Kasta said impatiently, waiting for Bristol to get to the point.

"My father. He's at Judge's Walk, inside a pillar. He said your name."

Kasta glanced away briefly, the corner of her mouth pulling, but then her gaze landed squarely back on Bristol, her shoulders widening, unapologetic. "Well, that's unexpected. Leave it to Kierus. Those prisoners usually can't move a finger, much less utter a word. What were you doing way out at Judge's Walk?"

Fire flashed in Bristol's eyes. "What fucking difference does it make? I want you to free my father!"

Kasta smiled at Bristol's outburst. "Too late, it's done. The council ordered a thousand years for his crime, and I carried out the sentence."

"Tyghan promised to stop the hunt for my father."

"People say and do a lot of things when they're in love. I wouldn't put too much stock in anything Tygh told you. He's king. Trust me, he holds the laws of Elphame higher than you. Besides, even he can't override a full council vote. And they refused to convene for a new one. They're a powerful lot. I thought we already made that clear to you."

"Then let me make something clear to you, Kasta. I'm commuting his sentence right now. As the only bloodmarked in this nation, I'm powerful too."

"Think so?" She strolled over to a rack holding her sheathed sword and weapon belt.

"You won't kill me, Kasta. You know my value to Danu."

"Maybe you overestimate your value."

"I don't think so, and I definitely know what your value will be if I tell Tyghan about your role in his stabbing. That you found my father first and let him walk away? Yes, I know all about it. Tyghan nearly died because of your very unknightly actions, and he still suffers from the horrors of it."

Kasta's cool composure vanished. She ran stiff fingers through her spiked hair, like she was trying to think of a fitting comeback or a way out of this, but the truth was too damning. She shook her head, and all she could manage was, "Your father told you?"

"Yes. And if I tell Tyghan, you'll be banished, or worse, you'll end up in a pillar right beside my father."

Kasta's breaths were coming faster now. "Tyghan wouldn't do that to me."

Bristol smiled. "I'll make sure the council knows what you did too. Almost an accessory to the crime. As you said, they're a powerful lot."

Color blazed across Kasta's cheekbones. "You conniving little bitch. I helped your father once, and now you're going to turn on me?"

"Life stinks, doesn't it, Kasta? But what did you expect? That I would play nice after you imprisoned him in a block of marble? You made a choice. Now I'm making one. All you need to do right now is help me save him again. One last time. You can do that, can't you?"

Kasta didn't budge, her dark eyes lethal, like she was planning Bristol's demise. At best, it was a stalemate.

"Come on, we can both win at this game," Bristol said softly. "You help me release my father, and no one will know your secret. You can go on with your precious life as a noble knight, and I will be able to save a man who doesn't deserve a thousand years of hell."

Kasta leapt, slamming Bristol against the bookcase, her grip fierce around Bristol's throat. "How can you say what he deserves?" she hissed between gritted teeth. "You barely know him! You barely know me!" Her fingers dug into Bristol's skin. "Did you know that, besides summoning water from the air, I can also draw every last drop of it out of your body? Every drop, until all that's left is your dried up leather carcass. How does it feel?"

Bristol was already feeling the effects, the weakening of her knees, her arms unable to push Kasta away. The muscles of her throat grew taut. "Go ahead, kill me," she choked out. "You'll become the new scourge of Danu, a traitor worse than my father." She coughed, her tongue and lips dry. "Elphame needs me. Commit your last traitorous act and doom it forever. Just think of it, Kasta. Your disgrace will be legend."

Kasta squeezed harder, her eyes wild, but then suddenly let go and stepped away.

Bristol rubbed her throat, coughing as moisture returned to her mouth. "How do I get him out?" she asked. "That's all you have to tell me. I'll take care of the rest."

Kasta glanced at a small golden bottle on her bookshelf. It was like one of the many potion bottles from Madame Chastain's workshop.

"That?" Bristol asked.

Kasta's jaw was razor sharp as she gave a single nod. "Four drops on the pillar imprisoned him. Four more drops, with the command *aira mathemis*, will release him."

"Are you sure that's it? I'll go straight to Tyghan with what I know if it doesn't work."

"That's it. Now get out of my sight. And make sure he stays out of sight too. If anyone spots him, he's a dead man."

CHAPTER 58

Bristol ran with her cloak and sword in one hand and a pack with food and water in the other. The potion was secure in her pocket, and she repeated the spell, *aira mathemis*, over and over in her head so she wouldn't forget it. She glanced over her shoulder as she ran, afraid Kasta might change her mind and come after her. But there were no footsteps, no surprises, even when she made it to Judge's Walk.

She ran up the steps, her chest burning, and took in the two long rows of columns. Terror struck her. Which one? The column was somewhere in the middle on the right side, but now she wasn't sure which one. They all looked alike. *The wine bottle*, she remembered. *It was near the wine bottle*. She hurried to the middle section, searching for it and found the bottle on its side—it had rolled to the edge of the walkway. She must have knocked it over in the shock of finding her father there.

"Daddy?" she whispered, hoping for a response, but there was nothing.

That one, she thought, staring at one of the pillars, a vein in the marble familiar, the white line that ran across her father's face when he pressed forward. "That's it."

She dropped her gear to the ground and pulled the potion from her vest pocket. Her hand shook as she pulled the dropper from the bottle, and then she was uncertain where to put the drops. Every step was overwhelming. Her father's life was at stake. She squeezed the dropper, and one glistening bead slid onto the pillar. She put three more drops near it and said, "*Aira mathemis.*"

The drops began smoking and spreading, and she let out a shaky breath. *It's working.* The marble undulated, like it was alive, and then it rumbled, the low groaning sound of someone waking. She stepped back, uncertain what would happen next, wondering if the whole pillar would collapse.

She saw a marbled elbow, a hand, a back, all trying to emerge like a moth from a cocoon.

"You can do it," she said. "Press harder."

And he did. Then a knee. A shoulder. Finally, a man broke free and tumbled out. A tall man like her father.

But it wasn't him.

She had freed the wrong person.

The man got his bearings, straightening, standing tall, and studied her. He was a striking figure and wore a long black velvet coat that matched his coal-black hair. "Ah, Miss Keats, the king's paramour." His arm swept to his middle, and he bowed. "Pengary, in your debt, my lady."

Bristol stared at him, horrified and speechless. What had she done? "First, I am not the king's paramour, and second, how do you know my name?"

"On the first point, I'm pleased to learn I was wrong, and on the second point, here I have nothing but time to listen, and your name comes up in passing conversations frequently." He smiled. "Besides, I knew you'd come back. There are so few of us, and our kind always stick together."

Her horror turned to fury. "*Me?* I am not one of your kind! I am nothing like you. I don't burn queens and children to death and then eat them."

Pengary sighed, shaking his head. "The stories . . . how they grow.

The centuries have their ways of embellishing them. Be wary of the legends you hear. Who knows, one day you may be a legend yourself." He took her hand before she could pull away and kissed it. "Until then, I am indebted to you, Miss Keats. And our kind never forget their debts."

With that, he turned, like he was throwing on a cape, and his body transformed, golden scales surfacing where skin had once been, claws sprouting from his fingers, his head growing sharp teeth, horns, and an enormous snout. Finally, thick leathery wings stretched from his shoulders until they spanned over thirty feet across. A dragon. If he was only the "fair-size" one that Cully described, how large were the wild dragons of the north seas? Bristol found herself stepping farther back, until the twelve-foot-tall creature gave her one last knowing glance, lifted his wings, and launched into the air, the strong draft blowing her hair behind her. He flew away, gliding over the spires of the palace, and disappeared into the clouds.

Bristol stared at the sky where he had once been. "I am *not* one of your kind," she murmured to herself again.

The bottle of potion was still tight in her grip. Her father. She had to get him out. She ran to the next pillar.

CHAPTER 59

Tyghan stormed toward the rotunda door.

"Where are you going?" Eris called.

"To kill my brother. It won't take long. I'll be back before the meeting is over."

No one followed him. They probably all hoped he meant what he said.

A string of curses rattled through Tyghan's head as he made his way to Cael's quarters. *An asset.* Tyghan saw gold glittering in Csorba's eyes. *She could provide us with advantages for centuries to come.* And suggesting she wear a collar so they could control her? *You won't be king much longer.* Tyghan had never cared about being king, but now it seemed essential he maintain the position. He couldn't trust Cael to keep the council in line, with his constant gallivanting around Elphame.

And to reveal himself to council members? All Tyghan needed right now was for Kormick to find out and send a fleet of his rotting restless dead to the palace in retribution.

Melizan stopped short when Tyghan almost rammed into her around a corner. "Whoa, I recognize that blood in your eye. Who are you off to dismember?" She fell into step with him.

Tyghan didn't slow. "Our brother," he answered.

"It's about time. Need help?"

"I can manage. You go on to the meeting."

"I know you can manage, but I owe you so much after that wedding. I could spare you from getting blood under your nails?"

"I don't mind blood. Where's Cosette?"

"Down at the river saying goodbye to her family. They all loved you, by the way. What did the bread head do this time?"

Bread head. Tyghan would have laughed if he wasn't so enraged. When they were children and forbidden from cursing or calling each other names, Melizan got away with bread head, claiming she loved dry tasteless things. He hadn't heard her say it in years. Now she used words that could singe an ogre's hair. Tyghan explained to her in a few terse sentences what Cael had done.

"Definitely coming," she said. "Besides, I haven't seen you two in a good row in a long time."

Blood ran from Cael's nose, but Tyghan had a bloody face too, from a gash across his cheekbone. Cael always wore those nasty rings.

Melizan watched the two brothers tire as they fought, neither one truly wanting to kill the other. The hot fury at their temples slowly faded. As mismatched as the three siblings were, none of them had any other family, and there was something comforting about sharing a history, having someone who had known you from the beginning and shared the same blood, the same losses. Someone who tolerated you in spite of all your blunders. Cael was definitely the king of bad choices, and Melizan had throttled him herself a few times, but she and Tyghan had made their share of stupid mistakes too.

Her brothers were equally matched in height and stature, their swings predictable, and Cael had gained most of his weight back, and apparently his strength too, thanks to the High Witch. Still, Cael was a sloppy fighter, and Tyghan wasn't. Tygh had embraced his training as a knight. Cael never did. He never learned that in a fight, he really had no chance against Tyghan—or her. It was like he always believed that, one day, fate would turn, and his blows would land magnificently. He was king, after all. That had to be worth something.

Melizan and Cael were both twelve when her father died, Tyghan only seven. She remembered Cael coming over to her with puddles in his eyes when he heard the news. *This is going to kill my mother, please don't let it kill you.* He had nodded toward Tyghan and said, *We both need to be here for the brat.* He said it with the sincerity and bluntness that only Cael could muster, but she heard a softness in it too, and she pulled her arm back and hit him in the jaw. She didn't want to be necessary for anyone else, for making sure they survived, because she wasn't sure she would survive herself. She had already lost too much in her short life. But she always remembered, Cael *knew*, through all his own worries, that this would break his mother, and he needed Melizan to lean on. There were so many times over the years, as he floundered and grew into his role as king, when she hated him, but she didn't forget that moment when he shared his fear and needed her. And maybe that gave her something to need too.

"I swear, it was an accident," Cael said, wiping a stream of blood from his mouth. "I thought I had my glamour in place."

"You *thought?*" Tyghan yelled. "Are you still a child, Cael? You're the king of the second most powerful kingdom in Elphame! That's right, *second*, soon to be no kingdom at all, if you don't stop fucking things up!"

Cael took a weak swing, barely grazing Tyghan's jaw. "I'm not king!" he yelled. "Not anymore. You stole that from me!"

The blaze returned to Tyghan's temples. "*Stole?* I didn't ask for this! I had no choice. You disappeared because of another one of your selfish escapades. I stepped up to be king because I had to! And that's what we're expecting of you! Step up! There is no room for any more reckless mistakes!"

Cael slipped to his knees, out of breath, and raised one hand in surrender. "I will stay in my room until the ceremony."

Tyghan's chest still heaved, and he nodded.

"Well, that was quick," Melizan said. "I thought you two would go at least a few more rounds."

"Shut up, Melizan," Cael snapped.

She walked over and scooped her hand under his arm and helped him to his feet. "Come on, brother, let's get your face cleaned up. I'm sure if you grovel a bit, Tyghan will heal that darling fat lip of yours and make it kissable again."

And Cael leaned on her all the way to his bath chamber, because he knew he could.

"Am I groveling enough?"

"Never enough," Tyghan answered as he dabbed a small cut over Cael's brow and then pressed his finger to it.

Cael winced. "I never wanted to be king, you know? At least not at age twelve. But I had no choice. Now it's all I have. Without it, I'm nothing." And then, even more glumly, he added, "I never had the same powers as you."

It was a sore spot, the one thing they never talked about. Cael was decent enough at glamour and the standard array of spells. He could also control the air in small bursts by summoning an occasional strong gust, but it could barely be called a kinship, and he had no kinship whatsoever with the other elements. They had different fathers, and Tyghan attributed it to that. But he was good at parties, and that explained his favor with the kingdoms.

"You'll be king again soon enough, but you'll have to do better at keeping the council in line. You're a good ruler when you stay focused."

"I'm always a good ruler, little brother. I am fair. But even kings need to take breaks."

"And you take more than your share."

"Don't question me on everything I do. Besides, when I step up on the Stone of Destiny, I'll be spending a lot of time at the Elphame court, and when I'm away, you'll be regent here. You're the one who will need to keep the council in line."

"Or Eris. He's played that role before. I have my duties as Knight Commander."

"You're managing both jobs now," Cael answered. "And if things are settled with Kormick and there's peace in Elphame, there will be far less for you to do. What else could you want to be besides regent in my absence?"

A memory flashed behind Tyghan's eyes. He saw a golden scythe clutched in his small hands, a field ripe with wheat, and Amaetheon, the only great god he had ever spoken with face-to-face, asking him a question: *Will you help with the harvest?* For a few weeks, being a farmer became Tyghan's burning passion, but then after his father died and his mother left, it was the knighthood that consumed him. It was who and what he was now. But now he wanted even more. He wanted a life with Bristol too.

Cael didn't wait for Tyghan to respond. "Yes, that's what I want, you taking care of things here when I'm away. Together, the Trénallis brothers will watch over both ends of Elphame and make sure the likes of Kormick are never seen again. Until then, I will stay in my room."

Tyghan wiped his hands with a towel and threw it in the basin. "When did you become so agreeable, Cael?"

"When your fist smashed into my face."

"You threw the first punch."

"Just trying to get a head start. That's what kings do."

CHAPTER 60

Bristol forced her hand to stop shaking. She couldn't risk wasting a single drop. There were barely four left in the bottle. She carefully squeezed one drop at a time onto the marble, whispering the spell in her head, but not saying it until the last drop touched the stone.

"*Aira mathemis.*"

The drops smoked, as before, and then began spreading, searching for the prisoner within. "This has to be the right pillar," she whispered. *Please let it be the right one*. How much time had she wasted already? What if someone came along and stopped her? She willed the glistening drops to move faster. Her nails dug into her palms.

The process repeated itself, and finally a human form pressed and stretched against the magic casing of the pillar. She still couldn't tell if it was her father. But then an arm broke through . . . a leg, and then there was a horrible moan. It shivered through Bristol. Finally, a man fell to the walkway in front of her, on his hands and knees. He shook his head as if dazed, still looking down at the marble floor.

"Daddy," Bristol said quietly. She grabbed his arm and tried to help him stand. "You're free. *You're free.*"

Logan Keats dragged himself to his feet, then looked into Bristol's eyes like she was the whole of the universe. He drew her into his arms.

"You're safe," he said, rubbing her back. "Thank the gods." His chest jumped as he muffled a sob. "How long have I been in there? I tried to count the days, but it was impossible. Every time I closed my eyes, I thought another whole day had passed and knew I had a thousand years of them to go."

Bristol shivered. *A thousand years*. How could they do this? "I don't know how long you've been in there, but the Choosing Ceremony is in four days. You have to find a safe place to hide until it's over. I'm bloodmarked, Daddy—just like Mother. I can stop all this."

His face clouded over then, his dark eyes glistening, and Bristol's heart stabbed with all the pain she saw in them. Even if he had made mistakes, in that moment she was certain there was never a man who loved his family more. He understood what being bloodmarked might mean for her. "No," he said, shaking his head. "We didn't want this for you. We never wanted this—"

She cupped his face in her hands, his skin damp with tears. "I'll be fine, Daddy. I am not Mother, and Tyghan is not Kormick. I can handle this, but I need you safe. No one knows I've released you yet. They still want you imprisoned." She couldn't bring herself to mention Tyghan's name. She refused to believe he was part of this. It had to have been the council. Tyghan would not do this to her. The pain of it burned inside her, a scream wanting to tear free. She grabbed the cloak and supplies from the floor. If there was one good thing she had learned from a lifetime of being on the run, it was to move faster than what hunted you, find the next safe place. "You need to go quickly. Take these and hide," she said, handing her father the sword and pack. "In five days, return to the barn where we last met. From there, I will take you and Mother home."

"*Brije*—"

"No arguments this time." She swept the cloak over his shoulder, telling him it was an invisibility cloak. He already knew how to invoke its magic, and nodded.

But before he kissed her goodbye, before he pulled the hood of the cloak up and disappeared, she saw the familiar determined glint in his eyes, the one that made her chest swell with pride. She saw the power-ful, skilled knight he had always been, and the creative artist who had raised and protected her, but mostly she saw the worry he still had for her mother. And in the tilt of his head, she saw the certainty he pos-sessed that only he could save her. And maybe he was right. He was a man who loved deeply and beyond reason. He couldn't help who he was, and really, she didn't want him to be anyone else.

Free. He was free now.

CHAPTER 61

Pengary soared high above the palace grounds, circling for the sheer joy of it, reveling in every enormous bone of the beast within him, feeling the strength of his expanded rib cage, the crisp wind gliding over his wingtips, the air filling his wide nostrils with the scent of clouds and freedom. He roared, a burst of flame jumping from his throat, the powerful sound scorching the air, his heart truly alive again. He couldn't wait to eat something, to swallow it whole and feel it tumble down his long throat. He had almost given up hope—until she passed by. Her voice was the sweetest sound he had ever heard. The scent of her blood had pricked him from his numb existence, and even when he was pushed back into his pillar by Cully, he knew she would return to help him.

He peered down at the palace and nation he had once served. Never again. He banked to his right and beat a straight line to the northern isles. *Home*. But he wouldn't forget his debt to Miss Keats. His kind never did.

The meeting in Lir Rotunda was just adjourning when Kasta hurried through the door. She nodded to Tyghan, indicating she had what he wanted.

"Go on," he told the others, "I'll review this alone with her."

No one had questioned him when he had returned to the rotunda meeting earlier, but now as they filed out, Madame Chastain stopped and pressed a finger to Tyghan's cheekbone, ordering him to hold still. "You two," she said, shaking her head. "Always at it." Tyghan reached up and felt his cheek. He had healed Cael's wounds, but in his rush to return to the meeting, he had neglected to heal his own. "There. Done," she said. "Still a bloody mess, but I'm not going to wash you up too. I'm assuming he looks worse."

"I cleaned him up," Tyghan answered, "but he got my message. He won't be leaving his room again, even with glamour." She nodded and left, but Tyghan noted that Eris had already left without her, and he wondered what his rush was.

He and Kasta pulled out chairs and sat side by side at the huge round table. He liked the peace of the rotunda when it was nearly empty, the small echoes almost like whispers of the gods. With only him and Kasta, there was no shouting across the table, only soft agreements as he reviewed her list. "Good," he said, reading the choices and balance of skills. "Very good."

He finally slid the roster back to Kasta. "Nice work. Let's get them outfitted. We'll do a dry run tomorrow to make sure everyone knows who is who."

Kasta smiled, but she didn't look happy. Her face was drawn, as though she had been awake for days. "Tailors are ready and waiting. I'll let them know immediately," she said, her voice strangely flat. "It's a brilliant idea. I'm sorry I questioned you when you first proposed it. More fawning nobles in their bright party clothes to witness his ascent will make Kormick fucking giddy. When he——"

"Are you all right?" Tyghan asked. "You seem off."

She sat up taller in her chair. "Of course, I'm fine. Just a lot on my mind. I——"

Someone pounded on the rotunda door, and Kasta jumped like she was expecting a monster to burst through it. Instead, the door flew open and a young cadet rushed in. "Your Majesty! Forgive the intrusion, but Commander Maddox——" The cadet bent over, gulping for air.

Once he caught his breath, Tyghan said, "Go on."

"She wanted me to inform you immediately that an avydra was spotted flying directly over the palace. She saw it herself. It circled several times, but it's gone now. It was last seen flying north."

An avydra? Surely there was some mistake. As far as Tyghan knew, there hadn't been an avydra in Danu in decades. The creatures knew to stay clear, so his next thought was the winged creatures from the Abyss. *Hyagen.* They had pointed wings too, but Maddox was well versed in both. She wouldn't make such a mistake. "Thank you," Tyghan told the cadet. "Perhaps it was blown off course. As long as it has moved on, that's all that matters, but I'll check on it."

The cadet left and Tyghan rose to leave too, but then he noticed Kasta leaning forward with her hands pressed between her knees, like she was about to implode. "What's wrong with you?"

"Nothing."

"Then go rest, Kasta. Or go blow off some steam. You're wound as tight as Eris on a bad day. I'll check on the sighting."

"*Pengary,*" Kasta murmured to herself as Tyghan walked to the door. Her thoughts flew out of control. *It was Pengary. She fucking let the wrong one out. What if the beast had killed and eaten her?*

Tyghan turned. "What?"

She gaped at him and reached for a lie. And then another. But all she saw was a long swirling tunnel of lies, black as the Abyss, and she was being sucked into it. It would never end, not now. Kierus had lied to her again. He did tell someone. And now Kasta would always be under Bristol's thumb. How long before she was back, blackmailing Kasta again with another demand?

Her breath seized in her lungs. "The avydra is Pengary."

Tyghan's expression darkened. "He has centuries to go. You know that. What's really wrong with you?"

A lie. Tell him another lie. But instead, she whispered, "I did something."

🗝

Tyghan sat at the table, listening, and Kasta talked. He stared at her, trying to absorb it. Her eyes reddened as she confessed things in broken sentences, things he had never suspected, especially not from his trusted First Officer.

"He begged me, Tyghan. He begged. You know how we—I had loved him for years, and I knew he didn't feel the same about me, but, right then, he needed me so much, and I hoped—" She shook her head. "I don't know what I hoped, but he promised me that he'd leave with her immediately, and I believed him. It was a gift, I thought. I was giving him a gift, and he—I had no idea you would come along so soon. I'd left you a mile away on another trail. I never thought he would—"

She looked down, unable to say it.

"Stab me with Maire's knife?"

She nodded.

Tyghan couldn't think. He could find no words. He felt the sting of the blade going into his gut again. The shock. He stared at her and saw Kierus. She hadn't even come to warn him, hiding from her decision instead. It was Dalagorn who scooped him up from the mud of the forest floor.

"I will resign my position," she said.

He stared at her, that dark bloody day swimming in his head again, but the Choosing Ceremony was swimming there too. She was already an integral part of every step of their strategies. He rubbed his temple. "No," he said. "You will not resign. It's too close to the ceremony. You'll fulfill your duties without error, and I'll figure out later what to do about this."

She nodded without meeting his eyes.

"What does all this have to do with Pengary?" he asked.

As she spoke, Tyghan's blood went cold. She told him about the blackmail and trading the potion to release Kierus. "I gave Bristol the potion in return for her silence, but I think she got the wrong pillar and released Pengary instead."

Pengary, the one who burned and ate his victims? Tyghan was on his feet.

"I'll come with you," Kasta said, but he was already nightjumping to Judge's Walk.

🔑

"Bristol!" he called into the darkness as he ran down the walkway, but there was no reply and no sign of a disturbance. When he got to Pengary's column, he searched the ground for blood or some other evidence, holding his hand up to amplify the light of the moon. There was nothing out of place but an empty wine bottle. He slammed his hand against the column and put his ear to it, listening for the faintest heartbeat, but there was only silence. He pressed his ear to the next column, which belonged to Kierus, but it was silent too.

CHAPTER 62

With Beltane now past, and many gentry and nobles off to their summer homes in the country, evening festivities had grown quieter. Only one group of musicians played a tune near the base of the grand staircase, and a few fae danced nearby.

A half-moon peeked over Bristol's shoulder, illuminating the porcelain plate shivering in her hands. She viewed the delicacies that the Sun Court buffet tables offered. *Food*, she thought. *I only need food*. She still hadn't eaten since that morning. Her stomach was eager, but her mind still wrestled with Pengary's words. *Our kind always stick together.*

She swallowed, her stomach spinning uneasily. Details kept jabbing her like darts: her affinity with fire, Pengary's golden scales, his claws that were blue at the root. And then another detail stabbed her—the drawing. Her lifelong obsession with da Vinci's dragon. And then Cully's words when Pengary tried to leap from the pillar: *That hasn't happened in years. He must have sniffed new blood passing by*. Her blood. Heat flashed across her face.

Circumstantial, she told herself, forcing a shallow breath. *Everyone is six degrees from something*. Her stomach wobbled as much as the plate in her hand. She heaped a large spoonful of hot thyme potatoes onto it. And then salmon puffs drizzled with dill béarnaise. She breathed in the rich, warm aroma, her cheeks swelling with anticipation. It was a welcome

and needed distraction. Of course she was rattled. She had just released
her father from a fucking slab of marble. She was being bombarded with
too many emotions. *Food—that's what I need to concentrate on.* She moved
down the line, piling her plate with more, both sweet and savory, down-
ing a palm-size vanilla tart as she went.

But Kasta's words haunted her. *If anyone spots him, he's a dead man.*
No one would find him, she assured herself. Not Logan Keats, the
wonder of Danu—

But they had found him once, or he wouldn't have been imprisoned. He wasn't impervious. He was a man.

She held her plate steady in one hand and poured herself a glass of
wine with the other. And then she felt a presence close at her back, hot
and angry. She didn't turn around.

"I've been looking everywhere for you," Tyghan said.

Her spine stiffened, her back becoming a wall. "The only thing I
want to hear out of your mouth is if you knew what she did. Did you
know he was in the pillar?"

"I knew."

His answer, quick and unrepentant, jolted her, but she steadied herself. And then the same demanding voice. "Where is he?"

She felt his scowl, and the sharp edge of his words. He had no idea
what anger was, but she remembered what her friends said: *With you
two at war, the other war looked grimmer.* She still intended to win this
war, and all the battles between, including the one at hand.

"Smile, Your Majesty. In case you hadn't noticed, every eye in Sun
Court is on us."

He pressed closer, his heat radiating onto her. He whispered quietly
against her neck. "I don't give a fuck who's watching us."

She set her plate down and turned to face him, and flinched at
the burn of his eyes. "You should care," she said. "Because the two
of us happily working together inspires faith and trust in a victory
to those watching. Appearances matter. Of course, you know how
to make quite a show of that already, don't you? Wasn't that the
whole purpose of your grand gesture last week, when you held my

hand over our heads for your troops?" She drew out her next words, coating them with sugary sarcasm. "And what are we without *faith* and *trust*?"

"Exactly," he replied, still set on getting what he wanted. "How long have you known that it was Kasta who found your father first?"

Kasta had confessed? "Weeks ago, when I met with him in the barn."

"And yet you didn't tell me?"

"She had helped him. I didn't want to condemn her for that."

"But when she no longer served your purpose, you blackmailed her?"

She definitely confessed. "Don't you dare judge me for that. All my father is guilty of is wanting to save my mother. Kasta was no longer helping him—and I found a fast way to change her mind. In case you forgot what I told you when you were wrestling with demons, I love my father."

"Over everything else apparently."

He turned to leave but she grabbed his arm. "Where are you going?"

"To get my things out of your room, before I find them out in the hallway. I'm moving back to my room."

She tightened her grip on his arm. "There will be no moving. Look around you."

This time he did. It was clear they were having a heated conversation and, indeed, every head had turned their way. He pulled his arm free, his gaze locked onto hers, thoughts steaming in his eyes. "You don't even know Kierus."

"I know my own father."

"Open your eyes, Bristol. You know the man from the mortal world, the artist who raised you. That's not who he is here. Here he's a knight on a mission. I know *that* man, and I know him far better than you do. We trained and worked together for eighteen years. I know how he thinks, how he moves, and what lengths he'll go to to get what he wants—and he wants Maire." He raked his fingers through his hair. "Yes, he was the wonder of Danu, but he's a mortal, dammit! How do you think he got that reputation? We were best friends. How many times do you think I saved him? I was the one covering his back, time after time, keeping him alive. I was watching his back this time, too, until you interfered."

"Are you insane? How is putting him in a pillar for a thousand years watching his back?"

"One month. That's all I gave him, just long enough to keep him out of the way, and out of the council's hands. To keep him from being captured again by someone else—like Kormick. Because that's what will happen."

A mocking laugh jumped from her chest. "One month? You expect me to buy that? Cully said from the start that it was a thousand years. My father said the same. He was already feeling hopeless. Everyone knows the sentence for Judge's Walk. If it was truly only a month, why didn't you just tell me?"

"The way you told me about Kasta and your father? The way you blackmailed her behind my back? The way you released a dangerous beast to add to our worries? I wish just once you would trust my judgment as Knight Commander and king." His jaw clenched, like fury was about to explode out of his head, but he kept his words tight and low. "I didn't tell you because I am trying to juggle a thousand details for a nation on the brink of war. Because I have to make some decisions without announcing them to the whole world. Because every eye in court is always on me, just like you said. Because . . . *because I'm the fucking king. La-di-da!*"

She glanced at the suddenly silent plaza, even the musicians pausing their play, straining to hear their words.

Tyghan shook his head with disgust. He stepped forward and pulled her into his arms, kissing her long and hard, but there was no tenderness or love in his touch. He pulled away. "There. Do you think that convinced them? I agree. Appearances matter."

He turned and walked away.

CHAPTER 63

Her room was dark and silent when she returned, but her stomach was loud and churning. She ran for the bath chamber and dropped in front of the commode, losing her dinner in several waves. She was not prone to a weak stomach, but after Tyghan had left Sun Court, she wolfed down her piled plate of food, and her empty stomach had not been ready for it. Now it was empty again.

She fell back on the floor, weak, and wiped her clammy forehead with her palm, then felt a cold nose nudging her elbow. She opened her eyes. It was Reggie, checking on her. "I'm all right," she said, and got to her feet, splashing her face in the basin, and brushing and gargling until her mouth was fresh again. She snapped her fingers, illuminating a single candle on the chandelier, and got into the shower, trying to wash away the day.

If anyone spots him, he's a dead man. Fine advice from someone who imprisoned him for a thousand years. He'd rather be dead. So would she. And that was the precise point of Judge's Walk. The horror of seeing his face pressed against the marble made her woozy again. She got out of the shower and was drying off when she heard her door slam.

Fucking appearances. He was here. She wished she had never suggested it. She quickly threw on her nightgown and wrapped her hair in a towel. Tyghan gave her a cursory glance as he entered, and she left the bath chamber. "The sofa," she said as she passed. "Yours."

He didn't respond, but he crashed around the bath chamber like he was a trapped bear instead of a man. When he finally finished, he exited with only a towel around his waist and scooped her up from her side of the bed.

"What are—"

"Appearances. Your idea." He deposited her on the sofa. "The sofa is yours." He returned with a blanket and threw it at her.

♟

Tyghan lay in the dark, staring at a ceiling he couldn't see. She was awake too. He heard her rolling over on the couch and then rolling back again.

She was just as stubborn as her father. And arrogant. *Smile, Your Majesty. Every eye in Sun Court is on us*. Like he didn't already know that after a lifetime of being watched. His business became everyone's business in the blink of an eye.

He had been crazed with worry when she disappeared, searching all over the palace for her, ready to call out a whole regiment to search the skies for Pengary and pull her from his jaws—and then he found her filling a plate at the buffet tables? His momentary rush of relief had turned to rage. Rage at everything she had done.

I gave her the potion in return for her silence. Blackmail. Bristol knew what Kasta had done for weeks, and she didn't tell him. She chose to blackmail Kasta instead, then compounded it all by releasing Pengary too. And now Kierus was out there somewhere, doing the gods knew what.

♟

Bristol rolled over, unable to get comfortable, but not because of the sofa.

I know him better than you do. Open your eyes, Bristol. He's a knight on a mission.

That's what she had seen when she said goodbye to her father. A determined man on a mission to save his wife—but he was also mortal. A man who had already been captured once. *A month. That's all I gave him.*

A month? A thousand years was what the council ordered. And that's what her father and Kasta had both said. But when Tyghan said one month, he didn't hesitate. It was not new information he had plucked from the air as an excuse. His eyes never strayed from hers. He believed it. The difference between a month and a thousand years was the difference between choking on a sip of water and drowning in an ocean.

But her father never should have been imprisoned in the first place.

"You promised to call off the hunt," Bristol said into the darkness.

Tyghan didn't answer.

"And the kill order for my mother. Did you really rescind that, or was that a lie too?"

She heard the rustle of bedcovers and then the slam of the door.

He didn't return until dawn, a minute before a servant arrived with breakfast.

Just in time for appearances.

The servant hummed as he laid breakfast out on the table, removing warming covers, pouring coffee for her and juice for him—their usual fare.

When everything was set and they still hadn't moved toward the table, he asked, "Anything else?"

If this was for appearances, they were both failing miserably at it. Usually at the first sniff of hot biscuits, Tyghan was crawling out of bed and peeking under warmers, reciting the dishes to Bristol as she brushed her hair in the bath chamber. Instead, today they were both dressed and groomed like they were ready to move on with their day, and they hovered at a safe distance from the table and each other.

"Nothing else," Bristol said cheerily, and finally sat down. Tyghan did the same, and the servant left.

They stared silently at the dishes for a moment and then Tyghan dug in, his fork and knife clinking in place of conversation. He cleaned his plate in minutes and stood, his eyes grazing her still full plate. All she had managed was half a biscuit.

"You haven't touched your food."

"I had something last night that disagreed with me."

He stared at her, wondering if that something was him. "Then see Esmee about it. We have a full day." He went to the wardrobe, grabbing some of his things.

She shouldn't have been irked, considering the enormity of everything else that had transpired, but Bristol was peeved that his only concern for her stomach was that it might interrupt his schedule. She stared at his back as he slipped a jacket on. Sometimes it was the small things that unleashed tongues.

"Last night you proclaimed that I interfered. Well, guilty as charged. I was on a walkway and suddenly I was caught in the horror of my father's tortured face jumping out at me from a pillar. Yes, I interfered. And I will not apologize for blackmail."

Tyghan turned, color tinging his temples. "*You* had a fright? Last night I did a record number of nightjumps. Ten at least, to the point I could barely breathe, because I was frantically searching for *you*. I was terrified that you might be in the jaws of that beast you released. Instead, I find you happily piling food on a plate, because apparently *blackmail* agrees with you! Don't talk to me about horror."

"It's not the same thing at all."

"I agree. Not even close. And I didn't promise to call off the hunt. I promised to convene the council for a new vote. They refused!" He grabbed his weapon belt from the chaise and headed for the door.

She screamed at his back, her voice on the brink of collapsing.

"*Safe?* How could you look me straight in the eye yesterday and tell me he was safe?"

He was halfway out the door, and turned, his expression blank. "Because yesterday he *was* safe. Safer than he is today." He left, not bothering to close the door behind him.

Bristol ran over and slammed it shut, so he'd be sure to hear.

CHAPTER 64

I t was a first, having an extravagant party in the Winterwood ballroom so early in the day. Midmorning, most fae were still asleep. But
this affair was not for most fae. It was a dry run for the parley that
would take place in a few days because that part of the ceremony needed
to go off without a hitch. It would set the tone for the entire ceremony
and, like everything else, needed to be perfect. Every knight who played
the role of a noble needed the finesse, knowledge, and nuance that would
seduce Kormick into believing that he had already won.

Winterwood was chosen, again, because of its inner sanctum status.
With no exterior walls, windows, or doors, no one would be there but
those waved past secure checkpoints manned by sorcerers and guards
posted in the long hallways.

As Tyghan walked down one of those long hallways, a question
snaked through him, making his skin crawl. He was afraid he knew
the answer already, but he still had to ask, and he wanted to do so before there was an audience looking on.

Kasta would be the first of his crew at Winterwood, busy getting
things ready, so he arrived early, hoping to catch her alone. He found
her speaking to the guards. As soon as she saw him, she broke away
and came over to where he waited some distance away—where even
the guards wouldn't hear.

"Everything is set," she said. "The tailors worked all night. The knights are in the salon getting ready for—"

"I need to ask you something," Tyghan said. Kasta froze, knowing by his tone it wasn't a question about the parley. "How long did you tell Kierus he was being sentenced for?"

Kasta blinked, her chest rising in a slow guilty breath. "I told him a thousand years."

"And how long did you *actually* give him?"

She stared at him, the answer already in her eyes.

Tyghan only nodded. A menacing nod, not one of acceptance.

Kasta became earnest then. "I thought you'd come around," she explained. "I was trying to protect you from the council. He didn't deserve—"

"Don't. Don't even try to make this about me. You're a knight, and your commander gave you orders. This was about resentment, revenge, and hiding what you had done."

She abandoned excuses and squared her shoulders, standing tall as if she expected him to strike her down. She rolled her lips over her teeth, bracing herself. "Now what?" she asked, expecting to be dismissed immediately—or worse.

But he needed her. At this point he couldn't rip apart his team and reorganize it. He couldn't put someone else in charge of all the duties she was midway in executing. She was his First Officer, and a hundred details were in her head alone. He curled his fingers into his palm, trying to avoid hurling a fireball down the empty hallway. There was no perfect solution. She hadn't done anything to directly jeopardize the mission, only his trust. "I don't know what comes next," he said, "except for you to follow the same orders I gave you last night. Finish your duties without error."

"I will. I—"

He turned and walked away before she could finish, but he had nowhere to go.

"Going the wrong direction, aren't you? You passed the ballroom quite some distance back."

Tyghan glanced to the side. Eris sat on a bench that hugged the wall, shadows nearly obscuring him. "Looks like you're in the wrong place too," he replied.

Eris shuffled through some papers in his lap. "Just sorting out a few things."

"I guess that's what I'm doing too."

Eris stood, the papers rustling in his hands. "We should go back. It's starting soon."

They walked at a slow pace, neither of them eager to go where they needed to be.

"What's troubling you?" Eris asked.

Tyghan shrugged. "What makes you think something is troubling me?"

"Your face. Your voice. I know the signs. When you stop yelling and issuing orders you're troubled. Deeply. You're well past the anger stage."

Tyghan didn't try to ease the blow with tactful words. There were none. "Bristol found her father in the pillar, then blackmailed Kasta to get him out. Kierus is free. Somewhere."

Eris was silent. This was far more troubling than what he had expected to hear. "How?" he finally said. "How could she ever blackmail Kasta? With what? She's a stellar knight."

"Yesterday, that's what I would have thought too." Tyghan told him the details of what Bristol had learned from her father that day in the barn. The papers crinkled in Eris's fist. He gazed at the floor, trying to process this new turn of events. They arrived at the ballroom entrance but remained in the empty hallway, reluctant to go inside.

"I don't know what to do about Kasta," Tyghan said. "My mind says she's the best. But my gut is wary—and it's too late to put her duties on anyone else. It's three short days until the ceremony."

"And what is Bristol's state of mind?"

Tyghan hissed. "Not good."

"You two are at odds?"

"Odds? That's like saying—" Tyghan looked up at the soaring ceiling, shaking his head, unable to answer.

"All right," Eris said, nodding. "It's bad, but it doesn't have to stay bad. You should go to her and—"

"It's not that easy, Eris. We've agreed to keep up appearances, but—"

Eris hissed out an angry breath. "Please, don't talk to me about appearances! Everyone can see through them. They're as worthless as shoes on a snake. Don't—"

The ballroom door slivered open, and Madame Chastain emerged, her condemning gaze landing first on Eris, then on Tyghan. "Must you be late everywhere?"

"When you can add ten hours to his day, the king will be on time," Eris snapped. "In the meantime, give us some privacy. Our conversation does not concern you."

Tyghan wasn't sure if he should duck or run. Madame Chastain shot Eris a glare so sharp, he expected Eris to be cut in half, but before blood was shed, she turned and went back into the ballroom.

A clumsy silence followed. "What was that?" Tyghan finally asked.

Eris's brows pulled together, a crease forming between them. "I suppose we're at odds too. More than at odds actually. We're not together anymore."

Tyghan thought he had shared the most stunning news of the day, but Eris's was a close second. "You've been together for seven years."

"Eight," Eris said, his eyes drilling into the ballroom door that the High Witch had just disappeared behind.

"You're not going to tell me what happened?"

He looked back at Tyghan. "It's what didn't happen. Words that were never said between us. Actions never taken." He shook his head. "It doesn't matter. We should go inside." But with his first step toward the door he added, "You were wrong earlier about Kasta. She's not the best. I am. If you decide you need a new First Officer, I can step in."

CHAPTER 65

The ballroom burned with curiosity, everyone waiting for the extra twenty witnesses, or the "Noble Knights," as they were now being called, to join them.

Hollis and Quin held hands near the ballroom entrance, ignoring the excitement, far too enraptured with each other. Not far away, Melizan and Cosette sipped strawberry mint mimosas, their little fingers hooked together, looking like the very picture of newlyweds. Apparently, mimosas were the festive brunch choice for the morning gathering. Bristol passed on them. Esmee had given her something for her stomach, and it worked, but she wasn't ready to press her luck beyond the dry toast she had for breakfast. Not to mention, she didn't want to be the least bit relaxed by a mimosa, not with Kasta hovering near the entrance to the ballroom. Their gazes had met twice, and it hadn't been pleasant. Bristol remained on alert.

"What do you think the big surprise is?" Rose asked. "Monsters?"

"I'm afraid twenty monsters wouldn't impress Kormick," Julia answered, sipping some nectar. "He has plenty of those already."

"There he is," Avery said. "I was beginning to wonder if the Knight Commander was going to make it at all. You know what a punctuality freak he is."

Sashka tapped an imaginary watch on her wrist and laughed. "Five laps!"

Bristol glanced up. Tyghan and Eris walked through open ballroom doors that were immediately closed behind them by guards. He was greeted by a few of his officers, and he stopped to speak to them. The Knight Commander. The one who led thousands of troops. *I was the one covering his back . . . until you interfered.*

How could she believe him? Why wouldn't he just tell her? *The same way you told me about Kasta?* Their words warred in her head.

Tyghan stepped away and scanned the sea of faces in the ballroom, and his eyes landed on Bristol. After two seconds and no acknowledgment, he looked away and engaged Eris.

Bristol's face burned.

Avery startled, thinking the flash of color on Bristol's cheeks was because of her remark. "No insult intended, Bri. Really. I was only—"

"No—no—I know that. It was only a joke," Bristol said, her voice a touch too breathless.

Julia hooked her arm through Bristol's, claiming she needed to show her a piece of art on the other side of the ballroom, and dragged her a safe distance away. "What's going on with you two?" she asked.

♟

Julia waited while Bristol squirmed for a moment, hugging herself like it would keep everything trapped inside. Julia wished they weren't in a crowded ballroom. She longed to draw Bristol into her arms and let her collapse, to carry her load for a while, because Julia had never seen any woman burdened with so much. The future of twelve kingdoms rested on her shoulders in this world, and an orphaned family needed her in another.

"Can you see through me that easily, Julia?" Bristol finally asked.

"No. Not at all," Julia answered softly, aching at the pain she saw in Bristol's eyes. "You're an incredibly complicated and smart woman who excels at keeping things in check. And you're quite possibly the bravest one I've ever met, but don't forget, you and I have a history of sharing, and I saw the signs in you the minute you walked through the doors of the ballroom. You're struggling with something. If it's none of my business, just say so, but if you want to talk, I'm here."

Bristol's heart tumbled, like everything inside her was coming loose. "You were right, Julia. About me and Tyghan. Our differences caught up with us."

"You couldn't talk them out?"

Her brows knitted together. "We tried at first, and he made some efforts. So did I. But after my encounter with my mother, and everything that happened with Glennis, we mostly stopped talking about my parents. It was easy to do, we were so busy with so many other things, and I knew it was difficult for him. Difficult for both of us. I assumed both of my parents were safe and off-limits, and he assumed something else."

"Oh." Julia rubbed her brow. "So things came to a head?"

Bristol nodded, like she didn't trust her voice.

"Is it too late to talk things out now?"

"I don't know."

"Let me pose a better question: Do you *want* to talk things out?"

Bristol angled her head to the side, and Julia saw an impenetrable wall in her eyes. "He captured my father and imprisoned him, and then I blackmailed Kasta to get him back out. We're on opposite sides of this issue, and we have been since the day we met. I'm not sure we can find a middle ground."

Julia couldn't hide her reaction. She whistled out a surprised breath. "Well, when you two do it, you do it up big."

"Big in a bad way," Bristol agreed.

So Kierus was captured again, Julia thought. She had known he wouldn't take her advice about returning to the mortal world. He was not a man who gave up, even when facing insurmountable odds. It was a trait he had passed on to his daughter, and Julia admired him for that.

She eyed Bristol staring up at the ceiling, like she was studying the intricate floral designs, but she knew Bristol was only seeing the painful breach between her and Tyghan. It was one time Julia wished she had been completely wrong, that the couple's differences wouldn't matter, that they would just miraculously disappear. Sometimes it didn't feel good to be right.

"Bri," Julia said, drawing Bristol's gaze back to hers. "From the beginning, the gods gave you two an impossible mountain to climb. It doesn't mean you can't do it, assuming you still have a common goal."

"Don't worry, Julia, nothing will get in the way of me stopping Kormick." Julia saw the steel return to Bristol's eyes, the resolve she always managed to summon no matter how bad things were. Julia had seen it on their first day of field training, when Bristol was pushed and tested harder than the others because of who she was. It hadn't deterred her. Bristol had hidden scars in her that made her tough, and yet she never abandoned her soft side. It was the ballast that kept her on course. "My goal hasn't changed," she continued. "Kormick started something the day he took a broken girl from a forest and manipulated her for his own purposes, and I am going to finish what he started." Her hazel eyes narrowed like she was already envisioning it. "Trust me, I haven't given up on Elphame just because of Tyghan. My goals don't revolve around him. He's just one more man and relationship gone wrong, and I've had plenty of them."

And this was the hurting side of Bristol. The defensive side ready to tear apart the world. Julia stared at her, waiting for more, and Bristol blinked, glancing at the ceiling again as if she felt every heavy second.

"All right, he is not just one more man," She admitted. "I say things when I'm angry, and so does he."

Julia still waited.

Bristol sighed. "You are so damn good at this," she grumbled, like Julia was forcing the words out of her. "Yes, I want to talk things out. Maybe. I don't know."

"Listening is what makes the talking part successful," Julia replied. "It's completely up to you. And him."

"I suppose so," she said, still resisting the thought.

"I want to help, Bri. You know that. I can step in if you need me to. You only have to say the word."

Bristol's gaze settled on Julia's. She nodded. "You're helping now, Julia. You're listening. Thank you."

"Always here for that," Julia said. She was about to venture a hug, even in the crowded ballroom, when her eyes darted past Bristol's shoulder. "Okay, he's walking over."

"Tyghan?"

"Yes."

There he was again, almost instantly, a wall of heat burning her back. "Kasta's about to announce the parley," he said. "Officers and commanders are lining up in formation. Two lines. We should be standing together as they enter." An intense sadness inched up her throat at the cool distance in his voice.

She swallowed and turned to face him. "Appearances. Of course."

They walked elbow to elbow across the room. "Esmee gave you something for your stomach?" he asked.

"Don't worry, I won't be delaying any proceedings."

"Did I say I was worried?" he replied. "Smile. People are watching."

"Touché, Your Royal Assness," she mumbled, but he pretended he didn't hear.

As soon as they took their places in line, Kasta announced, "And now I'd like to introduce you to the new premier nobles of the Danu court." The ballroom doors opened, and the twenty new witnesses flooded in like concertgoers rushing for seats. They circled in the center of the room, fae of all sorts, elven, ogre, spriggan, and Tuatha de, becoming an elegant whirlwind of tailcoats, bright buttons, swishing satin, colorful capes, and feathered hats. The laughter and chatter of the dazzling storm of nobles filled the air, until all of them settled at the other end of the room, except for one—a flamboyant Tuatha de dressed in a richly embroidered crimson coat. His long black hair fell in waves around his face.

He stepped up to Bristol and lifted her hand. "Lord Dowly," he said, nodding. "Dance, my lady?" She reminded herself that this was a dry run, a parley of knights disguised as nobles, but it all felt very real. Her heart skipped, uneasy at the charade, but she stepped forward, and he led her to the middle of the room.

A fiddle played somewhere in the crowd, and the dance began, a strange unknown one, halfway between a minuet and a jitterbug. Not knowing the steps, Bristol mostly stood still as he danced around her, but he occasionally grabbed her hand and gave her a spin. On one of those turns, she saw Tyghan, his eyes cold steel, glued on her. Lord Dowly laughed and chatted with her, so everyone could hear—just like a tipsy noble. "It's the latest dance in Eideris," he exclaimed, "at least according to my tailor. Dashing, isn't it?" And then he swung her into his arms, holding her snug for a long beat like he was trying to create a lasting picture, a story that would leave a mark. The music stopped, every eye fixed on them—especially Tyghan's—and then the enthusiastic noble released her.

He stepped back and bowed deeply. "Officer Reve Perry at your service, madame." Several of those present gasped, finally recognizing him. His demeanor changed from an excited noble to serious officer. He turned to the audience and bowed again. "And at the service of the Danu Nation." Kasta read off his service record and special skills, including his exceptional kinship with air and sounds.

As soon as Bristol returned to Tyghan's side, another knight broke free from the group, her flamboyant leafy gown trailing behind her as she descended on Avery and pulled her to the middle of the room. "Pleased to make your acquaintance. Lady Beechwood of Crown House," she said, patting Avery's hand as they circled the room. "Surely you've heard of the Beechwoods?" She fluffed her spriggan crown of leaves and moss and sighed dramatically. "Isn't it a chore to keep our ferns looking their best this time of year? But I do have a few secrets. I'd be happy to share with you. Do you have a moment?" She chattered mindlessly at the speechless Avery, the crowd tittering, until she stopped and bowed, introducing herself as third-year knight Sage Jarvis. "At your service, madame, and to all the damn court." There were more laughs, until Kasta read her extensive skills—and kills.

And so it went, witness by witness, knight by knight, as they made themselves known to everyone in the Winterwood ballroom, their names, personalities, and skills indelibly stamped in everyone's memories like they had always known them. *Walk-ons in a play*, Bristol thought. Each was an archetype—the show-off, the chatterbox, the empath, the wide-eyed ingenue, the know-it-all, the optimist, and more. A brilliantly selected team. They understood their mission: to flatter, infatuate, beguile Kormick, catch him off guard just long enough to give the Elphame troops the edge they needed to move in.

The room broke into applause, including Tyghan. "I'm convinced," he said. "Well done."

"We'll be covering all the logistics shortly," Kasta said, "but for now, spend some time getting to know your fellow knights as they will appear at the parley—and memorize their noble names and histories. Kormick will test you."

Memorization was Bristol's strong suit—her parents used to make her and her sisters memorize the plays of Shakespeare as part of their studies—so she already knew all the names by heart, but when the two lines broke formation and she started to walk over to the chatterbox and the optimist, Tyghan grabbed her arm. "We need to talk. Privately," he said and pulled her toward the door.

"You're making a scene," she whispered, but as soon as they were out the door, he stopped short, noting the guards milling in the hallway. And then he was pulling her tight against his chest and they were nightjumping, but this time his lips were not on hers and she felt none of his warmth.

CHAPTER 66

T he jump was short, and he released her as soon as her feet touched the floor. They were in a dark parlor she could barely see, but with a sweep of his hand, Tyghan roused a small flame in a stone hearth and it crackled to life, illuminating the aged log walls around them. The interior was nothing like the rest of the palace. It looked more like a one-room cabin in the mountains.

"A little notice would have been nice before you grabbed me," she said, rubbing her chilled arms. "Where are we?"

"The deepest heart of Winterwood. The first queen's quarters. It's rarely used anymore. I knew we could be alone."

"Someone could be here. There was a fire burning."

"The fire was started by the daughter of winter thousands of years ago. It never goes out."

A fire that burns forever? Through every storm? The thought intrigued her. She looked around at the small rustic room. It appeared to be lovingly tended, even if rarely used. The roughly hewn timbers surrounding them glowed in the flickering firelight, and multiple furs graced a simple bed on the other side of the room. She felt the room's safety and magic—at least until Tyghan spoke again and scattered her thoughts.

"We need to talk," he repeated, and folded his arms across his chest. It sounded more like an order than an offer.

Like the small flame in the fireplace that burst to life, resentment flared in her again. "So you said. You didn't want to talk last night. You ignored my questions and then walked out on me. And now I guess I'm just forced to listen to whatever you have to say."

His arms dropped awkwardly back to his sides. His eyes were fully focused on her. "I'm sorry. I should have asked you first. I didn't want to talk back there in front of others and—" He shook his head. "We don't have to talk. I can take you back if that's what you prefer."

Bristol remembered her parents' arguments. They were loud and passionate, usually ending with her mother storming out and going for a long walk. Bristol didn't want to drag this out for another day, or even another hour. However it played out, she wanted it settled.

"Go on," she said, determined to listen this time before she opened her mouth—because she still had plenty to say.

He motioned to two chairs in front of the fire. They walked stiffly to them and sat down, like they were facing a challenger in a game. A game that had no winners. Bristol waited—the same way Julia would. Tyghan leaned forward, his arms resting on his thighs, glancing at her, then away. He stared at his hands, clasping and unclasping them. She still waited.

"I couldn't talk last night, and I want to explain now." He looked up, his jaw tight, his eyes sharp glass, like he was trying to hold the entire world together. "I'm hurting, Bristol. I always try to pretend I'm not, that I'm fine. I have to be fine for everyone. But the other day, you told me I had to share my feelings." He bit his lower lip. "That's what I'm trying to do now, and I know I'm not doing it well, but I'm doing it the best way that I know how." He raked his fingers through his hair, searching for all the ways to avoid speaking, any distraction, but there were no hazelnuts to pluck from a tree and throw, no grove to swallow him up. He had initiated this talk, and he had nowhere to run. Against her will, she ached for him, and the struggle she saw in his face. "I want you to understand," he finally continued, "six months ago I almost lost my life—at the hands of someone I loved. I'm not sure I ever told you that, but it's impossible to explain what that does to a person. I still don't have the words. In that same exact moment, I lost my closest friend. As crazy as it sounds, I've mourned that loss for months, that lifelong friendship. Kierus was like a brother to me. And then, seeing him again once he was in custody—" He squeezed his eyes shut for a moment. "Hearing his voice. It gutted me all over again. It was like a day hadn't passed. It dredged up all the betrayal, anger, and pain still inside me. And all the loss. I didn't tell you about your father, because I'm still trying to figure this out myself. I just know it hurts. Maybe it always will."

The ache in her reached deeper. She wasn't sure if he was finished, but she remained silent, because he pursed his lips like he was still trying to get out more words. She waited, and they came.

"And then last night—" He gripped the arms of the chair. "I didn't expect an apology from you for the blackmail, but maybe . . ." His eyes shot up, fixed on her. "*Dammit*, maybe I did expect one for not telling me about Kasta in the first place. It was like you didn't grasp what it meant and how that day had changed me forever. Like you didn't think that I even had a right to know. For weeks you kept it a secret. What she did *mattered* to me. I lost my sense of trust that day and I've been trying to reclaim it ever since."

Bristol swallowed, seeing his pain—and her silence—in a new light.

He shook his head, his jaw rigid. "And just a few minutes ago in the ballroom—" He rose, pulling her to her feet, and turned her to face the small mirror on the wall. "When you were dancing, I saw this." He drew back her hair. She saw the bruising on the side of her neck, and the distinct dark impressions of three fingers. "Someone tried to kill you? Another thing you didn't think to tell me? That it wouldn't matter either? If not to me personally, then at least to all of Elphame?"

Bristol stared, shocked by the bruises too. Kasta's deadly grip left evidence. Yes, it mattered. And yes, she could have died and ruined everything if she hadn't been able to talk Kasta into letting her go. She would have told him, but her mind had been bursting with other things, things that mattered to her too. She whirled back to face him.

"How am I supposed to know all the things you do and don't want to hear, Tyghan? I can't read your mind! Every time I try to say anything about my parents, you shut down. So I keep those things bottled up inside me to spare you, things you've never heard and never wanted to hear, but they matter to me too."

He studied her, as if sifting through all the times he had changed and avoided the subject of her mother and father. "Then tell me now. I'm listening."

He returned to his chair, but Bristol didn't sit. Instead, she paced in front of the fireplace. "The pain you've suffered these past months is un-imaginable—I know that—but so was my lifetime of running from monsters I couldn't see. I don't think any of you have truly understood that. I always felt like I was being hunted. Every single day of my life. There were no breaks. The duffle bags always ready to go. The disturbed glances between my parents. The rushed departures just as we were settling in.

"My sisters endured the same. No one should have to grow up that way—distanced from everyone. Even in the mortal world I always felt like I was an outcast, that I didn't belong. Unlike you, I never had a best friend at all—I had no friends—only my sisters. We've both suffered, Tyghan, in different and unjust ways.

"But when it comes to my mother and the things she's done, I—" She drew a shaky breath. "I always hold the losing cards, and that weighs on me every hour of every day. How can I convince you of any-thing concerning her? Even around everyone else, I hear the silences when her name is brought up in my presence. I feel it like a burn on my skin. What do they say when I'm not there? *Kill the bitch*, like Cael shouted at the portico? I'm trying to make amends, to make things right, but who wants to make things right for her? No one. But I know things about my mother no one else wants to know, including you. You only see the monster."

She stopped pacing and faced him, swallowing back tears. "I know a woman whose parents were murdered in a raid when she was just a girl, a woman who was terrified and wanted a different life, who strug-gled to figure out how to live in a completely new world, a woman who played string games in laundromats, and cried at sunsets, a woman who loved teaching her daughters about the stars in the sky and who fiercely wanted another life, but she couldn't make it happen, because others wouldn't let her. A woman who had a gift, and Kormick twisted it into something ugly. And she had no one, *no one* else to turn to, only him—until my father came along. And maybe, maybe she is a monster now. Maybe that's all she is. But at one time, she wanted to be something else."

She took a step closer, her gaze fixed on his, her cheeks wet.

"I don't want to just save Elphame. I want to save *her*. There, I've said it. I want to give her something no one else will. Maybe something she doesn't even deserve. And maybe that's how my father and I are alike.

"I've held on to your promise to rescind the kill order for my mother, but last night after finding my father, I wondered if that was a lie too, and that terrified me." She reached up and swiped at her nose. "So yes, those are the things I never told you."

Tyghan pushed up from the chair and stood. "It wasn't a lie," he said. "I swear. I can't control the council and force them to change a sentence, but I do control my troops. I promise you, I did rescind that kill order, and that still stands, and will always stand." His gaze was unwavering. "I need you to believe that."

She searched his face—his eyes glistening—and she finally nodded, brushing at her lashes. "Julia said our differences would catch up with us if we didn't talk them out, and now they have."

He rubbed the back of his neck then nodded. "Then let's talk them out. Let's not leave this room until we've talked about everything."

And they did. They talked, and they listened, their conversation spilling out of order, one thought triggering another, biting their tongues, trying not to interrupt, but mostly following each other's lead. Mostly listening because they truly wanted to understand, more than they wanted to scream anymore.

Why didn't you tell me it was only a month?

I struggled with my choice and didn't tell anyone, not even Eris. I wasn't sure if I had done the right thing. He didn't just betray me. He betrayed an entire kingdom. If the council found out what I did, they'd convene and put

Cael back on the throne faster than I could blink. That could be disastrous. He's not ready. Too many plans are already in the works . . .

When I questioned her, Kasta confessed to me that she gave him a thousand years. She thought I was making a mistake to shorten his sentence. She tried to talk me out of it.

    But you shortened it anyway. Why? Have you forgiven him?

    No—I'm not sure—I don't know. I'm still confused by my own feelings, but one thing I know with certainty is that you love your father. I didn't do it for him. I did it for you . . .

My father called out Kasta's name from the pillar, that's why I ran to her instead of you. I was still in shock. And then I was angry. All I saw was red, and not all the consequences.

    I'm sorry, Bri, for the way you found him. I never meant for that to happen. What did he say when you let him out?

    He sobbed when I told him I was bloodmarked. He said they never wanted that for me. He was afraid for me. I told him that you were not Kormick . . .

Eris and I were shocked when we learned Kierus had a family already, with adult children, but mortal time is unpredictable and takes us by surprise too. It was only six months in our world, not your lifetime. That was the timeframe we thought in. Months. We had no idea that you even existed. If we had known . . .

All the times I shut you down. I'm sorry. I thought I was protecting you, but I was only protecting myself. You can talk about her, and I will listen.

    I sold her a dream, Tyghan, in order to get Cael back. It still feels like I sold part of my soul that day . . .

My father's a mortal. Fully mortal. When I let him out of the pillar, I told him to wait for me at the barn, but I knew almost immediately that he wouldn't. Now I've put him at risk.

Your father has always had a compass of his own. You're not responsible for what he does.

You were watching his back. You wanted to keep him out of trouble. Is it so hard for you to admit that at least some part of you doesn't want him to die?

No, not so hard. A big part of me doesn't want him to die.

Did Pengary try to hurt you?

No. He kissed my hand and thanked me for helping him, telling me not to believe all the stories I've heard about him. He said the centuries twist them and that one day I might be a legend too. And then he turned into an enormous beast and flew away . . .

A dragon.

Yes, a dragon with sharp claws and teeth, but he didn't use them on me.

They sat silently for a while, their words and feelings settling in, the only sound the crackling of the fire. Bristol's fingers strummed the arm of her chair, another thought still tugging at her. "In the last letter I wrote, I told my sisters my mother was alive, that I was bringing her home. Bringing both of my parents home. I shouldn't have said it. But I wanted it to be true. I'm afraid now. I can't let them down."

Tyghan leaned forward, his forearms on his thighs again, repeating the words she had said to him a few days earlier: "All of us are given powers from small to great. There is only so much one person can control." His brows rose. "See? I do listen to you. Every word."

She stared at him. A lock of hair dangled over his forehead. He looked as drained as she felt. "What are we doing, Tyghan?" she asked.

He was silent, his dark eyes simmering with thoughts, but still locked on her. His shoulders rose then, in a bare shrug. "We're stumbling, messing up, and loving each other."

"We're quite good at the first two," Bristol replied.

A faint smile creased his eyes. "But most of the time we're spectacular at the last one."

A weak laugh stirred in her chest.

He stood. "Are you ready to go back?"

She pushed against the arms of the chair, standing too. She took one last look at the room, the fire still flickering, casting warm shadows. "Yes, I suppose it's time." Tyghan walked toward the door, apparently intending to walk back instead of nightjump, the urgency gone. But something inside her wasn't ready to leave. She still needed more. More healing. More closure. More of each other.

"No," she said. "Not yet."

Tyghan turned, trying to understand what she was saying, and his eyes soaked her in. He took a hesitant step forward. "I'm not sure what—"

"I'm not ready to leave."

It was her eyes that spoke to him, more than her words. He swallowed.

"You can touch me, Tyghan. If you want to."

His eyes slowly swept over her. He stepped forward, his movement slow and considered, stepping close until heat radiated between them. "I want to." He raised his hand, swiping a strand of hair from her brow. "Bri," he whispered. Something was different between them now. It wasn't just desire driving them forward. A new reverence reverberated between them, a shared vulnerability.

His finger grazed the hollow of her neck and trailed across her collarbone, and then down to the first button of her shirt. Needles of heat shot through her, his fingers searing her skin. He worked the button loose like he was unlocking a treasure he had almost lost. One by one, each button was freed, and he slipped her shirt from her shoulders. It fell, whisper quiet, to the rug beneath their feet. His words were spent, but she felt his love in every measured move, every glance, even in the flutter of his lashes as he gazed at her.

Heat blazed over her skin, but she didn't want to rush the moment. She wanted to savor his breath, his touch, his gaze devouring her. His mouth came down, his tongue parting her lips, his hand at her back, expertly popping her bra free. He moved on to her trousers, no fumbling. He knew exactly how to make everything come undone, including her.

His lips slid across her cheek to her earlobe. "You are my soul, Bri, my light, and I will die before I ever hurt you again."

"Never say the word *die*," she whispered back. "We have a lifetime ahead of us. I don't care how many times we stumble, I will always come back to you."

She reached up and slipped his buttons free, a slow languid parting of his clothes, belt, shirt, trousers, all falling to the floor until every bit of his flesh and muscle was exposed, the hard planes and angles carved by firelight. He was still and yielded everything to her touch, even the scar he had once tried to hide. Her finger traced its jagged line, not in curiosity but in love, acknowledgment of what he had shared with her and her new understanding. She skimmed her hand up his arm, following the hard rise of his biceps, his skin burning beneath her palm. Her hand swept to the side then, pressing against the broad firmness of his chest, and her thumb circled his nipple.

His eyes drank her in, his breath grew husky, and then he gathered her up in his arms, his lips on hers again, and the darkness of the room swallowed them whole as he carried her to the bed.

He laid her down gently, the soft furs of another era beneath her back, the feeling of something ageless gripping them. Something inevitable. It vibrated in the air. History was written within these walls, not in great swaths of time but in fragmented moments like these. They were another layer of that history.

Bristol sank into the softness of the furs, waiting for Tyghan to join her. He was a black silhouette at the side of the bed, flames licking his outline like he was a dark specter about to consume her. Her skin burned. She wanted to be consumed. By him.

And he did, touch by touch. Her mouth, her breasts, her nipples, even places she didn't know that drove her to madness, his tongue skating down her spine, then nipping at the flesh of her lower back. They explored each other's bodies like it was the first time, taking nothing for granted. His fingers reached into her, plundering the slick wetness between her legs, stroking her, her pleasure building, breaths skipping, the throb growing. Her fingers dug into the blankets beneath her, and her breaths and moans intensified as she lost her grip and her mind crushed into one blinding thought. But then she let held breaths slip loose, and nudged his hand away. *Not yet*, she thought, and rolled over, pushing Tyghan onto his back. She wanted this single moment to be long, torturous. A memory they would never recover from.

She sat on his thighs, her fingernail barely grazing the full length of his shaft. "Let's talk," she said.

His breaths quivered. "*Now?* You expect me to talk while you do that?"

"I expect you to *try* to talk."

Her finger grazed him again. He swallowed, his arousal making his brain and mouth stop working together. "You want to play? How about if we change positions?"

"See, I knew you could talk. The Knight Commander always has something to say. But I staked out this position first. And I know you're well versed in strategic maneuvers."

His eyes narrowed, their blue ice piercing her. "You're a wicked vixen, but if you order me to lie here for a century, I will."

"Good. Because I want this moment to last forever. I want it burned into us. I want to see your eyes needing and wanting and loving me, and I want you to see the same in mine. I want to memorize every touch and whisper between us."

"This isn't going to be our last time."

"I know that. But it won't be the last time we stumble either. And when we do, this moment will be engraved in us. We'll remember. We can get past anything."

She leaned down, her lips lightly grazing across his like a signature on a precious document.

The fire popped then, as if in agreement, and they laughed against each other's lips. "Got it, Knight Commander?"

"Got it, Keats. And speaking of maneuvers—"

And with a flip that overtook her so fast she didn't see how he did it, she was beneath him again. "Time for more games," he whispered.

♟

Somewhere along the way, Bristol had gained the upper position again, and Tyghan's breath caught as she eased down between his legs, her mouth closing around him, squeezing, her tongue swirling, and his eyes clamped shut. His legs, his abdomen, every muscle in him tightened in response to her touch. *Mercy*, he thought, his groin burning as he searched for control. She slowed her movement, teasing him, drawing it out. Her taste and scent were still in his own mouth, assaulting his thoughts, and her moans undid him, his head lost, weak. But whatever glorious torture this was, he wasn't ready to let loose, not yet. He reached down, guiding her up onto his chest, holding her in his arms, a hunger so deep inside him, he never wanted to let her go. His hand glided over the curve of her hip and he breathed in her hair, her skin. He burned for every part of her. He wanted to loose the throbbing inside him, but when he did, he wanted it to come loose inside her. To press deep into her until they both were lost to each other.

"I love you," she whispered as her lips brushed his ear. Three quiet words, but they tumbled into him like something solid, something that held him together.

She gently ground against him, her breaths shivering. "Now," she said. "Go into me, now."

He didn't need a second invitation. He rolled over her and slipped his hand behind her knee, lifting her thigh. She wrapped her legs around him, inviting him to go deep, and he did. He was hard, eager, and she was wet. He plunged to the root, filling her completely, and she gasped, but screamed her pleasure at the same time. He paused mid-thrust. "Easier?" he whispered.

"No, all of it," she groaned, and her hips rocked up to meet his.

She was ripe, ready, and the sounds of her coming shot through him like fire. He felt her spasm around him, and he couldn't see any more, his blood molten, every part of him pulsing and pushing and pulling her closer, until their screams were not his, or hers, but theirs.

♟

They lay there for a long while, their hands entwined, soaking in each other, the moment, the crackle of the logs. Engraved. Bristol gazed at the small quarters, the rustic walls, the aged timbers, the fire that never stopped burning. The daughter of winter had built this room as a refuge in the middle of a blizzard. It had sheltered the first queen of Danu, and hundreds since then. Now it sheltered Bristol and Tyghan as they navigated their own storm.

They finally dressed because the world waited for them. Tyghan opened the door—they were going back the old-fashioned way— walking, so Bristol would know how to get there again if she chose to return.

Tyghan stopped in the threshold of the doorway, hesitating. "Before we leave, I have one last question. I need to know." He gently swept back the hair from her neck. "Who did this to you?"

CHAPTER 67

For once, everything on Eris's desk seemed to be in order. No messages to send, no meetings to call to order, no fires to stamp out. The trivialities had ceased to matter in these last days, so he had no squabbles to settle. Not even his own.

He and Dahlia mostly avoided each other, and that freed up time too. Evenings were spent at his desk now, instead of with her. She only seemed to grow angrier at his decision, digging in her heels that everything about their relationship had been just fine—that he was the one who had broken something that didn't need fixing. She hadn't actually said anything of consequence to him since he gathered his things from her room, but he knew all her ways, her silences, her glances, even the soft beat of her heart. But she didn't know his.

He shuffled through a few parchments that needed to be filed into the archives, but they weren't urgent. There was no rush—

There was a brief knock, and his door flew open. Tyghan walked in, disheveled, both in grooming and spirit. He was breathless, his hair uncombed. "Busy?" he asked.

"No. I—"

"Good. Was your offer in jest? I need a First Officer."

Eris studied Tyghan. Clearly something had transpired since they talked earlier. "I never make offers I can't deliver on. What happened?"

"Something else came up. Kasta is on limited duty until she can communicate all her responsibilities to you."

"And after that?"

"She'll be dismissed."

Eris nodded, wondering what further offense Kasta had committed. Dismissal was at least better than the punishment that the council would inflict. "What about Melizan or Sloan stepping in?"

"They're both leading critical regiments. Quin and Dalagorn too. I think you're the only one who can pull together all the duties Kasta handled. I've already set up a meeting between you and Commander Maddox at the garrison. Right now, in fact. She's waiting. She'll help outfit you—unless this is something that—"

"I'll do it." Old feelings came to life in Eris, like no time had passed since he last commanded troops at the Elphame court all those years ago.

"Good. I'll let her know."

"Thank you for believing in me."

Tyghan looked at him, perplexed. "I've always believed in you. If you say you can do it, you can. You always have. You found Bristol for us at the eleventh hour. Come down to the garrison as soon as you can." He turned to leave, but Eris called out to him.

"Tyghan, if you have just a moment, there's something I need to tell you."

🔒

Tyghan froze, his back to Eris. He knew what Eris was about to say. He heard it in his tone. His heart pounded. Afraid to believe it. Afraid not to.

"It's something I've put off for too long."

Tyghan gripped the latch, still facing the door. "I know," he said, and turned. Eris's eyes were locked on his. "I know you're my father."

Eris looked like he'd been punched in the gut. His mouth fell open, a question hanging in it that he couldn't even utter.

"I've suspected for a long time. Probably first when I was a child and my parents were gone and I didn't want to be alone—"

"You were never alone."

"I know. Even then I noticed you were always there for me. For everything. But you never said anything, so I assumed I was wrong. And you always talked so highly of my father too. Like you revered him."

"I did revere him. He was a good and respected man—and I wasn't. And he was raising my son with love and devotion." Eris swallowed, his expression stricken, and he motioned to the chairs by his desk. "Please. I know we need to go, but I'll make this quick."

Even though Commander Maddox was waiting for them, Tyghan nodded, and they sat down opposite each other. Eris told the story he began a week ago on the rooftop, but this time he shared details he had held back before. Everything he had wanted to say poured out, including the first time he held Tyghan, just hours after his birth. "I loved you the first time I held you in my arms, and when you opened your eyes and peered at me, I thought I was going to die with joy and grief because I wanted to tell the world I had a son, but I couldn't. In the years that followed, I ached to tell you, but it wasn't my place. Your mother had been through so much, and she was finally happy again, and Lord Jannison was a good man who adored you."

"What about my mother . . . Did you love her?" Tyghan asked.

Eris's composure faltered. "I—"

"Did you *love* her? Not as a queen but the way a man loves a woman."

The question swelled in Eris's chest. His chin finally dipped once in affirmation. "It was a brief affair. We were only together for a few months, but it seemed like a lifetime. Yes, I loved her very much."

"I always thought so," Tyghan said. "Whenever you mentioned her, there was something different about you. You never said her name in haste. Caroline. You'd bite the corner of your lip and pause like you were remembering some tender detail about her."

"I remember many things about her, things she told only me, and

I'll share them with you one day when we have more time. Commander Maddox is waiting."

They both rose from their chairs, but then Tyghan paused, facing the man who had been there for Danu and for him for twenty-six years. "I just want you to know, you're wrong, Eris. You are a good and respected man."

🔑

Dahlia swept into Ivy's office. "Eris isn't in his study. I have an important matter to discuss with him. Where is he?"

Ivy hesitated, aware something was going on between the counselor and the High Witch. Something as prickly as a pine cone.

"Ivy!" the High Witch snapped.

Ivy swallowed. "It's a delicate matter."

"And I am the senior-most member of the council, just below the king. I expect an answer, *now*."

"He left an hour ago. He was on his way to the garrison to meet with Commander Maddox and to get outfitted for the ceremony."

Dahlia was flummoxed. *Outfitted?* What else did he need besides his formal robes? And what could Commander Maddox have to do with it? She hovered over Ivy's desk. "Outfitted for *what*?"

Ivy's wings fluttered nervously. "No one is supposed to know yet, but . . . he is the king's new First Officer."

CHAPTER 68

Across Elphame, from the tiniest villages in the Whelky Lands, to the darkest lanes of Bogshollow, to the sparkling high towers of Lugh Bridge, windows were being shuttered. The Choosing Ceremony was in two days.

Creatures, from nobles to witches to trolls, were packing up and seeking refuge in the less traveled countryside, or in ancient mounds beneath the earth. Wild things tumbled in the wind, flying in hasty flocks to the southern islands to wait things out in caves, and forest sprites disappeared into the deep crevices of ageless trees.

It's almost time, a warning message whispered from fae to fae, whisked through hearts and hollows.

Mae packed up too, but when she came to her chest of gold, she paused, and her eyes glittered. It was getting harder to lift, but that was what centuries of prudent hoarding accomplished. She would need to employ some stronger magic to lift it this time. It warmed her gristled heart to know how much she had acquired in the last century, and usually in the easiest of ways. Fae were foolish things. But with the city shuttering windows and locking doors in anticipation of the ceremony, there were no customers coming to her store anyway, and that meant no more gold to fill her chest. It was best to move on, at least for now, to someplace in the country, away from the nonsense of kings and queens. Maybe she would return to Queen's Cliff, and stir up sightings of hungry dragons. She could always count on royals to give up handfuls of gold for information, whether it was true or not.

She peeped through her shutters. Yes, the streets were empty, everyone fleeing for less tempting targets in the country. There was no sense in staying. She swept her hand over a lustrous bolt of silk as she went back for her chest. It was an expensive fabric, and she hated to leave it behind. She paused, rubbing her bristly chin. *Why leave any of it behind?* She opened her bag of belongings and swept her hand through the store, all the bolts and goods tumbling and swirling and disappearing into her small bag. The goods would never come out quite the same on the other end, but it was better than losing it all. It would still have some worth. She prided herself on being a shrewd businesswoman. She hoisted up her chest of gold and left. In the end, she would come out ahead. She always did.

Of all the fae packing up, the steward of Elphame was surely the most reluctant and frightened. He was charged with bringing the Cauldron of Plenty to the Choosing Ceremony. He carefully wrapped and packed up the cauldron, sealing it in a sturdy crate for transport. He had dreaded this day ever since the queen died suddenly and her duties fell to him. Within days, the first attack on Elphame was launched. Fomoria had mostly been a forgotten, brutish territory on the northern border of Elphame, but always kept in check by the larger and stronger kingdoms. Not anymore. The power Fomoria wielded was crushing. The steward had never expected to be in this position. Would he even survive handing it over to the new ruler of Elphame?

CHAPTER 69

Kormick beamed at Maire in her green velvet gown. "You're magnificent, my dear."

"As are you," Maire replied. "Battle clothes become you."

He gazed in the mirror, admiring his newly tailored clothes fit for both battle and coronation. His cream-colored tunic and cloak would gleam in the sun as he stepped up on the Stone of Destiny. "It's all for show. There will be no battle, thanks to you."

The wizard who had prepared the amulets embedded in Maire's crown fastened the headpiece to the horns on her head. The diamonds shimmered against her copper hair. "My best work yet," the wizard boasted. "Step to the side, Your Majesty, and I'll demonstrate."

Kormick did as he was advised, and the wizard instructed Maire not to worry. He drew the broad sword at his side, slashing upward before bringing it down toward Maire's skull. Maire flinched, but a few inches from her head, the blade recoiled like it had hit a wall and flew from the wizard's hand, clattering to the floor on the other side of the room.

"The magic is good for at least ten direct blows. If any trouble should break out, not a hair on her precious head will be harmed," the wizard proclaimed. "Nor on yours," he added, pointing to the other crown he had prepared for Kormick. The antique gold was rich and dignified, which would be perfect for the ceremony. Kormick wanted every aspect of the day to be etched in the witnesses' memories. They would carry stories back to their cities, praising the day—and him. And with the cauldron in his possession, even kings and queens would be bending their knee to him. Especially kings like Trénallis, if he let him live at all.

"There will be no direct blows," Kormick said, but thanked the wizard for his craft and artistry. He dismissed him before turning to Maire. "Does that ease your worries?"

"I'm not worried," she said. "I only detest being in the middle of these large affairs. Besides, no one is going to challenge you, unless they're fools. You've already proven your strength to them."

Kormick lifted her hand and kissed the back of it. "I agree. But you deserve this moment. I deserve this moment. No kingdom will ever ignore us again. We've earned this, Maire. Let's see it through to the end. I need you there. Just in case. Please, I believe in you. Believe in me too."

And she did. He had always been there for her. He gave her what no else would. Power.

CHAPTER 70

It was the damnedest thing. Quin didn't know quite what to think. Seeing the Royal Counselor suited up in leathers for battle, instead of robes for tackling contracts and statutes, made his head hurt. Like he was watching some warped sleight of hand that was going to explode in his face.

"Stop gawking," Cosette said.

"Tyghan will explain what happened when he's ready," Melizan added.

"Maybe Kasta is ill," Sloan suggested. "When we have more privacy, he'll tell us."

"Ill?" Cully said warily. "She seemed fine this morning. A little jumpy maybe, but that's the only explanation that makes sense."

Quin rubbed his chin. "If she's so sick that even the High Witch can't get her back on her feet, then it must be serious."

All Tyghan had said so far was that Kasta was taking care of other matters in private, and that Eris was now his First Officer.

"He seems to know what he's doing," Dalagorn grumbled, as mystified as Quin. They watched Eris walking alongside Tyghan and Commander Maddox, just ahead of them, checking the wagons that would depart that evening. The wagons carried the tents and supplies to set up for the parley. The advance teams would also secure Danu's place on the rim of the valley and set up the tents so they were ready when the "witnesses" arrived. With forty witnesses, they'd have the biggest spread of tents on the rim. Eris gave the advance team specifics, the order of the tents, and exactly how far each should be set back from the rim—like he understood tactical maneuvers.

"One thing is certain," Cully said, "the counselor will scrutinize every last detail."

"And where the hell did he get that Gildan sword?" Quin asked. It had gemstones in it they didn't recognize. It was decorated with the three traditional rubies of a Danu knight, but also had an enormous trillion-cut emerald. No one, not even Tyghan, had an emerald like that.

Melizan silently noted Eris's physique, which his robes and loose clothing had always hidden. He appeared fit for the role of First Officer, but did he actually know how to use that sword on his back? But there was something in his walk, a certain swagger, not unlike Tyghan's, that told her, yes, he knew how to use it.

Tyghan and Eris signed off on the last wagon and headed back toward the officers.

"Thanks for waiting," Tyghan said, feeling six sets of eyes burning into him. "I wanted to speak to you when I had you all together." The news still turned his stomach, but he knew they were eager for an explanation. It was the last one he wanted to deliver. He remembered when he was crowned king, still on his sickbed and half-conscious. He had called Kasta to his side. She was the most detail minded of all his officers—and his close friend. Through gasps and moans, he asked her to be his First Officer—the *king's* officer. She had cried. He'd never seen Kasta cry before, and he'd thought it was for him. Now he wondered if it was actually because of her guilt.

"Is Kasta sick?" Cully asked.

Tyghan swallowed. "No. Before you feel relieved, I want you to know she has resigned her position." There was a murmur of disbelief, but before he was bombarded with questions, he continued. "I will not be sharing details, but Kasta has disobeyed direct orders and put lives

and the mission in jeopardy. Once she has shared all her tactical information with Eris, she'll be dismissed."

"No punishment?" Sloan asked.

Tyghan was silent.

Melizan saw him struggling for an answer, his chin dimpling as he
bit back words. "We all know Kasta," Melizan said. "Knighthood is
her life. Her resignation and dismissal are her punishment."

Tyghan's gaze met hers, and he nodded.

Eris motioned to the full wagons. "Everything is done here. Take
the afternoon to give your horses a last go-over, gather your things together, and turn in early. We leave two hours before dawn tomorrow."

Quin squinted. "You sure you're up for this, counselor?" He motioned to Eris's back. "That sword and all?"

"Hmm," Eris said, drawing the sword from its scabbard. "This
thing? I thought it was just for show. Maybe we should give it a go?"

Tyghan knew this moment had to come. Better they see it with
their own eyes. "Sure, Quin," Tyghan said. "Put the counselor through
a few paces."

CHAPTER 71

A lmost done here," Esmee said, brushing a curly lock from her forehead. "Just the powders to get in order." The cupboards of Madame Chastain's workshop were flung open as the witches searched for necessary supplies.

Olivia wedged another bottle into the box of potions she was packing. "All labeled, but I'll go over these with the sorcerers, just to be sure."

Dahlia rubbed her temple, trying to ease the tension pulsing there. Besides a handful of palace sorcerers, they had recruited twelve healers from the city to attend wounds—and there would be wounds. Her face pinched as she packed another box, bottles rattling. *First Officer? Has he lost his mind? And Tyghan! How could he even allow this? And without consulting her. She was the High Witch, dammit!*

Every potion she packed made her head hurt worse. Potions for bites! Claws! Bloody slashes! Suffocating spells! Potions to bring you back from the brink of death! The bottles clanked and rattled as she arranged them. Why was Eris doing this? To get back at her? All because of a few words? He had no business carrying a sword, now of all times. His powers were better suited elsewhere, like supporting her, Esmee, and Olivia.

She grabbed another box and moved on to bandages. All this for a few flowery words? It was nonsense. But—

It mattered to him. She had never seen him look so angry. At least not at her.

Why couldn't she say it? Why was it so hard?

"Dahlia?" Esmee said, her brows squiggled in a question mark. "I can finish that for you?"

Dahlia looked down. She was stuffing the bandages in a disorderly fashion—and Dahlia liked order. She quickly began re-sorting them. "I've got it," she replied, unhappy that she had let Eris invade her thoughts so completely. If he hadn't made this foolish decision—

But he had. He was done with her, and she with him. So be it. He hadn't fought in battle in thirty years, and now he was going to go off and get himself killed.

She stilled, her hands sinking into the bandages.

What if he does die? What if he dies over all this nonsense?

She tried to force her attention back on her work, but instead she heard Eris's last words before he walked out. *I won't keep paying for the sins of your past lovers.*

It wasn't that simple. Dahlia thought about Daiedes and all the lovers who came before him. Those wasted years. Until Dahlia came along, Eris had only had two lovers in his whole life—his wife and the queen, both good, loving relationships. But Dahlia had squandered her love on countless people who didn't love her back. Lovers who cheated, lied, and made a fool of her. She was incredibly good at making bad choices. Daiedes was her third husband, and he had especially broken her, being the greatest cheat of them all, carrying on behind her back, but in front of others. Of course she was cautious with her heart. *After eight years, maybe I am not the right man for you.*

She pressed two fingers to her brow, Eris's voice impossible to shake.

"You have a headache, Dahlia?" Olivia asked. "I can pull some of those tense energies for you?"

Dahlia shook her head. "No, it's fine now."

"It's a wonder we don't all have pounding heads," Esmee said as she latched her box. "We're packing enough supplies to treat every knight in Danu. We can only pray to the gods that we don't need it." She sighed, eyeing the other two. "I hear the city is emptied out, everyone packing up for less obvious targets. It's all becoming very real, isn't it?"

Dahlia's breath pooled in her chest.

Olivia shook her head. "Very real. The supply teams are leaving tonight from the garrison," she said. "I guess we're getting these loaded just in time."

"Yes," Dahlia agreed, "just in time." She fumbled with the bandages she was loading. They seemed to unravel in her hands no matter what she did.

Eris's voice broke in again, destroying her focus. *Whatever you're holding on to, it's time to let it go.*

Dahlia slid the box in front of Olivia. "Finish loading this one for me. I have some unfinished business to take care of."

CHAPTER 72

Cully sat in the shade of a tree near the reflection ponds, whittling his arrows. Curious fish broke the surface occasionally, wondering what he was doing. It was a peaceful place for such serious work. He had finished a full quiver already, but he reached for another thin ash branch.

Curled shavings fell in his lap as his knife slid along the wood, a soothing sound, the *scrape, scrape, scrape* of his blade against the dried branch. It was a rhythm he liked, and he let every ounce of his hatred flow into the small limb, making it even more powerful. He would fletch them tonight, but only half of them would be tipped. Without a forged tip, an arrow wouldn't fly as far or sink as deep, but it could slip past the cleverest of wards. And it would kill just like the others. Every single time.

Elven archers were a tight-knit group and took pride in the power of their arrows. Cully and his team had been honing and stockpiling them for weeks, and they were going to need them all. Fomoria would be paying for the terror they had inflicted on Elphame, for the many they had taken—like Glennis. He held his arrow up against the blue sky, examining its tip, so sharp it would barely be felt piercing a heart. Perfect. He added it to the quiver and started another.

Fresh-faced buckling, he thought, and smiled. His cheeks had burned the first time Glennis called him that, but now he missed it. There was no one to call him that anymore. Glennis had taken Cully under her wing from the time he was a young knight at the garrison. She would chide him, telling him to stand straighter, be smarter, work harder, but she did it in a way that made him want to do better, be better. She said it in a way that made him believe he could be the knight she expected him to be. And then she recommended him to Tyghan to join their squad as a junior officer.

He paused from his whittling as a young woman approached on the pathway that bordered the pond. She looked lost, out of place. As she neared, she spotted him and walked across the lawn to where he sat. "Excuse me, sir," she said, "I apologize for interrupting your peace, but I think I may have taken a wrong turn. Can you point me in the direction of the Ceridwen Library?" She explained she was a guest of the ambassador of Silverwing, who was meeting with King Trénallis, and the king had directed her to the library to pass the time because of her love of books. She was excited to peruse the volumes, but had strayed from his precise directions when she became curious about a flock of wild things flying overhead, trying to take notes about them in the journal she carried.

A mortal, Cully thought, judging by her demeanor. They always tended to be guileless when they first came. "Where are you from?" he asked.

"A place called Indiana," she said. "You've probably never heard of it. It's in the mortal world."

"Oh," Cully said, like he was surprised. "How did you come to be here?"

"It's an interesting story, actually. I was at a train station on my way to see President Roosevelt's inauguration when I saw a man walk straight into a brick wall. He disappeared. I stood there shocked, staring at the wall, and then he walked right back through it again. Of course, I accosted him with my burning questions. The man turned out to be Ambassador Thornbush. He was very kind and gave me a gold coin, a timemark he called it, and said he would be happy to show me where he was from. Since I had my bag all packed, I went. That was two weeks ago. I've been taking notes in my journal ever since."

"You're the adventurous sort?"

She smiled and nodded, her blond upswept curls bouncing. "I suppose I am."

Cully hoped the ambassador wasn't showing her too much. She seemed like a nice young woman. "I hope you have a pleasant stay. You're close to the library now. Just turn at that corner." He pointed the way to her. "Enjoy your book browsing, Miss—?"

"Wiggins," she replied. "My friends call me Ana. I'm only here for a short time and trying to gather as much information as I can about this world. Your kingdom is so different from Silverwing."

"That it is," Cully agreed. "But our differences keep it interesting. Most of the time. You know about the ceremony, right?"

"Oh yes." She hugged her journal to her chest. "If at all possible, I plan to be gone before then."

"Good," Cully said. "It won't be safe here for your kind."

She thanked him for his help and left, and he returned to his whittling.

Mortal or fae, it wouldn't be safe for anyone.

CHAPTER 73

Daiedes bemoaned the lump in his stomach. It weighed him down, making it impossible to move. He couldn't even sleep properly. And worse, the ferret had been tasteless when he swallowed it. He had dreamed of the moment for *ssso* long, but it turned out to be as unsatisfying as swallowing a rock—and it lay like one in his belly. He couldn't even remember why he had sought revenge on the creature, only that it had irked him by its very presence. Now he was stuck in this horrible position with a miserable ball of fur hanging in his middle. If only it had tasted the slightest bit *sssweet*. If only someone had warned him.

Madame Chastain stood before the mirror in Tyghan's foyer, looking at the pathetic snake and its sagging middle. She had cursed Daiedes two decades ago, sentencing him to be a mere decoration on a wall, yet to always be on watch so he might not be as completely useless as he was in life. But even her most powerful curses couldn't ensure worth.

"Wake," she ordered.

Daiedes moaned. "I can't."

"*Wake!*"

The snake stirred. "It's *so* heavy. It's hard to wake."

"Give up the ferret, Daiedes."

"What? It took so long to get it. I won't! I won't give it up. The king said I could have it."

"Shall I cut it from your belly? I will, you know. And that would be the end of you."

The snake groaned and hissed as, scale by scale, it shivered free from the mirror frame and fell with an inglorious thump to the floor.

"*It'ssss* humiliating," he cried.

How well Dahlia knew the sting of humiliation. Daiedes's cheating had cost her far more than she was ever able to admit. She'd been the last to know and had guarded her heart ever since.

"Give it up. Now."

Daiedes began twisting, regurgitating, inch by inch, the lump moving forward through the snake's sleek body, bulging and stretching scale and skin as it went. Daiedes wept with each convulsion. "It's mine. It's mine."

"Keep going," she said.

Finally, his jaws stretched wide, and with one last violent heave, the ferret popped out of his mouth onto the floor.

The ferret's fur was dry, the snake having none of the juicy insides needed to digest anything. Daiedes only had the memory of what a meal tasted like, from when he had been a human so long ago. If he ever truly was one.

The ferret was dazed, slowly stretching.

Dahlia nudged him with her shoe. "You too, Angus. Wake up!"

Angus startled, instantly shape-shifting to his human form.

"Fritz," Madame Chastain said, scrutinizing the large hulk of the former doorward of Celwyth.

"Madame," he returned, fear edging his voice. Fritz stared at her, weighing his choices. He was strong of muscle, but the High Witch was strong in deadlier ways. He avoided powerful creatures like her by stealing through the shadows in his ferret form. But there was no avoiding her now. He could tell by her gaze that she knew of his secret wanderings. Was this his true end? He squared his shoulders, waiting.

"Go back to Bowskeep, Fritz. Stop burrowing through the palace. Stop stealing art. Stay true to Kierus's last orders. Watch over his daughters."

Fritz's furry brows pulled together, and he sputtered over his words. "How— how do you know about Bowskeep?"

"We saw the wards you keep at the house there. They won't last forever. Go back where you're needed. Kierus is on his own mission now, and it doesn't include you."

"You're just letting me go?" he asked suspiciously.

Daiedes writhed on the floor. "Noooo. Sssstop."

"Yes," Dahlia said to Fritz. "Go back and fulfill your orders in Bowskeep—and stay there. Those girls need you."

Fritz nodded, and just as swiftly as he had changed to his human form, he shifted back to the ferret Angus, the form he liked best, and disappeared out the door.

The High Witch looked down at Daiedes.

She thought about all the time she had wasted on him, all the things he had taken from her, and the lesson she thought she had taught him. Instead, for years his garish presence had only been a constant reminder of her own foolish mistakes.

She knelt down, stroking his scales. He squirmed beneath her touch, afraid. "*Temeesh, arri sen fini.* Your curse is lifted."

The snake writhed, a hissing screech escaping from his mouth, his forked tongue whipping wildly about as he transformed, the golden scales becoming the hair she once loved, his sleek body growing in width and stature, his mouth becoming as perfectly beautiful and dangerous as it had once been.

He scrambled to his feet, staring at her, terror shining in his golden eyes. "What are you going to do with me now?"

"Nothing," she answered. "Nothing but let you go."

His eyes grew wider, still waiting for retribution, but when none came, he shuffled slightly, then bolted for the door. Dahlia didn't care where he went, but knew he would never cross her path again, not even in her thoughts, and that was what mattered most.

CHAPTER 74

Ceridwen Hall echoed with laughter. It came in nervous bursts, but any kind of laughter was welcome. Bristol and her squad were taking turns glamouring a book as they waited for Reuben. He was bringing them amulets for the ceremony, newly infused with strong protective magics. It was their final meeting with him before the ceremony.

Besides passing the time as they waited, the point of their glamouring exercise was to shave time off their techniques. Sashka was the best at it, barely waving a finger before the book was a wild tusked boar leaping off the table. But that didn't surprise any of them. Sashka was nimble, a sprinter, a graceful gazelle, who knew exactly which way to turn and when. She sat on the end of one of the other tables, her legs swinging back and forth.

"There!" Rose said with triumph, as she turned the boar into a vase of pink roses.

Avery laughed. "Well, that's sure to frighten an enemy."

"But it certainly would distract them," Julia quipped.

"If you shape-shifted to a lion," Hollis said, pointing at Julia, "*that* would distract them."

Bristol tipped back her chair, her feet propped up on another one. "We're prepared for this," Bristol said. "That's what matters."

"And that's why we need amulets?" Hollis asked.

"As prepared as we can be," Bristol conceded.

The door rattled, and Sashka groaned. "Here we go."

Reuben walked in, one of his precious satchels clutched in each hand. His normally sleek hair was disheveled, and some green foliage clung to it. With his hands full, he reached back with his foot and slammed the door behind him. It wasn't his usual stiff entrance. "Good morning, ladies," he said as he walked across the room toward them. "Sorry to keep you waiting."

"Okay . . ." Sashka leaned toward the others and whispered, "Who glamoured Reuben? Not even close."

"I can hear you, Sashka," Reuben said in a singsong voice. "We all have our off days."

He set his satchels on the front table and got down to business, telling them to gather round. He pulled out six sets of the thinnest chain mail wrist cuffs they had ever seen—and that was it. The squad arched their brows, almost in unison. *No belts? No buckles?* When they went to Timbercrest, they even had a full array of amulets sewn into their clothes.

"Esmee, Olivia, and I have been working on these for months," he said. "The problem with some amulets is that they can be cumbersome, or torn away in combat—not that any of you will see combat. These cuffs only come off at your will, or when their energy has been exhausted." He looked up, his dark eyes circling the table. "But it would take several direct hits of either blunt force or magic for that to happen."

His gaze settled into them to underline his point: *Don't get hit.*

"I have full confidence in all of you," he added, then looked down as if embarrassed, color lighting his sallow cheeks. He distributed the wrist cuffs, then opened the other case and pulled out a small tin. "I concocted it myself," he said, handing it to Bristol. "A balm in case you suffer any more burns when you close the Abyss and we're not there to help you. Some things you have to take care of yourself when you're in the field. It's powerful and effective, if I do say so myself. And finally . . ." He reached into the case one more time and set out six perfect apples. His lips pursed like he was deep in thought. His cheeks colored again. "A little memento of our first day together and all the weeks that followed. I know sometimes I can be exacting. And tiresome. Which is why I am keeping this short. Your stamina is to be commended."

There were a few seconds of stunned silence and then Reuben added, "Miss Keats, the shanty you inquired about is gone. I've been to the forest twice now looking for it, and it's completely erased, its occupant gone as well." His face looked like it was going to break, much like it did when she barged into his cottage and mentioned Willow's name. "If that's all, I'll be going." Bristol reached up, and plucked the leaf from his hair. He blinked several times, but couldn't hide the sadness in his eyes.

"Thank you, Reuben," she replied.

"If any of you need anything, I will be in my workshop. Otherwise, I'll see you at the ceremony." He left, his head bowed.

When the door was firmly shut, Sashka hooted. "What was that? When did he get so . . . *nice*?" She said the word like it was something frightening. And it rather was, since it was so out of the ordinary.

Hollis picked up an apple, carefully examining it. "Think they're poison?"

Avery took a chance and bit into hers. "It's delicious." When she didn't instantly die, the others picked up theirs.

"What happened to him?" Julia wondered.

Rose shrugged. "I don't know. I just wish it had happened sooner."

Bristol stared at the door Reuben had just closed, feeling both relieved that Willow wouldn't be complicating her father's effort to hide and sad for the loss she saw in Reuben's eyes. *It was magical*, he had told her just a few days ago. Now he had nothing to go back to. Not even rickety shanty walls that held memories of a lost love.

Reuben had never been the man any of them had thought he was.

CHAPTER 75

Pounding hammered through the darkness from the moment the first Danu contingent landed on the rim, the sounds of tents being raised. But as the first purple hues of dawn rose on the valley, Tyghan saw the tent city that Shane had described. *Breathtaking*, Tyghan thought.

Colorful tents trimmed in silver and gold, with scalloped edging that flapped in the breeze, glowed with the morning light. If he had been there for a different reason, the fullness in his chest might have even felt like pride. *Jewels*, Shane called them. Tyghan had a sudden deep ache, wishing Bristol was by his side to see it with him. It had only been a few hours since he kissed her goodbye, but he missed her already. He also had a nagging need to watch for threats, to sleep beside her, his arm tucked safely around her ribs. He couldn't help but worry, especially after Csorba referred to her as an asset, like she was a piece of property to be caged and used. Who else, right beneath his nose, had similar thoughts? Greed was never in short supply, not even in Danu.

Her squad was with her, and that eased his worries. The six were skilled and devoted to one another, a rare union, almost as if the gods had interceded to match their skills and temperaments perfectly. Or maybe he just had Eris to thank for that. Tonight Bristol would be with him, but by tomorrow she might end up in the middle of it all if Maire opened another portal. *If only Maire were dead*. Guilt clawed inside him for even thinking it. Not only because of his promise to Bristol but because he hated that Maire had been used—in the same way Csorba wanted to use Bristol. He knew Bristol would never stoop to the depths her mother had reached—there were always choices along the way— but he wished Maire could have had more of those choices.

His attention returned to the city of colorful tents. Sounds drifted across the valley, shouts of cooperation as more tents were hoisted, frying pans clanked, fires stoked. He heard the hope swelling, kings and queens preparing for a parley, a peaceful one, because none of them could take on the endless army of the restless dead.

Neither could Danu.

As he scanned the rim, Tyghan recognized their colors—the green and gold of Cernunnos, the maroon and red of Greymarch, the white and silver of Amisterre. Every kingdom was present, their banners already fluttering in the morning breeze. Every kingdom except Fomoria.

The spot on the rim Shane had pointed out as their usual place to set up for the parley was empty. Tyghan had no doubt they were coming, but Kormick would make a dramatic entrance, just like he had at Timbercrest. Tyghan squinted at the empty spot and smiled. He slowly rubbed his fingers together, then flicked one, carefully casting a focused bit of energy across the valley. No one would feel or know he was bending the light around them. The blank spot rippled, like a finger touched to a still pond. He breathed out a satisfied breath. Good. Fomoria was there. They were only glamouring it from everyone's eyes until their grand entrance. What did Kormick expect? For everyone to fucking applaud?

But what was an outrageous thought for most was a perfectly rational one for Kormick.

Tyghan glanced behind him, the Danu tents still going up—because they had more tents than everyone else. The Danu reds and golds taking up so much space would be an irksome, brilliant sight that Kormick couldn't miss. He was probably watching already.

The first rays of the rising sun were just eclipsing the hills, the purple hues of the sky transforming to vivid blue. Eris walked away from the tents to join Tyghan. "It's almost time," he said.

Quin, Dalagorn, and Cosette ambled up behind him, ready to stand watch. The opening of the garrison portals had been perfectly timed. They couldn't open them too soon and risk someone stumbling through them accidentally, but neither could they wait too long. Bristol could only be in so many places at once, and tomorrow morning she would be closing the most important portal of all—the Abyss. As the rising sun lit up the city of tents, Tyghan grabbed some of that light and amplified it, just enough to make those on the other side of the valley squint and look away, as anyone might. It was going to be a spectacular sunrise.

♟

Bristol stood in front of the rock with the symbol of the crescent moon. Her squad and Commander Maddox stood behind her—and a whole garrison of knights were behind them.

"Now," Maddox said. Bristol raised her hand, concentrating on the first coordinate in the valley. It was high above the stand of oaks where she and Tyghan had made love and she told him for the first time that she loved him. Energy flared from her hand, up her arm, and her lashes sparked with brilliance. She forced the light to go wider. Wide enough that a regiment could ride through it, twenty abreast. And when she saw blue sky over a distant valley, she said, "Now," and Avery tossed the bird cupped in her hands through the portal.

♟

Tyghan and his officers waited, their breaths held.

"There's one!" Cosette finally said.

Only seconds later, Dalagorn whispered, "Another. That's two."

They watched discreetly for the third and fourth. A small bird in the sky was nothing of note for those in the valley, and the glaring sunrise covered any light that might have escaped with them. But when the fourth bird emerged, it was hard for any of them to contain their smiles. Four in a row were a signal of success for Danu. Bristol had opened the portals. Tyghan relaxed his hand, and the glare from the rising sun returned to normal.

Only a minute later, another tent appeared on the rim. Its silver and black banners shimmered in the bright morning light. Fomoria had arrived, and a hush fell over the city of tents.

🔑

And so the parley began. Kings, queens, knights, and witnesses slowly ventured out, putting on the show that Kormick required. Even the white stags of Cernunnos draped their antlers with strings of pearls, and the goblins of Bleakwood wore their best silk jackets and gowns, pulling at the ill-fitting collars and sleeves. The pungent scent of roseclaw, mugwort, and cloves wafted through the air, depending on which tent you were near, every kingdom hoping to summon whatever protections they could, but they walked the rim with chins held high, putting on a show, discussing nothing but good weather and good food.

Sizing up the competition? The notion almost made Tyghan laugh. Not one of the kingdoms came with forces—including Danu. Behind their beautiful billowing tents you could see miles of hills, and they were all empty. Only the twenty witnesses that Kormick had allowed were there, and it made for an odd affair. Tyghan loathed strolling to greet other monarchs, sharing chitchat like they were at a village fair after the summer harvest. No one was sizing up anyone. They were enduring. Every king and queen met Tyghan's eyes with trepidation. *What is Danu going to do? Step up? Or bend a knee? Where is your army?* Tyghan could tell them nothing without the risk of tipping his hand.

Four tents away from Danu, the king of Silverwing put on an especially extravagant spread. Spits turned over fires, and the spicy aroma of roasted game drew dozens for a taste. This was something Cael would excel at, drinking and eating with other royals until the stars came out. It was a skill Tyghan hadn't appreciated until now.

"Will this ever be over?" Melizan whispered between gritted teeth.

Quin groaned. "Never. We still have eight kingdoms to go."

"Let's go back," Tyghan said. "We've made our appearance. We'll do the rest later. They know we're here."

They, meaning Fomoria.

Sloan and Dalagorn didn't miss a beat and were already turning around.

Quin and Eris walked just behind them, Quin plying Eris with more questions about their sparring practice from the day before. Quin was a stout, strong knight, and he was both annoyed and awed that Eris had played him, roundly disarming him in a burst of cuts. Tyghan hadn't told anyone yet that Eris was his father. There hadn't been time, and he was still getting used to it himself, even if some deep part of him had always known.

As they approached their tents, they saw that their Noble Knights—in full costume—had arrived. They were already putting on an amusing show for other kingdom participants strolling past. Seconds later, Cully, Madame Chastain, Reuben, and the rest of their entourage arrived. Reuben proceeded to ward the tents, and Madame Chastain nodded to Tyghan, indicating Cael was delivered and safely sequestered. Cael would hate being cooped up in a tent until the ceremony, even if it was less than a day away. Madame Chastain's eyes shifted to Eris, but he seemed to make it a point to not look her way.

The Noble Knights were especially loud and lusty with their laughter. Everything was just as Tyghan had envisioned after speaking with Shane. *It was a once-in-a-century affair. Nobles who had no business being there tagged along too. It gave them bragging rights to history.*

Cosette sucked in a sudden breath. "Behind you. Ten lengths," she said. "They're coming."

CHAPTER 76

That didn't take long, Tyghan thought.

A crowd drew Kormick like a moth to a candle. "Remember," Tyghan whispered to his officers. "We're not amused by the nobles' presence. We're annoyed."

Tyghan turned.

Twelve Fomorians approached on enormous gray steeds with silky black manes. Tyghan had to admit, their horses were magnificent. If Fomorians knew how to do anything right, it was breeding the beautiful beasts. And Kormick cut quite a regal picture atop one. But his warriors were a scarred, monstrous lot, their muscular shoulders barely contained by uniforms. And they looked thirsty, but not for drink. They eyed the crowd like they were already bludgeoning heads.

"Trénallis," Kormick said, shaking his head. "It seems all the other kingdoms understood the agreement. Twenty *only*. What do you have to say for yourself?"

Tyghan remained silent, defiant, like a ruler who was cornered but unbowed.

"Beating your pathetic chest by flaunting the rules? It's what we all agreed to."

Is that him? An excited whisper from the crowd of nobles behind Tyghan. The chatterbox.

I think so. He looks like a king. The know-it-all.

Ohhh, I'd love to meet him. The ingenue.

"Quiet!" Tyghan growled at them. He turned back to Kormick. "They insisted on attending. Nobles and council members. I warned them not to come. They tagged along anyway."

Kormick raised a quizzical brow. "You can't even control your own subjects?" He scoffed with contempt and swung his leg over his horse to dismount.

We should have listened to the king and stayed home. The rule follower.

But I didn't want to miss this! It's the event of the century! The adventurer.

He's more handsome than I expected. The flirt.

Kormick stood eye to eye with Tyghan. His warriors dismounted too.

"Go ahead," Tyghan said, his gaze steely as he met Kormick's. "Get rid of them. You'd be doing me a favor."

Kormick remained planted in place, like he was searching for a lie in Tyghan's face. "My scouts tell me you have no troops behind you. As long as it remains that way, you won't have to be watching the skies for dark clouds. See how reasonable I can be, Trénallis? And unlike you, *I* can control my subjects." He pushed past Tyghan. "Now to meet your rule breakers, to see if they stay or perish."

The crowd received him and his warriors, offering up a believable amount of fear at first, with a chaser of curious adulation. Officer Perry crowed convincingly about how much he had heard about the king of Fomoria, and Sage Jarvis made sure there was a continuous hum of excited chatter.

Time ticked by as Kormick moved through the group, speaking with one noble after another. Eris's gaze met Tyghan's. *This is either going to go well, or very, very badly.* A smile on Kormick's face was no indication of anything positive. Melizan, Cosette, and Sloan discreetly circled around to be in position, if events turned violent.

Finally, Kormick stepped away to where Tyghan waited. "They can remain. They only wish to be witnesses to history, and they will have

that wish. It seems your subjects are looking forward to the transition."
He and his warriors got back on their horses. He leaned forward and
said quietly to Tyghan, "Remember, little king, if any blood is shed in
this valley tomorrow, it will be by your hands."

"The only blood I will shed is yours, if I don't have my brother
back by the end of the day tomorrow. I've met your demand and come
without troops."

"Of course," Kormick replied. "I'll be glad to be rid of him."

After he rode away, Eris stepped up and said, "Nice touch. You
exuded reckless bravado and frustration. He expected nothing less."

Dahlia intercepted Eris as he walked to his tent to get his jacket. "What
are you doing, Eris? You haven't been a knight in thirty years. What
is this all about?"

"Isn't it obvious? I'm doing what I've always done, working to pre-
serve a nation."

"Not as a knight! A sword does not belong on your back!"

"My son asked me to take on this position."

Dahlia's next words stalled on her tongue. "Your son? You told
him?"

"Yes, when *my* timing was right. And I hope you give him the grace
to tell you on his own. Stay out of his personal business, Dahlia."

Her face caved. "Please, can we go into your tent and talk? I only
need five minutes."

Eris looked over his shoulder. Tyghan was waiting for him. "As you
can see, now is not the time. But when we get back to the palace, I'm
sure Ivy can find a place in my schedule for you."

Dahlia watched him walk away. Was this what she had done?
Shoved him into one little compartment of her life that was safe and
scheduled? She rubbed her brow. She wanted to tell him she had let
the past go. That she only wanted to move forward and focus on their
future. She sighed. He never looked back as he walked away, but she
wouldn't give up. When this was over, she would make an appointment

with Ivy, if that was what it took, to tell him exactly what he deserved to hear.

🔑

The evening wore on as bonfires were lit, more game was roasted on spits, and casks were opened. Cully scoffed at all the food. "Do they think this is their last meal?"

"Could be," Dalagorn said, unbothered by the plethora of food. "At least something worthwhile is coming out of all this wallowing."

But the dancing was the last straw. When Bogshollow struck up their drums and fiddles, the Danu contingent headed back to their camp. This wasn't a party, and even Fomoria wouldn't buy that Danu was celebrating.

When they reached their encampment, Tyghan spotted Sashka, and then Hollis talking with Officer Perry, and finally his eyes landed on Julia. She was standing outside his tent, and he hurried over.

"Julia," he said, breathless.

She smiled. "I suggest you retire for the night, Your Majesty. Tomorrow will be a long day. I will stand watch for you."

He nodded and went in.

His tent was dark, only a tiny flame flickering in a lantern cast a thin light. His gaze swept the shadowy corners. As she pushed her hood back, Bristol appeared, an ethereal apparition becoming flesh. He ran to her and held her, his hands rubbing her back, his lips brushing hers, her mouth eagerly opening to his. "I missed you," he finally said.

"What will we do if we're ever apart for more than a day?"

"Die," he answered. "How long have you been here?"

"Only a few minutes." She told him she slipped inside as planned while the others gathered information outside. "You saw the birds?" she asked.

"All four. Like clockwork."

She smiled. "Thank god."

He assured her it all went according to plan, and Kormick suspected nothing. "It's all going perfectly, Bri."

She asked him a hundred questions about the parley and the other kingdoms and the city of tents. "It's impressive," he said. "I wish we were here for another reason. You'll see it tomorrow."

She told him more about what was going on at the garrison. "The regiments from Eideris and Greymarch arrived. Maddox is getting them positioned for tomorrow." She bit the corner of her lip, her eyes suddenly dark. "And my mother. Have you seen her?"

"No," he answered. "We didn't see her, but we rarely do. He keeps her out of sight. But I'm certain she'll be here and visible tomorrow. Kormick wants a spectacle." He squeezed her hand. "I know it's going to be hard for you to see her, especially beside him. You'll be okay?"

"Of course," she answered. "I have no other choice."

Her lashes fluttered downward for a moment and when she looked back up, he recognized the mischief in her eyes. "Now that we have a few private minutes . . ." She slipped a finger in his belt and tugged him closer.

"So what kind of sex is this going to be?" he asked.

"Quiet sex. The walls are thin, and the tents are close. You don't want your knights to think you're having more fun than they are, do you?"

He shrugged. "Maybe?"

"Don't you like a challenge?"

"I'm up for it. But it *will* be a challenge, especially with what I'm going to do to you."

Julia, Avery, and Rose cleaned out their saddlebags, making room for new provisions. They startled at a sudden crash and crack of wood from the king's tent. Rose and Avery jumped to their feet, drawing their daggers. "Slow down," Julia said. "Bristol is in there with the king."

Rose wasn't convinced. "But the noise. Something might be wrong."

Julia smiled. "I think the king's cot was just a casualty of enthusiasm."

They heard muffled laughter coming from within the tent, a pleasant sound at the end of a tense day.

♟

Tyghan and Bristol lay sprawled across the floor of the tent, trying to suppress their laughter. "Shhh!" Bristol said, pressing a finger to his lips.

He still laughed against it and pulled her hand away. "At least the cot held up until the important parts were over."

Bristol fell into more suppressed giggles. It felt good to laugh with him. Necessary. It had been too long, and who knew how long it would be before they could laugh again. She remembered the first time they made love and he confessed to her that he loved her laugh. She loved his too. It was a sound that made her feel like everything wasn't madly wrong with the world, and for at least a little while, some things were exactly right.

CHAPTER 77

The squad left under the cover of predawn darkness. The Abyss wasn't far away, and their steeds were fast. They could get there, close it, and be back long before the ceremony started at noon, leaving plenty of time for anything extra that came up, like burns. Bad ones. Bristol had Reuben's balm with her, just in case.

When they were high enough and far away enough, they finally broke their suffocating silence.

"I threw up last night," Rose said. "I'm not sure if it was because of the excitement or because I found out I was eating goose for dinner."

Rose didn't eat fowl, which was understandable. Even when she was a hawk, Rose wouldn't eat other birds. Too much of her human sensibility stuck with her.

"I have a potion Esmee gave me for my stomach if you need any," Bristol said. "Mine's been a little touchy too."

"I'll take some of that," Hollis said, rubbing her belly. "I think it's just the tension."

"I should have asked Esmee for a six-pack," Bristol replied, and they laughed.

"A six-pack?" Avery said. "I'll take one, but make it a good pale ale, with pretzels."

"You're in luck," Hollis said. "When I was shopping, I saw a pub in town that can set you up with that—just like back home."

"I heard the town was empty," Avery answered. "Everyone is leaving for safer places."

Julia sighed. "True, but they'll be back when this is over."

The words hung in the air. *When this is over*. It all hinged on so much going right. Every time Bristol thought about facing her mother again, she felt queasy, not about her own lies and deceptions to get Cael but at the thought of her mother standing at Kormick's side.

Sashka broke the grim silence. "Okay, these aren't last words or anything. Don't read too much into it, but I want you all to know, I love you. You know, before everything goes down. That's all. I love you. All."

Hollis laughed. Rose teared up and wiped her eyes. Julia grinned. "We know that, Sashka. You've shown us every day. But it's still nice to hear. You know, before everything goes down. We love you too."

Sashka nodded. "I knew that."

"Remember that first day we all met?" Hollis mused. "I was terrified when Julia shifted into a cat, never mind a lion. There wasn't a chance I would shift into a mouse at that point."

Julia suppressed a laugh. "Luckily, mice have never been on my menu."

"I was terrified by Ceridwen Hall," Avery confessed. "It was so big. All those floors of books above us? I thought I had gotten in way over my head."

Bristol chuckled. "I was certain I had. I was trying to figure out how to gracefully sneak out of the room."

"Nah," Rose said, "you were tough from the moment you got there."

"Tough and reckless are two different things."

They reminisced about their first days together and how far they had come, what they had learned, and the wonders they had seen. And the sorrows.

Hollis sighed. "So much has happened. It seems like a lifetime already."

The others murmured their agreement.

They descended over the ridge of mountains and down the gorge, until they came to the steep cliff that held the Abyss portal. They hovered for a moment, making sure there were no Fomorians or demons present outside the hellhole.

"This is it," Bristol whispered. The others nodded their readiness and drew their swords, ready to be her ears, eyes, and shields so she could concentrate only on the Abyss. Bristol landed on the ledge, a fair distance from the portal in case any tentacles reached out. She stared at the towering rock and felt its corrosive darkness reaching out to her already. Instead of bees humming in her chest, she felt the loud drone of misery, the pounding and screams of centuries. A suffocating gloom clutched her throat.

She stepped closer, eager to get it over with, then gave a last glance at her palm, smooth and unburned, and wondered if she would ever see it that way again. She punched her hand into the portal before the wretched drone could consume her. Her hand sparked with brilliant dark light. Purple and black tendrils twisted around her arm, traveling up to her shoulders, lashes, and hair. A powerful *whirr* buzzed over her skin and blinding sparks flew from her hand. It was intoxicating in a different way from the other portals, a thrilling fear streaming through her like the light was inviting her in. *Join us.* Instead, her grip tightened on the light. It tugged back, the dark power of the ages, but then she knew she had it. She controlled it. She saw demons within screeching, writhing, knowing the power she had over them, and they clawed their way toward the portal. She closed her fist and yanked hard on the buzzing light, saying, *Duseen o duras nay tulay—may this portal be no more.*

And just like that, the screams, the demons, and the Abyss portal were gone.

She looked down at her palm, and there wasn't a single blister.

She blew out a cleansing breath. Tyghan was right. *It's all going perfectly.*

CHAPTER 78

This time when dawn arrived, it was greeted with bleak silence. There was a new addition to the landscape. Tyghan and the Danu contingent looked down at the valley.

Melizan cursed. "I don't think that's part of the traditional pageantry."

"Doesn't trust us much, does he?" Eris said.

Tyghan's nostrils flared. "Now who's beating his chest?"

Below them, Kormick's warriors, witches, and wizards stood shoulder to shoulder, five deep, creating an impassable circular wall around the tall stones that made up the Mother Ring, ensuring that no last-minute contenders got past them and entered the sacred grounds.

Dalagorn dragged his hand over his knotty cheek. "There must be a thousand of them."

"Eight hundred forty by my calculations," Eris said.

"Is that all?" Cully said. "I feel much better now."

Tyghan eyed the circle, already contemplating changes to their plan. "We'll need to adjust our timing."

Quin cracked his knuckles. "Fuck. Look up."

They were so busy looking down at the valley, they hadn't noticed a small black cloud looming in the distance.

Cosette squinted one eye. "Think it's rain?"

They reconvened in the main tent, Esmee and Olivia casting fresh wards to keep their words within.

"We can get through their wall. Divide and scatter," Tyghan said. "That's not a force meant to scare off a whole army. It's meant to scare off kingdoms that only came with twenty witnesses."

"Fast and quick. That's our strategy," Eris said. "Kormick has this orchestrated down to the last breath. We're going to jostle his applecart. Take them by surprise and don't give them a chance to regroup."

Tyghan agreed. "Once we've thinned their numbers, we can bring out Cael."

Officer Ailes shook his head. "But he likely has an army of more warriors standing by, possibly thousands, only a few hills away."

"Sure he does," Eris said. "But so do we, and ours are far closer."

"What about that cloud on the horizon?" Officer Perry asked.

"I don't think it's any bigger than the one we beat back at the palace," Sloan said. "We can handle it."

Sage Jarvis cursed under her breath, the leaves on her head stirring. "One cloud maybe, but there could be a lot more on the way."

More. The small word tripped through the silent room. More restless dead that could put an end to all their well-laid plans.

"No more."

A new voice rose from the back of the tent. Every head turned toward it.

"The Abyss is sealed." Bristol raised her palms. "And no blisters."

The sun was high. In minutes, the Stone of Destiny would be ready to break its hundred-year silence. Queens, kings, and their witnesses dotted the valley floor, and the steward of Elphame read from his scroll, hailing the rich history of the Stone and the cauldron. He stood on a distant knoll, far from the ring of warriors glaring at him. His voice wobbled. On either side of him were two powerful kings, and next to one of them was the Darkland monster.

Tyghan had watched Kormick enter the valley. Everyone had. When

Kormick dismounted from his magnificent horse, there was a hush. His cream-colored cape shone in the sun, and his crown glowed against his golden locks like he was an anointed god. But when Maire shed her invisibility beside him, there was an oppressive silence. Mouths fell open. Few had ever seen the Darkland monster, and she was not what they expected. Maire was stunning. Her long copper hair gleamed like a fiery sunset, and the horns twisting around her head twinkled with a sparkling diamond crown. She was only visible for a few moments because the same guards who protected her at Queen's Cliff provided a barrier between her and everyone else. But the spectacle Kormick wanted was achieved, and it would wipe the word *monster* from their mouths and minds. She was a beautiful symbol of his power, and no one would forget it.

Tyghan wondered how Bristol was feeling, seeing her mother this way, a unified force with the enemy. *I'll be okay. I have no other choice.* He wanted to give her other choices. She stood somewhere behind him, invisible, but prepared to act if her mother reopened the portal.

A timeless heartbeat thumped the ground beneath Bristol's boots, a new century of rule poised to begin. Even though her cloak kept her invisible, the sun beat on her just the same. Sweat trickled down her back, and the fury simmering beneath her sternum felt like it was about to blaze through her shirt. Seeing her mother quietly standing beside Kormick almost shattered the restraint inside her. He hadn't saved her mother out of charity, like he made her believe. He saved her because she was a prize. A possession to achieve his goals. He had been anticipating this moment for years. Bristol had her father's tiny switchblade in her pocket. She hoped to gift it to Kormick. Right in his throat.

"His crown is a powerful ward. So is hers," Madame Chastain whispered, as if she could read Bristol's thoughts. "It would do you no good to attack him yet. Wait until the magic is spent by others."

Bristol rubbed the cuff on her wrist, still full of protective magic. Unlike her, Kormick had great powers within him, even when the magic of his crown was spent. She remembered Melizan's long-ago warning. *He's a demigod, same as Tyghan. You'd be a fool to underestimate him.*

The parchment shook in the steward's hand as he continued to read the proclamation. "Now is the time for any who believe they are worthy to come forward. Let yourselves be known. There is no magic within the inner circle of the Mother Ring, only the magic of the Stone of Destiny dwells there. It will judge those who step forward, and choose the new ruler of Elphame, and the custodian of the cauldron for the next one hundred years."

The warriors surrounding the ring pounded their thick spears on the ground in unison. It rattled like a death cry across the valley.

No one moved.

Kormick smiled, soaking in all the eyes fixed on him, and took a step forward.

But then Tyghan stepped forward too.

Kormick's glare was swift and sharp. "Are you begging me to destroy you, Trénallis?"

"No," Tyghan answered. "I was just giving my troops the signal to destroy you."

And then the sky opened up.

CHAPTER 79

Tyghan was already moving forward, while his officers behind him shouted orders to their squads. Kormick shoved Maire toward the protection of the Mother Ring, shouting, "Summon more! Summon them all!"

The ring swallowed her up, but three lines of warriors stormed forward, shields raised, as the sky above them filled with Danu troops on horses. Kormick drew his sword, and Tyghan charged him. Their blades rang out when he blocked Tyghan's strike. "You've made a deadly mistake, Trénallis."

Tyghan had anticipated this moment, but Kormick was three seconds behind him, his plan gone awry, and it showed in his eyes. He was using rage to push forward, not strategy.

The blows between the kings were fierce and fast, years of resentment boiling between them, Tyghan forcing Kormick backward, step by step. Five of his strikes hit home—Kormick's chest, shoulder, and gut—only to bounce off, almost making Tyghan lose the grip on his own sword— but even a protective ward couldn't withstand direct hits forever, and he saw the worry on Kormick's face. Blood from a clash somewhere overhead spurted down on them, spraying Kormick's pristine cape.

"What's taking you so long?" Tyghan taunted. "Go ahead, destroy me, Kormick." He swung hard, sending Kormick back several steps.

As Kormick stumbled, he fisted his free hand and threw a desperate, vicious punch into the air. A stinging burst of energy as sharp as knives knocked Tyghan backward, cutting into his neck and arms, and he rolled across the ground. He lost sight of Kormick as he disappeared behind warriors, and now six enormous brutes bore down on him.

🔑

Bristol could barely hear Cully shouting orders. An explosion of pandemonium made it hard to hear anyone. Everything moved fast. Kingdom witnesses were screaming and running back toward their camps. The first troops to come through the portal gathered them onto their horses two and three at a time to carry them to safety. Cully summoned the knights' horses while Eris, Quin, and Melizan shouted more orders, until they were drawn into the battle too. Officers Perry and Jarvis took to the air, directing incoming regiments, and the other Noble Knights dispersed to direct ground troops. Bristol ran forward, hidden by her cloak, her squad surrounding her.

They circled wide around the warriors protecting the Mother Ring, searching for an opening for Bristol, and hid in the shadows of a stand of oaks. The warriors' barrier had thinned as hundreds of them leapt forward to fight off the knights descending upon them, but there was still a tight line two warriors deep. Wizards between them worked to maintain a protective ward above the Stone of Destiny.

Her mother was somewhere past the warriors, and Bristol had heard Kormick's last order to her, *Summon them all!* How long before she discovered she couldn't summon them and opened a new portal? Bristol had to reach her—quickly. They searched for a gap, a way for Bristol to get past the warriors, but then a new threat bore down on them. The small cloud that had been so far in the distance was now overhead. The restless dead. The cloud didn't look so small anymore. It cast an ominous fluttering shadow, and she heard the familiar screeches. This time, Tyghan couldn't summon his dark web of lightning because Danu troops were still flying in through the portals.

Two hideous hyagen with thick leather wings and sharp claws

swooped down between the trees, their jaws snapping as their riders prodded them lower and lower. They circled the squad like wolves, ready to devour them. Rose gasped, turning in all directions, the terror of the maze and the day they were stalked gripping her. *Sweet fuck*, Bristol thought. *Not again. Not this time.* Bristol pushed back her hood, shedding her invisibility, and drew her sword. Their squad stood back-to-back, slashing at the creatures as they darted down at them. Sashka leapt upward like a swift gazelle, nicking the underside of one, and it spiraled high into the air, screeching. The other swooped again, and Avery swung on its retreat, slashing off the end of one of its wings. It squealed and tumbled, falling to the ground, and Julia plunged her sword into its heart. When the other hyagen came back to investigate, Bristol had the perfect angle and sliced its head from its torso. A bloody last breath spewed from the stump of its neck, but there was only a split second of relief. The rider who had tumbled from it jumped to his feet and drew the sword on his back. His hair was brilliant red, like a blazing sunset, but with none of the wonder, and his skin still looked like it was turned inside out, thick veins crawling across it like worms.

"Do you know me?" he asked softly, in the same refined voice that didn't match his monstrous exterior, a voice that sent chills down Bristol's spine. He was still obsessed with being known. Being remembered. Even if it was for all the wrong reasons. She recalled his boastful banter with Tyghan as he held a sword to her throat, reliving his past glory.

"I could never forget you, Braegor."

He smiled, his yellow eyes glowing, delighting in the recognition. "Bris-tull Keats and Rose. So nice to see you again—and this time you brought two friends." He eyed Sashka and Avery. His sharp sword flashed in the shadowy light. "Ready to join our army? I promise we have a nice space for you."

"Five friends," Bristol corrected him. "You never learn, do you, Braegor?"

Before he could speak another word, Julia and Hollis sank their swords into his hideous back, and the sharp tips punched out through his chest. His smile and his glory were gone, and his patched-together body crumpled to the ground.

How many times has he died this way? Bristol wondered. Maybe clinging to his infamous name and past glory was the only solace he had in his miserable existence.

Glory. Kormick searched for the same thing. And he used anyone in his path—like her mother—to get it. The fury inside her burned to a sharp point.

"Gods, they stink," Hollis said, wiping the rancid mucus off her sword onto Braegor's shredded pants. Julia did the same, and then Rose pointed in the other direction, at the ring of warriors.

A barrage from a platoon of spear bearers above them took out four Fomorian shield warriors, a split-second gap in their human wall appearing. Bristol lifted the hood of her cloak and ran for it. Her squad already knew what to do—stay behind, stay invisible, and listen for her. *I'll search between the stones and the shadows for her. My mother will balk if she sees you. If I scream, you'll know I need help.* Bristol knew it would be excruciating for them to let her go—they were a team—but she had to do this part on her own. She would not be delivering false hopes and dreams to her mother this time. There would be truth between them. She had to reach the woman she had once been. Beneath the hard exterior, she knew her mother was in there. Somewhere.

🔑

Dahlia and Reuben stood on a protected plateau just below the rim of the valley. From there, they had a view of it all, especially the hottest battlegrounds. Their hands were busy casting blinding mists over stampeding Fomorian warriors just entering the valley. Word had reached them at their fortress, or they had been nearby all along. Dahlia prayed to the gods that their numbers would dwindle soon.

She and Reuben also provided cover for injured knights as they were carried away to be treated by Esmee, Olivia, or one of the other healers in the tents above them. It kept the witch and wizard alert and busy. Dahlia glanced at the sky fighters at the north end of the valley.

Eris was somewhere in there, but the blur of battle and blood made it impossible to see him. Every time a body fell, her heart fell too.

"Now they're coming from the south as well," Reuben groaned, sweeping his arm out and casting a mist so thick it would blind them. Unfortunately, wizards who traveled with them dispersed those same mists with spells of their own. It was a task that was never finished.

Dahlia noticed a ward on one of the supply tents was fading, and she cast another spell to strengthen it. All magic was being tested beyond limits. They had all heard Kormick's shouts, *summon them all*, and she hoped that Bristol had reached her mother and was able to prevent the Abyss from being reopened. No magic or will could survive an endless assault of evil.

♟

"*Maire!*"

She heard the faint shout, chopped up by the sound of screams, clanking metal, and her own pounding temples. More Fomorian warriors flew overhead, joining the battle. *Maire!* A fist tightened in her heart, the sound too familiar. Too impossible. Maire angled her head, listening, but the screeches high above her wiped out the sound.

She stood between two of the standing stones, hidden by a shadow. *Summon them all!*

She had never done that before. A small number of the demons were deadly, but all the evil of millennia would block out the sun—and she liked the sun. Still, she would release a large number of the restless dead, enough to end this quickly.

The small cloud of demons she had summoned last night had already spread across the valley, but when she summoned more from the Abyss, she didn't feel the usual tremor in her veins, nor the intoxicating surge of power in her lungs. She tried again, calling the demons to her, but there was only deadness in her chest. The thrum that made her safe— that made her invincible—was gone. Cold sweat sprang to her brow. She panicked, searching for the rush of power. She needed it. *Come to me! Come to your liberator!* There was nothing. No hum, no rush, no exhilaration. Was it her crown? Was the ward blocking her power? She reached up and threw it from her head, and tried again. Only an empty echo. Her belly turned to ice. Why couldn't they hear her?

A clear voice spoke behind her.

"They're not coming, Mother. I closed the Abyss."

"Where's Tyghan?" Dalagorn shouted as he maneuvered his horse through the sky. "He should have been here by now."

But neither Eris nor Quin had time to answer as they slashed and dodged one restless dead after another. The cloud may have been small from a distance, but it was dense, almost a solid wall of stench, claws, and blades, swirling around them.

Melizan and Cosette fought in tandem, as they always did, not far away. They were a machine together, stabbing and slicing methodically, more united and determined than ever not to be headed for Paradise anytime soon, even if it would be together. The bloody remains of their victims fell in a steady stream below them.

Cully fought on the other side of the valley, leading platoons of archers from Eideris through the sky, targeting warriors below, their aim so perfect their arrows slipped between the seams of thick leather vests.

"He'll be here!" Eris finally called to Dalagorn, then yelled to Quin, "Watch below!" Dalagorn and Eris made a nosedive, circling to stop two restless dead speeding up from below. They speared them both before they reached Quin, but the thrashing hyagen slashed Eris's shoulder on its way down. "I'll tend to it later," Eris said when Dalagorn told him to have a healer search the gash for claws. It could wait. Eris knew exactly how long a claw could remain in his flesh before it started consuming him, and right then, more important things mattered.

Only seconds later, a mist that Dahlia had cast cleared in a breeze, and Eris saw her working as hard as he was to save the nation they both loved. He felt a tug in his chest and wished he hadn't been so sharp with her outside his tent. On the heels of that thought, a demon dove past Dahlia. Its hyagen grabbed her in its jaws, then tossed her over the plateau to the ground below.

Eris's heart plunged as he raced to reach her.

♟

Tyghan couldn't nightjump, not in the midst of this chaos. He might jump right into the path of a swinging blade. And his sword was beneath the enormous boots of one of the outsized warriors.

The brutes closed in on him and his hand swept the air, barreling a ball of fire into the face of the closest warrior. With his other hand he sent a freezing mist into the eyes of the next one. Both of them fell to the ground screaming, but the third stabbed a spear toward Tyghan's head that he barely escaped by rolling, and the fourth swung an ax toward his chest. He leapt to his feet and summoned his now freed sword back to his hands. More warriors descended on him. He couldn't get a break. And then he felt heat behind him. A secure shoulder against his.

"Always have someone covering your back. Isn't that what you taught me? I've got your back, brother. I'm here to help."

The voice made Tyghan's breath stop up in his lungs. An ache squeezed his throat. "Better late than never," he answered. "Horses are on the way."

And then they moved in synchrony. Like they always had.

"On the count of two," Kierus said. And they charged forward, beating back the enemies, one after another.

CHAPTER 80

What new hell is this?" Quin shouted.

There was a break in the onslaught, and the others turned. In the distance, two huge, shadowy figures swooped through the sky, long tails trailing behind them. Their enormous pointed wings banked, and the creatures dove, the scales on their backs reflecting the sun.

Cosette gasped. "Fucking dragons."

"Avydra," Dalagorn said, his thick ogre lip twisting. "The smaller ones."

"But big enough to swallow *you* whole," Quin assured him. "First, they'll roast you." He hissed. "How many more beasts can we take on? Especially ones that size."

Melizan squinted. "Look," she said. "Look closely at those small shadows around them. They're hunting an incoming regiment. *Of Fomorians.* I think they're helping us."

"God, I've missed this. Never thought I'd say that," Kierus said.

"It's a surprise to me too," Tyghan grunted as he halved a hyagen.

Their horses had come, and Tyghan and Kierus fought side by side with other sky fighters, Perry, Sloan, and Jarvis nearby. Sloan had only briefly raised his brows. Kierus was fierce and holding his own, making as many kills as the rest of them, so for now, he was on their side, and nothing else mattered.

"I'm sorry," Kierus said after they dispatched another restless dead. "I should have thought of another way. I'm sorry I made a bad choice. A frightened choice."

"I know. I saw your painting."

"But in some ways, it was a good choice too."

"In some ways, yes," Tyghan reluctantly agreed.

"She is smart, Bristol."

"I know." It seemed that was all Tyghan could say. And discussing this *now*, of all times? While they were fighting for their lives? He couldn't understand, but it felt good. Good to have something back, maybe something that could never be lost or destroyed.

They spoke between dives, dodges, and stabs, their words punctuated by the heavy breaths and grunts of battle.

"You love my daughter?"

"Completely."

"You'd do anything for her?"

"Is this an interview? Now?"

Kierus laughed. "Sounds like it."

"Anything."

"Then you know. You know what it's like. Bank right!"

Yes, Tyghan thought. *I know.*

A huge piece of carcass fell between them.

"You like it?"

"Like what?"

"The painting."

"*Like* isn't the right word. I hate it. But it's good."

"I hate it too. Its why I have to keep painting it. I'm sorry," he said again.

"I know," Tyghan said again. He knew.

"Behind you!"

They both spun instinctively, like a precise timepiece, still remembering how they moved together, and a restless dead was split in three clean pieces.

Tyghan spotted a flash beneath another hot spot of the battle. It was Eris, making a crazy, dangerous dive toward the floor of the valley. Something was wrong.

"Team with Sloan!" Tyghan told Kierus. "I have to check on Eris!"

But Kierus had other places to be—and another person to find. Someone who needed him. He hadn't seen her brilliant copper hair anywhere. He had even called her name near the Mother Ring. The battle only drowned him out. But the skies had thinned now. His chances were better. Or he would hunt down Kormick. The coward always kept her close.

Eris dodged hyagen, restless dead, and Fomorian warriors as he dove in a straight line to where Dahlia had fallen from the plateau to the shadows below. He refused to lose sight of her. The short distance seemed to take forever. He finally landed near her still body and jumped from his horse. All he saw was blood. Pools of blood. "Dahlia!" he cried as he ran to her, hoping for any signs of life. He fell to his knees and brushed her silver hair from her forehead. He called her name again, and looked at the gashes around her abdomen. He pressed his hands to them, but the blood only gushed through his fingers. *Cantes! Shant!* He shouted every spell he knew to close, weave, and stop. The flow slowed, but he had to get her to Esmee or Olivia.

He scooped her gently into his arms. "It's all right, my love," he whispered. "You're going to be fine."

Her eyes fluttered open. "Eris?"

"Yes, it's me. I'm taking you to Esmee. Everything is—"

"Eris, I'm sorry. At the tent, I was going to say—"

"Don't talk. Save your strength," he ordered. "There's nothing you need to say. We—"

"Yes," she said weakly, "I need to tell you." Her gaze rose to meet his, her pale blue eyes glassy. "I love you," she said. "I've always loved you."

"I know. Hold on, Dahlia. You are my rain. Without you I am the scorched earth."

He pulled her onto his horse, holding her tight against him, and then Tyghan was there, clearing the way for him as they rushed to get help.

"Where are they?" Kormick screamed, not expecting an answer from the twelve guards who surrounded him. He scanned the sky. The restless dead were already thinning—and no more clouds were in sight. His army of warriors was thinning too. How long could they last without the endless supply of demons streaming in to support them?

Below him, there were still too many archers for him to take a chance and make a run for the Stone of Destiny. The protective ward above the ring and his wall of shield warriors would keep it secure for now. He circled, trying to get a glimpse of Maire, but he was too high to see her. Only the tops of stones and the dark shadows they cast were visible. Had she summoned the dead as he ordered? She had to be there, safe in the shadows somewhere. "Go down," he ordered one of his guards. "See what's taking her so long!"

The guard had just reached the ground when he was shot by an arrow, killing him instantly. Elven arrows. Kormick hated the creatures. He ordered another guard to go down, and he left hesitantly.

And then Kormick spotted a figure skirting the standing stones. Maire? He flew a little lower on his horse, and saw her weaving among the stones again. Chestnut hair. No horns. *It was Bristol*. She hadn't left as promised. Was she the one thwarting Maire? He reached up and touched the crown on his head, its protective magic humming beneath his fingers. Other than with Tyghan, and a small skirmish as he escaped him, he hadn't encountered any other combat that would deplete its magic. He could risk a few arrows—and use his remaining guards as a shield for the rest.

Maire whirled, her eyes flaming. "What have you done?" she said, not as a question but as an accusation. "You promised me you would leave."

"I lied. You know about lying, Mother. Can we stop now? Can we finally stop?"

"You said if I gave you Cael—"

"You aren't listening, Mother. *I lied.* I said what you wanted to hear."

"For *Cael*?"

"No. For Elphame. For Father. For Cat and Harper. For you. I'm taking you home. Your time here is over."

She shook her head like Bristol was speaking gibberish. "How were you able to close the portal?"

"Isn't it obvious? I'm bloodmarked just like you. The tick is gone."

Guilt flashed through her mother's eyes. She glanced down at her palms, like they itched. The power. Bristol understood. She had felt its enticing allure too. "You don't understand," Maire said. "I need—" She turned away and lifted her hand to a stone on the outer perimeter. A bright stream of energy burst from her palm making the stone light up. She began to name coordinates, "The caves, the—"

Bristol raised her palm too, allowing her own energy to stream out and wind around her mother's, and then pulled back. She felt the sharp tug of her mother's energy snapping. Maire's light and power disappeared.

"Stop!" her mother screamed, her chest shaking as she gasped for breath. She lifted her hand again, brilliant light streaming out once more, and Bristol did the same, choking her power, closing it up before it could even take hold.

"I will do this all day with you, Mother. You are not reopening the Abyss. Please. Come home with me."

Maire's eyes glistened in the shadows. "You don't understand this world. You haven't been here long enough. Kormick—"

"Kormick is done! Can't you see his power waning already? You owe him nothing!" Bristol stepped closer and grabbed her mother's shoulders. "Listen to me! Sometimes you get another chance, Mother. This is yours."

Her mother's eyes locked on to hers, and the pain Bristol saw in them was bottomless, the depth endless. Bristol ached for her, but she wouldn't back down. She kept a firm grip on her shoulders. "Remember, Mother. Listen to my voice, and remember. Listen to Cat and Harper and all of us laughing around a campfire, Daddy playing a tune on his harmonica. *Listen*. You are the strongest woman I know. You found the dream once, and you can find it again—and this time, you'll keep it."

She saw the panic in her mother's face, still resisting, but Bristol wouldn't stop, not trying to sell her something false this time, but something true, something her mother once had: her love of her loom, the seashore, powdered doughnuts, rose oil baths, orange soda, and her family. "Your family wants you. We want you back."

Bristol watched her mother's eyes transform, like Bristol had finally shaken something loose inside her. The cold glass faded, and her eyes became the ones that searched the night with Bristol and pointed out the stars, the eyes that sparked with pride when her daughters recited a play without missing a line, the eyes that held dreams as she wove another colorful scarf. The eyes that looked over her husband's shoulder, admiring his new painting. Her green irises shimmered with puddles.

"I love you, Mother. It's not too late."

And then a furious shout destroyed the moment, and they both turned toward it.

It was Kormick, surrounded by guards, spears in hand. "Open the portal!" he shouted at Maire. "Summon them now!" And then to Bristol, "Step away from your mother. Closer to me."

Closer? His gaze was deadly. He didn't want her closer for old times' sake. He wasn't Mick with his eyes full of lust. He was Kormick, filled with hate. He wanted a clean shot at her. He wanted to kill Bristol without harming Maire. But then she noticed a glimpse of something else in his gaze. Terror? A shine in his frozen eyes pinned her in place, and his parted lips were set with dread. The dawning was sudden, cold needles pricking her spine. She stood near the inner ring of standing stones, closer than him, only one stride away from a place where the earth felt footsteps—and judged them. If he charged her, she had only one direction to run—straight to the Stone of Destiny itself.

Her mother moved fully in front of Bristol. "Kormick, she's my daughter."

Distant shouts erupted from the opposite direction.

"Bring her forward, Maire," he said more urgently. "And she'll be fine."

Metal clanked and golden spears beat against shields, the sound of combat getting closer. A wall of knights pounded a path through the warriors still protecting the ring—clearing it for another squad that ran toward it. Cael was in the middle of them.

"No!" Maire cried out. "No!" Bristol wasn't sure if she was shouting at the knights or Kormick, but she grabbed Bristol and swept her behind the inner standing stones and into the Mother Ring. Kormick screamed and ran after them. Maire kept going, her grip iron around Bristol's wrist. The Stone of Destiny was only thirty feet away.

"Mother—" Bristol knew her intent and strained against her grip, like the time her mother dragged her toward the portal to send her home, but this time nothing could stop Maire. She was thwarting Cael, Kormick, maybe all of Elphame. She was summoning a different kind of power. *Come to me.* She was a mother dragging her daughter away from a park and rubbing herbs in her hair and whispering spells to protect her. Determined. She dragged her to the center, more screams erupting, not just Kormick's anymore, and just before Maire reached the center, she stopped and pushed Bristol onto the Stone of Destiny.

CHAPTER 81

Tyghan and his officers saw their chance. Their troops had overcome and killed the restless dead, and thanks to some bizarre intervention of the gods, dragons in the distance were culling the incoming troops of Fomoria. Their warriors were either roasted or retreating. It was a mystery to all of them, but it gave Danu the edge they needed to snuff out hot spots on the valley floor.

Now they attacked Kormick's last precious stronghold, the already diminished shield guard of warriors and wizards around the Mother Ring. Danu hit them from all sides, Cully attacking with archers on the other side of the ring and Tyghan leading forces who paved the way for Cael. Bristol's squad had reported that she made it into the interior, and it was clear she had been successful in stopping her mother from reopening the Abyss, but Tyghan was desperate to reach her, to hold her—to tell her that her father was here and fighting on their side. Fighting with Tyghan.

His platoon broke through the wall of warriors, and as they charged through the standing stones, he caught a glimpse between them. A tunic. An arm. A flash of brown hair. They emerged onto the sacred grounds, but after only a few steps in, a sound he had never heard before drowned out all the chaos. Everyone froze, unsure where it came from. It swept upward through the stones, like wind plucking a tune through the trees, exultant. Decisive. The sound vibrated through Tyghan's bones. *The Stone of Destiny*. It was hailing a new ruler of Elphame.

🔑

Bristol dragged herself to her feet, her legs weak, every part of her unbelieving. She turned. Every direction she looked, she was met with blank stares. Disbelief. Cael. Tyghan. Kormick. Shocked. Silent. "No," she said, "No. No." She couldn't think what else to say. To do. This was a mistake.

The silence was fractured by Kormick's enraged scream. He yanked someone out from behind one of his guards—a man bound and gagged—and held a wide dagger to his heart.

Panic gripped Bristol. She couldn't summon even the smallest fireball to her fingertips. Magic didn't work within the sacred ring. But a dagger—

"Let him go!" Tyghan yelled. "It's over."

There was a crazed glint in Kormick's eyes. "It's never over."

Maire screamed. "Don't," she pleaded. "Please—"

"You did this, Bristol," Kormick said. "Remember that every day of your miserable reign. You should have left when you promised."

Before any of them could move, he plunged the dagger into her father's chest, then ran through the stones, disappearing instantly. A nightjump. His guards fled too, knights in pursuit. Maire ran to her husband. Tyghan was there first, pulling Kierus into his arms as he collapsed. "Outside the ring!" he yelled to everyone else—where magic would work. Dalagorn helped him carry her father out to the meadow, and they laid him on the grass. Maire fell to his side and pulled away his gag.

"Do something!" Bristol screamed at Tyghan. He was already pressing on the wound and whispering spells, Kierus's blood pumping through his fingers.

Bristol vaguely heard shouts to summon the High Witch. *Get her! Now!* Sashka raced away. Tyghan worked furiously to heal the wound to Kierus's chest. Julia dropped to her knees beside Tyghan, using all her healing powers to help him too.

"Maire," Bristol's father whispered, a peaceful sound among the panic. "Maire. I've saved you. Again, my love."

"Yes," Maire answered desperately, her hand cupping his cheek. "Yes. Again. We'll go home now. We'll go home to our daughters."

He smiled, so faint his lips barely moved, and then his eyes stilled.

Maire stared at him, like she didn't understand, or maybe she was just absorbing the peace in his face.

Something snapped inside Bristol then. Something behind her sternum, kindling set afire.

Tyghan still worked on Kierus, refusing to believe he was gone. "Come on, you bastard. Come on." She heard the tears in his throat.

Bristol stood and stepped back, pulling up her hood as she walked away so no one would follow. She summoned Zandra and took to the sky, her face numb, her hands numb, but a blaze burned in her chest. No nightjump was far enough away that she couldn't find him.

Never over. And she believed him. One day he would come back for her mother. Or for Bristol.

From high in the sky, she saw a few hot spots still flaring in the valley below. But her sights were set elsewhere, and it didn't take long to spot Mick far ahead of her, his creamy regal cape flashing in the wind and sun. He was retreating toward Fomoria with his guards, five altogether. *No, Mick, you're not running off. Not this time.* She eyed them, sizing them up like game. A fool's challenge. She was ready to be a fool. Zandra was fast, and they were quickly closing the gap.

She heard Camille's warning.

Some never change back. They forget their old lives.

Ignore it. That's all you have to do.

But she couldn't ignore it. She didn't want to.

A guard flying ahead turned, pointing her out to the others. Kormick saw her and circled back, because they were alone in the sky and his vengeance on her father wasn't enough. Bristol had taken something from him, and no revenge would ever be enough.

Nor for Bristol. The burn glowed inside her, no longer foreign but something she had always owned.

You soar far above it all . . .

Every part of your body moves differently . . .

Something calls to you to forget your other self . . .

New instincts overtake you . . .

It's seductive, the incredible power . . .

Kormick was close now. She could already see the smile on his face. A demigod raging with power and eager to use it. He circled around her, like she was a trapped bird. "Your father came after me, and look what happened to him. He wouldn't give up. Just like his daughter. How do you wish to die, Bristol? Fire? Sword? Quick? Slow? You've never seen everything I can do."

Bristol glanced at her fingers, knowing it might be the last time she saw them, then leaned forward and whispered to Zandra, "It is time for you to go home now, Queen. Swiftly." Then Bristol rolled from her saddle and plunged toward the ground.

Instead of resisting the burn beneath her breastbone, she welcomed it, and the flame inside her exploded into something blinding and hot. She felt the claws first, not just the gentle blue moons beneath her nails but long, sharp claws unfurling that were meant to tear and shred. The ground was coming up fast. She thought she heard Kormick's laugh, and then her ribs expanded, her arms and throat grew, and finally a loud popping sound rent the air, like a sail catching wind, and she felt the updraft beneath her wings. Its power was intoxicating, and she breathed it in deeply, like it was everything she had been waiting for, *living for*. Her fear was gone.

You want to fully sink into who and what you are . . .

She was a beast, and she sank into it, embracing every scale, tooth, and claw.

Mick shouted for his guards, his voice different, all sounds different, even the monstrous rumble of air over wings. She sucked it in, her massive lungs hot and glorious. His guards returned, creating a tiny wall between her and their king, their swords drawn and raised. She wondered if the smile she felt could be seen, if it glimmered beneath her nostrils. She swooped and banked, felt the battering and pinpricks of their weapons, a pain in her underside, and then the rush, the *bump bump bump* of her wing knocking them from their steeds. They became screaming shadows plunging back to earth.

She angled her enormous head then, studying Mick, her large golden eyes seeing him differently. Seeing him as prey. A thing to be roasted and eaten. He hurled a fireball at her, and then another, the flames singeing her wings, and she heard a squeal. Her own. And then a painful roar when he hurled his sword through the air and it pierced her shoulder. She recoiled, thrashing, and the sharp movement shook it free.

She slowly turned her gaze back on him. *Quick? Or slow?*

She saw it in his face, his parted lips, his eyes. The terror he inflicted becoming his own. He knew.

Now it's over, Mick, she hummed in the back of her throat.

She swooped, plucking him from his horse, her teeth sinking in gently at first, feeling the snap of his ribs, his back, his agonized shriek echoing inside her mouth, and the surging bloodthirsty scream inside her wanted more.

New instincts will overtake you . . .

You'll forget your other self . . .

But enough of her remembered who she still wanted to be. She didn't need more than what she had already taken.

She released his broken body and watched him plummet to the earth.

Go to your glory, Mick, she said to him, *and strut with your demons in hell.*

She watched him land, a crushed blot on the ground, twisted and still, and she banked, turning toward home.

Dragons who had been in the distance soared closer, their work finished too, the skies finally clear.

Pengary didn't speak aloud, but she understood the language of his nod. The language of his breath. The faint rumble in his throat. She was one of his kind.

I never forget my debts, and mine are paid. Farewell, Miss Keats. I wish you peace in this world. Pengary and his companion flew away, their strong wings swiftly carrying them north.

CHAPTER 82

Bristol heard shouts as she circled to land, and saw the knights below drawing swords and readying spears. Melizan and Cosette ran forward, their arms outspread. "Stand down!" they yelled. "Stand down!"

She heard other screams from the rim. Horrified ones. *Avydra. Beast. Dragon.* She landed some distance from the Mother Ring, giving her space to transform back into a woman with arms and legs and wounds. Her clothes were singed and shredded, but she didn't feel the burns and cuts. Other wounds consumed her. She had won, but she had lost. Elphame was saved from a tyrant, the cauldron secure for both the fae and mortal world for another hundred years, but Bristol lost what she had come there for in the first place. The reason she left her sisters and Bowskeep. Her father.

She was numb again as she walked back to be with her mother. *I'm bringing them both home.* But she wasn't. Stringent shouts nearby pulled her from her stupor.

"Kill her!" King Merriwind of Mistriven yelled to a knight as he pointed at Bristol. "Kill her now!"

The knight's chin dipped as he sheepishly looked at Merriwind. "But, Your Majesty, the Stone just named her the new queen of Elphame."

"It was a trick!" he yelled, the once timid king now emboldened by Kormick's death. "She and the Darkland monster were working together all along!" He stepped into Bristol's path to block her. "Arrest her! Her kind aren't even legal in Elphame!" Bristol didn't stop, prepared to walk through him.

But then the king of Mistriven was flying through the air, launched by Cael. "Shut up, Merriwind! A dozen other feet were planted in that ring, including mine and Tyghan's, when the Stone called out. It could have waited for any one of us to step up, but it didn't. *It chose her*. It's not a trick! She's the new queen of Elphame! Bend your knee!"

Bristol registered surprise that it was Cael defending her. In fact, he even looked relieved.

"That's right," the queen of Cernunnos agreed, and bowed her head to Bristol. "Your Majesty."

The king of Greymarch did the same, as did many of those who were starting to gather now that the battle was over.

Cael followed suit, dropping to one knee. "Your Majesty."

Bristol paused in front of him uncertainly, a jumble of emotions stopping up in her chest, but she then continued toward her destination. Her mother.

Merriwind got back to his feet. "But—"

Tyghan shot him a lethal stare to shut him up, as his long strides closed the space between him and Bristol. "You're bleeding," he said.

She saw his shirt for the first time. He was drenched in blood. Her father's blood. Agony still lined his face. "I'm all right," she said, wondering if he saw her as a beast now. "I need to go to my mother." She tried to step around him, and he caught her arm.

"Bristol, wait—"

"What?" And then she noticed the unnatural silence. She saw Julia's anguished face. And Sashka's. And—

Every face was frozen in time, frozen on her. *The quiet*. There were no screams or sobs. Her stomach hollowed to an empty pit, and she ran. "Mother—"

"Bristol!" She heard Tyghan call. "Don't—"

She stumbled to the other side of the ring, where she had left her father, and stopped short. Her mother's cheek was pressed to her father's chest like she was listening to his heartbeat. One of her arms draped over his middle in a tender embrace. Her graceful form was relaxed beside him. But the back of her elegant green velvet gown had a large stain. Blood. In the middle of the stain was an arrow.

Elven arrows. They kill every time.

Cully stepped forward. "I'm sorry," he said. "It must have been a stray."

Bristol stared at him in disbelief. "In the middle of her back?"

A dozen Eideris archers stood by him, empty bows in hand, impossible to know who it came from. Was that the point?

"She was the Darkland monster," one of the archers said, like it was no great loss. "All of us know someone who died at her hands."

Bristol spun toward Tyghan. "You promised me! You promised!"

"I had just stepped away for a minute after Kierus—" His voice shook. "I'll get to the bottom of it. I'll find out—"

"The bottom of it? What fucking difference does the bottom make now? She's dead. You promised me—"

Bristol stumbled, weak, waving Tyghan away when he came toward her. "Leave me alone!" Julia ran to her instead, slipping an arm around Bristol's waist just as her knees gave out. Hollis ran to her other side.

"Where's the High Witch?" Melizan shouted at Sashka. "I thought I told you to summon her!"

"I tried," Sashka said, her voice shaking. "The High Witch is dead."

CHAPTER 83

S he's here!" Deek whispered to his cadre of thugs. Deek didn't
know what a thug was, but he liked the word. It sounded important. And she had called him that once. And he liked *her*.

He was relieved to finally find Bristol here in Julia's room. He had
heard they had arrived back in Danu hours ago. He and his thugs had
looked all over for her. The nation was celebrating, the news already
buzzing from rooftops and windows, flowers raining down and covering the streets. Elphame had a new ruler. Her. The one he liked.
He and his thugs had gone to her windowsill to bring her a crown of
chamomile flowers, but she wasn't there.

Deek pressed his face to the window, trying to get a better look.
Bristol looked sad. He didn't understand why. *A thimble of nectar*, he
thought. That's what they would bring her. Maybe it would make the
dark circles beneath her eyes disappear.

"Last one," Julia said. The worst one. It required actual stitching.

Was it a demon blade that made this gash? Bristol wondered. Not
likely since those were rare and ugly, forged by demons, and Kormick's
sword had been gleaming and beautiful. But it felt every bit as ugly.

Bristol winced as Julia pushed the needle in again. Julia had offered her a potion for the pain, but Bristol refused. She wanted to come out of her numb world, not go back into it.

"Here," Avery said, handing her a cup of tea. "Drink this. You need to get your strength back." Her friends were gathered in Julia's room, all of them caring for Bristol, cleaning her wounds, putting balm on her burns, bringing her food in small portions. She was propped up on Julia's chaise. Rose brought a soft blanket for her legs when she noticed them shaking.

Julia tied off the last stitch and bandaged the wound as Bristol's mind skated through questions, then turned away from them. As long as they were tucked in her mind, maybe they weren't real. Finally one slipped off her tongue.

"How did Madame Chastain die?"

All eyes turned toward Sashka. "It was—" Sashka looked sick, like it was the last answer she wanted to give Bristol. "It was a demon. Eris rushed her to Olivia, but it was too late."

Another demon released by her mother.

A sorrowful weight hung inside Bristol. She and Madame Chastain had their conflicts, but the High Witch had cared for her too, healing her wounds, healing the wounds of so many she loved. Without her, even Tyghan wouldn't be alive. The most powerful woman in Danu was dead, just like—

Bristol remembered her last moments with her mother, the promises she made.

Sometimes you get another chance, Mother. This is yours. It's not too late. Come home with me.

She remembered her mother's gaze resting in hers. The connection they made. Her mother believing Bristol. Believing the dream.

Bristol's nails curled into her palm. The dream Bristol didn't deliver. What was her mother thinking about just before she died? Bristol wondered. *Betrayal or dreams?* "Did my mother have any last words?" she asked.

Hollis knelt on the floor beside the chaise and gently laid her hand on Bristol's leg. "Yes," she answered. "I had just stepped up after—" Hollis cleared her throat, searching for the right words. "She was looking at your father like he was still alive—for the longest time—and then she said his name, Kierus. She was serene, Bristol. *Kierus*, that was her last word."

Avery's chest shuddered, and Rose pressed her hand over her mouth.

And *Maire* was one of her father's last words. My love. Each of her parents holding on to the other at the end. She remembered his last smile, *I've saved you.* He died believing that.

"Where was Tyghan?" Bristol asked. "He said he stepped away."

"He worked on your father long after you left," Julia said. "He refused to give up. I finally had to touch his arm and tell him he was done. He stood and walked away, trying to pull himself together. That's where he was, in the shadows of the stones."

"We were all surprised," Avery said. "We thought there was bad blood between them."

Tears trickled down Bristol's face. "There was," she said. "But people change."

Somewhere along the way, Tyghan had forgiven him. Maybe even he didn't see it coming. But there were signs. He had reduced a thousand-year sentence to one month, defying a council vote.

He was safe. Safer than he is today. Until Bristol let him out of the column. He would still be alive if she hadn't. In some ways, Tyghan did know her father better than she did.

"He was only gone for a minute when we heard a thump," Avery said, "and then your mother slumped forward."

♟

Bristol spent the night in Julia's room. They all did. Like a tangle of pups in the back of a van, fitting in where they could, sprawled on the chaise, the bed, the sofa. A family. They talked about wounds, food, and funerals. Bristol already loved them, and she loved them even more for that. For not shying away from something painful because they knew, whether they talked about it or not, it was there—a bruise in Bristol's heart to be healed. There would be many funerals in the coming days, and her parents deserved one too. A funeral together, just as they died together. A real one this time. It might only be the six of them attending, but they would have one.

She lay on the sofa, her head at one end and Avery's at the other, their feet overlapping, her shoulder hurting, Sashka snoring. It felt like home.

"Did you know you could shift?" Rose whispered into the darkness.

It was the last elephant in the room, and Bristol was grateful that someone finally brought it up.

"The Sisters told me, but they said to never do it. Now I know why. Was I hideous?" It was an honest question, not one fishing for a *no*. It was a question that had eaten at her since she saw the scales on her back, long before she heard the screams from those who spotted her from the rim of the valley.

"Frightening," Julia said. "But definitely not hideous."

Frightening was a word Bristol could live with, although she didn't want to be frightening to her sisters if one day something made her snap and she shifted again. At the thought of her sisters, tears sprang to her eyes. How would she tell them about their parents? Because of her broken promises, they would have to live through their deaths all over again—as she was now.

Rose sighed. "I thought you were beautiful."

"Majestic," Sashka said, suddenly awake again. "Those fucking wings!"

"Breathtaking," Avery agreed.

"But illegal," Bristol replied. "Merriwind made that clear."

"Not everyone agrees with that beanhead," Hollis said. "The queen of Cernunnos was quick to bow."

"Because she was frightened?" Bristol asked.

"Because the Stone made the right choice," Julia said.

But it didn't, Bristol thought. Sometimes even revered stones made bad decisions. She could not become the queen of Elphame, not now. She had sisters to go home to.

🔑

Early the next morning, there was a loud knock at the door. Julia groaned and stretched in her bed. "I told the guards, no visitors."

Hollis stumbled from the chaise to the door to see who was there, her tangled pink curls flying in all directions. They heard her talking to someone in hushed tones. *Now is not the time. No. All right. I'll check.*

She came back into the room. "It's the steward of Elphame. He has something for you, Bristol. He says it can't wait."

🔑

The steward set a crate on the floor beside Bristol. The Cauldron of Plenty. Bristol didn't say a word as he told her about the cauldron, her responsibilities, choosing her officers, and the court of Elphame that now awaited her. When he was finished, she asked only one question. "How does one appoint a steward to take one's place?"

He looked at her, bewildered. "You simply name them, and if one day the time should come—"

"Thank you," she said. "That's all I need to know."

CHAPTER 84

When Tyghan walked into the treatment tent, Eris was sitting beside Madame Chastain's body. He held her hand. She was covered in a blanket, up to her shoulders, that hid her fatal injuries. Her silver hair fell in soft waves around her face, and her expression was peaceful. She could have been sleeping.

It was still hard for Tyghan to believe she was dead. She was badly injured when he and Eris got her to Olivia, but the High Witch was powerful and strong, with an incredible will. Larger than life and bigger than death, he had always thought. She'd been a constant in his life since he was a child, and he couldn't imagine anything overcoming her.

Tyghan's eyes stung. Too much was happening too fast.

"He's been like that for two hours," Olivia whispered to him. "I healed the wound on his shoulder, but his heart . . ." She shook her head, her skin splotched from tears. Madame Chastain had been her mentor and friend. "Injured are still coming in. I need to get back to help Esmee."

Tyghan nodded. "I'll take care of him."

He stepped over to Eris and squeezed his shoulder. Eris didn't look up, continuing to skim his thumb over the back of Dahlia's hand.

"Five minutes," he finally said. "She asked me for five minutes, and I wouldn't give it to her. I clung to my hurt pride instead."

"You couldn't know—"

"I had five minutes to spare. Everyone has five minutes to spare for someone they love." He leaned forward, holding her hand to his lips, and sobbed.

Tyghan's lungs burned. He remembered Eris pulling him into his robes after his mother died, when it was too hard for him to be brave. *When you can't be strong, I'll be strong for you.*

He gently pulled Madame Chastain's hand from Eris's and laid it across her chest. "I promise, she will be taken care of properly, with all the honors she deserves." He tugged on Eris's arm, nudging him to his feet. "Come on, Counselor. Let's go home."

Once Eris was settled in his quarters back at the palace, Tyghan went to Julia's room, where Bristol and her squad were staying. Bristol came to the door, but he wasn't invited in. She came out into the hallway, a large bandage on her shoulder. Kormick could have killed her, even in her beast form. Time seemed to pause—a stubborn space slipping between them. *Fuck space*, he thought, and he gently nudged her into his arms. She melted into him. "I'm sorry," he said.

She shook her head. "I can't talk about what happened. Not now." She pushed back to look into his face. "But I want a funeral for them. I want their bodies and a place where they can rest together."

He nodded. "Of course. I'll take care of it."

Her expression hardened then, like she was bracing herself. "Did you see me?" she asked.

He knew what she meant. "Only as you flew back to the Mother Ring," he answered.

Flew. The word hit him in his gut. The reality.

"What do you think?"

He had been frightened. Not of her, but for her. From the first time he saw the scales on her back, he had wondered. It wasn't until he saw Bristol shift in the sky that his suspicions were confirmed. "I think you saved Danu. I think you're the queen of Elphame."

"That's not what I meant. What do you think of *me*?"

"I think you're Bristol Keats, the woman I love."

CHAPTER 85

Bristol climbed the hill to the isolated, windswept glade over-looking the sea. Far from the heart of Danu, Bristol's parents were laid in a cradle of stones.

Unlike Logan's and Leanna's funerals in Bowskeep, where dozens crowded into a mortuary parlor, or Glennis's funeral, where hundreds dotted the hills to pay their respects for a fallen knight, here there were exactly seven in attendance. Other than Bristol and her friends, only Tyghan was there. A hush of cold wind shivered through knee-deep grass.

The sight of their wrapped bodies lying on the stones gripped Bristol with finality. *No more second chances*. New truths would have to be shared with her sisters. The thought made her queasy. Instead of reciting the revered laws of the gods, or recalling history and valor, Bristol spoke about the lessons they taught their daughters, like perseverance, protection, and joy in the simplest moments: gathering stones for a campfire, strolling a museum gallery, dancing in the rain.

Bristol paused as images raced through her head, and it was always hands reaching out for them, her father, her mother, finding them, pulling them along, keeping them safe, loading them in the van for the next place and the next, hiding their worry, never giving up on their family.

"Never giving up," Bristol whispered. "That's what they taught us."

She looked at their wrapped bodies, snug against each other, but she saw Mick's sneering face hovering between them. *You did this, Bristol. Remember that every day of your miserable reign. You should have left when you promised.* She squeezed her eyes shut, blinking the horror away.

"Bri?" Rose said uncertainly. Bristol looked at her and nodded. Rose had plucked a handful of wildflowers along the way and she laid it between them.

Tyghan laid a bottle of whiskey and two shot glasses beside her father and whispered some words Bristol couldn't hear, but when he turned back, his eyes were red.

Last, Bristol stepped forward with a pocketful of tiny stones, and pressed them into the dirt at their feet the way Cat would have done if she were there, creating their initials, LK, LK. Leanna Keats and Logan Keats. The people they tried to be.

Bristol's throat closed as she set the last stone. She couldn't deliver the final goodbye, so Julia stepped up for her. "Through the mists and over the golden waters to where the sun sets, the gods and Paradise await you. Go to your deserved rest, Logan and Leanna Keats."

The winds blew in answer, a mournful whine, and Bristol wasn't sure if it was the gods answering, or Willow, or maybe her own heart.

It was a small but fitting funeral. Bristol would remember the details, because her sisters would want to know. Cat would cry but soak in every word, especially the part about their initials, happy that they were honored, remembered, no matter where the stones were placed.

Tyghan hugged Bristol for a long while, not just for her sake but for his too. He had been to Madame Chastain's funeral earlier, and his heart was already low. Tomorrow he had five more funerals to attend, among them Officer Perry's and two cadets who had been minding a supply tent. They lost seventy in all and the battle was hailed as a resounding victory—except for the families who had lost loved ones, like him and Bristol. Because in the end, Madame Chastain was more than a mentor to him, and Kierus was still Tyghan's brother. He had proven that in their last minutes together. It was going to be hard getting through these next days, but for Eris's sake, and everyone else's, he had to keep going. For now, he was still king, and Knight Commander.

Tyghan finally ordered the sealing stones set on the vault, and fell into step beside Bristol as they walked back down the hill.

Halfway down, she said, "I'm going home, Tyghan."

This didn't catch him by complete surprise. He knew she would want to break the news to her sisters. "I understand. For how long?" he asked.

"For a while."

"What does that mean?"

"I don't know."

But she needed to know. A few days of mourning were expected, but everyone would be clamoring to know when she would set up court and be accepting petitioners and making the first tithe for the cauldron. It was her right and duty. "You're the new queen of Elphame, Bristol. You can't just leave without—"

"I'll be gone indefinitely," she said firmly. "My sisters need me. I've named Julia as my steward while I'm gone, and my squad as my officers."

Tyghan was silent until they reached the bottom of the hill. *Julia?* No one in Elphame even knew who she was. Bristol was enough of an unknown—it would take days and weeks for Elphame to adjust to all the changes without adding to them. He could understand leaving for a few days, but . . . "You've only just become queen, Bristol. It's an important—"

"My family is important too!" she snapped. "What's *left* of it."

He heard the accusation in her words. That it was his fault. Maybe it was, her mother's death at least. Tyghan had questioned the archers, just as he promised her. They confirmed there was one last Fomorian attack near the stones, and one of their own fell to an axe. Arrows flew fast, and it could have been a stray. But Bristol's disbelief still rang in his ears. *In the middle of her back?* Unlikely, but Tyghan couldn't prove it was intentional. At least not yet. Even Cully swore it was an accident, but Tyghan saw no remorse in his eyes either. Tyghan should have made his orders more clear, more imperative, not just rescinding the kill order but adding protection for Maire too.

But her father's death, he had tried to protect Kierus, to keep him out of the council's hands—and Kormick's. He wouldn't push the point now, though. Bristol was still raw, her parents freshly buried—and Maire's death seemed like a betrayal from the world Bristol was trying to protect. "I'm sorry, Bri. I didn't wish for your mother to die."

"And yet she's still dead. I need to go, Tyghan. I need time. I can't just jump in to take care of your world when my own is shattered."

"You're not the only one who is hurting. I tried to keep your father safe. I—"

"You're blaming me now? That I was the one—"

He grabbed her by the shoulders. "Hold on. Let's both just take a breath here." He put his arm around her, and they walked silently back to their horses. "I have to take care of a few things when we get back to the palace, but I'll have a meal brought to your room for us, and we'll talk more then."

She only nodded.

Had she grasped the gravity of her new position yet? She wasn't just under the scrutiny of many kingdoms who expected her to claim her throne now, but under the greedy eyes of many lords, like Csorba, who might seek to use her in other ways. She couldn't leave indefinitely. She needed the protection a full court could offer.

♟

Bristol thought about Tyghan as she walked back to her room. *We'll talk later*. He couldn't hide his disappointment at her decision, but she needed this. A touchstone to her old life. A reminder that she once existed elsewhere, as someone else. Not as a bloodmarked or a shapeshifter but as a sister. That was all. She needed Harper and Cat as much as they needed her. Their hearts all needed to heal, and she didn't know how long it would take.

She pushed open her door, already planning her departure, but when she stepped inside, she froze. For a moment she thought she had stepped into the wrong room. It was a war zone. All of her bedding was stripped and tossed. Pillows slashed. Her wardrobe emptied out. Piles of clothes were strewn everywhere. Even her mattress lay askew, half off her bed.

Ransacked. Her room had been ransacked.

Like she was staying at a shoddy motel along a lonely highway, and someone came looking for quick cash. But she had no cash, or anything of value other than her fancy gowns, and those had been left behind, scattered everywhere.

She drew her knife and readied her other hand to summon fire. "Hello?" she called, aware that intruders could still be inside. The room remained silent. She carefully checked her bath chamber. It was ransacked too, towels, brushes, soaps scattered everywhere.

Bristol returned to her room and stared at the chaos. Complete and utter turmoil. And anger. This had been a vicious rampage. Slashed pillows? Someone had wished her head had been lying on those pillows. Why? But then she noticed one out-of-place detail that was neatly arranged. And then it was all she could see. Her heart hammered in one continuous beat as she walked toward it. Her sneakers sat alone on the middle of the breakfast table, perfectly aligned like shoes in a store window inviting you to notice them.

"No," Bristol said, the word slipping off her tongue like a reflex. "No, no."

She looked down at her sneakers. A note was tucked in one of them. Her hand trembled as she pulled it out.

> *You stole my life. You stole everything that ever mattered to me. Now I'm stealing yours from you. Don't bother searching. It's lying somewhere at the bottom of the sea. Blackmail has a price. Was it worth it?*

Bristol couldn't breathe. She grabbed her shoes, frantically ripping out the insoles, plunging her hands inside, searching for a cold metal disk. *There was nothing*. Her fingers shook, skimming the insides again, and again. Both sneakers were bare. Empty. *Empty*. Her knees gave way, and she fell to the floor. A curdling scream tore from her throat. Her timemark was gone.

🔑

A servant heard the scream and found Bristol on the floor, inconsolable. The urisk immediately summoned Tyghan. By the time he got to Bristol's room, she was madly searching through piles of scattered clothes, stuffing her old tattered jeans into her backpack, her black tank top, then looking for something else.

He took in the mayhem. "What happened?"

Bristol paused her frantic search and slammed the crumpled note in her fist into his palm, then went back to searching.

Tyghan's breath pooled in his chest as he read it. He hadn't seen the depth of Kasta's rage—only his own when he discovered her handprint around Bristol's neck. He had offered her the mercy of leaving Danu and disappearing somewhere in the wilds, instead of being tried by the council. He had escorted her to the palace gates himself, but it was a mercy he shouldn't have given her.

He looked back at Bristol, caught in a feverish pursuit. "We'll find it," he said. "Somehow. We'll search—"

Bristol whirled, fury overtaking her. "At the bottom of the sea? Which one, Tyghan? Where will you start? How many more years of my life will it rob? Stop!" she screamed. "Stop making promises you can't keep!"

She picked up a trampled toothbrush and shoved it into her bag.

"What are you doing?" he asked.

"I'm getting out of here. I'm going home."

He reached for her arm, and she yanked it away. "I'm angry, Tyghan, and I'm staying angry! Don't try to change that!"

"I wasn't. I'm just trying to make you slow down and think. You're distraught."

"I'm not distraught. I'm *done*. I can't do this anymore. My father's dead. My mother's dead. I made promises to her in her last breathing moments on this earth. I promised her another chance. I made her believe in the dream. I lured my mother to her own death. I can never forgive myself for that—or you. I gave Elphame everything, and it gave me nothing. And my sisters? I may never see them again. But there is one promise to my mother I'm going to keep. I'm going home! I'm suffocating here. My whole time in Elphame has been one long nightjump, and I'm not getting anywhere."

"Give it some time, Bri—"

"Time? There is no more time! I've lost time! I've lost everything!" she said, furiously zipping her pack shut. "I'm on my way to tell Julia I'm leaving. She will take possession of the Cauldron of Plenty. And then I'm riding Zandra to a far place to create a portal where no one will find it. A portal back to Bowskeep."

She headed for the door, and he grabbed her wrist to stop her. "You can't do this."

Her gaze was cold steel. "You forget. I'm the queen of Elphame. I can do whatever I want." She looked at his hand on her wrist. "Now let go of me. I need to go speak with my steward."

CHAPTER 86

I'm sorry," Bristol said. "I have no choice."

"Shhh," Julia said, her arms wrapped tight around Bristol. "You don't need to apologize to anyone."

Bristol huddled with her friends, a mass of tears and arms holding on to one another. "We don't want you to go," Rose cried. Bristol had told them about the stolen timemark, and that she likely would never be able to return to Elphame once she left. This wasn't just leaving for a little while, but maybe forever. Her friends worked through their own anger and disbelief, Avery wondering if she could substitute her own timemark for Bristol's.

"It won't work," Julia said. "Each timemark was imprinted to us when we passed through the portal to Elphame."

It took every bit of Bristol's will to speak coherently, because inside she was a raw mess. "I'm sorry to leave, but at least you have each other. My sisters don't have—" Her chest shuddered. "I can't—" She felt she was going to be sick.

"It's all right," Hollis murmured, rubbing Bristol's back. "You've lost too much. Witnessed too much. More than anyone should have to bear. Both of your parents and now this. I'm sorry. I'm so sorry, my friend."

"You'll be back," Avery said, her chin dimpling like an orange, refusing to believe they might not see each other again.

"Damn straight she will," Sashka said. Tears streamed down her cheeks.

"We could go with you?" Rose cried hopefully.

Bristol shook her head. "No, your life is here. Help Julia as she watches over Elphame. She'll need you. You're my First Officers. And hers. Please—" She choked on her words.

She bit her lip, unable to say anything else, and they understood, as they always had. Pushing forward, pulling back, trusting her when she didn't trust herself. She kissed each of their cheeks.

"We'll always be your other family, Bri," Rose said, her long lashes spiked with tears.

Bristol nodded and left.

Her other family. She sobbed as she walked away. Bristol had never felt so out of control, like every decision she had made and would ever make again would be wrong. Hollis was right, the weight of her parents' deaths was more than she could bear. She needed home. That's all she knew. And home was Cat and Harper.

♟

Bowskeep. Bristol was already considering the coordinates for the portal after she said goodbye to her friends. Desperate logic overtook her, her mind jumping from one shattered maybe to the next. Maybe if she chose just the right coordinates, if she said them just right, if she did a skip and a dance and wished on a star, she would make it back to her sisters. There had to be a way. *There was always a way.* She was already thinking of a hidden place for the portal too. A secret place where no one ever went.

When she arrived at the barn to get Zandra, Tyghan, Quin, Dalagorn, Olivia, and Reuben were waiting for her. Or barring her. They were a wall across the entrance.

"Is this the farewell committee? Or are you all here to stop me? Am I a prisoner already?"

"We're here to talk," Tyghan said. "If I can't convince you, maybe one of them can."

She looked at them, but none of them spoke, like they were afraid. Of her? Or did they hate her? Madame Chastain was dead. And so many of their comrades—knights she didn't even know—were dead too. Did they blame her? The panic in her grew. Who was she to anyone here anymore? She didn't even know herself.

"Look at me, Tyghan. I don't need your backup squad to tell me what I already know. I'm bloodmarked. A prize just like my mother. And everyone knows it. You think I'm not aware that I have a target on my back now? To be used or killed the way she was? Besides that, I'm an *avydra*, the most hated of dragons. I heard the screams as I landed. Merriwind's accusations. I'm illegal and reviled. I'm facing double jeopardy. How long before I'm dead too? Tomorrow? I'm all my sisters have left. Even the great king of Danu couldn't keep my parents safe."

Dalagorn winced. Quin looked down and shook his head.

Tyghan stared at her like she had kicked him in the gut.

Olivia eased half a step forward. "We could keep you safe—"

"I don't want to be kept safe!" Bristol shouted. "That's what my parents did for my whole life, running from one town to the next to keep us safe! I want to own my life and live it as I please! That's why I came here in the first place, so I could stop looking over my shoulder! So I could finally take a deep breath! So my sisters could do that too!"

She barged past them into the barn and began saddling Zandra.

Tyghan followed her. "What do you want from me, Bristol? Just to let you go into the unknown?"

"Yes," she answered as she smoothed a blanket over Zandra's back, refusing to meet his gaze, her head pounding, her eyes stinging, everything inside her torn to tiny pieces. "My mind is made up. I'm empty. Can't you see that? I have nothing left inside me for anyone, including you. I have a small chance to reclaim part of my life, and I'm taking it. I'm going home. My last wish before I leave is that I never see Elphame or anyone in it again." She turned to face him.

"Stay away from Bowskeep. Let me live my life. And make sure no one else follows me either. Do whatever you have to do so I am dead to this world. So no one knows I exist. Promise me you will do that and you'll actually make this final promise stick."

"There's no undoing this, Bristol. You're half mortal. Without a timemark, you don't even know what you're going back to. Everything could be gone. Don't make the biggest mistake of your life."

"I already made the biggest mistake of my life when I came here. I sacrificed one family to save another. Haven't I given Elphame enough already?"

Tyghan was gutted, afraid, not knowing how to make any of this right. He was grieving for so much already and now he was grieving for what she seemed set on. How much more could one person take? Tyghan knew the answer to that now. Bristol had reached her limit. And maybe he had too.

"Please," he said. "Don't lose the family you have here too. Take this." He pressed something into her hand. "It's another timemark. This one will at least keep the two of us connected in time so you can return here. So centuries won't keep us apart, in case there's nothing for you in Bowskeep. I will always be here for you."

Bristol looked at the timemark, a useless coin that couldn't give her back what she had lost. She tossed it away, and it clattered somewhere against another stall. "I'm never coming back."

Tyghan's hands trembled. He wasn't sure if it was rage or fear. "Dammit, Bristol! You want to just throw it all away? You're not the only one hurting!"

She continued saddling Zandra, ignoring him.

"Sure! Go ahead! Forget me! Forget us! I'll forget you too!" Tyghan stormed out of the barn before she could answer. She watched him leave, rage rolling off him. *Forget us.* If only she could. If only there was a potion for forgetting, maybe everything inside her wouldn't feel like it was dying.

Reuben stepped up to her, a wistful smile on his face. "You can't outrun your heart or your past, Miss Keats. Trust me, I know. Someday you may want to reach out." He held out her backpack. "Don't forget this. I truly wish you the best."

Stay away. Do whatever you have to do so I am dead to this world.

The words floated in the air, through the walls of the ancient barn, to the vaulted ceilings of the throne room, to the trees of the sacred forest. The ancient sentinels sighed in unison, and as witnesses. When the queen of Elphame made a request, especially a last wish, it was always to be granted. So on a small dark terrace just below Sun Court, Olivia glamoured herself to look like Bristol, and she and Tyghan offered up a heated argument that drew the eyes of onlookers. A bitter lovers' quarrel. It was convincing. Bristol wasn't the only one who was broken. Guilt and anger ravaged Tyghan. He played his role a bit too well. Olivia, who made a compelling Bristol, drew a knife at the height of their argument, and that was when Tyghan turned her into a frog, in self-defense, of course. Though it was actually Reuben who performed the sleight of hand, including the swooping crow that carried the frog away. It was the perfect solution. No one would be hunting down or stalking Bristol. She was presumed eaten, and word spread at lightning speed among the gentry, the story taking on a delicious life of its own.

Bristol Keats no longer existed in the realm of Elphame—except to a secret few.

CHAPTER 87

The Willoughby Inn. The great oak tree. The abandoned parking lot. Zandra leapt through the portal. Bristol's insides were jumbled, everything floating in all the wrong places. When they emerged on the other end and raced toward the town, heads turned, wondering at the unusual appearance of a woman on a great white horse. Where had she come from? Bristol sat back in the saddle, signaling Zandra to slow. *Bowskeep*. She gulped in a sobbing breath. She had done it. Main Street. The giant fig tree was still a massive umbrella casting its shade. A gaggle of Georgie's chickens on the sidewalk flapped their wings at her. Starky's neon sign still glowed in the window. *She was back*. But then she noticed that every storefront had a new paint color, new shutters, new touches. Was Georgie on another one of her sprucing-up campaigns? And then she saw that Miriam's Nail Emporium had gone out of business and was replaced with a trendy hair salon. Best Threads was gone too. Her heart sped, and she galloped toward Oak Leaf Lane.

The house was still there. But now it had a fresh coat of paint and a manicured green lawn, and the porch no longer sagged. *Of course*, she thought, trying to control her panic, *they used funds from the art to fix up the old place*. Everything else was the same. Even the lace curtains in the front window. She dismounted and whispered against Zandra's soft muzzle. "I thank you for your service, sweet queen. Now it's time for you to go home too, return to your family where you belong." Zandra lowered her head, like she was bowing to another queen, and disappeared.

Bristol turned back to the house and dashed up the stairs. The front door was locked, so she ran to the back steps of the mudroom and found the key, still in the same pot by the door. When she threw open the door, she slowed. A pile of envelopes lay atop the washing machine, and a dusty bicycle was propped against the wall just beyond it. Every envelope had her name on it. She desperately ripped them open. Birthday cards. Every single one.

We miss you, Bri.

Happy Birthday, dear sister.

We still hold hope that one day you will come home.

And then a switch to, *I still hold hope that one day I will see you again.*

Thirty birthday cards.

Bristol heard screeching brakes, and then the front door slammed. She stumbled out to the hallway. A middle-aged woman with dark hair stood there with a small child. She had fine lines fanning from her eyes, and her hair was gray at her temples. But her big dark eyes and lashes—minus the glasses—were the same. The eyes of their father. "Bri," she said breathlessly. "It's you. It's really you."

Bristol stared. Her voice. "Harper?"

She nodded.

"How long have I been gone?"

"Thirty years."

"Cat? Where's Cat?"

Harper's eyes creased. She shook her head. "She's gone, Bri. Cat died nine years ago in a plane crash."

♟

Even though the coming days and weeks would pass in a blur, years later, Bristol would still remember every detail of that moment like it was burned somewhere behind her eyes. A permanent record of what had happened so she wouldn't think it was just a dream. *Thirty years.* In the blink of an eye, they were gone. Bristol's old life was gone. Her knees had given way, and Harper had to help her up off the floor. For a long time, she couldn't quite grasp it, or maybe she just couldn't accept it. Her younger sister was now her much older sister, and her oldest sister was dead. Harper nursed Bristol back to health.

There now. Eat this. Drink this. Do this. Rest. Breathe. You can do it.

Harper put Bristol back together, one day and one piece at a time, always knowing just what to do, what word to say. She was older. More experienced. Harper found the time to care for Bristol among all of her other responsibilities. She had four children. A doting husband. And she was principal of Bowskeep High School. She was a wonder. Apparently, Cat had been a wonder too. She'd gone back to her music and became world-famous for her pitch-perfect voice. She performed at opera houses all over the world, making audiences cry, the same way she used to make Bristol tear up.

Her sisters had both lived full lives in the few months Bristol was gone.

Harper told her about Sal, dead from a heart attack just weeks after Bristol left, and Sonja, in an elder care facility. Harper visited her regularly. And they had a new mayor. Georgie Topz was called home after her mother passed to help with the family business. Between all of Harper's news, Bristol confessed her own grief and shame over the promises she didn't keep. It poured out in ragged breaths and fits and Harper tried to console her, reminding Bristol that she wasn't responsible for their parents' choices. "In their last moments, they were together. You honored them, Bri. Focus on what you did do. I know you're grieving right now. It's all fresh for you and hitting you all at once. Go ahead, grieve, cry, scream, but do not take on the weight of guilt. You don't deserve that."

But on one particularly bad day, when grief crashed over her again and Bristol couldn't stop crying and saying she was sorry, Harper grabbed her by the shoulders and gave her a good shake. "Stop feeling guilty! Do you understand? Cat and I were the ones who felt guilty!

You ran so we didn't have to. *You did that for us.* Cat and I built lives. Good ones, even though we missed you. Everything you always said you wanted for me, I have it here, Bri. I'm happy."

She ran to get a letter and pulled it from its envelope. Bristol recognized the paper. Her stationery from Elphame. "Listen to this, Bri. This is what you told us. *While I'm gone, I hope you're putting down the deepest roots ever, because we are never going to have to run again.*" She smoothed the letter in her lap. "That's what *you* gave us. Roots so we could build dreams. You sacrificed everything for us. It's your turn now—your turn to have dreams."

She looked back at the letter, skimming to another part. "And this: *We can't choose every road we're destined to travel—and we've been down a lifetime of roads together.*" She grabbed Bristol's hand like she would never let it go. "We've got this road too, sis. Hold on to me. Let me be the strong one for a while."

When a new memory, misstep, or numbing guilt would send Bristol into a downward spiral, she held Harper's words tighter. *We've got this road too.* She'd been home three weeks, still dazed and unable to keep food down, when Harper looked at her strangely and asked, "When did you last have your period?"

Bristol was stunned by the question. "Oh god," she finally whispered. "The aspirin." The High Witch's words slammed into her. *Because of the changes in your body, the aspirin no longer works.* Her body had changed. Her other pills hadn't worked either.

The new reality sent her into another nosedive, but Harper was there for that too. She taught Bristol how to move forward, one step at a time, because there was no going back.

CHAPTER 88

EIGHT YEARS LATER

Over the weeks and months as Bristol healed, she thought a lot about choices. Sometimes when you were afraid or hurting, you only wanted the fear or pain to stop, and you made a decision that would forever alter your life. You might wish you could go back and make that decision over again with your new eyes and new self, but that moment was forever gone.

Sometimes there was no going back. You had to move on with what you had left, but without forgiveness, there was no moving forward. *I will never forgive myself or you.* She had felt every one of those words to the depths of her soul when she said them, but somewhere along the way she had found forgiveness for both herself and for others.

Julia was right, forgiveness was a thing of the heart, and her heart was wounded and mended in its own way.

Harper had found her happy ending without Bristol's help. Even through the hardships and sorrows, Harper had found her way. Happy endings can't be given—they have to be claimed. And that was what Bristol was doing now.

One corner of that happiness was the Menagerium, the coffee shop she had once dreamed of owning. It had everything she had imagined, from gourmet doughnuts to handmade mugs, to local art on the walls to flowers she had grown in her own garden. And yes, books that Harper curated. Bristol had stayed on in the old house on Oak Leaf Lane. Some things from the past she didn't want to let go of. Harper and her family were in a newer house closer to town—along with Angus. He was old and gray and mostly slept his days away now. Though Bristol tried to coax him, he never once turned into Fritz. She guessed that part of his life was behind him, just as she had left things behind too.

Bristol also claimed another corner of happiness by acquiring an advanced degree in art history at the local university, something she had dreamed of but never thought would be possible. She taught two courses there now, on Renaissance art. When she covered the unit on da Vinci, she always smiled, knowing the secrets about him that she could never share.

And sometimes the deepest happiness was found in acceptance, and embracing the things you never planned to be. Bristol welcomed the beast in her now. Every scale, tooth, and claw. She breathed in the beauty and power of the animal inside her, and drove to a remote mountaintop once a month to practice the full depth of her magic— and to shift. She was no longer afraid. She was prepared.

She had something vital to be fierce for now. Something that mattered to her above all else: Her greatest happiness and the light of her life. Her son. Tyghan's son. Rían Trénallis Keats.

🔑

Bristol had just finished grinding a pound of Jamaican Blue for one of her regulars when the bell on the door jingled. It was Harper, with Bristol's son in tow. Harper picked him up from school two days a week and dropped him off at the coffee shop. He held an ice pack to his cheek.

"Rían Trénallis Keats!" Bristol snapped. "If you got into another fight—"

"It wasn't my fault," he cried. "They were making fun of me again. They don't believe that my father's a king."

Bristol knelt and hugged him to her chest. She sighed. "All right. Let me see." He stepped back and removed the ice pack. It was only a small bruise, but his second scuffle. Rían was curious about his father, as any child would be. She had never wanted to lie to him the way she had been lied to, so she told him his father was a king but lived far away in another world. The other children teased him about it. Sometimes a lie, or another version of the truth, was necessary.

"I told you, tell them he's a soldier instead and works far away. Now, go get your sprinkle doughnut," she said, "then start your homework."

Harper shook her head as he went to the doughnut case. "He's only seven. The questions aren't going to go away. He asked me on his way here if his father was ashamed of him. If that was why he never comes to see him."

Bristol's stomach caved. How could she tell her son that his father didn't even know about him? That they weren't just separated by magical portals and distance but by time? Maybe centuries. Tyghan might even be dead. Even considering the possibility made her chest ache. Rían was still too young to understand it all.

Harper's left brow rose—that principal's brow of hers when she wanted to discuss something serious. "I found something. Yesterday when we were going through the pockets of the clothes you donated for the rummage fundraiser, I went through your old backpack too."

Bristol grimaced. "Sorry I didn't clean it out first. What was in there, old moldy jeans?" She had thrown it onto a shelf in the hall closet under the stairs when she returned and forgot about it when other things, like a new baby, were more important.

"I found this." She pulled something from her wallet, hiding it in her hand. "I looked it up today in Anastasia's *Encyclopedia of Faerieland*."

Ah, Bristol thought. *The infamous book by Anastasia Wiggins*. Bristol had left her copy behind in Elphame, but Harper found another one in a used bookstore. "Well?" Bristol asked.

Harper opened her palm. "Is this a timemark?"

Bristol gasped.

"So it *is* one," Harper said.

Bristol took it from her. This was in her pack all this time? How? She had thrown it away. She had—

This will keep us connected in time. And then she remembered Reuben's odd smile as he handed her the pack. She tried to retrace her steps, his steps, but in that chaotic moment, she had been too distraught to remember her own moves, much less anyone else's.

"I read all about it in the encyclopedia," Harper said. "This is your chance, Bri. Rían deserves to know his father. And maybe there could be a second chance for you two."

Bristol's breath caught for a moment. "What? It's been eight years, Harp. Stop being such a romantic."

"I just know what I see. I know you've never stopped loving him. You've never had more than a single date with anyone. No one else measures up to him."

"You're wrong. I'm just busy," Bristol answered, but it was true. Once the broken parts inside her healed, she still had feelings for Tyghan. *Yes, no one else even comes close.* She watched Rían happily eating the last bite of his doughnut, colorful rainbow sprinkles pasted around his mouth. He was her whole life. Going back to Elphame was impossible. She couldn't take a chance mixing the two worlds again. It was too risky—even with a timemark. Timemarks could be stolen. She already found that out the hard way. *No. Absolutely not.* She wouldn't risk losing her son, not after what she had lost the last time. She shook her head. "It's been eight years, Harp. It's too late."

"But it's not centuries like you thought. Eight years isn't that much. I waited thirty years for you."

"We're different people now. He could be married."

"Or he might not be."

Bristol looked back at Rían, the same blue eyes and black hair as his father's. He was the most beautiful, joyful thing in her life. Tyghan would never forgive her for not telling him. It wouldn't go well.

Harper leaned closer and whispered, "Are you the same Bristol Keats who took a huge chance for the sake of her sisters? Take a chance, Bri. Take a chance on yourself."

She punched a key on the cash drawer and tossed the timemark in with the quarters, like the matter was settled and forgotten.

Rían saw her throw it in. "Can't I keep it, Mommy?" he called.

"It's only a useless coin, Rían. It even has a hole in it. I'll give you a better one." She gave him a quarter instead.

"Hey, Ri," Harper said, "want to come back to the house with me? Uncle Jake is making pancakes for dinner tonight." Then she shot Bristol a knowing glance. *Do it for him—and yourself.*

Rían was rushing to the door with his aunt before Bristol could say a word. Harper looked slyly over her shoulder as she left. Sometimes her older little sister was infuriating.

But as Bristol closed up the shop for the evening, she wondered about Tyghan, wondered about the years that had passed, and wondered about chance and a timemark that surfaced after all this time. She heard Tyghan's voice like he was right in the room with her. *A million chances happen every day. The difference is what we make of them.* She opened the cash drawer and pulled out the timemark, slipping it into her pocket. Just for safekeeping.

CHAPTER 89

Tyghan heard the sound of galloping hooves and looked out his window. It was Eris approaching on horseback. Not his usual day to come to the farm, so that meant there was some problem Tyghan needed to fix. He mostly stayed at his farm now, only going to the palace and garrison for monthly check-ins. Cael had been right. With Elphame at peace, his duties were now light. Cael was king again, and Tyghan and his brother had fallen into a rhythm, Tyghan taking care of kingdom business, and Cael mostly acting as Danu's ambassador—which was what he was best at. The division of duties worked out well, and Cael became the kind of king he could have been all along, a good one, something settling inside him at last. Melizan and Cosette had a baby girl now, and he and Cael were dutiful uncles, spoiling her at every turn. *Babies, adventures, and dreams—*

He snuffed the words from his mind. It was easy to do. He had years of practice.

The front door of the farmhouse flew open.

"My boy."

"Father."

It was a tradition they had. Their new names for each other were awkward at first, but only on the tongue, not the way they felt inside.

"You're a day early," Tyghan said.

Eris shrugged off his jacket and went to the larder for a pastry. "I received a message for you."

Tyghan poured some sweet milk for Eris to go with his apple muffin that Ahbriya had baked that morning. "It couldn't wait until tomorrow?"

Eris settled in at the kitchen table, taking a bite, and gave an approving nod. "The message came special delivery from an outlier. It's from the queen of Elphame. She's asked—"

Tyghan sighed. He didn't care who had delivered it. Whenever Julia asked him for something, it always led to other topics or needing him to come to court. Eris spent a lot of time with Julia these days and Tyghan doubted it was only because of kingdom business. "Tell Julia she can put her asks on hold. I'm in the middle of harvesting a field. I have a farm to—"

"It's not from the steward."

Tyghan angled his head, not understanding.

"It's from the actual queen of Elphame."

A sick feeling spread through Tyghan's stomach. Impossible.

"It's a message from Bristol," Eris went on. "She says she releases you from your promise and requests that you come to Bowskeep. She has something she wishes to show you."

At the mention of Bristol's name, Tyghan's breath turned leaden in his chest. For eight years, no one had mentioned her name in his presence. It conjured up feelings he had worked to forget. And now, after eight years, he was supposed to drop everything and run to Bowskeep so she could show him something? She released him from his promise?

He felt something inside him splitting in two, one part that wanted to guard his heart, and the other part that was already racing to Bowskeep. He leaned forward to brace himself against the table, the dead weight in his chest igniting to fire. She could wait another eight years for his answer.

He walked out of the farmhouse with no reply, which was his answer. But for the rest of the day he was in a foul mood. He hacked away at the ripe wheat like he was battling a monster.

For grueling weeks, months, and years, he had waited for her to forgive him, to come back, to send him a message like this one. Her silence had pounded the guilt in him into a sharp blade, until there was nothing left inside of him to bleed. *Eight years?*

When he went back to the farmhouse at dusk, his hands blistered and his face streaked with sweat, the message still ate through him. He burst into Eris's room. "She has shirked her duties here in Elphame for years. And now she summons me like I'm a minion in her court? All this time I have waited— See *what?* She wants me to see what?"

Eris took his time marking his place in his book before setting it aside. "I don't know."

"Tell the queen she can go f—"

"Mind your words, Tyghan," Eris said sharply. "I know you're hurt. But what many of us wouldn't give for a second chance—just to talk. Would giving her five minutes of your time cost you so much? Or perhaps . . . you're afraid it could give you everything you really want?"

"I am not hurt. And I don't want anything. She wished me out of her life eight years ago, and I've honored that wish."

Eris sighed. "Eight years ago, you were both swept into a maelstrom of epic proportions. You were both so caught up trying to save everyone else, that you lost yourselves. Bristol was crushed when she left, beaten down by this world, just as your mother once was. Don't hold her to every shattered word. That last wish was *hers*. It doesn't have to be yours too."

Tyghan felt everything inside him harden, an old familiar armor he reached for that kept the pain away. "I'm busy," he answered. "Reuben put the timemark back in her pack. If it's important, she can come to me."

CHAPTER 90

Bristol's heart sagged. It had been three weeks since she sent the message to Tyghan. Three weeks of watching and waiting, her breath skipping in her chest every time she imagined seeing him again—imagined telling him about Rían. She had hoped, for their son's sake, that he would come, even though part of her was terrified at how it might turn out. But no response at all? It hurt—more than she thought possible. She had tortured herself these past weeks with memories of him. The timemark had given her hope, but the silence had taken it away. She guessed she wasn't even a memory for him anymore.

She remembered that long ago night at the waterfall when she feared how much she might forget when the tick was removed, and Tyghan said he would dance beneath the moon with her every night until the end of his days, until she fell in love with him again. Instead, he was the one who had forgotten.

Or maybe he just hated her and never wanted to see her again. She could understand that.

You are my destiny, Tyghan. She still felt those words, even if he didn't. She wished Harper had never found the timemark. It stirred up too many old feelings.

Bristol returned to her work, refilling the creamer, putting mugs in the dishwasher. She had reached out. She had tried. That was all she could do. But her son, how many excuses could she keep giving him?

🔑

Harper had just parked her car when she saw him—a man lurking near the coffee shop—and she didn't like what she saw. A scowl that meant trouble. But it was his hair and eyes that gave him away. It was like she was looking at a grown up Rían. She jumped out of her car and intercepted him.

"Hold on there," she said. "I know who you are."

Tyghan looked at the petite woman, somewhere in her fifties. "I don't think so. I'm afraid we've never met. If you'll excuse me—"

"I didn't say we had met. You're here to see Bristol?"

He stopped, wary. And then he noted the woman's familiar eyes—Kierus's eyes, fierce and protective. "Maybe?" he answered.

"Maybe is not good enough."

"Who are you?"

"I'm Bristol's older sister, but I used to be her younger sister, Harper. Our sister Cat is dead. Bristol never got to see her again. She lost thirty years when she came back from your world, including her old life. As you might imagine, it devastated her, and she carried overwhelming guilt about our parents too. More than any person should bear."

"I'm sorry for what she's been through," he said, and he was sorry. Old instincts he thought he had banished, rose in him. His instinct to comfort her.

"I had to put Bristol back together piece by piece when she got here," Harper continued. "She's doing well now, but I don't want you to go messing things up. Tread carefully. She only just discovered that she still had that timemark a few weeks ago. It took a lot of courage for her to write you that letter. *Remember that.*"

He got Harper's message loud and clear. Protection ran strong in both sisters. "I'm not here to start something. She summoned me, so I came, and then I'm leaving. That's all. I didn't come for trouble."

"Good," she said.

"Do you know why she summoned me here?"

Harper's eyes narrowed. "Yes, I do. But that's for her to tell you. Not me."

"Sounds serious."

She only shrugged, which meant it was serious. "Go on." She brushed her hand toward the coffee shop. "She's in there." Harper left, walking to a library at the end of the street, but she glanced over her shoulder once, making another brushing movement with her hand.

He walked over to the shop and looked through the window. His eyes landed on Bristol immediately, and he felt like he'd been slammed in the chest. He turned away, trying to force sense back into his head. He didn't expect that seeing her would be so hard. It all seemed so fragile now, like he could break everything just by opening his mouth. What did she want? What if she wanted him here for all the wrong reasons?

🔒

"Latte half caf to go," Bristol called as she marked a paper cup. The shop was busy, three of them on the schedule that day, and she had just ground a half pound of espresso for a customer when something outside caught her eye. A glimpse that passed quickly. Something she wouldn't ordinarily even pay attention to. Bowskeep was a busy town on Saturdays. Still, she walked out from behind the counter, her heart skipping as she followed the flash of color like a fish following a lure— and then she got a better view. Her stomach flipped over. The lettering on the window covered much of his face, but she'd know that scowl anywhere. She glanced at Rían who was happily involved with his puzzle. Bristol didn't want Tyghan coming inside and making a scene, so she quickly pulled off her apron and slipped out of the shop. He was right outside the door, like he was waiting for her.

"Hello," she said.

"Hello."

There was a long silent moment as they both tried to act as if seeing each other for the first time in eight years was no big deal, but she could tell he was as jolted as she was. Everything about him, from his jaw to his shoulders, became stiff like he was bracing himself against a storm.

"I wasn't sure you were going to come," she said.

"I was busy."

"Everything okay in Elphame?"

"Yes. Everything is peaceful. Crops are good."

She noted his skin had a golden cast now, and his hands were more calloused. His gaze was more intense than ever, the blue ice cutting into her, or maybe she was just feeling his scrutiny. She was thirty now. What did he see? The lines around her eyes? That she was trying to be brave but was as nervous as the first time she met him at the Willoughby Inn?

His lips rolled over his teeth like he was trying to hold back eight years' worth of words. She was sure he had a lot more to say than hello. "You summoned me, so I'm here," he finally said, an edge to his tone. He wanted her to get to the point.

She didn't want to spring such big news on him before they at least had a few friendly words first. "Can we walk?" she asked. "Just to the end of the block and back?"

He looked at her cautiously, then nodded.

As they walked, their conversation continued to be stilted like they were strangers, and yet when she stole a glance at him, it was like yesterday, all her old feelings bubbling up hot and bright. She wished he would look at her too, but he seemed to purposely keep his gaze averted. The guard he kept up made the conversation pure torture. It was like every word was costing him something. He only shared the polite bare events of his life, so she did the same. He was balancing farming with lighter duties as Knight Commander. She owned a coffee shop and was an art professor at the local university. She tried to move to some deeper conversation that might engage him more—things he might find surprising.

"I shift regularly now, a long way from here of course, and I've increased my repertoire of magic. I'm able to—"

The corner of his mouth pulled in a frown. "Why? This is the mortal world. You don't need that here."

"Maybe I do. I need to be ready, just in case."

"In case of what? No one knows you're here but a trusted few. We faked your death. Just as you ordered."

Was she imagining the resentment she heard in his tone? *As you ordered?* Or maybe he just wanted to remind her of her last tirade. She'd been so shattered and ashamed she barely remembered it—only that she begged to be left alone.

"Thank you, but I still have my reasons for wanting to keep my skills sharp." She explained about just discovering the timemark, which was why she summoned him now.

He stopped walking and finally faced her. "Eight years and you never went through your pack?"

"There were circumstances that occupied my time. I forgot about it."

"Those must have been some circumstances," he said suspiciously.

"Yes, they were."

She wondered if now was the best time to tell him about Rían, but then he blurted out, "Marriage? Was that it? Are you married?"

"No. Are you?"

"No."

He looked different for a moment, his eyes resting in hers, questions simmering behind them. She tried to nudge him for more. "Anything else you want to know?" The distance between them seemed to be closing. He studied her and her hope spiked.

"I think I—" He rubbed the back of his neck and looked away, glancing down the street like there was somewhere else he had to be—or wanted to be. "We should go back," he said. "I don't have a lot of time." He was agitated for the rest of their walk, and Bristol's spirits sank, but for Rían's sake, she would see this through. She had to. This wasn't about her but about her son who was still curious about his father. As soon as they arrived at the coffee shop, he said, "So I came as you asked. What's so important for me to see, that I had to come all the way here?"

Fair enough, she thought. He owed her nothing. She braced herself, then pushed open the door of the shop and said, "Your son."

Tyghan froze, staring past a shop full of customers, looking at a boy who unmistakably shared his likeness. *His son?*

"His name is Rían Trénallis Keats," Bristol said. "He's seven and a half. I've told him about you. But I need you to be—"

Gentle, she thought. *He's just a child.* But he was already walking into the shop.

Tyghan maneuvered past customers and tables until he was standing beside the one where the boy sat. Rían looked up from the puzzle he was working on and scrutinized Tyghan, like he was noting the similarities too. Tyghan knelt so he was eye level with the boy. "Hello."

Rían squinted one eye. "Are you my father?"

Tyghan nodded, swallowing back the knot in his throat. "I believe so."

"You're a king?"

"No, not anymore. I'm a prince."

"You got demoted?"

Tyghan's brows rose. "That's a big word for a seven-year-old."

"Seven and a half," Rían corrected. "My mom reads to me a lot. I know a lot of big words. Are you still a soldier, or did you lose that job too?"

"Yes," Tyghan said, fighting back a smile. "I'm still a soldier."

"Will you tell me about it?"

Tyghan looked up at Bristol. She was standing nearby, watching them, and he was certain she had stopped breathing.

"Rían, can you hold on for just a minute? I need to talk to your mother." Tyghan stood and grabbed Bristol's hand, dragging her behind the counter and through a door to a supply room.

When he finally let go of her hand, Bristol steadied herself with one hand on a shelf. Her heart pounded so hard she felt faint. "I'm sorry, Tyghan. I am so sorry. I messed up." She stared at him, trying to catch her breath. They were surrounded by bags of flour, sugar, and coffee beans in the cramped storeroom, and heat poured off him like he was ready to combust. "I didn't discover I was pregnant until I got back here and—"

"You thought you had tossed out the timemark and had no way back."

She nodded, tears filling her eyes. "I'm sorry."

He stepped closer to her, his gaze as stern as the Knight Commander at drills. "Yes, you messed up," he said.

"I know," she whispered.

He hovered over her. "But I stumbled like a complete fool in a hundred different ways, especially when I told you to forget me and I walked out. I'm the one who's sorry. Maybe we should just skip the messing up and stumbling and get to the last part—the part we're spectacular at. Loving each other. Because I haven't stopped loving you, Bri. Not for a single day. Because if I can't take you into my arms and kiss you right now, I'm certain I will die."

Bristol's mouth fell open, her thoughts jolting to a sudden stop.

"This would be your chance to say something," Tyghan said.

She nodded. "I wouldn't want you to die."

Tyghan closed the space between them, and they bumped against the shelves, dishes clattering, utensils falling, the rest of the world disappearing. He cupped her face in his hands, and his mouth met hers, her tongue warm against his, and she tasted of tears, hunger, and hope, and all the things he'd been afraid to dream of, forgiveness, tomorrows, and home. Bristol was his home, not a place in one world or another but a place where his heart resided. She was sewn into every part of him that mattered and always would be. "I love you," she whispered against his lips, tears streaming down her face, and his arms swept around her like they had never been apart.

They heard a tiny knock and looked over.

It was Rían, standing in the doorway. "Does this mean you're staying?"

EPILOGUE

1 YEAR LATER

Bristol sat alone in her favorite place in the garden, not too far from the house, so she was always within earshot. It was summer, the season she loved the most, bees buzzing over the rows of yarrow, cosmos, and chamomile she had planted, the trees ripe with fruit—especially the peach trees. Those were Rían's favorites. And there was something about sound in this part of the garden—the way it wove together like a song—the *whiiish* of the breeze skimming flowers, the chirps of goldfinches, and the laughter—there was always more of that now. She had bought the fields behind her house years ago, but now, besides flowers, every acre was planted, because Bristol had married a farmer.

From her chair beneath a willow tree she saw Rían running waist-deep down the rows of chamomile. Eris was in pursuit just behind him. *His grandfather.* Rían loved all the new additions to his family. A little boy could never have too much love, but he especially adored his father. He and Tyghan were inseparable, except when Eris visited. They ran toward the pasture now, where more than a dozen horses grazed, including August and Zandra. Of course, there weren't always that many here, but today was a special day.

Does this mean you're staying?

When Rían asked them that a year ago, it had never been a question in either her or Tyghan's head. They had nodded to their son in unison, and then Tyghan got down on one knee to make it official, but she and Rían were both saying yes, even before he could get the question out. And then they had all hugged, Rían sandwiched between them, and even Tyghan cried.

"Hey." A gentle whisper. A kiss on her shoulder. "I'm going to start dinner soon." And then his lips brushed hers. "Ready?"

"Always ready for you. But shouldn't we get dinner on first?" He laughed and she pulled his mouth back to hers, kissing him leisurely, appreciating every touch, never taking a day—or a kiss—for granted.

Sashka's voice broke through the calm. "Dear gods! Will you two ever get a room?"

"Don't encourage them," Melizan said. "That's what got her into her last predicament."

"Dinner will be on soon," Tyghan told them. "Why don't you two run along?"

"Better hurry," Melizan said. "Dalagorn's stomach is growling and I think he's about to eat one of the children." She rushed off after her toddler, who was drinking out of Reggie's water bowl over on the porch.

"You come along too, freeloader," Tyghan said to Reggie, who lay curled at Bristol's feet. After she left Elphame, Tyghan fed Reggie a snack every day, and then brought him along when he moved to Oak Leaf Lane. Reggie stretched and got to his feet, never one to turn down a treat.

Melizan shrieked as she pulled the toddler from the bowl, but it melded with all the other noise of children playing, dishes clattering, and Harper yelling for Jake to get more ice. "Family," Tyghan said, but Bristol heard his heart swell with the word.

When she and Tyghan walked over to get dinner underway, they found Quin scratching his head as he looked into the fiery dome that would cook their meals. "What did you call this thing again?" he asked.

"A pizza oven," Tyghan answered. He discovered that he loved pizza on his first day in Bowskeep, and insisted on having his own oven. "Choose your toppings and I'll make you one."

Quin perused the dishes full of olives, pepperoni, and salami. "Nah. It's all round. I don't eat round stuff."

"Oh come on, you old coot," Rose said, not the least bit timid anymore. Apparently eight years of defending the realm had shaken that out of her. "Try something new. You won't die!"

"I promise you, Quin," Jake said, "Tyghan makes a mean pizza." Harper's husband took his unusual new family in stride, even the enormous and intimidating Dalagorn. Harper had married a winner. She beamed not far away, loving the chaos of a large family.

Quin remained skeptical, and Hollis elbowed him. "Mean means good. Be a good example for your children." They had two now, adorable little boys who stared at him, waiting to see what he would do. Under Hollis's stern stare, he reluctantly began piling his pizza with round stuff. After it was cooked, he devoured it and made a second one, reluctant to admit that it was delicious.

There was plenty of other food to eat too, though. Everyone brought something to share. They all sat around their long farm table, Rían and his cousins at one end, their eyes like saucers, as Rose, Avery, and Cael entertained them with amusing magics. Cael was perhaps the most changed of everyone. As Avery observed, he was comfortable in his own skin now, not trying to prove anything to anyone, and his duties as king were tailored to his strengths.

"Hey, everyone, look who's awake!" Eris called out. "Come meet the newest member of the family." He walked down the back porch steps with his granddaughter tenderly tucked in his arms, Catarina Trénallis Keats. Julia was at his side, both of them cooing over her.

"Looks like he stole our thunder," Tyghan whispered. Bristol knew he didn't mind and he loved seeing the pride in his father's face, but it was also the healing that Bristol saw in Eris's expression, and maybe that healed a part of her too. Catarina was the first child or grandchild Eris had ever gotten to announce to the world. But she wouldn't be his last.

Tyghan put his arm around Bristol, pulling her close as they watched everyone oohing and ahhing over their precious daughter. "Do you think she's bloodmarked?" Tyghan asked. A protective glint lit his eyes. Catarina was only a week old. They hadn't discussed the possibility yet, but it was something they had to consider.

"She will be whatever she is meant to be." A passionate blaze ignited behind Bristol's sternum. The enormous power of both beast and mother. "And we will protect her, until she is old enough to protect herself."

Julia brought Catarina over and kissed Bristol's cheek as she laid the baby in Bristol's arms. "She is beautiful, Your Majesty, just like her mother." She glanced over at Tyghan and winked. "And her father too."

Bristol looked down at Catarina, her baby's eyes swallowing her whole. She'd thought her heart was already full after she had Rían, but that was the miracle of hearts—they were limitless in what they could hold.

The wonder of it all made Bristol think about chance, about a long-ago letter in her mailbox, a meeting at an abandoned inn, and finding a forgotten timemark in a backpack. A million chances happened every day. The difference was what we made of them. She and Tyghan didn't let this chance slip past them. Day by day, they fiercely claimed it, and were turning their chance into something that would last forever.

ACKNOWLEDGMENTS

First and foremost, I want to thank my husband, Dennis. From the very first spark of this story, he gave me the courage to embark on something new. His support was unflagging, from listening to me talk out plot points, to babbling on about my excitement for this world and these characters. He *shared* that excitement. And when the writing hours I had to put in were long, he was beyond heroic in helping me to get this second book done. Even with all his own work responsibilities, he took on more so I could finish this book on time. He is a superhero, cheerleader, and savior all wrapped up in one amazing package. Thank you, my love.

I'm forever thankful for my supportive family, Karen, Ben, Jessica, Dan, and their mischievous sprites, Ava, Emily, Leah, and Riley. They are my deepest joy, and make me believe in the future and all the good things of the world.

So much gratitude to my publisher, Flatiron Books, and their stellar team for bringing first *Courting*, and then *Last Wish* to readers, with so much creativity and dedication. Enormous thanks to Deb Futter, Megan Lynch, Marlena Bittner, Brittany Leddy, Malati Chavali, Kate Keating, Maris Tasaka, Louis Grilli, Emily Walters, Molly Bloom, EmmaPaige West, Steve Wagner, Drew Kilman, Eva Diaz, Bria Strothers, Claire McLaughlin, Mary Retta, and the countless others working behind the scenes. Thanks, and smiles, to my longtime copy-editor, Ana Deboo, who wouldn't let me overlook that August needed an apple too, because those are his favorites. Her care and attention for the little details are so appreciated.

Again, the book cover and design are mesmerizing. I love the colors and the magic they evoke, and I continue to be in awe of the art and design team, Laywan Kwan, Jim Tierney, Donna S. Noetzel, and Kelly Gatesman, who make that all happen.

I am such a map person, and in the writing of this second book, I often referred to Virginia Allyn's whimsical map of Elphame as a reference and reminder of where everything was, from kingdoms to faraway islands. I know readers loved the map and found it helpful too, and I'm grateful for Virginia's talent and creativity.

I cannot begin to gather enough words and praise for my editor, Caroline Bleeke. Where do I start? Her patience and enthusiasm exceeded the bounds of mortals. She was always there with a cheerful word and immediate guidance and advice whenever I needed it. She is definitely part fae and wields magic because she helped me achieve the impossible. Whatever you are Caroline, fae, mortal, or both, I am grateful for your tenacity and kindness. Thank you.

My fellow writers Tricia Levenseller, Jodi Meadows, Melissa Wyatt, Marlene Perez, Isabel Ibañez, and Stephanie Garber were true gems and offered infinite support, wisdom, laughs, and so many helpful insights, and I am thankful for these very smart friends.

Again, many thanks to Dr. Allyson B. Williams, SDSU art history professor, for answering my questions about art and the pursuit of art degrees. I'm happy that in this second book Bristol did indeed achieve her goal of studying and teaching art history, which has so many lessons to offer on humankind.

Supremely grateful to my fantastic agents, Rosemary Stimola and Allison Remcheck, who have been there every step of the way with this book too, cheering me on and always offering wise counsel. I'm also thankful to the whole Stimola Literary Studio team for all the incredible work they do to help books like mine become realities, here and in faraway places. They are the best.

And speaking of faraway places, a huge thank-you to my foreign publishers and teams who ushered in these books with such passion and beautiful artwork, bringing *Courting* and *Last Wish* to so many book lovers around the world.

As always, I am incredibly thankful to all the readers, bookstagrammers, and book pushers everywhere, who have shared and shouted out about Bristol, Tyghan, love, and this magical corner of Elphame. Your excitement fueled my own and helped me reach the finish line. I wish I could jump through a portal and give each one of you a hug.

xo,

Mary

ABOUT THE AUTHOR

Mary E. Pearson is the *New York Times* and internationally bestselling author of the Dance of Thieves duology, the Remnant Chronicles trilogy, the Jenna Fox Chronicles, and more books for young readers. The Bristol Keats duology is her debut series for adults. She writes from her home in California.